From *Murder is a Serious Business*

"All you chaps," he said, "I want to make you a sporting proposition."

Emma groaned. Jeff ignored her and went on.

"I have here the names of all the people who could have killed Amos. For a mere fifty dollars you can draw a name; for one hundred you can draw two. Step right up, gents. Winner take all."

"Yippee," said Shay. "The Murder Sweepstakes. Who holds the money? Will you take a check?"

Emma put the bowl down on the table with a bang. "I never heard of such a thing," she said indignantly. "The idea of betting that one of us killed Amos—this is serious."

"—and him not yet cold in his grave." Shay mimicked her indignation. "Well, one of us did kill him and I, personal, intend to prove that the guy I draw done it."

Hank abandoned his operations at the sink and came toward them, grinning. "You got something there," he said. "Ellis will be glad of the help."

"Nix," said Shay. "I won't even help you, this is strictly my investigation. You draw your own client."

"I agree with Miss Marsh," Eddie put in. "It doesn't seem quite right, and fifty dollars is a lot of money."

"Don't be a heel," said Shay.

"Loosen up," said Jeff. "You get in on this or you get no more policies out of me. Emma can hold the stakes."

"Daddy first," said Shay. He put his hand in the bowl and turned to Eddie. "See what I'm doing? Perfectly simple; no trick at all."

He withdrew his hand, looked at the slip and grinned.

"Get a good one, Jack?" asked Hank.

"I should hope to whinny."

"Who is it?" Emma's curiosity got the better of her scruples.

"Don't you wish you knew?"

The Emma Marsh Mysteries

Murder is a Serious Business

by ELIZABETH DEAN

The Rue Morgue Press
Boulder, Colorado

Murder is a
Serious Business

About Elizabeth Dean

Like Emma Marsh, Elizabeth Dean worked in an antiques shop in Boston in the 1930s. After graduating from Pembroke College (now part of Brown University) and obtaining a masters degree from Radcliffe, Dean worked in the famous Boston antiques shop owned by George McMahon, who provided the model for the irascible but tender-hearted Jeff Graham.

When asked what made her books stand out from the pack, Dean would always cite their spontaneity. She refused to work from either and outline or a synopsis, knowing only the setting, the pivotal incident, and the identity of the murderer.

Written on a dare, *Murder is a Collector's Item* was published in the spring of 1939, and introduced to the world Emma Marsh, a young, pretty big-footed woman living on her own in Boston just after the Great Depression. In Emma, Dean created one of the most memorable women characters in American crime fiction. Very much her own woman, she trades barbs and insults with boyfriend Hank, and makes her own way.

She followed up that maiden effort with two more novels featuring Emma, *Murder is a Serious Business* (1940), once again set in Boston, and *Murder a Mile High* (1944), set in Colorado where Liz Dean and husband Abbott, an ophthalmologist, maintained a ranch near Evergreen.

She used the royalties from her first book to furnish her Council Bluffs, Iowa, home with antiques, all purchased in New England except for one table which had been transported by oxcart to Boulder, Colorado. The rest of her royalties went to buying purebred Aberdeen Angus cattle to stock the ranch she called Buckshot and in 1951 she finished first in the Jefferson County (Colorado) Angus field trials.

Her third and final mystery was published while she was living in Warrington, Florida, near Pensacola, where her husband was stationed during World War II. Upon her return to Council Bluffs at the end of the war, Dean abandoned her career as a mystery writer and threw herself into the activities of the local historical society, spearheading a drive to save the historic Squirrel Cage Jail with its revolving cylindrical cellblock.

Born in New York City in 1901, she died in Council Bluffs in 1985 at the age of 84.

Chapter 1

MISS EMMA MARSH, assistant to the proprietor of "J. Graham, Antiques," was feeling very happy. In spite of the sweltering heat that had driven any prospective customers, along with most of the inhabitants of Greater Boston, to the beaches and Jeff to an air-cooled spot where the laws of chance were persistently ignored, Emma was industriously rearranging a window. The awnings had been down since morning and the doors closed. The shop was possibly two degrees cooler than the street but it was permeated with the woodshed odor, that musty, slightly acrid scent that revealed the last refuge of many a discarded treasure. Emma was sure she smelled of it but she kept the doors closed anyway.

Emma speared the woolly hair of a rag doll with the point of a steeple-topped fire shovel and suspended it over a pair of matching andirons. The shovel was supported by the rungs of an overturned five-slat chair. Emma decided to call her composition "Daybreak" and was grateful to Jeff for pointing out that Surrealism at least gave them something new to do with antiques. Jeff was full of ideas; she thought that was the only way he kept in business. That, and his fine assistant. It had been her fine idea to pick up a lot of the odd earrings, baby lockets and stickpin heads that the gals were putting on bangle bracelets. Jeff was a fine fellow, too, if only he wouldn't put the rent money on a horse that had invariably had the wrong thing for breakfast.

Emma laid a purple overlay lamp on a bed of excelsior, discarded the excelsior as suggesting the too sensible idea of packing and substituted a cracked blue-and-white platter which didn't mean anything that she could think of.

Mr. Finegold, their next-door competitor, wandering about in search of any kind of breeze, stopped in front of the window and gaped in amazement. When his eye lit on the purple overlay lamp he came quickly into the shop.

"Shut the door," said Emma patiently.

"I got a customer—" began Mr. Finegold.

"You're lucky," said Emma. "Hang onto him."

"It's Mrs. Garfinkle," said Mr. Finegold unguardedly.

Emma pursed her lips. Mrs. Garfinkle's taste might not be so good as her checks but she was a customer of Emma's too.

"The lamp," said Mr. Finegold, "is it cracked? And how much for the lamp?"

"More than you can afford," said Emma sociably, "and it's perfect."

"Look"—Mr. Finegold became confidential—"last week I am selling her a purple overlay lamp just like that one." He peered at the lamp. "Maybe the base is a little better—"

Emma bridled.

"—maybe not quite so good"—Mr. Finegold was trying to be diplomatic—"but close enough for a pair. She wants a pair. I can sell her this one, and you know how business is."

"Why don't I sell the lamp to Mrs. Garfinkle?" Emma wanted to know.

"Look." Mr. Finegold became pleading. "Anybody can sell a lamp. But you take Jeff, he sells rag dolls, he sells old barns and mustache cups. He sells insurance—"

"No," said Emma, "not insurance."

"Phooey," said Mr. Finegold. "You make the inventories?"

"Yes," said Emma.

Mr. Finegold nodded, satisfied. "But me, I can't sell anything even if it's good. But I can sell that lamp. I got a customer—"

Emma knew it was only a question of time before she gave in.

There was a certain amount of truth in Mr. Finegold's remarks. Jeff did a good business in good times because his honesty was as outspoken as it was reliable, and he missed no angle that would supply his customer's wants. Frequently he created a want by pointing out a new use for some curious object. Less imaginative dealers wished they could suspect him of chicanery or hypnotism, but to most of them he was generosity itself in the matter of customers and prices. Only a few, whose imagination had led them along the way of adding inlay to a plain piece or reconstructing a chair from a single leg, had felt the sting of Jeff's tongue and waited hopefully for a misstep on his part. Mr. Finegold's remark about the insurance indicated the stories some of them were telling. Jeff didn't sell insurance but he recommended it highly.

Concerning investments Jeff was inclined to be notional. First it had been stocks, but some of the gilt-edged shares recommended by his customers had let him down rather badly. Then it had been farm loans, but the farms as well as the profits had blown away. Now it was insurance. He bought it himself, he made Emma buy it; he was a pest to his customers and a gold mine to Eddie Rawlins, the agent who had first sold him. He was particularly insistent that customers whose country houses contained fine antiques insure their furniture, although the absence of fire and police protection frequently sent the premiums soaring, and the companies were reluctant to accept any but an expert's appraisal of value. Emma told herself that it was Jeff's reputation for honesty and knowledge that had resulted in his making out most of the inventories and not any fee splitting between him and Eddie Rawlins. If it hadn't been so hot and she hadn't been feeling so amiable, Emma would have argued with Mr. Finegold about the insurance. She knew Jeff would never bother to explain and she knew that Jeff would sell Mr. Finegold the overlay lamp.

"I suppose," Emma began with mock sadness, "that I'm not to make any profit."

"How much did you pay for it?" asked Mr. Finegold quickly.

"Sh-sh," said Emma. "That's a secret. There's the overhead, and my salary, and Mrs. Graham's cruise, and you know yourself there's no profit in this game." Jeff had brought the lamp in that morning and by some mutual omission it had not been marked. A quick turnover was a quick turnover, however, and Mr. Finegold would have no respect for her if she asked too little. She would take a chance on the profit and not look in the stock book for the cost. She was so jovial about the whole transaction that Mr. Finegold, once the lamp was safely in his hands, was moved to comment.

"You feel good today?"

"Yes," said Emma. "I feel swell."

Mr. Finegold peered into the little office and down the high-piled rows of furniture, although he knew that the shop was empty except for the two of them.

"Where is he?" he asked. "I don't see him, but he is coming?"

"Yes." Emma smiled with a coyness that would have made Jeff snort. Mr. Finegold nodded wisely again and hurried out.

Emma's smile broadened as she put a bootjack in the place left vacant by the sale of the lamp. Oh yes, he was coming, she supposed; he always did. He'd show up any time that suited his fancy and assume that she was going to dinner with him, just because it was Saturday night. Well, Emma dusted off her hands with a gesture of finality

and went into the washroom next the office to powder her nose; this
time he was due for a surprise.

There were times, when she had broken something or failed to
make a sale, that Emma felt she was unappreciated, put upon and
doubly crossed. Only a particularly malign fate would have given her
the irascible Jefferson Graham for an employer and then heaped up
the coals of fire by adding Mr. Henry Fairbanks to the top of the heap.
A boss who had tantrums was bad enough, but a beau who did nothing was worse. She patted with one hand and prodded with the other:
a complicated process for one who was only twenty-six and normally
impulsive.

Jeff snapped at her for forgetting to lock the corner door of the
shop, for omitting to make out sales slips and for smoking the last of
his cigarettes. Hank sat around with a dreamy look of what he called
contemplation in his eyes and let her trip over his long legs. For Jeff
she assured the customers that Mr. Graham hadn't meant it when he
said that nobody but a fool would try to combine Empire with Early
American furniture; for Hank she clipped notices of interesting murders from the papers. Over the telephone she told Jeff's wife that Jeff
had gone to see a dealer in Hingham when she knew perfectly well
that he was somewhere making another assault on the laws of chance;
she tried to be equally tactful when Hank's hard-bitten office girl called
and said, "Mr. Fairbanks is there, I presume?"

Emma could reconcile herself to such of Jeff's ways as she could
not change; but over Hank she still fretted. A mother will defend a
wayward child, but Emma's feeling toward Hank was not maternal.
She refused to admit exactly what her feeling was, not wishing to be
the first to make a positive statement of their relationship, but it was
significant that she did not want Hank to be President. All she desired was that he be industrious, ambitious and, after the proper
amount of hard work, successful in his chosen field of the prevention
and detection of crime.

To be sure Hank had hired an office with "Fairbanks, Inc., Inves-
tigators," on the outside of the door and a secretary inside, but he still
sat, and he still preferred to do his sitting in the shop of J. Graham,
Antiques. Emma sometimes wished that Hank's uncle, the late Richard Norwitch, club man, antiquarian and perennial board member,
had left his money instead of his furniture to the Museum. Without
money Hank might have done something for himself instead of being content to pull occasional chestnuts out of the fire for his friend,
Police Lieutenant Donovan.

Hank claimed that the police department got a higher class of business than a private detective agency. He preferred, he said, a nice murder any day to the shoddy task of securing evidence of infidelity. To Emma's protest that hiding his light under Donovan's bushel buttered no parsnips Hank replied that he didn't like parsnips so how could he want butter on them?

The trouble with Hank, Emma had decided, was not that he had too much but that he didn't want anything. Aside from sleeping quarters for himself and Oscar, also inherited, Hank had not refurnished the Chestnut Street house after the removal of his uncle's Early Americana to the Museum. Hank ate breakfast at home, just to give Oscar something to do. He bought four new suits a year, to cheer up his uncle's tailor. Emma said that he kept the house, Oscar and the tailor only because he was used to them and not at all because he wanted them. Sometimes Emma felt that Hank sat in Jeff's shop merely out of habit and not because he wanted her company. Sometimes he didn't even talk to her; he wandered in and sat and wandered out again. This casual procedure had been going on for three years.

Emma wasn't even sure just how much she was Hank's girl. He was always saying, "When we are married I shall beat you;" and planning extraordinary honeymoons in lighthouses, igloos or the Carlsbad Caverns; but he only sighed when Emma said that she couldn't possibly leave Jeff and by the next day apparently forgot all about it.

Considering the freckles on her nose and her big mouth, she supposed that she ought to be grateful for Hank, but the freckles only came out in summer and Amos Currier had told her that she had nice eyes.

She was carefully applying lipstick when she heard the shop door open.

"Shut the door," called Emma.

"Woosh," said a man's voice. "I verily believe this is the day for the annual egg frying. Ah." The sigh was followed by a long creak as the Chippendale sofa outside the office relaxed under the weight put upon it.

"Oh, it's you, is it?" Emma calmly finished putting on the lipstick. When she had quite done she came out of the washroom and surveyed the long angular figure stretched out on the sofa. Gray flannel suit, white shirt, blue tie; neat, and only slightly mussed. But beside the figure lay an ancient battered Panama hat, its crown creased and darkened, its brim bent to shapelessness, its band frayed and sweat-stained.

Emma had disliked that hat for a long time. No man, not even Henry Norwitch Fairbanks, should be able to present a well-dressed appearance with a hat like that. Such indifferent composure came, she supposed, from not wanting anything and being perfectly well able to have it. Emma had her eye on Hank's composure.

"All right," said Henry Fairbanks, "wipe the canary feathers off your chin and tell Papa all about it."

Emma tried to keep the corners of her mouth firm.

"I don't know," said she, "what you're talking about."

"You've done something. That open book you carry around for a face is just itching to be read, but I've had a hard day and excitement is bad for me. You don't have a cold can of beer anywhere, do you?"

"No," said Emma, annoyed at Hank's short-lived curiosity. "Jeff has decided that beer gives him indigestion."

"It's not the beer," said Hank, "it's the whiskey chaser."

"Look who's here."

A small but very neat coupe had drawn up outside the door bearing an impeccably dressed young man and a bag of shiny new golf clubs. The young man carefully adjusted the golf clubs before approaching the shop.

"Our Eddie," said Emma, "is certainly putting on the dog."

Eddie Rawlins was blond with nice teeth and a hearty tan. Emma admired the tan and wished that Hank would try something more athletic than an occasional swim in the club pool.

"Hello, Emma," said Eddie. "Hello, Hank. Is Jeff here?"

"Jeff," said Emma, "is in conference."

"Eddie," said Hank, "how would you like a nice cold can of beer?"

Eddie looked at his watch. "But fine," he said. "Just one. I'm meeting Hornsby at four-thirty at the Country Club for a round."

Eddie put it all in because Hornsby was one of the vice-presidents of Old Cape and he was proud to be playing the Country Club course with him.

Hank grinned. "Nice work. You'll be a vice-president first thing you know."

Eddie grinned shyly back. He was grateful to Jeff Graham for the business he had brought him. He was grateful to be playing golf with Hornsby and to be on terms of easy familiarity with Henry Fairbanks, who was also a vice-president of Old Cape, though privately Eddie didn't think he looked it.

"Angel face," said Hank, "both of your guests want beer and both of them are tired businessmen."

Emma said, "Of all the lazy—" and went across the street for the beer. When she got back Hank was explaining to a bewildered tourist that a Stiegel sugar bowl was genuine Early Sandwich.

Emma hastily dropped the beer on the sofa and took over the customer. By the time she had sold her an ivory pie crimper Eddie had finished his beer and gone. It wouldn't, Hank explained, do to keep a vice-president waiting.

"I think he's cute," said Emma. "He's so pleased to be doing well and he has cute ears."

"Yah," said Hank, "you leave Eddie's ears alone. He wants to go to dinner with us some Saturday night. I told him we always went to the Ritz and had fried nightingale's tongues. He's a social climber."

"You flatter yourself," Emma said. "Your family's name may be on all the bronze plaques around town, but you've ruined your reputation going around with me."

"Uncle said it would be like that."

Jeff Graham, his coat over his arm and his tie slightly askew, threw the shop door open wide and sniffed the air disgustedly. "Beats me," he said, "how you chaps stand it."

"Do you smell anything?" asked Emma of Hank.

"Just now," said Hank, "I thought I caught a faint odor of whiskey. I hadn't noticed it before."

Jeff stalked into the office and put a small paper-wrapped object in his bottom desk drawer.

"Sociable as usual," said Hank. "Where do we eat?"

"That reminds me." Emma spoke very casually. "I'm not going to dinner with you."

"Why not?" asked Hank.

Jeff came out of the office and looked curiously at Emma.

"Because"—Emma wished somebody would laugh or do something, she hadn't realized that it was going to be this hard to say it—"because I'm going to dinner with Amos Currier."

"Swell!" Hank's voice rang with sincerity. "You know," he went on confidentially, "I think you've sort of got Amos going."

Emma was distinctly taken back. This was hardly the effect she had anticipated.

"Of course he's a little old," Hank continued, "but the Curriers are a long-lived bunch and Amos is well preserved. I don't think he looks a day over sixty "

"Sixty-five," said Jeff, "his teeth, you know."

"You dogs," said Emma, "Amos is fifty-five and he has all his teeth."

Hank and Jeff exchanged a knowing look.

"There's something about an older man," Hank went on, "a certain considerateness, a sureness—shall we call it the result of experience?—that must be very intriguing. Then there is the Currier name, and the Currier money, and the Currier silver, and the Currier furniture. It would turn any girl's head."

"Speaking of the Currier furniture " Jeff began.

"And so," Hank went on, "I say, God bless you, my children, and for once Jeff and I can have a peaceful meal."

"The Currier furniture"—Jeff abandoned the game in midair and spoke to Emma—"is going to be insured. And you're not going to dinner with Amos, at least not alone, because I just left him and he's not going to New York. He wants us to get Eddie and go out to the farm and talk over the inventory. He wants Hank there too."

"Why didn't you say so in the first place?" Emma's little explosion had backfired and she was annoyed that she had been unnecessarily singed.

"Cripes! Did I have a chance? Now I better call Eddie because this affair is going to take the roof right off Old Cape."

"Eddie's playing golf with a vice-president."

Jeff picked up the phone. "I'll call the office anyway. Maybe he'll call back."

"The office'll be closed. It's only people with very disagreeable employers who have to work on Saturday afternoon."

"Why don't you quit then? I'll call his boardinghouse."

"Eddie'll be pleased." Emma spoke almost timidly to Hank. "Amos has stalled so long on this that I think he's given up hope."

Jeff hung up the phone. "I suppose," he said, "that you'll want to go home and change your clothes and get a toothbrush. You hop to it and Hank and I'll pick you up in half an hour."

"Count me out." Hank's tone was final.

"Now what the—" began Jeff.

"Please, Hank—"

Hank was not looking at Emma or he might have relented.

"The house is lovely and it'll be cool out there—"

"Thank you," said Hank, "but I'm not going."

"Forevermore, why not?"

"Because," said Hank sharply, "I don't like the idea of your wheedling Amos Currier into buying insurance and I don't like the idea of your weekending at his house."

Emma's eyes snapped. "I didn't wheedle him, and you ought to know that it's a crime for that houseful of stuff to go uninsured. It's worth two hundred and fifty thousand, not counting the silver. And as for staying out there all night, when did you get so fussy? And besides Miss Currier is there."

"Of course she's deaf as a post," said Jeff helpfully. "But, anyway, Amos really wants you."

The ringing of the telephone cut across their wrangling.

"You answer it. I'm not here, unless it's Eddie."

"Hello," said Emma, anger still tingeing her voice. Then, "Hel-lo, darling, how were the beetles? Oh, you have not. I bet you never thought of me once."

"That sounds like the O'Shay," said Jeff, "bring God's gift to women and newspapers along, Eddie wants some pictures of the house, and Amos wants—"

Hank, who had been nearly to the door, came back and took the phone. "Hi, my friend, when did you get back? No, not a thing. No, they're busy. All right. In about ten minutes."

"Look," said Jeff, "Eddie wants some pictures, and Shay might just as well—"

"Sorry," said Hank cheerfully. "Shay just got in, but he must have come all the way down in the club car, and he doesn't sound as though he could tell a camera from a pair of bifocals."

Hank went out the door and hailed a cab.

"The hell with him," said Jeff. "We can get along."

Emma looked ready to cry, but the telephone rang again.

"It's for you," she said warningly. "I think it's a cable."

Jeff took the receiver reluctantly; after a moment he hung up with a resounding crash.

"You saw that letter of credit," he accused Emma. "Am I supposed to be made of money?"

Emma said nothing. She tried to maintain a neutral position in the constant war over money waged between Jeff Graham and his wife. She should have warned him, she thought, that Rio was called the Paris of South America. She should have warned Jeff, or he should have thought of it himself, but the vision of a summer free from nagging telephone calls and supercilious visits had appealed to both of them.

"Money, money, money," Jeff was repeating. "If Amos Currier goes back on this deal, I'll break his neck."

Chapter 2

AMOS CURRIER, master, at twenty-two, of the barque *Mary Nickerson,* decided, at the age of forty, to give up the sea and marry. In later years he liked to tell that he had marched inland from Marblehead, an oar upon his shoulder, until he finally met a man who asked him the nature of the contraption he was carrying, and that on that very spot, where he would be untroubled by mention of the sea, he had built his house. The tale was a greater credit to the captain's classical education than to his veracity. It was unlikely that chance would have chosen the sightly knoll on which the house stood, facing the distant mountains; it was doubtful if a man so foresighted as the captain would have left anything to chance. On his last voyages Captain Amos had shopped for his house furnishings with the precision and discretion of a canny housewife. In Belfast he bought linens, in Antwerp, feather beds. In London he left orders for furniture that showed him to have the size, if not the location, of his house well in mind. In Hong Kong he purchased a set of monogrammed Lowestoft as well as a supply of blue-and-white Canton for daily use and had had painted the portrait of the *Mary Nickerson* that was to hang over the parlor mantel. The original Amos was a man of taste, or at least he was happy in the almost unfailing good taste of his period. His dining-room chairs were graceful Sheraton, as were his sideboard and table. He set them against pale green woodwork in 1791, and so they stayed.

Wing chairs, side chairs, "fancy chairs"; books, cellarets, lowboys, plant stands, knife cases fitted with the best Birmingham steel—Amos Currier bought them all. Perhaps it was Amos' bride-to-be who helped him with the lists and added yards of copperplate chintz for bed hangings; perhaps it was she who put in a word for the cabinetmakers of her own country and was responsible for the Goddard block-front secretary and the pair of delicate card tables, in the Hepplewhite fashion, made, according to the label, by J. Seymour of Boston.

And whether to assure his bride-to-be that he had fulfilled all her wishes or for the comfort of his own careful soul, Amos Currier inventoried all his purchases, together with their cost and the place or person from which he had bought them; and the inventory, together with his house and furnishings, had come down, through his careful descendants, to the present day. Some of the Canton cups were missing, linen sheets had worn out, a careless hand had cracked the Lowestoft sugar bowl and "one brass idol, small," had been lost for generations, made away with, possibly, by a righteous Currier. Windsor chairs, country-made tables and the knickknacks of many people had found their way into the house, but nothing of importance had ever found its way out.

This unusual circumstance, coupled with the fact the Curriers continued to be people of mild importance in the legislature, the courts and the schools, had given the house the deserved reputation of a museum piece. The Goddard desk had been described in *Antiques,* the dining room had been photographed for *House Beautiful* and the *Transcript* had done a careful article tracing the family back to a "courier" who had pleased William the Conqueror. The Society for the Preservation of Massachusetts Antiquities hoped that the present Amos Currier would remain a bachelor, and the Museum invited him to be a patron when it opened its American Wing.

Emma and Jeff left the turnpike and drove to the village of Westham. At a point where the North-of-Boston aspect of the village green was marred by a filling station they took a narrow road that wound between stone walls beneath the thick shade of avenues of maples.

After the bustle and racket of the turnpike on a Saturday afternoon it was very quiet. Emma relaxed and Jeff slowed down to a mere forty. About five miles from the village, on the crest of a long hill, Jeff stopped the car entirely. Before them a waving meadow climbed another hill, and there, framed by two gigantic elms, stood the Currier house. Broad and square it faced them, its small-paned windows twinkling in the late afternoon sun, its great chimneys breaking the angles of its tripped roof. It was not unlike many other houses of its period—it boasted no unusual cornice or fanlight—but there was something about the proportions, the balance of windows on either side of the massive door, that was especially pleasing. It sat its hilltop with a gracious dignity, with an air of permanence that ignored a changing world.

"Yep," said Jeff, "that is a house. I don't know as I blame you."

"You hush up," said Emma, and then reopened the subject by asking, "Do you think Hank was really sore about the insurance, or just because I said I was going to dinner with Amos?"

"I think"—Jeff shot the car down into the valley—"that you're going to get caught in the wringer, and it'll serve you right."

One side of the Currier house rambled on through pantry, kitchen ell and woodshed until it joined the stable. The road skirted this side of the house and was separated from it by a thick lilac hedge. At a break in the hedge Jeff swung sharply left up a short gravel drive, passed beneath the keystoned archways of the woodshed and came out into the yard at the rear of the house.

Amos Currier rose from a deck chair in the shadow of the gazebo and came to meet them. Emma was glad that the lawn was large and the deck chair a long way off. She was furious with herself for a sudden self-consciousness about Amos.

Until very recently Emma had accepted Amos Currier as a friend of Jeff's, a gentleman-farmer with some furniture that ought to be insured, whose occasional deferential squiring was a change from the somewhat cavalier treatment accorded her by Jeff and Hank. Until last week Amos had never taken her out alone except to lunch. But on the previous Wednesday Jeff had been out of town and Hank had been busy and Amos had asked her to the Copley for dinner. She hadn't told Hank or Jeff about that because of what had happened. It hadn't been Amos' fault that his niece, Eunice Chandler, had occupied the table next to them; it hadn't been Amos' fault that his niece had been a little tipsy and rather more than a little nasty. Emma hadn't minded when Eunice told her escort in clear, ringing tones to look at the shopgirl who was running after her uncle, but Amos had. He had made the mistake of going to Eunice's table and telling her escort to take her home. Eunice had advised him that he was the one who had better be taken home before he made a fool of himself. Disturbed and apologetic, Amos had suggested dinner on Saturday night to make up for their spoiled party. Emma had accepted, though all that evening she had sensed a change in Amos' manner toward her, a heightened interest in what she said, an intensity in the way he looked at her; and Emma, whose life had not been as devoid of men as she sometimes pretended, recognized the signs. If Amos was falling for her, Emma was natural enough to be pleased, and normal enough to be amused; Amos was just one of a number of people that she liked because they were nice to her. If she had had anything more than a friendly interest in Amos she would not have planned to use him to bait Hank. She would have thought nothing of spending the weekend at Amos' house, Miss Currier or no Miss Currier, because making inventories was part of her job.

But now, watching Amos' well-set-up figure striding toward them,

Emma was conscious of a changed feeling on her own part. Amos' interest in her had been a pleasant little secret. She hadn't cared when Eunice Chandler accused her of running after Amos, because that had been untrue; but when Jeff and Hank indicated that Amos' interest in her was common knowledge Emma began to wonder how interested Amos was. And then Hank, who had pretended to joke about Amos' taking her to dinner, had blown up at the suggestion that she had helped talk Amos into taking out insurance. That didn't make sense, and when Hank was irrational it was a sign that he was greatly disturbed. She had succeeded in shattering his composure, if that was any comfort to her.

What made Emma self-conscious now was that for the first time she noticed that Amos' shoulders were broad, that he walked smoothly and easily, that his head was well set on his neck and that his iron-gray hair showed no sign of thinning. Emma knew that Amos was fifty-five but she had not realized how attractive he was. Emma was reminded of a long-ago and unrequited passion for her high school's football coach.

"Hi," said Jeff, climbing out of the car.

Amos opened the door for Emma. "Hello," he said. "It's nice to see you. I hope you didn't mind the sudden change of plan?"

He took her arm as he always did, but this time Emma was acutely aware of his strong fingers and felt herself blushing.

"Where's the booze?" asked Jeff. "We don't have to work until tomorrow."

Amos led the way to the kitchen door, his hand still on Emma's elbow. At a table by the kitchen window a tall spare woman about Amos' age was chopping cabbage.

"Sally," said Amos Currier, "this is Miss Marsh and Jeff Graham: Mrs. Leavitt."

Mrs. Leavitt "did" for Amos and his aunt; she lived on the adjoining farm with her husband, Amos' assistant in the farming of the Currier two hundred acres; she put down the chopping knife and wiped her hands on her blue percale apron before she greeted Emma. Mrs. Leavitt's eyes were keen and she folded her lips together after she spoke. Emma drew away from Amos.

"Miss Amy said to tell you," Mrs. Leavitt began, "that she would see the folks tomorrow; she's busy." She looked toward a kitchen calendar and Emma, following the look, saw that the thirtieth of June was circled with red pencil. She wondered what anniversary Miss Amy Currier was celebrating alone in her room.

Jeff was already in the buttery, impatiently fingering the glasses that Amos had set out on the counter. The buttery extended across the ell, conveniently joining it with the dining room, and Amos used it for a bar. Except for the doorways to kitchen and dining room, a counter ran clear around the buttery, affording ample space for mixing. There was plenty of room for bottles among the thinning ranks of Canton china in the cupboards that lined the two long sides, and windows at either end, over the counters, let in sufficient light. On the counter there was ice in a tub and a piece of ice was already darkening a thick canvas bag. Amos opened a drawer and took out a hammerlike crusher that had a scoop in place of claws.

"With this," said Amos, handing the crusher to Jeff, "you can occupy yourself in pounding up the ice."

Amos went into the kitchen, and Jeff attacked the bag, muttering that fancy drinks were just a waste of time. Amos returned with a jar in which mint and sugar and bourbon were by now pleasantly blended and set to work.

Emma peeked through the swing door into the dining room, anxious to see if the furniture was as lovely as she had remembered it, her mind busily tabulating chairs and table and wondering what value Jeff would put upon them. The table was a honey all right. Fifteen, seventeen hundred? Her eyes traveled around the room from left to right. (Jeff always started to inventory at the left of a door and progressed around a room, rattling off objects and prices at a speed that made her head swim.) The sideboard was faced with crotched mahogany, paneled and inlaid; she thought two thousand would be about it. The knife boxes? Two hundred if they were empty. Behind the doors of the corner cupboard, to the left of the fireplace, Emma could see the rows of blue-and-white Lowestoft. The blue borders were gold starred, Jeff had said so, but she gave up trying to estimate because she could not count the pieces. The soup tureen had a cover and if it had a platter it would be worth at least three hundred dollars. She skipped the cellaret beside the fireplace and opened the door a little wider to see the corner cupboard to the right. There were five shelves in this cupboard and on every shelf thick-packed silver gleamed darkly, unpolished, disregarded. Emma shook her head at the careless waste. There were supposed to be pieces there by Dummer, Coney and Savage, though Emma wondered about that, because those workers antedated the building of the house. Emma pulled her head back into the buttery.

"How come," she asked, "that you've got silver from the sixteen hundreds when the house wasn't built until seventeen ninety?"

"Seventeen ninety-one." Amos paused in the concoction of his drinks to correct her. "Didn't I ever tell you about that? My namesake, Captain Amos, was an upright man but he was pretty cute just the same. When the date for his marriage was finally set he wrote to all the outlying relatives—the ones who wouldn't think that they had to send a present because they lived too far away to get to the wedding. To each and every one he expressed deep regret at their inability to attend the festivities, but if, he added, they cared to send his bride a little remembrance, he thought that she would be most charmed with Great-grandfather's candle cup, or Uncle Zeke's mug, or whatever particular piece he was after. Most of the relations bit. Captain Amos may have been an antiquarian before his time, or more likely he simply liked property, for he appended all his presents to the inventory."

"What a slick idea," said Emma.

"Yah," said Jeff. "You can use it when you get married. Are we going to get that drink?"

Again on the lawn, sitting in the lengthening shadows, Emma looked away over the rolling fields, the orchards and the stone-grayed green of pasture to the distant hills. It was very peaceful.

"This," said Emma honestly, "is a swell place."

"It could burn down," said Jeff, "just like that."

"Did you get Rawlins?" Amos asked.

"No, but I left a message; he'll be out later."

"There's no hurry. I might change my mind."

"Cripes, have we got to go all over that again?"

Emma thought Amos was joking; she had assumed from the way Jeff had spoken that everything was settled. But if Jeff got waspish she would have to be the oil on the troubled waters or they would be out a much needed fee. It might be wise to change the subject.

"Who lives over there?" she asked, pointing to a gable end that showed through the trees perhaps a mile away.

"That's the Chandler place," Amos explained. "They came out about a week ago. They only come in the summer. It's pretty rural for Eunice."

"Oh," said Emma, wondering what kind of man Amos' dead sister could have married to produce such a disagreeable girl as Eunice Chandler.

"That was a good drink," said Jeff.

"Well," said Amos, "you saw how I made it. Are you ready for another, my dear?"

"Not yet," said Emma, "and I haven't seen Slocomb yet."

She got up, expecting that Amos would go with Jeff; instead Amos followed her to the stable.

Jeff went into the house. He wanted a drink and his interest in horses was purely academic.

The big barn, over the brow of the hill, was used only for the storage of hay. Amos' work team was kept in the Leavitt barn and the stable was occupied in solitary splendor by Slocomb. The Leavitt boys complained that the quarter mile added to their round of chores when Amos was away, but Amos would have it so. Mrs. Leavitt had been heard to remark that he would have kept Slocomb in the house if it hadn't been for Miss Amy.

In the stable door Emma paused and carefully put out her cigarette. From the aromatic depths within came a sociable nicker. At the first box stall Amos unsnapped a chain. A dark bay horse stepped briskly out. Slocomb, b. g. 15.2, had the good fortune to have been foaled with extraordinary willingness to please and to have developed a perfect conformation. The ribbons in the tack room attested to both. Now he nuzzled Amos' pocket suggestively.

"Pig," said Amos. "Where are your manners? Say how-de-do to the lady."

Slocomb turned to Emma, removed with sensitive lips her broad-brimmed straw hat and bowed politely three times; then, with the carelessness of a child, he dropped the hat and stretched out his neck for the deserved carrot. Emma, who was used to waiting on herself, reached for the hat; Amos reached too, and their hands met. With his other hand Amos picked up the hat, then he drew Emma to her feet. Emma could have laughed, she could have reached for her hat, she could have done any one of a number of things to turn the situation off lightly, instead she made the mistake of looking at Amos.

"There is something I want to tell you," Amos began.

For a long instant their eyes held, then a dark head was thrust between them, demanding attention, and it was Amos who laughed.

"Always be good to Slocomb," he said, "he's a very smart horse."

Before Emma had time to decide whether or not it was relief that she detected in Amos' tone a voice came from the doorway.

"Mrs. Leavitt said to tell you that the baskets are packed."

As Amos led Slocomb back into his stall, Jeff spoke to Emma.

"Leave the customers alone," he said, "we don't need the inventory that bad."

And the worst of it was, Emma thought, she hadn't been thinking of the inventory.

As they walked back to the house Emma found nothing to say. She felt as though she had reached for the cookies and received a punishing whack on the fingers. It was embarrassing enough to be caught in the throes of an emotion, however transitory, without having the added wonder if, perhaps, Amos had not been glad of Slocomb's interruption. Emma began to be quite disgusted with herself and a little annoyed at Amos. After all, she thought, maybe women deserved to be knocked over the head and dragged by the hair to a cave. She wished Hank were there.

They carried the baskets to a pine grove at the foot of the hill, some distance from the house. There were benches there and a table and a fireplace for cooler nights. Jeff had replenished his glass, not for the first time. He breathed rather heavily through his nose and, the incident in the stable apparently forgotten, sat himself down and told Emma what to do next.

Emma laid the cloth and set out the knives and forks meekly under his direction. "About the inventory," she began, just to show that she could be as prosaic as the next one, "it oughtn't to take so very long, because of that one of the first Amos' that you told me about. We can check off the things that are on that and add the rest."

Jeff looked at Amos.

"No," Amos said quickly, "we won't use the old inventory. It's not made out by rooms, naturally, and you'd spend half of the time running from attic to cellar trying to find something."

"Oh." Emma was interested. "What's it like? Does it say twelve leather-seated chairs, so many pounds, shillings and pence, when it means twelve shield-back Hepplewhite mahogany dining chairs, curved seats, molded and tapered square legs with spade feet and stretchers?"

"You left out 'carved ears of wheat and pendant honeysuckle ornament,'" Jeff reprimanded her.

"Good heavens," said Amos, "do you have to put things like that in? Why, it'll take you forever."

"When we do a job," said Emma, "we do a job. If you don't put down a description how can you tell which set of chairs got burned up? We're expensive but we're worth it."

Amos set a pot of beans on the table and shook his head. "It sounds to me like a lot of trouble and expense. I don't know that I can afford it."

"For shame," said Emma. "All your gorgeous things and the inventory to prove that they've always been there—why, they're a sacred trust, a connoisseur's dream, an historical heritage."

"You sound like my brother-in-law," said Amos dryly. He leaned against the table and spoke slowly. "I don't believe you understand how I feel about my house and its furnishing and because—of certain things, I should like to tell you."

He looked at Emma intently and, ignoring Jeff, spoke only to her.

"When I was six my father thrashed me because I tried out a new jackknife on one of the ladder-backed Chippendales. I deserved a thrashing, but it seemed to me that the fact that it was Great-great-grandfather's chair was unduly stressed. I could never play in the house. My mother was always polishing something, and my father could never be disturbed because he was always in his room writing a paper for some historical society. It wasn't until Aunt Amy took me in hand with her stories of typhoons and waterspouts and killer whales that I began to appreciate old Amos and to have some respect for his furniture, but I never let it dominate me the way it did my father. I like the house because it is mine and I like the furniture because it is beautiful, and perhaps I am not so immune to its value as I have led you to think. The man who built this house had earned the right to it; his descendants deserved it as long as they farmed the land. My father was proud of his ancestors but he spent his days writing about them, supported by the labor of girls in a mill. I myself am not much better but at least I try to grow apple trees. After—" Amos broke off with a shrug of his shoulders. "I am being much too serious and probably boring; but remember that I do not like useless things. A chair is not good if there is no one to sit in it. Do you see a big spoon for the beans anywhere?"

Emma didn't and offered to go back to the house for one. She was rather surprised that Amos let her go. Perhaps she overrated his manners. But as she climbed the hill she thought of the little boy who had been unhappy in a home that was no better than a museum and her irritation gave way to tenderness.

Still deep in thought Emma turned the corner of the house toward the kitchen door and almost ran into a sorrel mare who promptly reached forward with one white-stockinged foot and kicked sidewise. Emma saw the flash of white, ducked and landed one shoe neatly in the pan of milk set out for the barn cats.

"Now that's too bad," said Mrs. Leavitt. "That Agnes is a mean one."

The redheaded girl in boots and breeches laid a hand on the mare's neck. "Darling precious," she said, "Mamma loves you."

A bangle bracelet clattered on her arm as she patted the mare, almost approvingly. It was a cute bracelet, Emma thought. And wouldn't Eunice Chandler have one composed almost entirely of fraternity pins?

"Hello," said Emma flatly. She supposed that Eunice Chandler had a perfect right to ride over to her uncle's any time she wished, but Emma would have preferred that she had picked another time. She had assumed that Eunice had not been quite herself the night at the Copley but she would a little rather that Eunice had not come upon her ensconced in the bosom of the family for the weekend. Eunice would undoubtedly have remarks to make about that.

"Isn't it marvelous out here?" she asked politely, shaking her wet foot. "It's the first time I've been cool in days." Without waiting for an answer she turned to Mrs. Leavitt. "Could we have a big spoon for the beans?"

"You tell Amos," said Mrs. Leavitt, "that I packed one in the basket, but I'll get you another one anyway." She went into the kitchen.

"I mean, really, Amos must be getting as senile as Aunt Amy."

The remark seemed directed more to Agnes than Emma, so Emma ignored it and sought to make peace by stretching out a tentative hand to the mare who put back her ears and struck at Emma, snake-like, teeth bared. Eunice laughed.

"Oh, for heaven's sake," said Emma, "put her in the barn and come on down and have some beans."

"Precious," said Eunice venomously, "will you listen to her inviting us, just like a lady?"

Emma couldn't have sworn to it but she was sure that Eunice jerked on the bits, for Agnes reared and struck out with her forefeet.

"Damn it," said Emma, forced to another undignified jump, "are you trying to kill me?"

"What a perfectly dreadful way to talk. We wouldn't dream of doing such a thing, would we?"

"I wouldn't put it past either of you," said Emma, beginning to be a little annoyed at being talked to through a horse interpreter.

"We just came over to get a look at that man"—Eunice still spoke to the mare—"that she calls her employer."

"You stop talking to that horse," said Emma, "and listen to me. If you're sore because Amos takes me out, go ahead and be sore. I don't see that it's any of your business anyway. But Jeff Graham is my em-

ployer and we came out here because we were invited. I tried to be
civil. It's the last time I'll ever do it."

Eunice whirled around. "What do you mean?" she asked.

Emma hadn't meant anything special but she had gained an advantage and she was not going to back down. "I mean," she heard
herself saying quite calmly, "that if I marry Amos, you needn't bother
to send a present."

Eunice's face was very white. "You'll never marry Amos," she said.
"I'm warning you. Now go ahead and try it."

Until that moment Emma had had no idea of marrying Amos;
she still didn't but she wasn't going to let Eunice Chandler out-bluff
her. "Just for that," she said, "I will."

"I said, 'Here's the spoon.'" Mrs. Leavitt was behind them.

Emma muttered a thank-you and departed, conscious that two
pairs of eyes were boring into her back.

All the way down to the grove she was furious with herself. If Eunice
hadn't insinuated things about Jeff, she wouldn't have lost her temper. If people hadn't been throwing Amos at her all day, it never would
have occurred to her to say that she might marry him—would marry
him; she had gone as far as that. And Mrs. Leavitt had overheard her.
And either she or Eunice would tell Amos and he would look down
his nose at her and say, "I hear that you are going to marry me. Well,
well, isn't that nice?" and she would feel like a fool, because, after all,
she did like Amos. Emma kicked at the pine needles and tried to
compose her face if not her feelings.

"What the hell," said Jeff as she came up, "did you go back to
Boston for that spoon?"

"I'm sorry," said Amos apologetically, "I found one in the basket."

Emma said nothing and took her place at the table.

"Beans and hot brown bread, on a night like this." Jeff sucked
plaintively at the melted ice in the bottom of the glass he had brought
down from the house.

"It's Saturday night," said Amos, "and it seems very comfortable
here to me. You aren't too hot, are you, my dear?"

Emma, who was boiling inwardly, said that she was delightfully
cool and that the coleslaw was delicious.

Apparently Eunice wasn't coming down. Emma didn't see how
she'd have the nerve to after saying what she had, the nasty snob.
Emma had half a mind to marry Amos, just to spite her; he'd die
pretty soon anyway—Emma stopped, aghast at the idea her mind had
presented to her, but she went on playing with the notion, almost in

spite of herself. She could marry Amos, and then when he died she'd have a lot of money and could loan it to Jeff. She'd feel better, too, about marrying Hank if she had something beside a salary which, generous as it was, always seemed to have been spent in advance. What was the matter with her? She couldn't marry Hank and Amos both. Emma tried to think of something else.

Maybe Hank didn't want to marry her any more; he hadn't mentioned it for at least a month; and Amos— Well, she couldn't quite decide about Amos until she had sorted out the meaning of the remarks in the stable. What had Amos wanted to tell her?

What had he meant by saying that Slocomb was a wise horse? What had he meant by telling her to take care of Slocomb? An idea came to Emma, an idea so fantastic, so improbable, that she put it away from her at once. But she looked at Amos speculatively.

"What's the matter with you, gone deaf?" Jeff's voice broke into her thoughts. "I've asked you three times if there's any reason why you can't stay out here Monday and finish the inventory if we get a good start tomorrow?"

"No . . . yes. I mean of course I can, if you do something tomorrow beside sit around with a glass in your hand."

"I've got a glass in my hand now," said Jeff, "but there's nothing in it."

Amos laughed. "There is no fruit of the field or the vine," he said, "that goes with beans. After we get back to the house and I've given you the key to the silver cupboard, you can drink all you want."

"You still keep the barn locked?"

Emma didn't think the remark made much sense and didn't think Amos thought so either, judging from the queer look he gave Jeff.

The shattering blast of an automobile horn made them drop their thoughts. The blasts continued and wound up with a jocular ta, da-da, da-da, tum-tum.

"Somebody ringing the doorbell?" said Jeff. "It must be Eddie."

"It sounds a little fresh for Eddie," said Emma.

Amos stood up. "I think perhaps I better go up."

"I think perhaps I better go up and get a drink," said Jeff.

"What am I supposed to do?" Emma wanted to know. "Wash the dishes?"

"Of course not," said Amos literally. "Come along if you've quite finished."

Jeff nudged Emma. "If it's company," he said, "we can go sit in the kitchen."

"If it's company," said Emma, "you'll sit in the parlor and be-have yourself."

As they came out of the pines they heard voices and a great shout of laughter. Somebody was admonishing Jack to hold 'er steady.

"That sounds like Shay," said Emma, and Jeff hurried forward, scenting companionship.

In front of the kitchen door they found Hank holding a laughing Eunice, tilting her face in various angles at the direction of a man who looked like a badly arranged haystack. His blond hair stood in every direction, his ears stood out, too, and his tan suit was as rumpled as an ill-fitting slip cover.

"O'Shay can you see—" Jeff had thought up the paraphrase and used it persistently.

Shay Horrigan had been Hank's friend for years, but life as a wan-dering photographer for various papers had taken him away from Boston before the shop of J. Graham, Antiques, had become Hank's favorite resting place. Returning, to work for the *American*, Shay had accepted Emma as not the worst that could have happened to a friend and Jeff as one who could occasionally be persuaded to abandon busi-ness for pleasure.

"That's it," Shay yelled and his flashlight popped in the semi-twi-light.

"Lookit," said Hank; "customers."

Shay turned to the others. "Step right up, folks," he called, "only three for a quarter, good for passports, albums and the college an-nual." Then, as he spied Emma, "Light of my life and star of my morn-ing, you look perfectly gorgeous—that means knockout—and you look gorgeouser every time I see you—"

"I know," Emma interrupted him. "I've heard you before. You love me, but I'm not photogenic." It was good, she thought, to be able to talk nonsense to someone without having to think what the words meant. She was glad that Shay and Hank were there and she hoped Amos wouldn't mind the fact that they were a little squiffed.

"I love you very much," said Shay, "but you repulse me, so I shall go for the redheaded beetle. How do you do, sir," as Emma went firmly through the routine of introductions, and, "H'are yuh, Jeff, still on the ragged edge of ruin?"

"Amos, old pal, old pal," said Hank, "why didn't you tell me you had a beautiful—" "And photogenic," Shay put in—"niece?"

"Her visits are rare," said Amos. "Her being here is surely a coinci-dence." His voice was calm and cool; it was more cool than calm when he spoke to Eunice. "Where is your father, my dear?"

"In Worcester." Eunice's voice was defensive. "I just stopped in; I was out riding."

"So I observe"—Amos' voice was imperturbable—"from your clothes."

The words that they said were all right, Emma thought, but there was an undercurrent in their tones. Apparently Amos hadn't forgiven Eunice for her remarks at the Copley.

Jeff asked, "What are we waiting for?"

Amos asked, "Would anybody like a drink?"

"You want a drink, Jack?" Hank asked.

"I dunno. What you think, Jack?"

"Well, maybe just one."

"Just one teensie-weensie, itsy-bitsy?"

"Oh, for God's sake," said Jeff as Amos led the way into the kitchen.

Emma maneuvered herself to Hank's side. "You might speak to me," she said. "And what have you two been doing?"

"Why, my dear Miss Marsh"—Hank was very formal—"how could I have overlooked speaking to my hostess? Lovely place you have here. Does it cost you much to run it?"

"You go soak your head," Emma advised.

"Fancy," said Shay. "Hand-hewn beams, just like in the movies. Swing your pardners!" He caught Eunice around the waist, whirled her off her feet and delivered her to Hank, who sashayed her the length of the room. Not to be outdone, Jeff seized Emma and followed them. When they turned, Emma, at least, was surprised to see Amos and Mrs. Leavitt, elbows locked, following each other in a skillful side shuffle.

"Hey, you cats," yelled Shay, "get a load of this."

But Mrs. Leavitt fell back with a, "Mercy sakes, I haven't done that for forty years" and asked Amos if he was going to bring up the baskets. Amos went out, laughing and reluctant.

Hank came across the room to Emma. "In answer to yours of recent date," he began, "in re to where we have been at. Don't ask stupid questions."

It was an offer of peace and Emma accepted it as such, "I don't have to ask," she said. "I bet you hit every bar in town."

"We may have missed a few of the smaller ones," Hank conceded modestly. "But Shay knows a lot of people."

Chapter 3

WHEN AMOS RETURNED everyone was in the buttery trying to mix drinks and getting in each other's way, and everyone was being very jovial and all the hatchets seemed to be buried, or at least ignored. Jeff pounded the big piece of ice in the bucket with the crusher because Hank was stirring his drink with the ice pick. Eunice sat on the counter beside Shay, who was playing "She loves me, she loves me not" with the charms on Eunice's bracelet. Emma, with a piece of ice that she kept putting in her mouth and plopping out into her hand when her mouth got cold, wondered whether Eunice had decided to stay to protect Amos or because she liked Shay's looks. Shay took a picture of Emma with the ice cube tucked in her cheek like a chipmunk's nut.

"We don't have to stay in the buttery," said Amos. "There are other rooms in the house."

"The best is none too good for me," said Shay. "Where's the parlor?"

"You won't like it," said Eunice; "it looks like a morgue." But she got down to show him.

Hank turned to Emma with a glass in his hand. "Here," he said, "Drink this and stop trying to act like a lady, unless you're afraid to have Amos see you with your nose wet."

"What's that?" said Amos.

Emma took a long swallow of her drink. Then she smiled sweetly at both of them and said, "Hank wants to know why I don't join the party."

"Why doesn't he?" asked Amos. "I rather imagine," he went on to Hank, "that Eunice intends to spend the night here. There is plenty of room and if you and Mr. Horrigan will stay you can drink as much as you like with no thought of smashed fenders or the state police, and tomorrow your friend can take some pictures. What do you say?"

Hank looked at Emma. "It's fine with me."

"Good."

Now Jeff was stirring his drink with the ice pick, so Hank picked up the crusher to compensate himself for the drink he had given Emma.

"Ah, sweet mystery of life," sang Jeff. "Amos! Got a pair of dice?"

Emma said, "Must you?" but Jeff followed Amos through the dining room and across the hall to the library. Emma went after them, protesting, but paused to listen to Shay and Eunice, who were peering in at the parlor door, as though afraid to enter.

"Isn't it awful?" Eunice was saying. "All set up for a funeral. Nobody's been in there since the last one. And the worst of it is that those goofy chairs are worth five hundred dollars apiece."

Emma knew that the chairs referred to were Gothic Chippendale and that Eunice was not far wrong on their value; she also thought that the parlor furniture, ranged as it was around the edge of the Turkey carpet did give the room a distinctly funereal effect. Shay took a picture of the parlor. "For our posterity," he said—"that means children."

Hank came up behind Emma and said, "Leave the young folks alone, can't you?"

Emma turned around and started for the dining room. Hank had proposed the truce and she was not going to be the one to break it, but if he was going to keep picking at her . . . Jeff whizzed out of the library with an, "Out of my way, woman," and Emma wondered if there was any place where she would be welcome. She went into the pantry and gloomily fixed herself a drink. She was a long time at it because she couldn't find the ice pick and because the ice seemed impervious to her inexpert blows with the crusher. She wondered what had become of Eddie; not that it would do him any good to come now. Sense was the last thing anyone seemed to want to talk, let alone business.

When she went back into the hall the crap game was in full swing. Shay took Emma's drink without so much as a thank you and handed it to Eunice. Eunice shot a seven and handed the dice to Shay.

"Are you sure you can afford this, my dear?" asked Amos.

Eunice did not seem to hear him.

"By the way," Amos went on, "if Mr. Horrigan will back his car into the shed, then Jeff can put his away and I can lock the doors."

Shay's point was a five.

"You can't five with a five," said Jeff. "Ten dollars he don't."

"As I said," Amos began again, "If Mr. Horrigan will back his car—"

"It's not my car," said Shay. "Come on, dice."

"You've got the keys," Hank reminded him.

Shay rolled a three and two, but the two was off the edge of the rug.

"No dice," said Amos.

"Great balls of fire," said Shay. "Here"—he pulled the keys from his pocket and flung them to Emma—"go put the damn thing wherever it is he wants it."

Emma left quickly. Somebody was going to get mad and she didn't want to be there to see it. Amos ought to know better than to heckle the man with the dice. She backed Hank's car in beside Amos'. The woodshed was long and there was plenty of room left for Jeff's car. The lights were on in the shed and as soon as she was in the car she couldn't help seeing it. It was a map, drawn in pencil on the back of an envelope and stuck in the gadget trap. Emma looked at the long straight line with the longer waggly line swung to the right. Why, Emma thought, it looked like the road to the farm. *W* certainly stood for Westham and the turns were right. Emma opened the compartment door and took out the letter. Sure enough, the map ended at the little square set beside the road. Someone had given Hank and Shay directions and drawn them a map, or perhaps they had drawn the map for themselves. It was good stationery. She wondered whether it was Hank's letter or Shay's. She turned the letter over and sat looking at it. It was Shay's letter all right, but printed across the corner in flaring letters was: Eunice Chandler, Pond Road Farm, Westham. But Shay didn't know Eunice. Stuff and nonsense, it was obvious that Shay did know Eunice but that for some reason they had pretended to be strangers. For what reason? Emma looked quickly around, then she put the letter back as she had found it and got hastily out of the car before temptation could overcome her.

All the way back to the house she concocted questions she could ask Hank that might lead to a little information. She was reasonably sure that Hank had not known the exact location of Amos' house. She could ask him if they had inquired in the village. He might say yes and add that he had drawn a map from the directions given them. If, on the other hand, he said no, what did that mean? It might mean that someone had given Shay directions; but when? Shay had come back only that afternoon. And why? She didn't know and she was growing more and more curious. She wished she had read the letter because she was afraid that she would have no peace of mind until she found out why Eunice Chandler had written to Shay and then pretended not to know him. But had she? It occurred to Emma that she had not been present when Shay and Hank arrived but that Eunice had. She would have to get Hank into a corner.

Another round of drinks was nearly gone when Emma got back. The tension of the game was higher now, and there was more money on the floor than Emma liked to see. The others could afford it, she thought—though Jeff shouldn't—but she knew that Shay's financial condition was always balanced perilously between payday and the end of the month. Eunice, who was out of the game now, was sitting beside Shay on the floor, and he would doubtless be moved to extravagance.

"I'll take fifty," he said as Emma came up.

"He's already faded," said Amos.

Jeff had the dice and rolled them. They came up six and three, and Jeff said, "Shoot the hundred."

"Just a minute," Amos broke in, "your point was eight."

"The hell it was," said Jeff.

"Really—" Amos began.

"Just for once," said Hank, "Jeff's wrong. The point was eight."

"You're a bunch of liars," said Jeff, picking up the dice again. "I suppose you think I can't shoot an eight?"

"I think," said Amos, "that you could probably shoot anything you wanted to."

The blow was so quick that Emma had not had time to realize what Amos' words could mean before she saw him lying on the floor with Jeff glaring down at him. Jeff had leaped to his feet as he struck, and the glancing blow had merely toppled Amos over backward. He lay there looking up at Jeff's angry face, laughing.

"My dear man," he said, "I didn't mean to insult you. After all, you just called me a liar."

Hank helped Amos to his feet, and Emma found her voice. "Jeff Graham," she said, "I'm ashamed of you. I always thought you were the one person who could be both a gambler and a gentleman. I see that I was wrong and I think you better apologize and go to bed." With shaking fingers she picked up the dice. Shay, emboldened by her example, reached toward the money.

"See here," said Amos, "none of that's yours. I told you he was faded."

Emma turned on him. "I can't imagine what ails you," she snapped, "you've done nothing but try to boss this game ever since it began."

If Emma had turned into a bee and stung him, Amos couldn't have looked more surprised.

"How fantastically vulgar," said Eunice.

"That's me," said Emma. "I'm vulgar and I'm a shopgirl, but at least I say what I mean and I don't try to interfere with other people's business."

"Nothing," Hank remarked, "could be farther from the truth."

"See here," said Jeff, "you chaps shut up. This is my fight. I started it and I'm sorry. Let's all have a drink and forget about it."

" 'Let's all get stinkin',' said Abraham Linkin." Shay wavered to his feet and draped his arms over the shoulders of Jeff and Amos. "Jack," he went on, "at this time of strife and uncertainty let no man cry 'Havoc,' unplug the dike or take the first step on the downward path. Let us have peace, gentlemen, and when I say peace I mean—"

"He means a drink," said Hank, "and it's best to humor him. You want a drink, Jack?"

"Of course I want a drink, you dumb ox."

Shay seized Eunice by the arm and hurried her toward the buttery with a surprisingly steady gait. Had he tried to relieve the tension, Emma wondered, by pretending to be drunker than he was? He seemed to have succeeded, for Amos was laughing, and Jeff threw his keys to Emma with the quite normal demand that she put his car away for him. Amos said that he would go with her and lock the doors.

"My sole concession," Amos said as they went out the rear door of the hall, "to the valuables in this house is to lock up every night. That is why I wanted to get the cars put away before this unaccustomed festivity made me forget about it, but I'm afraid I only succeeded in annoying everyone."

Emma wanted to tell him that Jeff wasn't angry any more, that his tempers were as transient as they were ferocious and to please not let Jeff's disposition interfere with insuring the furniture. But Amos had acted all right; he had laughed off the blow when he might very well have asked them to leave his house. She hadn't been very polite herself. She guessed she would let sleeping dogs lie.

"Skip it," she said and backed Jeff's car into the woodshed.

Amos watched her, then he came over and leaned on the car door.

"You're a cool little person, aren't you?" he asked. "Right now, when I ought to realize that I have drunk too much and been a tactless host, I am conscious of but one thing—"

A car rounded the lilac hedge and spotlighted them with its headlights. This time there was no doubt about it; Amos was annoyed at the interruption.

"Now who the devil?" he asked. "This isn't the Wayside Inn."

A figure in spotless cream-colored flannels and tan jacket got out of the coupe and came into the lighted woodshed.

"Why, it's Eddie," said Emma. "Mr. Currier: Mr. Rawlins."

"How do you do, sir?" Eddie extended a hearty hand. "I must apologize for the lateness of my arrival. I played two rounds with Hornsby"—he paused to see if Amos would nod appreciatively or say "What Hornsby?", but Amos merely shifted his weight from one foot to the other—"and after I got Mr. Graham's message I had to change and go to the office, but here I am. Ha! Ha!"

"Now if you'll just drive your car inside so I can lock up."

Anyone else, Emma thought, would have waited until morning to come out; but not Eddie. He'd be a millionaire when the rest of them were on the county.

Amos shut and locked the doors that opened onto the highway and then did the same for those that opened into the yard. With the doorways closed the woodshed was itself again, and it's arched and keystoned doorways might have hidden nothing but firewood for all the passer-by could tell. Eddie looked at the wood stacked by the kitchen door, at the scythe and pruning shears that hung on the wall; took in the passageway that led to the barn and the steps that led above. "It looks like a woodshed," he said.

"It is," said Amos. "We'll go round to the front door if you'd rather."

"Oh no. No indeed . . . quite all right."

Eunice might have known that they would use the door from the woodshed to the kitchen. She might also have released herself a little less languorously from Shay's embrace.

"Must you," Amos snapped, "abuse my hospitality and this man's condition?" and then, remembering Eddie, "I beg your pardon. Mr. Rawlins: Mr. Horrigan and my niece."

"The man who solicits insurance!" quoted Shay. "I hate to trust you with him, but this horse's neck has to see a man about a dog."

"Upstairs," said Amos, "right overhead."

Eddie looked a little shocked. Hank came into the room, nearly colliding with Shay and making as though to strike him.

"Well, look who's here. Now I know we have to have some more ice."

"Hello," said Eddie. "Quite a party."

"You ain't seen nothin'. Everybody's taken a poke at everybody else, or wanted to." Hank attacked the ice trays. "But now we're as agreeable as little birds in their nests." He added under his breath, "I don't think."

Eunice was repeating her name for Eddie and watching the door for Shay.

"Here's a note from Mrs. Leavitt," said Emma. "It says: 'Remember tomorrow is Sunday and have someone put the coffee on.'"

Amos sighed. "That's right," he said, "I'd forgotten."

"I'll do it," said Emma, "I really don't mind. The rest of them will probably want to sleep till noon, but I don't mind a bit."

"She makes lousy coffee," Hank called from the sink. Amos ignored him with a grateful "Thank you" to Emma and started Eddie in the direction of the buttery.

"Quite the little hostess, aren't you?" Hank said.

For two cents Emma would have burst out crying. It seemed to her that everyone had suddenly failed her. It didn't matter about Amos; if he did make a pass at her, she could always scream. But Jeff and Hank were the two people in her world that she counted on; they were supposed to behave themselves and to understand that her motives were always the best, even when obscured by somewhat dubious actions. It did not occur to Emma that this was a rather one-sided arrangement; it did not occur to her to rationalize her feeling at all. All she knew was that Jeff had disappointed her by letting his temper get away from him and that Hank was being unpleasant. She turned her face away and followed the others into the buttery. Eunice was there ignoring Eddie, who was trying to find out from Jeff if Eunice was one of the Woolen Mill Chandlers, and Jeff was telling Eddie that if he tried to talk business he'd get locked in the barn. In a moment Hank was back, mixing a drink for Eddie that he claimed was called "The Policy Clincher." Eddie said it was pretty late for him to start catching up with them.

Then the dining-room door burst open, and Shay was upon them, wild eyed and more disarranged than ever.

"I'm telling you"—his voice was husky—"the house is haunted. I—I went to the bathroom and I heard somebody talking."

His terror was so vivid and his appearance so comic that everyone laughed. It was a true laugh and it bound them together again in friendliness that was more positive than all their bickering had been. They all began explaining at once.

"You dope—"

"Miss Currier, of course—"

"Up so late?"

"I really believe he is scared—"

"My aunt," Amos explained to Eddie, "being deaf, is not aware that she frequently talks out loud. I'm sorry—"

Shay collapsed like a pricked balloon and took two of the drinks offered him.

"Speaking of haunts—" Eddie began.

"Sainted or otherwise?" asked Hank, causing Shay to writhe.

All the old stories of the will-o'-the-wisp, the loup garrou and relatives with second sight were trotted out, cynically or half believingly. Under Jeff's telling the flying Dutchman became an abandoned U-boat; Eunice wanted to know if cats really sucked babies' breaths, and Amos told of the Currier seasickness, traceable to the bride who had seen her husband washed overboard.

Shay, again the skeptic, said it was a pity that one of the world's best horror stories had been ruined by the assumption that a dying man's eye took a picture that could be rephotographed. Hank wanted to know if he'd ever tried it and stuck his finger in Emma's mouth which was wide open in a sleepy yawn. Emma tried to bite the finger but couldn't get her jaws together fast enough.

Amos said it was time they all went to bed, and Eunice said promptly that she would take the front room across the hall from Miss Currier's. Amos shrugged his shoulders, counted noses and asked Eddie if he would prefer to sleep with Jeff or on the couch in the parlor. Jeff glowered and Eddie said the couch would be fine. The rest of them went upstairs.

Emma accepted the room behind Eunice's and told herself that the maple field bed was just as comfortable as the claw-and-ballfoot Chippendale in the front room. Hank and Shay drew the room behind Miss Currier's, and there Amos pulled a completely made-up buckle bed from beneath the Hepplewhite four-poster.

"I'll be darned," said Shay, "the thing has a cot."

He flung himself on it and assumed the aspect of a man already deep sunk in sleep.

A bathroom had been installed in one of the smaller rooms in the ell and Jeff had the room beyond it—the hired man's room, Amos explained, pointing out the stairs that led from that end of the hall to the woodshed below. Where Amos himself was going to sleep was not apparent. Hank realized, from the brushes on the swell-front bureau and boots under the bed, that he and Shay were occupying Amos' room. Shay obviously neither knew nor cared. Amos, after the conventional apologies for the single bathroom, took his strop and straight-edged razor, a pillow for Eddie and went downstairs.

Eddie gave the sofa assigned him a poke and felt a little sad. The sofa might be worth a lot of money but it didn't feel as though it would be worth a nickel as a place of rest. Eddie hadn't expected to sleep on a sofa in a front parlor at Amos Currier's.

Eddie wasn't quite sure what he had expected; servants, certainly, tea in a summerhouse—only, of course, he had come too late for that sort of thing. What he hadn't imagined was a houseful of strange people waiting on themselves in a drunken, sloppy sort of way. Eddie locked the door—the key screeched loudly in the brass lock—drew the shades and carefully divested himself of his clothes. Aha. Just as he had feared, the sofa was at least a foot too short. With a deep sigh Eddie turned out the light and composed himself for an uncomfortable night.

Emma turned out her lights, pulled a hassock to one of the open windows and leaned her chin on the sill. The summer night was black and moonless; all she could see were the squares of light from the rooms below. She supposed everything was all right now. Everyone had gone to bed amiable. But Emma knew that it was an alcoholic amiability, likely to shatter at the first light blow, too flimsy to be proof against the irritability of the next day's probable hangovers. Emma could hear the running of water and the impatient pacing of feet in the hall outside. She would wait, she decided, until everyone else was through. She did not want to risk meeting Eunice in the privacy of the hall. She remembered that she had not asked Hank about the map.

Emma lost the thread of her thought; she might have dozed, for she became conscious that the squares of light on the grass below had disappeared. Amos had turned out the lights and gone to bed; probably everybody had gone to bed. No, there was a stream of light from the room that Eunice had taken, the best bedroom, not that Emma cared.

Eunice Chandler was a funny girl. What else did people have to have besides money and looks to make them happy? Money and looks usually got you everything you wanted. She wondered if Hank would like her better if she had money.

She was getting morbid, Emma told herself; money didn't make any difference, really; only if you were happy, money made things easier. She was stupid to think about Hank's feeling for her in terms of money. She had been a little stupid all day; it had been the heat. She wished she hadn't tried to tease Hank with Amos; she was sorry that she had been cross to Jeff in the crap game, and most particularly she wished she had not made the threat to Eunice. Suppose Eunice told Amos. Emma could feel herself blushing in the dark. Well, there was one way she could keep Eunice from telling Amos.

Emma went quickly to the door and listened. The old house was settling itself for the night with creakings and rustlings. Was Eunice in the bath or back in her own room? Emma couldn't tell; she would have to take the chance. Quietly Emma opened the door of her room.

Shay waited until Hank was in the bathroom before he opened his eyes. He had been afraid that his feigned sleep would become real before he could get away. Women were a bunch of dopes, but Shay had found that it was usually profitable to put up with their foibles. He grimaced to himself in the dark. He wished he hadn't told her he had the letter along, then she wouldn't have got so steamed up about it. What earthly difference did it make? The stair carpet was soft and thick; he hoped no one would hear him.

Hank bowed Eunice politely into the bathroom. Now he knew where she was. Shay was asleep and Jeff had just yelled at him to hurry; if he were going to make a fool of himself, now was the time to do it. Hank went downstairs and out the front door.

Jeff counted the people that used the bathroom: Hank, then Eunice and then a third that moved quietly and was probably Emma. What did Amos want to talk to him about? He could guess.

He waited impatiently for Shay and then decided that Shay had really fallen asleep when he hit the bed. Jeff went into the bathroom, drank a glass of water in front of the mirror and saw the ice pick protruding from his breast pocket. It was an excuse, not that he needed one. Jeff took the ice pick by its point and threw it across the room. It stuck, quivering, in the doorjamb. Not bad at all, Jeff thought. He'd learned quite a few useful things kicking around carnivals in his youth, things he didn't often get a chance to use nowadays. Jeff pulled the ice pick from the wall and went down the back stairs—quietly because he was in his stocking feet.

Eunice looked at her boots, cursed and wished she had asked Hank to pull them off for her. There was probably a bootjack in Amos' room, though, and no earthly reason why she shouldn't get it. She found herself walking softly because the house was so still it gave her the creeps, and someone had turned off the light at the end of the hall. As she reached forward to tap she felt Amos' door give under her hand. It swung away from her into blackness, and instinctively Eunice drew back. It was curious, she thought, that they had fallen asleep so soon. She listened but the only sound she heard was that of water running; not a creak, not a breath came from the room in front of her. Eunice felt, rather than heard, a door open behind her and without stopping to think what she would do next stepped into Amos' room. Someone was moving in the hall outside, someone who had come from Emma's room. Eunice wondered if it was Emma and then smiled maliciously as she wondered if it might be Hank. The steps edged their way softly downstairs, and Eunice just as softly closed the door. She had to be sure. She turned on the light, whirling about as she did so, half expecting a sleepy outcry. None came. Both of the beds were empty. Well, she could get the bootjack. It was in the closet, neatly placed in a row of boots. Eunice fitted one heel into it and then the other. She ought to have been suspicious, she decided, as soon as Hank Fairbanks had appeared. Amos had found out, maybe not all, but something. A detective had nothing to do with making out an inventory, and she didn't believe a word of their story about just deciding to come out. Shay had had a reason all right, and so had Hank. Hank had said that Amos had asked him, and Amos wouldn't do that, feeling the way he did about Emma, unless he had some other reason. They were down there now, talking, talking. A cold sweat broke out on the palms of Eunice's hands. She set her boots neatly beside Amos', picked up the bootjack and went, like the others before her, downstairs.

Chapter 4

EMMA opened her eyes and lay still for a few moments, thinking what a difference sunlight made. The house was quiet now; there were no creakings nor murmurings; or, if there were, they were drowned in the cheerful chirpings, chatterings and trills that came from outside. She hadn't the faintest notion what time it was; she supposed she'd better find out. Somebody would be sure to ask her what time it was when she got up. Somebody like Hank was always wanting to know the exact time. Emma pawed through her bag, put on a pair of slacks, a shirt and some slippers and opened her door. The house was still quiet. She breathed a sigh of relief; she would be the first after all. As she reached the bottom of the stairway the tall clock, after a series of whirring grunts, delivered itself of nine strokes. Emma made a face at it. Last night it had frightened her but not today, not in the sunlight, but she would have to hurry; it was later than she had thought. Down the hall, into the dining room—the pantry door was partly ajar, which was odd, because it was a swinging door. It must have caught on something. When Emma had rounded the corner of the table she could see what it was, and she stood stock-still.

All she cared, she thought, was that it wasn't Hank or Jeff whose bloody head kept the door from shutting; then she knelt down and touched the iron-gray hair because, until last night, she had been fond of Amos. Her fingers touched Amos' forehead; it was quite cold, and Emma put her hand on the doorjamb because the floor seemed to be falling away beneath her.

Shay came into the room unsteadily, rubbing his eyes. He was draped in a striped bathrobe that belonged to Amos and his hair was wet but uncombed.

"'S matter," he asked, "couldn't he get to bed?"

Emma made a strangled, gulping sound and got up from Amos' body. Shay shut his eyes and then opened them again quickly to see if the image was still there.

Jeff's head appeared around the corner of Shay's bathrobe. He said "Cripes!" and bolted back upstairs, almost knocking down Hank, who was descending, yawning luxuriously. By the time Hank had got his jaws together Jeff had disappeared into his room. Hank ambled on down the hall and paused at the dining-room door.

"What you got there, Jack?" he asked affably.

Emma, in the relaxation of relief at Hank's presence, threw her arms around Shay and began to cry.

Shay said, "Take it easy, Jack," meaning Emma and realizing foggily that they were all in this thing together.

Hank walked toward them, his eyes focusing on Amos' head. He disengaged Emma from Shay's shoulder and leaned her against his own. "It's what you get," he said, "for weekending in the suburbs."

Jeff returned with the air of having attended to something important and being, therefore, ready for any little thing that might turn up.

"It's perfectly ridiculous," Hank went on. "I don't know what county we're in. There's a sheriff or a chief of police somewhere, but where? What do we do first?"

"Couldn't we just put him away and forget about him?" Shay wanted to know.

"If you'd sober up," Hank said, "maybe you'd be some help."

"Oh-h-h," wailed Emma, burrowing deeper into Hank's shirt.

"Do you have to make all that noise?" Hank spoke to the top of Emma's head. "Are you just crying or are you crying because Amos is dead?"

"No," Emma gulped. "I'm crying because he got killed!"

"She's got you there, Jack," said Shay.

"The great detective in action," said Jeff, "perfectly in command of the situation. It's very interesting."

Emma stopped in the middle of a sniffle to raise her head and glare at him. "You shut up," she said, "and quit heckling. You'll be glad he's here before this thing's over."

"What thing? What's the matter?"

Eunice was upon them in lounging pajamas of chartreuse and wine. Her red hair hung soft and loose, her mouth was very red. She was obviously arrayed for an entrance, but there was an air of indecision about her, as though she had walked on in the middle of a scene and not yet caught a familiar cue. For a moment no one spoke; they had forgotten that Eunice was in the play and did not know what line to give her.

Then Eunice came forward and looked at Amos. Her hand went to her throat.

"What's the matter with him?" she asked sharply; "why don't you do something?"

"There isn't anything to do," said Shay gently.

"No, no." Eunice's voice was shrill and her face worked. "He can't be dead. He mustn't be dead. Tell me he isn't dead and don't stand there staring like a pack of fools."

No one spoke.

Eunice reached slowly for the back of a chair and apparently forced herself to look at Amos.

"He's dead," she said, and now there was no surprise, no emotion, only a flat finality in her voice. Then she looked up at Emma and there was a flicker of triumph in her eyes. A triumph that was quickly concealed as she turned on them all again. "Say something. Somebody must know something. Or are all of you protecting each other?"

Still no one spoke. If Eunice had seemed at a loss for words when she first came in, now it was as though the rest were embarrassedly waiting for a director to correct her overplaying, to tell her that her interpretation of the part was not consistent with the performance she had given the night before.

Finally Shay stepped forward and struck an attitude, profile turned, fingers clutching upward. "I killed him," he said. "No man can insult the woman I love."

"You don't love anybody," Hank broke in, "you're a somnambulist. I had to coax you down off the roof this morning with a saucer of whiskey. Did Amos frighten you? Try to think."

"That's it," Shay admitted. "I'd forgotten, but that's it."

"Yeh?" asked Jeff. "What'd you hit him with?"

"A left-handed monkey wrench left by a careless workman—pure coincidence."

Eunice looked at them in honest amazement. People didn't talk that way; not about serious things. One tried to cover up—to pretend, but not by joking. One pretended innocence, not guilt.

"Say," said Hank suddenly, "where's Eddie?"

Everybody looked at everybody else.

"Where was he supposed to sleep?"

"In the parlor, I think."

Hank dashed from the room. The parlor door was locked. He pounded on it; there was no answer. He pounded again.

"Hello—hello," said a sleepy voice.

"Open up."

After a moment, in which Eddie apparently put a pongee dressing gown on over matching pajamas, the key screeched again in the lock.

"Ah, but I say"—Eddie was half apologetic, half protesting—"am I late for breakfast? I had sort of a time getting to sleep but I was certainly corking it off— Oh, but Hank, I say! Is something wrong?"

Hank stood twiddling the key in the lock; with each turn it emitted its mournful screech. Hank noticed that all the windows except one nearest the front door were closed; those on the west were shuttered.

"What's the matter?" Eddie repeated. "Do you have to keep doing that?"

"Sorry, old man," Hank said, "I was wondering how to break the news. I'm afraid you and Jeff are out of luck on that policy—"

"Why, what do you mean?"

"You see, Amos got himself killed last night—"

Hank thought Eddie was going to faint and shoved him onto a chair. Eddie moistened his lips.

"What? How?" he managed to get out. Then: "Oh, this is dreadful. What will the company think? I must get out of here."

He half rose from the chair but Hank put a hand on his arm.

"Steady," he said. "None of us can leave until the police have been here, you know."

"The police!" Eddie was aghast, then he collected himself. "Of course. I'm sorry. There are others to think of, aren't there? There were others here last night." He seemed to brighten perceptibly at the thought. "Miss Chandler . . . Dreadful shock . . . How—how was he killed?"

"Hit on the head."

A thud, thud, thud sounded from above and Eddie jumped.

Hank started for the door. "Get your clothes on," he said, "there's a lot to do." His long legs took him upstairs with unaccustomed speed.

In the dining room the others heard Eddie's voice with relief and then their own worries claimed them.

"I ought to see if Father is back from Worcester," Eunice said listlessly. "Somebody ought to tell Auntie."

Shay looked at her. "Right now," he said, "before you do anything else, there's a little matter that I'd like to straighten out."

Without a word Eunice turned and led the way across the hall.

Emma turned to Jeff.

"Don't look at me like that"—Jeff's voice was indignant—"I didn't do it, if that's what's worrying you."

"I know that, silly, but somebody did. And it's happened to us before, and they'll dig up the newspaper files—"

"—and find out that we were O.K.," Jeff reminded her. "Cripes, can't we cover him up, or get out of here, or do something?"

Emma went to the sideboard, opened a drawer, another drawer, found a napkin and handed it to Jeff. "You do it," she said. "I'll be sick."

Jeff spread the napkin over Amos' head.

"God," he said, "what a mess."

"Jeff," said Emma, "I'm afraid. She doesn't like me. And someone is going to ask questions."

"You're afraid." Jeff was scornful. "You didn't hit him in the crap game; you had sense enough to go to bed last night."

"Jeff!" Emma's voice was sharp with anxiety.

Hank came back into the room.

"Where's the telephone?" he asked. "And where's Eunice?"

"In the hall." Emma was wishing that she had had sense enough to go to bed and was sure that Jeff meant that he hadn't. "The telephone, I mean. Shay took Eunice into the library."

Emma led the way to the telephone and after a minute Jeff followed them.

"135 ring 4," said Hank.

"And see here," he spoke to Jeff. "You and Eddie go around and check up on all the doors and windows. Only don't touch them; don't touch anything. Hello."

Emma wondered why Jeff had been prowling around in the night. It was just like him to be doing something he shouldn't at the wrong time. It was a wonder he hadn't seen her. Maybe he had seen something else, heard something. If only he hadn't seen or heard her, everything would be all right.

"Mrs. Leavitt," Hank was saying, "Miss Currier asks that you come right over, and how do I reach the chief of police? Yes, there has been an accident. How do I— Thank you."

Emma liked the way Hank's hair grew on the back of his neck. She had been a fool to think that she could ever marry anyone else. It had taken last night to show her that. Guiltily Emma realized that there was a certain relief in knowing that she didn't have to face Amos again. There'd be no inventory now and Eddie would feel badly about the loss of the policy, although this wasn't the time to be thinking about that.

"Is this the chief of police?"

It was funny how you got used to people and didn't realize how much you liked them. She ought to be sorrier about Amos, but all she had thought of when she saw him there was how glad she was that it wasn't Hank. She wished she hadn't been such a fool as to try to talk to Amos, but at least nobody knew about it. She'd hate to have to explain that to Hank.

"Yes sir, right here until you come."

Hank hung up. "Now," he said, "until someone hires me I'll work for nothing."

He went back into the dining room. Emma followed him because she felt the need of human companionship and Jeff was in the parlor with Eddie. Hank swung one of the Sheraton chairs away from the table and sat down in it. Emma counted the chairs around the table; there were eight of them, and four against the wall. Amos had thought there were two more around the house somewhere. And the love seat in the hall matched them. At two hundred and fifty dollars apiece, that made—

"Slugged," said Hank, "just as he opened the door, by someone he caught in the buttery doing something they shouldn't."

"You dummy"—Jeff's voice came to them from the hall—"of course this furniture is valuable."

"It was probably Jeff snitching another drink."

"You know better than that."

Hank reached out and patted her hand. "All right, pussy," he said, "it was Shay necking Eunice."

"It was not," said Shay. "That was earlier."

Shay was fully, and almost neatly, dressed. He carried his camera and sack of bulbs.

"Exclusive. By our staff photographer who just happened to be walking by. I wondered how long it would take you to think of that. Where's Eunice?"

"She went to the barn to feed the horses. She has no intention," Shay went on as Hank got up quickly, "of leaving these premises." Hank sat down again.

"How many shots do you want?" Shay propped the buttery door open with a chair and twitched off the napkin that Jeff had placed over Amos' face.

Emma, who had been rather proud, thus far, of her usually uneasy stomach, caught a quick glimpse of the dark clots in Amos' hair, clapped her hand to her mouth and hastily left the room.

Shay looked at Hank questioningly. "What you got there, Jack?"

"My best girl," said Hank seriously. "Only she sort of fell for the middle-aged gentility and excitement always makes her vomit."

"Okay, boss." Shay climbed up on the chair for a better shot of Amos' body. "Only I sort of wish she'd stayed in her room last night."

"Go on."

"Somebody heard her go out but fortunately they're in no position to mention it."

"Look here, this sort of thing isn't going to get us anywhere. Come on, out with it."

"Nope." Shay screwed in a fresh bulb and threw the old one to Hank, who caught it automatically.

"Nope," Shay continued, squinting up at the ceiling. "I've traded Baron Rothschild and an old suit of clothes for Upper Silesia. If there's no coal in Upper Silesia, I'm stuck, but it looked like a good deal at the time. Hey, turn that light out for me."

"I will not," said Hank but he got up off the chair and went to the doorway. In the bright morning sunlight the light of the single overhead bulb in the buttery had gone unnoticed. It stared dimly down at the scene it had illuminated so brightly the night before.

Hank looked up at it and muttered softly under his breath. The light had been on when he came back from the gazebo and the back door had been unlocked. He had assumed that Amos hadn't gone to bed, but perhaps he had been dead then. He looked at the switch in the dining-room wall beside the buttery door and then turned his attention to the buttery. The buttery was apparently just as Hank had seen it last, except for Amos' sprawled out figure. The counter to the left was strewn with empty and half empty glasses; a partly filled bottle stood there beside two of its depleted brothers. On the counter to the right the tub that had held the ice was encircled by a wet ring. The ice pick lay there, the canvas bag and a crumpled package of cigarettes. Hank looked at the ice pick. Its heavy wooden handle lay in the puddle of water. The wood would be soaked and fibrous but perhaps only on one side.

"Is it heavy enough?" asked Shay.

Hank shrugged his shoulders. "As I remember it, yes. I can't tell without touching it. Take a shot of the place, will you?"

They heard the sound of a key in the rear hall door, the sound of firm, hurrying footsteps; then Mrs. Leavitt came into the dining room.

"What's going on here?" she began and then, because Shay had the buttery door open, she saw the body. For an instant she stood there, and it was impossible to say what thought passed through her mind; then without a word she turned and went upstairs.

"Aplomb," said Shay admiringly, "sheer aplomb. What does it take to get a rise out of a native?"

"A native"—Hank's tone was perfectly serious—"should have asked: 'Is he dead?' taking no stock in the fact that he looked dead. You noticed that she had a key?"

"*Ethan Frome,*" said Shay, "with an all-star cast. Not a movie."

"How do I know?" Hank was looking at the dining-room windows. "I just came to paint."

"What are Jeff and Eddie up to?"

"Checking the windows and doors."

Shay whistled softly. "Suppose that they find they were all locked?"

"Then," said Hank, "you'll be damn glad Mrs. Leavitt had a key and you won't go around having secrets with Eunice Chandler."

"Honest"—Shay looked up from his camera—"that didn't have anything to do with this."

"Little Sir Galahad."

Hank was examining the windows. Like those in the rest of the house they had been furnished with ordinary modern locks, but there were no weights in the window, and the sashes, when raised, had to be supported on the notched boards that hung beside them. In order that the shutters might be closed, when so desired, against the summer sun the windows had been fitted with thin-framed screens that slid in narrow zinc troughs at the sides of the windows. If the windows were open, the screens could be raised from the inside by means of a handle affixed to the bottom, and it required no very great imagination to see that they could be raised from the outside by the insertion of any thin blade between the screen and the sill. Both of the dining-room windows were locked.

"Any good burglar," said Hank, "could jimmy these windows or get in if the windows were unlocked. But he didn't."

Jeff and Eddie came across the hall from the library.

"There's a window open in there," Jeff informed them, "but it's got a different kind of screen that hooks on the inside. Nobody could've got in there unless they cut a hole in the screen, and there's no hole."

"That's where he was going to sleep," Eddie put in. "There's a comfortable couch in there."

Hank looked at Eddie admiringly. Eddie had quite recovered from his earlier panic; he inspected the dining-room windows seriously, hands in pockets, but he walked past Amos' body rather quickly and hurried into the kitchen, leaving Jeff to investigate the buttery. The buttery windows were higher up, over the counters; Jeff looked to see that both the locks were turned and went quickly after Eddie.

"Come on," said Shay, "this is beginning to get me."

They followed the other two into the kitchen. There also the locks were fast, and the outside kitchen door fastened with a heavy old-fashioned iron bolt that made the door impregnable to anything short of an ax. The door to the woodshed was unfastened and for a moment they thought they had something, but Amos had himself locked the folding doors, and the door to the stable passageway was held tight with a heavy iron hook. Hank went up the stairs that led above and came down again.

"Fine and dandy," he said, "for anyone that wanted to move around inside the house; otherwise, nix."

"Well," said Jeff, "that ties the can on somebody. Anyone want to hire a good detective?"

They looked at each other and tried to laugh but each one presumably had his own uneasy thought, for they followed Hank in silence back into the kitchen just as Mrs. Leavitt knocked at the bolted door.

"Open it for her," said Hank; "we're all witnesses that it was locked."

Mrs. Leavitt's lips were folded together and her face wore its customary look of composure. She put a small pan of water on the electric stove, got down the tea caddy and plugged in the toaster. The great fireplace at the end of the room had a full complement of utensils but Mrs. Leavitt was not one to prefer quaintness to utility. The four men watched her intently. No one saw Eunice as she crossed the yard and entered the house. No one spoke.

Finally Mrs. Leavitt wheeled around in front of the sink and said, almost defensively, "I'm making tea for Miss Amy."

"Sometimes"—Shay's voice was plaintive—"I take tea for breakfast."

"Mercy sakes," said Mrs. Leavitt, the meaning of their concentration dawning on her, "haven't you had anything to eat?"

Four heads made instant denial as Mrs. Leavitt, without waiting for their answer, got out the coffeepot and an iron skillet.

Upstairs Emma came out of the bathroom and saw Eunice standing in front of Amos' room, barring her way. Emma paused, instinctively not liking to meet Eunice, alone, there in the narrow hall but unwilling to retreat down the back stairs. Eunice waited, too, her look hostile, intent. Then an insistent thud, thud, thud sounded from the front of the house and Eunice turned impatiently to answer it.

Emma went hastily downstairs, sniffed the smell of frying bacon and told herself that it was foolish to be afraid of Eunice Chandler. She went across the yard to the kitchen, slowing her steps now that companionship was at hand.

"Where have you been?" Jeff greeted her.

"None of your business." Emma spoke shortly, partly because the encounter with Eunice had upset her and partly because Jeff should have known what excitement always did to her stomach.

"Everyone," said Hank, "cooperated willingly with the police and the mystery was soon solved."

"That's what we've got to do," said Emma, supremely illogical. "Work together and get this thing solved, I mean, before the police try to pin it on someone we know didn't do it." She looked at Jeff as she spoke.

"The cops might pass me up," said Jeff, "if you'd quit pointing at me like a setter dog."

"Setters don't point, they set," Emma corrected him patiently.

"Now that you speak of it," said Shay, "you do remind me of a mamma hen."

Mrs. Leavitt poured a strong brew of tea into a Canton cup, arranged it with some toast on a brass Benares tray and spoke to Emma.

"Will you take this up to Miss Currier?" she asked. "Go right in, because she can't hear you. I'll attend to the menfolks."

Emma took the tray and left the kitchen; if she met Eunice now she would have something to throw at her.

Eunice was coming out of Miss Currier's room. They passed in the hall, Emma giving Eunice as much space as possible, watching her. Eunice paused outside Amos' door, looked at Emma and then went on downstairs. Emma pushed open the door of Miss Currier's room hesitantly, not exactly sure what to expect, and waited politely to be recognized. Miss Currier sat in a big chintz-covered wing chair at the head of a spade-foot mahogany four-poster; she wore a dressing gown of black-sprigged muslin held together high at the throat with a mosaic brooch. Her gray hair was parted in the middle and pulled, not too severely, into a knot on the back of her neck. In her thin brownish hands was a heavy gold-knobbed ebony stick that gleamed dully as her restless hands moved it to and fro. Her feet, in low-heeled black slippers, rested on a low footstool, and across her knees was a one-legged iron-braced table, of the type used fifty years ago in hospitals. For how many years, Emma wondered, had Miss Currier known no other life than that involved in the short but tedious journey from bed to chair and back to bed?

"My dear Miss Marsh"—Miss Currier spoke in a voice that was surprisingly deep—"this is very kind of you. If you can spare a moment will you please sit down and tell me about this dreadful business?"

Emma bent over to deposit the tray on the table and did not see the black cane slip out and poke at something that caused the valance of the four-poster to hang, ever so slightly, askew. She sat down in the fiddle-backed slipper chair that Miss Currier indicated and wondered what to say and how to say it. She had the feeling, although Amos had told her that his aunt could read lips, that she must raise her voice, and she didn't want to sit there shouting that Amos was dead and that they didn't know what or who had killed him. Besides, Hank had told Miss Currier that. What else did she want to know? Emma looked at the old lined face, half expecting to see there a senile tremulousness that indicated a desire for sympathy, for commiseration. In spite of the lines, the face was firm and the bright dark eyes that looked out of it were not veiled with age or tears: they looked searchingly at Emma, and Emma realized that she was being asked for information, not consolation.

"We don't know anything about it," she began. "I went down to start the coffee because he'd asked me to and—and found him—" Were the searching eyes, Emma wondered, asking what Amos' death had meant to her? "Then the others came—Shay—and—"

"Shay?" Miss Currier's cane remained poised for an instant in midair. "I don't believe Amos told me about him."

"Shay Horrigan," Emma explained. "He came with Hank—Henry Fairbanks. They went to school together."

"Amos told me that you were coming, with your employer, Mr. Graham, I believe?"

Emma nodded.

"Had you met my niece, Eunice Chandler?"

"Once before," said Emma. "With Amos." That way of putting it, Emma thought, made it sound very polite and proper. As a matter of fact it hadn't been polite at all.

"Amos never liked her," said Miss Currier, "but I think it is most unlikely that she—"

The knocker, sounding on the door below them, drowned out the rest of the sentence. Emma could hear Hank's voice and decided that the knocking indicated the arrival of the chief of police. She might just as well, she thought, stay where she was and find out why Amos hadn't liked Eunice.

"She only thinks she is unhappy," Miss Currier was going on. "So many of the present generation are badly brought up." She broke off and went back to the subject of Amos' death. "In the night," she asked, "you didn't hear anything?"

Emma looked in the searching eyes and said, "Noises. Not what you mean." After all, she thought, she didn't have to tell Miss Currier

The ebony cane tapped the floor with vexation. "I would have heard something if I hadn't been deaf for thirty years."

"Em-ma." Hank's voice came insistently from below.

"Someone is calling me," said Emma. "I've got to go."

As the door closed behind Emma, Miss Currier's lips began to move.

"I was very young when it happened." Her words were half whispered. With her ebony stick Miss Currier lifted the bed valance, then she looked toward the door, sighed and applied herself to her cold tea.

Chapter 5

CHES DURRELL, the chief of police of Westham, had a slight stubble of beard and a large paunch. He stood meekly behind a truculent young man in the uniform of the state police who was firing questions at Hank. Hank was trying to explain the circumstances and the personalities of the gathering in Amos Currier's house and was being constantly interrupted.

"Miss Marsh found the body. As I told you, Miss Marsh is Mr. Graham's assistant. She came downstairs to—"

Hank caught sight of Emma. "Here she is now. Ask her about it."

"Miss Marsh: Lieutenant Ellis and Chief of Police Durrell."

"What were you doing downstairs before the rest were up?" Ellis shot the question at Emma without acknowledging the introduction.

"How do you do?" Emma said politely. "I was going to make the coffee."

"Did you kill Currier?"

"Oh no," said Emma. "Really I didn't."

"We'll see about that. Where's Miss Currier?"

Durrell opened his mouth to speak, but Hank pointed to the second floor, and Ellis stalked upstairs, Durrell and Hank trailing after him. Hank, at the end of the procession, said nothing but he extended his hand in a stiff-armed salute that caused Emma to suppress a giggle.

It was nice, she thought, to be friends with Hank again; it was comforting to have him joke with her. She knew that Hank was wishing that he could put Westham in Suffolk County and replace Ellis with Police Lieutenant Donovan; she herself thought that Donovon's suspicious aide, Sergeant Tim Connerton, would probably be more help than the stodgy Durrell. But Hank would take care of things. Even if there was no one to pay him he would see that Jeff was not accused of murder again. Some prowler had come in the night and killed Amos, and Hank would catch him.

Carefully avoiding so much as a look into the dining room, Emma went back along the hall, out the door at the rear and across the yard to the kitchen.

Eunice and Eddie were seated at the kitchen table, Shay had thrown himself into the Boston rocker and Jeff was pacing nervously up and down. Jeff stopped as Emma came in and glared at her as though everything was somehow her fault.

"You'll be glad to know," he said, "that the downstairs was shut up tighter 'n a drum."

"All except Eddie's window." Shay rocked placidly.

"I'm usually a very light sleeper; I should think I would have heard anyone—"

"You were pounding your ear hard enough this morning"—Jeff squelched Eddie—"but, anyhow, that lock on your door makes enough noise to wake the dead."

"Oh!" Emma looked at the faces around her. All the thoughts with which she had been consoling herself left her and for a second she knew something near panic. Someone in the house, then, had killed Amos. Any one of them, except Jeff and Hank.

Shay poured Emma a cup of coffee and she took it to a corner as far removed from Eunice as possible. She didn't want any bacon now, nor any toast; she didn't think she could swallow either.

"Come, come," said Shay. "Remember, the condemned ate a hearty breakfast."

Emma didn't think he was very funny. She realized that to Eunice, and possibly to Eddie and Shay, she might be the guilty one. Jeff, alone, wouldn't suspect her. Her eyes sought out Jeff, hoping for a glance of reassurance, but Jeff was scowling at a pair of pipe tongs that hung by the fireplace.

Well, Emma wondered, why didn't somebody start it? Why didn't somebody look at her and ask, "What time did you go to bed?"

No one did.

Mrs. Leavitt began to gather up the cups and saucers. Shay asked if anyone wanted more coffee. Eunice said she did, and then Emma remembered the letter. Emma was sure, at that moment, that Eunice and Shay had been downstairs together after they thought the others in bed and, considering what had happened, they were keeping very still about it. Their secret would come out. Emma was sure of that, just as she had no illusions about being able to keep her own descent unknown. She got cold enjoyment from the fact that Eunice was probably as uncomfortable as she was. She and Jeff and Shay and Eunice. That was why nobody wanted to ask if anyone had been downstairs, because they all had. All but Eddie. Eddie had, Emma thought, slept the sound sleep of the self-styled insomnia victim.

"What was he hit with?" asked Mrs. Leavitt.

Jeff said, "I dunno," and bent over to tie his shoelace.

Shay said, "The ice pick."

Jeff's shoelace snapped in his hand.

"Are you sure?" said Eddie.

No, Shay wasn't sure.

Jeff tied a knot in the shoelace.

A car stopped outside, and they heard Ellis call from upstairs for somebody to go around to the front door. Two more uniformed figures passed the kitchen windows and presently there were sounds of activity in the buttery.

"Fingerprints," said Shay gloomily. "The fringe from your cuff, the hair from your head—that's what got Sacco and Vanzetti the hot-squat."

"Stop it," said Eunice sharply.

Eddie shook visibly. "It's awful," he said, "having to sit here. I ought to call someone from the office to explain before this gets in the papers."

"You and your office," said Shay with mock seriousness. "My office is going to cut my throat from here to here"—he gestured suggestively with his finger while Eddie watched with horrified fascination—"for not giving them a chance to scoop this job. And when they look in the morgue, well, let it be said I died for friendship."

"I thought they only put you in the morgue if you didn't have any relatives," Eunice began.

"Sh-sh," said Jeff before Shay could explain, "I think they're moving him."

They were all quiet. At the sink Mrs. Leavitt held her dishrag suspended in the air. They heard the shuffling sound of heavy steps, the scrape of a chair on the dining-room floor. "Careful, there," Ellis' voice snapped out.

From her corner Emma could look across the yard to the rear hall door and through it she could see men moving. She looked quickly away.

"They're putting him in the library," said Jeff.

"Why did anybody want to do it?" asked Mrs. Leavitt. "Amos was a good man."

"Maybe it was just an accident," said Eddie. "Maybe it was—"

"What makes you think it was an accident?" said Jeff.

"But, Jeff," said Eddie, "what else could it have been? Of course you know these people better than I do, but what motive—" He broke off and began again. "Look, if one of the windows was unlocked, it needn't have been any of use'

"You saw yourself," Jeff interrupted him, "that everything was locked except your window."

"I had a key," said Mrs. Leavitt quietly, "don't forget that."

The door to the buttery opened; Ellis strode briskly in and planted himself in their midst. Durrell followed him, mopping his forehead, and Hank ambled along again in the rear. As Emma looked at Hank she thought that he looked apprehensive, then he ran his fingers through his hair—a sure sign of irritation—and winked at Shay. Emma had no idea what was going to happen.

Ellis hooked his thumbs in his belt. "Come on," he said harshly, "which one of you killed him?"

Shay looked quickly behind himself for a hidden culprit; Jeff snorted, Eddie gasped.

"All right," Ellis snapped at them, "let's not waste time. Whose is this?"

He extended his hand and moved it slowly before their astonished faces. In his palm lay a little gold skull with ruby eyes.

Eunice said "Oh" and her bracelet clattered as her hand went to it. No one spoke. With a great effort no one looked at Eunice, except Eddie, who said stupidly, "Is it yours?" Eddie had not been there when Shay counted the fraternity pins on Eunice's bracelet and offered to get her an elk's tooth. Eddie had not been there, but the others had.

"It's mine," said Eunice in a very low voice. "It must have come off last night. Where—where did you find it?"

"Gimme that bracelet," Ellis demanded.

The bracelet jangled under Eunice's unsteady fingers as she unfastened it. Ellis spread it out on the table, and there, next to a little golden pig dangled an empty ring. Ellis laid the skull in position and turned to Emma.

"You," he said, "can you identify that?"

Emma bristled. She didn't like Ellis' high-handed manner and she didn't like to be called "you." Ellis knew her name.

"No," she said shortly. "I saw the bracelet but I didn't notice what was on it."

Eunice looked at Emma, amazed.

"So"—Ellis stuck out his jaw—"you didn't notice; well, let me tell you—"

"You don't need to be disagreeable," Eunice cut in. "I said it was mine, didn't I?"

Hank coughed discreetly, warningly, but Ellis did not heed him, and if he had, it probably would have been too late. Emma and Eunice, whose frosty avoidance of one another had not gone unnoticed, had by their defense of each other set the pattern of the defense against Ellis. Sides had been chosen and, whether Ellis knew it or not, the kitchen was aligned against him.

Ellis abandoned Emma for Eunice. "If you're so sure it's yours," he went on, "what was it doing in Amos Currier's hand?"

There was a stir of astonishment in the kitchen.

"Oh, but then," Eddie began, "it doesn't matter—"

"Shut up," said Ellis.

"Could be," said Shay, "that he had picked it up off the floor—

"—in the dining room," said Jeff, "or the hall, or any damn place."

"That's what I told you," began Durrell while Hank kept prudently silent.

"And I tell you"—Ellis shouted them down—"that Currier snatched at this bracelet as he was struck and this thing came away in his hand." He whirled on Eunice again. "What did you kill him with, the ice pick?"

"No," said Eunice. "No."

"Why," Emma began suddenly, "I thought the ice pick was lost; I thought that was why we were using ice cubes."

"Premeditated!" Ellis shouted at Eunice. "You hid the ice pick so that you would be sure of a weapon."

"Cripes," said Jeff, "how could she? I had it in my pocket."

Everyone looked at Jeff. Ellis looked from Jeff back to Eunice again, as though loath to abandon his first victim.

"I'm telling you," Jeff went on, "I had it in my pocket."

"It ain't in your pocket now," said Durrell.

"Because I brought it back," Jeff snapped. "I saw it when I was undressing and brought it down. I talked to Amos, too, and I was probably the last person to see him alive, if you want to make something of it," he added belligerently, "because he said he was all locked up and going to bed. He told me to turn out the buttery light."

If that were so, Hank thought, then someone had turned it on again, possibly Amos, attracted by a noise.

"So"—Ellis chose the hotter scent—"you came back downstairs. What time was this?"

"About one. I heard the hall clock strike while we were talking."

"Oh, but it couldn't have been." Emma had listened aghast to Jeff's admission and could restrain herself no longer. "Because the clock struck one when I was going upstairs and scared me."

Shay clucked warningly and Hank had tried to catch Emma's eye, but she was too intent on her protection of Jeff to heed them. It was too much to expect that she would not leap to Jeff's defense if she thought him in danger.

"When you were going upstairs," said Ellis pointedly, "did you see Mr. er—Graham?"

"No, I didn't, so he must be wrong about being the last person to see Amos because I saw him."

"Shut up," said Jeff. "It was one o'clock and you couldn't see me because I used the back stairs."

"You shut up," said Ellis.

"Just a minute," began Durrell hesitantly.

"That means shut up too," said Shay under his breath.

"If you're talking about the tall clock in the hall," Durrell went on, "we've got one like that over to our house, and it strikes one just the way it strikes the half-hours. Maybe that's what's got them mixed up."

Jeff and Emma looked at each other foolishly. The tall clock in the hall was a rocking-ship Simon Willard which, because of the fame of the maker and the delicacy of the case, they would have put on the inventory as valued at fifteen hundred dollars. They knew all about that, but it took a country chief of police to tell them how such a clock struck.

"The trouble is," Shay explained for them, "none of their clocks run."

"Why, of course," said Emma. "It was twelve-thirty when Jeff heard the clock strike, and one when I went upstairs."

"Or one-thirty," said Durrell.

Emma nodded.

"Didn't you look at the clock?" asked Ellis.

"How could I?" asked Emma. "It was dark."

"All right." Ellis turned on Emma because she seemed to be the weakest prey he had caught yet. "Suppose you tell me what you were doing downstairs at one-thirty in the dark."

"I was talking to Amos," said Emma calmly. She was not, Ellis would find out, quite so easy as she looked.

"What about?"

"Insurance." Emma let her voice fall just in time. She had been going to go on but she realized that it would do Jeff no good if she said that she had been going to urge Amos not to give up the insurance just because Jeff had struck him. She supposed Ellis would get the story of the fight from someone but she didn't want to be the one.

"Where," Ellis asked sarcastically, "did this alleged conference take place?"

"In the sitting room."

"Not in the dining room?"

"No."

"Not in the buttery?"

"No."

"Why not? Did you have an appointment to meet him in the sitting room?"

"I did not. He just happened to be in there. He was locking the windows."

"You expect me to believe that you came downstairs at one-thirty to talk insurance with Amos Currier in the dark?"

Emma raised both her eyebrows and her shoulders, as though disdaining to estimate Ellis' powers of perception.

Durrell stopped mopping his neck for a moment. "From what Mr. Fairbanks told us upstairs," he said cautiously, "that would have been a big policy—"

A faint moaning sound came from Eddie.

"Was Amos thinking of backing out of the deal?"

"Was he? Was that it?" Ellis snapped up the suggestion without so much as a thank-you.

"Not that I know of," said Emma blandly, "and wouldn't he be more likely to discuss that with Mr. Graham or Mr. Rawlins?"

"Then what was the idea of you talking to him about it in the dark at half-past one? Come on, that story don't hold water."

Shay had been fidgeting in the Boston rocker, staring at Eunice, but Eunice was examining her nails. Now Shay spoke up.

"You're the boss," he said, "but you've got no more grounds for saying that she was down here at one-thirty than that Jeff was."

"What's it to you?" asked Ellis. "Were you down here too?"

"Oh yes," said Shay. "Now that you mention it, I was."

Ellis looked from Shay to Emma, and back to Shay. Like Eunice, he did not understand these people who made light of their presence at the scene of a crime, who, it seemed to him, fought for the spotlight of condemnation. Ellis knew nothing of the loyalties and friendships involved; nothing of the crosscurrents of emotion that Amos Currier and his niece had set up in a group of people ordinarily united in their affection for one another. Ellis knew Mrs. Leavitt and Eunice Chandler because he had been born in Westham. Mrs. Leavitt he regarded as a negligible old woman; Eunice Chandler he would willingly suspect because he considered her a snob. Ellis' family had moved to Billerica when he was eight; Billerica wasn't a very big town either but it got a lot of summer people, and Ellis' native's suspicion of the outsider had hardened into dislike by the time he was ten. Ellis had risen in the police force in spite of a disagreeable competence that irked his superiors almost as much as it did his victims. He had been warned concerning his manners, and the criticism infuriated him. He burned to demonstrate that he could handle things in his own way. This was his first murder case; his golden opportunity.

Miss Currier had told him that Henry Fairbanks was a detective, a friend of Graham's. Ellis was suspicious of him as an outsider and an amateur and desirous of impressing him as a detective. Ellis was anxious to solve the case one, two, three, without recourse to any citified hanky-panky.

Insurance was to Ellis a sound, understandable idea. He was always happy when the participants in an accident could exchange the names of their insurance companies, partly because he liked a neat, orderly investigation, and only partly because his own careful report would become part of the record. A man was a fool not to insure his car, his house and his life. Rawlins, as the representative of a reliable insurance company, was O.K. with Ellis. Of course he was an outsider, and Amos Currier would have done better to take out his insurance with Chester Durrell, who combined a fitful policy writing with the raising of Duroc-Jersey hogs, but that was a reflection on Currier and not on Rawlins.

The antique business, however, as contrasted with insurance, was shady, unimportant and a nuisance. Ellis knew that many an old farmhouse was actually the summer shop of a city dealer instead of the home of the spinster who seemed to inhabit it. He had heard complaints that sometimes the rent wasn't paid on the farmhouses. He couldn't imagine what women wanted with a lot of old spinning wheels and beds anyhow, and he wished they wouldn't clutter up the roads stopping to look at them. The presence of the antique dealer and his assistant looked crooked to Ellis because he didn't like what he had seen of antique dealers.

Fairbanks had told him that Horrigan was a photographer, an

occupation that Ellis thought sissified; Ellis didn't like smart cracks either, and Horrigan gave every evidence of being a wise guy.

To Ellis the case looked simple. Five strange people had spent the night locked in Amos Currier's house. It remained for Ellis to frighten or bully a confession out of the one who had killed Currier.

"You come into the dining room with me," he said to Shay.

At that moment one of the men in the buttery thrust his head ut the door.

"We're through in here," he said. "What next?"

"Can I clean up in there then?" Mrs. Leavitt cut in. "I've got a dinner to get."

"Not yet." Hank forgot his self-imposed nonintervention pact in protest. He wanted another look at the buttery himself.

Ellis might have suspected an insinuation that his examination had been cursory or he might have resented the usurpation of authority. He ignored Hank's protest and told Mrs. Leavitt to go ahead. He did, however, follow Mrs. Leavitt into the pantry, telling Shay to wait. Durrell panted after him.

Jeff thumbed his nose at Ellis' back.

"What do you suppose he'll do," Shay asked when the door had closed, "pull out my fingernails or just burn me with a lighted cigarette?"

"He wouldn't dare do that." Eddie was incredulous.

"I thought," said Emma, "that the state police went in for Courtesy, Kindness and Cooperation."

"You're thinking of the Camp Fire Girls," Hank corrected her.

"I'm not either. They give you beads for making beds and helping people across streets."

"You're all mixed up"—Shay came to her rescue—"them's the Boy Scouts."

"Couldn't we complain about him to the head office?" Eddie felt the others were taking the situation much too lightly.

"Oh, for cripes' sake," said Jeff, "shut up."

"I could write to my congressman," said Shay. "He hasn't had a letter from me for a long time."

"If you're after seeds," Hank advised him, "I'd ask for morning glories, they'd look nice on the bars of your cell."

"String beans would be more practical," Emma offered. "Tell him Kentucky Wonders—"

She broke off because Hank wasn't listening. He was eying the ice bucket that Mrs. Leavitt was bringing from the buttery.

"I'll empty that for you," he said, "go on and get the rest of the stuff."

Emma sidled over to the sink. Gallantry that involved physical effort was rarely indulged in by Henry Fairbanks, and practically never except when accompanied by an ulterior motive. Mrs. Leavitt might not know this, but Emma did. She peered into the bucket and saw through the faintly discolored water the ice crusher, now lightly coated with rust.

"Shut up," said Hank before Emma had a chance to say anything.

"Hey, gimme a pencil," Jeff yelled at Emma, "I got an idea."

Eddie reached in his pocket, but Jeff found one of his own and blandly ripped from the calendar the sheet on which the thirtieth of June was encircled with red. He tore the paper into strips and sat down at the table by the window, his face alight with the brilliance of his own cleverness.

"Mrs. Leavitt had a key," he remarked. "Hand that here." He pointed to a burled walnut bowl beside the fireplace and Emma dutifully brought it.

Jeff scribbled on one of his strips, tore off the part on which he had written and put it in the bowl. Looking in, Emma saw that Mrs. Leavitt's name was written on the slip.

"The old girl upstairs is practically bedridden, but she was here, so in she goes." Jeff put another slip in the bowl.

"What on earth are you doing?" Emma wanted to know.

"Shut up," said Jeff, writing his own name with a flourish.

"The next person that tells me to shut up," said Emma, "gets a poke in the puss."

"Shut up," said Jeff, warding off Emma's blow with his elbow. "And don't let that big lug in there get you down. Here, hold this." He handed Emma the bowl and stood up.

"All you chaps," he said, "I want to make you a sporting proposition."

Emma groaned. Jeff ignored her and went on.

"I have here the names of all the people who could have killed Amos. For a mere fifty dollars you can draw a name; for one hundred you can draw two. Step right up, gents. Winner take all."

"Yippee," said Shay. "The Murder Sweepstakes. Who holds the money? Will you take a check?"

Emma put the bowl down on the table with a bang. "I never heard of such a thing," she said indignantly. "The idea of betting that one of us killed Amos—this is serious."

"—and him not yet cold in his grave." Shay mimicked her indignation. "Well, one of us did kill him and I, personal, intend to prove that the guy I draw done it."

Hank abandoned his operations at the sink and came toward them, grinning. "You got something there," he said. "Ellis will be glad of the help."

"Nix," said Shay. "I won't even help you, this is strictly my investigation. You draw your own client."

"I agree with Miss Marsh," Eddie put in. "It doesn't seem quite right, and fifty dollars is a lot of money."

"Don't be a heel," said Shay.

"Loosen up," said Jeff. "You get in on this or you get no more policies out of me. Emma can hold the stakes."

"Daddy first," said Shay. He put his hand in the bowl and turned to Eddie. "See what I'm doing? Perfectly simple; no trick at all."

He withdrew his hand, looked at the slip and grinned.

"Get a good one, Jack?" asked Hank.

"I should hope to whinny."

"Who is it?" Emma's curiosity got the better of her scruples.

"Don't you wish you knew?"

"Put up or shut up," said Jeff, passing the bowl to Hank.

Hank drew and, like Shay, folded his slip in silence. Reluctantly Eddie took out a fat wallet and handed five bills to Emma.

"Folding money," said Shay with undisguised admiration.

Eddie drew and looked quickly at his name. It seemed to Emma, who was watching, that his face fell as he read it. Then Jeff drew, and the others drew again, all but Eddie.

"Honestly," he said, "I can't afford any more."

Jeff peered into the bowl. "There's a good one left," he said.

Emma looked, too, snatched the slip and tore it to bits. The name on the slip had been uppermost, and it had been Jeff's name.

"Highly irregular"—Jeff reproved her—"but that's one way to get rid of it."

"Now," said Shay, "every man a detective."

"That was my idea in the first place," said Emma.

"But you drew two names." Eunice sounded disturbed. "You can't prove that two people did it."

"Why not?" Shay looked at her quizzically. "For three hundred and fifty dollars I'd prove it was a corporation."

There was a callousness in Shay's tone that Emma did not like; she wondered if there was a different Shay than the jovial one she accepted as a friend of Hank's. She knew that Hank and Shay had been at school together, though Shay was older, having taken time out to put the finishing touches on making the world safe for the next war. She knew that Shay's father had been a ward politician, that Shay lived in an untidy room on Joy Street and was a photographer for the *American*. She realized that Shay's bad grammar was an affectation, but she suspected that his liking for "beetles," his generic term for women, was real. Shay was fun to have around; beyond that she had never given him much thought.

Her analysis was interrupted by the entrance of Mrs. Leavitt with an armful of bottles, of which Hank politely divested her.

"Where shall I put them?" he asked innocently.

Hank, Emma thought, was behaving very queerly.

"Out in the woodshed," said Mrs. Leavitt. "One of the boys will dump them in the gully."

But Hank put the bottles in the sink and proceeded to rinse one under the tap. Mrs. Leavitt paused to ask Eunice if she had heard from her father.

Eunice shook her head. "He's supposed to be back from Worcester this noon. I telephoned the house and left word for him to come right over."

Mrs. Leavitt sniffed and looked at the kitchen clock. It was nearly twelve-thirty.

"Mercy me," said Mrs. Leavitt, "I better make you some sandwiches."

At the sink Hank was filling the rinsed out bottle from the water in the ice bucket. Jeff, Shay and Eddie were in a huddle. Only Emma was watching Hank. He put the metal cap back on the bottle, took the crusher from the bucket and put it with the bottles in the sink, then he gathered up an armful and started for the woodshed door.

As he did so Ellis appeared from the buttery with a curt, "Come in here, all of you."

"Just a minute," said Hank cheerfully, "till I get rid of these."

Eunice looked apprehensive and went closer to Shay.

"Now what?" Jeff grumbled darkly, leading the way.

Emma lagged behind the others, half waiting for Hank, half loath to see the spot where Amos' body had lain. She noticed that Mrs. Leavitt had not finished her work in the buttery. A dustpan filled with litter and cigarette butts was on the floor, the glasses had been stacked and the bottles and the ice bucket removed; but the ice pick still lay in a puddle of water and the Canton saucers used for ashtrays were still on the counter. Emma heard Hank behind her and turned to him quickly. Hank met her inquiring look with a blank stare.

"Get on in there," he said, "before Ellis beats you."

Durrell, obviously ill at ease, was standing by the head of the table, the technicians were preparing to move into the kitchen, and Ellis was posted by the hall door.

"Line up," said Ellis. "I'm going to take each one of you into :he library to look at Currier. Then I'll talk to you separately."

The brutal disregard for the innocent and those who might have been fond of Amos left them speechless. Then Eunice sank into a chair and buried her face in her hands.

"I can't," she said. "I can't do it."

"Get up," Ellis said harshly. "You go first."

Eunice did not get up and Emma, crossing to her, put a hand on her shaking shoulder. Emma's hand was shaking too; she didn't know exactly why. She had looked at Amos once; she supposed she could stand to do it again, but she realized that Ellis was hoping for some break, some telltale giveaway of emotion that would be incriminating. Eunice's collapse might or might not mean that she was guilty, but that she was suffering was plain, and Emma could not bear to see a mouse suffer.

"Damn you," she said, "see what you've done."

"You're under arrest," Ellis roared, his face purpling. He started toward Emma but Jeff got in his way.

"You touch her," said Jeff, "you touch anybody, and I'll beat the hell out of you, so help me, cop or no cop."

From the side of the woodshed next the road came a pounding so violent that it could be heard above their angry words. A shrill voice was calling, "Eunice, Amy, Mrs. Leavitt!"

Mrs. Leavitt started automatically for the kitchen to open the doors.

"That must be Father," said Eunice. There was apprehension in her voice and she straightened up, wiping her eyes.

"The Chandler Woolen Mills," said Eddie.

"The Society for the Preservation of Massachusetts Antiquities," said Jeff, turning his back on Ellis and lighting a cigarette. "President of."

"Come again?" said Shay.

"They buy up old houses," Emma explained quickly, "really old ones that the Historical Society passes up because Washington didn't sleep in them, but ones that ought to be kept because they have an overhang or sliding shutters like those in the front room upstairs. I think he wanted Amos to will them this house."

The front screen door slammed violently, and the shrill voice repeated, "Amy, Eunice, Mrs. Leavitt!"

Eunice flew out into the hall, Eddie at her heels.

Jeff went to the buttery for an ashtray and put it on the dining-room table.

"Gimme a cigarette," said Emma. "I feel as though I'd been through that wringer you're always talking about."

From the hall they could hear Eunice attempting to explain that she had at once tried to let her father know what had happened and that Mr. Fairbanks had called the chief of police.

"Durrell's a fool," they heard the high voice cut in. "Sold the mantel out of his parlor and bought a pig. What Fairbanks? Where's the lawyer? Where's his will?"

Durrell stopped mopping his face and turned an embarrassed red; Ellis stepped to the door but fell back before the wave of Mr. Chandler's approach.

Against the background of his tall daughter and the stalwart Eddie, Lloyd Chandler's stature was miniature, and in contrast with their clothes his own were particularly outlandish.

He looked, Emma thought, like a composite caricature of a prohibition agent, a bank president and a man she had seen once at a college reunion. He wore old-fashioned side-elastic shoes, a suit of black alpaca, a white shirt, white wash tie and his yellowed straw hat was attached to something with a black cord.

"Who are all these people? What are they doing here?"

The question ended in a scream. Mr. Chandler hurled himself into the room as Jeff picked up his cigarette from the edge of the table and rubbed ruefully at an imaginary burn.

A moment ago, Emma knew, Jeff's cigarette had been safely in the Canton saucer and Jeff would have marred the table about as soon as he would have cut his own finger. Jeff must have acted deliberately to provoke Chandler. She wondered how well Jeff knew him.

Mr. Chandler glared at Jeff, clutched the Canton saucer to himself, regardless of the ashes and matches it contained, and pointed a shaking finger at the film of moisture that was spreading from Durrell's handkerchief.

"The original finish," he shouted, "ruined by a pack of hoodlums. The priceless patina—"

"In a pig's eye," said Jeff. "That table's been refinished."

"It has not!" Chandler's voice quavered with rage. "Get out of my house!"

Jeff pointed to Ellis. "Can't," he said. "The cops won't let me. And what makes you think it's your house?"

"It's my house now." Eunice, with family backing at hand, was sure of herself again. "That's what Father means."

It occurred to Emma that they were ignoring the old lady upstairs.

Mr. Chandler had managed to tangle the Canton saucer and the handkerchief with the cord of his hat. With a "Let me help you, sir," Eddie straightened him out, brushed him off and set the saucer carefully on the mantelpiece. Then Mr. Chandler shifted his attack.

"Who's in authority here? What's been done? Who killed him? Where's the medical examiner? Where's the doctor? Why doesn't Amy come downstairs? Speak up, somebody!"

Ellis opened his mouth to answer, but Mr. Chandler forestalled him with a tirade that charged incompetence, dillydallying and general mismanagement. His charges were as unfounded as they were abusive, but no one in the room raised a voice in protest, they were too thoroughly enjoying the sight of Ellis' discomfiture.

With Chandler's entrance Moses Ellis was to himself no longer the symbol of authority of the Commonwealth of Massachusetts, he was the little boy whom the Chandler gardener had caught stealing apples. The outsiders did not know this; all they realized was that Ellis had at last met his match, and whether awe of Chandler or sheer inability to get in a word was the cause, they did not care. Emma nudged Hank delightedly with her elbow.

It was inept Durrell who finally came to the rescue.

"If you'll keep still a minute," he said, "maybe you'll find out something. Amos was murdered and I don't know nothing about murder; all I know is hogs and insurance. Moses was the one to call so I called him. Doc Pratt is having a baby and the undertaker's having a funeral; one who gets through first'll be out here. These people are here because Amos invited them. Mr. Rawlins was going to write some insurance. That would have been a big policy . . . ."

His voice died away regretfully and Mr. Chandler leaped into :he pause.

"Insurance? What company? Who persuaded him? Was the policy written?"

Eddie shook his head.

"For years," Mr. Chandler went on, "I have entreated him, and now he is dead and I shall have to pay for it myself. You may not be aware"—Mr. Chandler addressed the room almost pleasantly—"that the objects in this house are of inestimable value. That chair an which that young man is leaning might go down on an inventory as valued at a paltry three hundred dollars "

"Two hundred and fifty," Jeff muttered out of the corner of his mouth as Shay removed his weight from the chair.

"—but actually," Chandler continued with only a slight raise in pitch, "it is irreplaceable because it is one of the chairs which Captain Amos Currier bought for this house. It is the same with the ornaments, the pictures. To a dealer"—there was delicate scorn in his voice—"that cabinet of Lowestoft would be a gold mine, because no matter what he paid for it he could sell it for more. To us"—he apparently considered himself a Currier, if only by marriage—"the matter of price has never occurred. There"—he waved his hand toward the other corner cupboard—"is a collection of silver finer than anything in the museums. We value it because, with the exception of the service that was presented to the Reverend John Currier after fifty years as pastor of the first Unitarian Church, every piece of that silver is listed on Captain Amos Currier's inventory. Let me show you."

Eagerly, almost pleasant in his enthusiasm, forgetful for the moment that he was speaking to people who were more interested in the manner of Amos Currier's death than in the value of his possessions, Chandler turned to the cupboard where, behind the arched doors, rows of silver gleamed dully. He tugged at the knob but the doors were locked.

Jeff pulled a key from his pocket and held it out to Chandler.

"Here," he said, "maybe this'll help."

Mr. Chandler snatched at the key. "Where did you get this?" he demanded suspiciously.

"It's none of your business but it just happens that Amos gave it to me yesterday."

"Amos was criminally careless." Mr. Chandler was plainly disturbed but his yearning to display his newly acquired treasures overcame, for the moment, his desire to find out what Jeff was doing with the key to the silver cupboard. He threw open the doors and stood back as though unveiling a monument.

"Gentlemen," he said, "superb examples of the work of most of the outstanding Massachusetts silversmiths."

He might have been, in fact was, quoting a speech that he had given before many an antiquarian society. Amos had possessed the silver but Mr. Chandler had had the glory of talking about it.

"Most important, for its historical associations," he went an, "the Revere porringer. I do not"—he looked archly at his audience—"need to give you Revere's dates. The teapot by Nathaniel Hurd, also of Boston, 1729 to 1777; the mug by John Burt, circa 1710, and that veritable treasure of delicacy, the Coney muffineer."

Chandler broke off suddenly and peered into the cupboard as though unable to believe his eyes.

"What's wrong here?" he said; then, his voice rising higher and higher, "it's been moved." He pawed among the silver. "It's not there at all! It's been stolen!"

Chandler whirled around, pointing to Jeff. "That man had the key. He's a thief. Who is he?"

Emma expected an explosion from Jeff. If he had knocked Chandler down, she would not have been surprised; instead Jeff sat still in his chair, an expression that she could only call sheepish on his face.

The room broke into an uproar of conversation. Eunice and Durrell were trying to calm Chandler; Ellis to get a definite statement from him.

"What's a muffineer?" asked Shay.

"A little thing like a salt shaker to put spice on hot muffins with."

"Father, Father, you mustn't say things like that!"

"Arrest him at once!"

"What's this what-d'you-call-it?"

"The Coney muffineer. It's worth a thousand dollars."

"Nine hundred," said Jeff with stubborn accuracy.

"Don't dispute me!" Mr. Chandler shook his finger under Jeff's nose.

"The name is Graham," said Jeff. "Remember me?"

"He's an antique dealer," Eunice put in. "A friend of Amos'."

She got no farther. Mr. Chandler seized Ellis by the shirt and shook him. "Arrest him," he shouted, "he had the key. He took it. He's a crook. He's the man who kept the Society from getting the Kimball-Haskett house and some of the leaded windows were still intact."

"Oh," said Emma on a rising note, remembering that Jeff had bought the Kimball-Haskett house for a customer, "that."

Ellis hadn't the faintest idea what they were talking about. He didn't have it clear in his mind yet what a muffineer was. He felt that he ought to stand behind Mr. Chandler but he couldn't keep his eyes off the little spot of blood on Mr. Chandler's necktie.

Hank was only slightly better informed than Ellis on leaded windows and muffineers but he sensed Ellis' indecision and felt that the time had come for him to do something. Jeff had been in possession of the key to the silver cupboard. If there was something missing, it was better to have the matter cleared up at once. Hank was in thorough agreement with Emma's opinion that Jeff had nothing to do with the murder. He disliked the idea of trading on the prestige of his family but he felt that Mr. Chandler would listen to him in the name of Norwitch.

"Mr. Chandler," he said, "you remember my uncle, Richard Norwitch?"

"Certainly," said Chandler, relaxing his grip on Ellis to peer at Hank. "He would have given his eyeteeth for that muffineer. What did you say your name was?"

Hank told him. "I appreciate your distress," he went on blandly, "but before we make any accusations we must establish the facts, get the picture clear."

Emma smiled to herself. Ordinarily she writhed at Hank's constant comparison of each and every situation to a picture, but when he used the word she knew that he had his nose to the ground, his ears open and his mind working. She had been a little annoyed at Hank's apparent willingness to let Ellis dominate the investigation. Ellis was a stranger, and Emma was not above wanting a friend at court.

"You say a muffineer is missing," Hank was going on, "but you must realize that first you will have to prove it was there."

Chandler stared at him, dumfounded. Then he remembered Jeff. "That man knew it," he began.

Hank stopped him. "Mr. Graham," he said, "would hardly be likely to admit the muffineer was there if he took it. Somebody call Mrs. Leavitt," he said without taking his eyes from Chandler's face.

Shay went out into the buttery.

"If Mrs. Leavitt," Hank went on, "can prove that the muffineer was in the cupboard yesterday, its absence may have some bearing on Amos' death. Otherwise I'm afraid it doesn't fit into our picture. You realize, of course, that our first concern is to find out who killed Amos."

Mr. Chandler fidgeted. The loss of Amos was not, to him, insupportable; the loss of the muffineer was. Richard Norwitch would have appreciated that, if his nephew didn't.

Mrs. Leavitt came in from the kitchen followed by Shay, happily munching a sandwich.

"Mrs. Leavitt," said Hank, "Mr. Chandler thinks something has been taken from this cupboard—"

"Lloyd Chandler"—Mrs. Leavitt's face flushed—"you've known me for forty years—"

"No," Hank interrupted her, "no one is accusing you. I am trying to establish whether or not there was a muffineer in this cupboard yesterday."

"A what?" asked Mrs. Leavitt.

"A silver thing, a—a—" Hank floundered.

"The Coney muffineer," Mr. Chandler began.

"Like a salt shaker," said Emma.

"Oh, that." Mrs. Leavitt was not impressed. "I guess so."

"You're not sure?"

Again Mrs. Leavitt avoided the issue. "That silver hasn't been cleaned for six months. Amos had the key and always kept putting me off. It was there the last time I cleaned it." Mrs. Leavitt folded her lips together and looked at Jeff.

"You see"—Hank spoke gently to Mr. Chandler—"she cannot prove that the muffineer was there yesterday."

"Can I go now?" Mrs. Leavitt was insistent. "I'm making sandwiches and I'll take some up to Miss Amy, but I've got a dinner to get."

Hank looked at Ellis.

"Sure. All right, I'll come and talk to you later."

The sight of Shay's sandwich was too much for Emma. Hank seemed to have the situation well in hand so she followed Mrs. Leavitt to the kitchen.

"Amy might know," said Mr. Chandler dubiously, "but"—his voice rose again with suspicion "that man had the key; he might have taken something else."

"Mr. Graham," said Hank firmly, "had every right to the key, he had been hired by Mr. Currier to make an inventory for the insurance company."

"The inventory," Chandler shouted. "That's it. That'll prove what was in there. That'll show if anything's been taken. Nothing's ever been sold out of this house and the inventory will prove it." He was becoming excited again, the more so because he was no longer the center of attention.

Ellis had decided that the muffineer, missing or not, was of no importance. Hank, who had belittled the absence of the muffineer, was wondering if he had made a mistake, and Durrell was gazing fixedly at the mantelpiece.

"Has the house been searched?" Chandler demanded. "Have their bags been searched?" He broke into a spasm of coughing and Eunice, going to the kitchen for a glass of water, came back with the report that the technicians were leaving unless Ellis had something else for them to do.

Ellis started for the kitchen but Mr. Chandler tugged at him.

"Somebody," said Ellis, "tell Morgan to get the prints developed but tell Zubinsky to go over the grounds. Tell him to look for a muffineer. Now see here." He turned to Chandler with almost a return of his old truculence. His childhood awe of Mr. Chandler was beginning to give way to the desire to put him in the wrong. "Nobody brought a bag except Miss Marsh and Mr. Rawlins and there's no muffineer in those. Graham hasn't made any inventory that I know of, because Currier was killed."

"The old inventory," Mr. Chandler said witheringly, "the original inventory, the one that lists everything in this house. You wouldn't know, but that's what I'm talking about."

"Yeah?" said Ellis. "Where is it?"

"Where?" Mr. Chandler's voice hung suspended on a high note. "Why, of course I don't know exactly."

Ellis started to walk away but Chandler pulled him back. "It's here somewhere. I know it is. I'll find it. I'll look for it."

"You'll not go pawing around, understand me?"

"It's my house. It's perfectly legal. It's on big sheets of paper sewn together at the top. I'll take somebody with me to prove I don't touch anything else. I have to find it. They may have taken something else. They may all be in this together."

He was screaming again in his insistence. Miss Currier, Emma thought, was the only one in the house who couldn't hear him, and that wasn't because she was upstairs. Eunice, half fearfully, put her hand on her father's arm to quiet him but he shook her off.

"You listen to me, Moses Ellis," he screamed. "It's your business to find it, just as much as it is to find out who killed Amos. That man's a crook." Again he pointed to Jeff. "He's worse than that." His face lit up with something just remembered. "He was suspected of killing Richard Norwitch."

Emma groaned; she had hoped Mr. Chandler wouldn't think of that.

"Mr. Chandler," said Hank quickly, "Mr. Graham was fully cleared of those suspicions."

A Chandler could be controlled only so long, even by a Norwitch, it seemed.

"He was not. Don't argue with me. Some woman got killed and they said he did it. He's a crook and he's probably a murderer as well as a thief."

"Don't you say that." Emma thrust herself forward. "He is not. She did it."

Jeff got up very deliberately from his chair. "I've stood just about enough of your lip, you narrow-minded little shrimp."

"Take it easy, buddy," said Shay.

"Please," said Hank, "please."

Eddie, with sandwich, stood goggle-eyed in the doorway.

Hank put himself between Jeff and Mr. Chandler. "Your lawyer," he said, addressing the latter firmly, "would advise you not to make any such accusations."

"Oh, dear me," said Mr. Chandler, "that's right, isn't it? I need a lawyer, but first I ought to find that inventory."

"Go look for it," said Ellis, by now willing to concede anything for peace and quiet. "Only you better take someone with you."

"Mr. Fairbanks," began Chandler, "if you would be so good?"

"I'm sorry," said Hank quickly, "but I'm trying to help down here."

Emma turned her back. Shay vanished toward the kitchen.

Chandler could see the impropriety of choosing his own daughter; there was no one left but Eddie and Chandler apparently found him suitable.

"Will you assist me, young man?" he said. "And what is your name?"

Eddie stepped forward with alacrity. "Rawlins," he said, "of Old Cape."

"Oh yes," said Chandler. "The insurance. That sandwich looks very good. I believe I will avail myself of one."

He slipped into the buttery before Eddie could offer his services and the dining room drew a breath of relief.

"The Napoleonic complex," said Hank. "Frequently present in small men and sometimes"—he did not look at Ellis—"in others."

"Too bad about the insurance." Chandler was back, sandwich in hand. "How much would it have amounted to? We'll go upstairs and ask Amy. She'll probably know right where it is."

Eddie and Mr. Chandler went down the hall in a cozy crossfire of figures and suppositions.

The tension in the dining room relaxed again. Ellis looked almost amiable; Durrell retrieved his handkerchief and gave his neck a thorough mopping; Jeff lit a cigarette and brazenly snapped the match into the fireplace, Shay stuck his neck in the door and asked if it was safe to come in. Eunice beckoned to him and the two of them followed Eddie and Mr. Chandler upstairs.

Ellis made no protest. "He had a spot of blood on his tie," he said, almost to himself.

"Must have cut himself shaving—" Hank broke off and looked more intently at Ellis. "You mean: where was he last night?"

Ellis nodded, glad that the suspicion had been voiced by someone else.

Hank sat down and stretched out his legs. "Is he always like that?" he asked. "Or was he just putting on an act to smear up the picture?"

Ellis looked at Durrell. Durrell did not speak for a moment and then he said:

"I guess Lloyd's all right. He's a bit hasty. His father worked in the mill. I don't mean that I hold that against him, but did you ever notice that converts is more rabid than them as turns them?"

Hank looked blank.

"You mean," Emma asked quickly, "that this house and its furnishings mean more to Mr. Chandler than they did to Amos?"

Durrell nodded. "He wanted to live here after they was married—him and Amos' sister, as was—but Amos wouldn't let 'em. Said Lloyd held his breath every time anyone sat down in a chair and wanted him to get some everyday china. Amos said he'd always et off the blue-and-white and he always calc'lated to. Lloyd was awful mad when he found out that Amos had title to the house and farm and his sister didn't. Said it warn't legal. But it was. But that's all water over the dam a long time ago."

"Doesn't Miss Amy Currier"—Hank wanted to know—"own any part of all this?"

"Nope. She can stay here so long as Amos lets her, but that's all. Place always went to the oldest son; that's how it stayed in the family so long, there always was a son. Only Sally married Ruel Leavitt instead of Amos."

"Mrs. Leavitt," asked Emma incredulously, "could have married Amos?"

"What's so funny about that?" Jeff's tone was malicious. "She's no older than Amos."

"Two years younger." Durrell saved Emma from further embarrassing comment. "Amos took it hard at the time. Sally was a mighty pretty girl and smart as a whip."

Zubinsky came down the hall with word that the doctor was there, and Ellis, who had been unimpressed with Durrell's local history, went across to the library. Zubinsky went back outdoors. Durrell got out paper and pencil.

"If nobody cares," said Emma, "I'll go upstairs and put on something besides pants."

"Go ahead," said Durrell. He turned to Jeff. "About that policy, now. I'd like to figure out what the premium would've been."

Jeff shrugged his shoulders. "Without an inventory," he said, "it's hard to tell. There's easily a quarter of a million dollars' worth of furniture here, maybe more; and the silver, from what Amos told me," he put in, "would come to twenty-four or -five thousand."

"Extended coverage?"

"Sure."

"That would have been a big policy."

"Not so bad. Rawlins figured his commission would be about six hundred and a quarter—"

Durrell sighed. "He'd have no call to kill Amos then, would he?"

"Cripes, no," said Jeff emphatically.

Durrell busied himself with his calculations and Jeff wandered out toward the kitchen.

Unlike Ellis, Hank was interested in Durrell's gossip. The facts seemed to show that Amos had been killed by someone in the house. But Mrs. Leavitt had had a key, and now Durrell told them that Mrs. Leavitt had once been engaged to Amos. Hank realized that he had hardly looked at Mrs. Leavitt twice. Except for the moment when she had danced with Amos, she had been as colorless and quiet as a shadow. She had made no outcry at the sight of Amos' body. How had she felt? Had her silence been that of control or lack of surprise? He wished Durrell would quit figuring and unbolt with a little more low-down. Was it pure coincidence that Amos had been killed just before he insured his property? Chandler claimed to have urged Amos to insure; he might have had a reason for not wanting him to do so. Antiquarians, Hank recalled his late uncle, were prey to curious idiosyncracies. Perhaps Chandler hadn't been in Worcester, perhaps Amos had caught him stealing the muffineer. Perhaps Chandler was anxious to know whether or not the policy had been written because he wondered if an insurance detective would be after him.

All that elaborate supposition was induced, Hank decided, by the blood spot to which Ellis had called his attention. He heard someone throw open a window upstairs; he heard a few footsteps. He wished he knew more about the old lady up there who was dependent on Amos' good will. He wished he had a long cold drink.

Failing either, Hank got up and locked the silver cupboard, and then he removed the key and unlocked the cupboard with a piece of wire from his pocket.

Durrell was watching him.

"See what I'm doing? Anybody could do it."

From the hall they heard Eddie's voice call. "Where would it be? Never mind, I'll find it myself."

Eddie came down the hall and into the dining room.

"Mr. Chandler wants pencil and paper." His eye lit on those Durrell was using.

Durrell laid his pencil on a sheet and shoved it across the table.

"I think"—Eddie took them into the confidence of the owner of the Chandler Woolen Mills with only a slight touch of condescension—"that he has found the inventory and wants me to make some kind of a statement. I'm a notary, you know."

"I always forget about notaries," said Hank. "Can they marry people or am I thinking of sea captains?"

Eddie looked faintly distressed at the facetiousness.

"The premium on that policy," said Durrell, "would have come to about sixteen hundred dollars."

"Sixteen ninety," said Eddie, "the way I figured it."

"Kinda tough to lose that commission."

Eddie looked at Durrell pityingly, then at Hank, not quite sure that this was the time to speak of business. "I think," he said, "that Chandler is going to give me the insurance. I have already spoken to him about it. Now I must be getting back."

Durrell's gaze remained fixed on the empty doorway.

"He don't let the grass grow under his feet none, does he?"

"Tell me—" Hank began.

"Help! Help!"

They heard the scream and the sudden thud of running feet; even Durrell was startled into action; they rushed into the hall just as Ellis and the doctor burst from the room opposite.

"Somebody! Quick!" Eddie clung to the bannister, his eyes staring wide with horror. He pointed a shaking finger upward. "It's Mr. Chandler. I—I think he's dead."

They swept around him and up the stairs, Hank in the lead. Emma was standing in the upper hall, wringing her hands and saying:

"I won't go in. I won't look at him."

Jeff was telling her that she'd do as she was told. After a moment Eunice came out the door of her room.

The beds had not yet been made. Mrs. Leavitt would explain that the sheets had to be changed and that, anyway, she couldn't do everything at once. The buckle bed in which Shay had slept was still pulled out, crowding the front of the slant-top desk, and on the buckle bed lay the body of Mr. Chandler. He looked very small and quite peaceful. It was fully a minute before Hank noticed the handle of the ice pick protruding from the left front of his alpaca coat.

Chapter 6

DOCTOR PRATT bent over Mr. Chandler and shook his head.

"He's dead all right."

With scissors the doctor cut coat, shirt and underwear away from Chandler's scrawny chest. The handle of the ice pick stood almost straight up. Above it the skin was taut; below, slightly puckered.

"Hmm," said the doctor, "didn't anybody hear him yell?"

"Did he have time?" Hank asked.

"I'd yell if somebody was tickling my ribs with an ice pick." The doctor pointed to the puckered skin. "Whoever did it felt for the space between the ribs with the point and then jabbed it in."

He undid Chandler's necktie and collar, looking for the marks of fingers that might have prevented an outcry. There were none.

"If a fellow committed suicide," Durrell said slowly, "he'd do it quiet-like."

Hank started to move one of the pillows on the bed.

"Don't touch things," Ellis snapped, "until Morgan gets here."

Ellis' face was ashen. He stood looking at Chandler's body as though unable to believe what he saw.

"I was right downstairs," he said, "all the time. Where's Zubinsky? Somebody get Zubinsky."

Hank didn't know whether Ellis wanted reinforcements or whether he held the optimistic view that a stranger might have entered the house and killed Chandler, but he sympathized with Ellis in the embarrassment of having the killing of the local bigwig take place right under his nose. He passed the huddled group in the hall, went to the window and called:

"Hey, come back here."

It was not to Zubinsky, who was even then running up the stairs, that he spoke, but to Mrs. Leavitt, who was walking away from the stable door as though she had just come out of it. Her back was toward Hank and it was only when she turned that he saw that she was carrying a large black pan, a deep old-fashioned biscuit sheet. There was something in it; what, Hank could not tell at that distance. Mrs. Leavitt went back in at the stable door.

When Hank turned around Shay was standing behind him; he hadn't noticed Shay before.

"Deaf, eh?" asked Shay, voicing Hank's wonder why Mrs. Leavitt was leaving when she must have heard Eddie's shouts. "I, personal, have an intense desire to know the contents of that there pan."

"Go ahead and find out," said Hank, following Zubinsky into Amos' room and closing the door.

Ellis was examining a yellowed piece of paper that had lain on the bed beside Mr. Chandler. It was a check, dated March 10, 1906, made out to Anthony Gillespie and signed Amos Currier. Across the face of the check was stamped "No Funds."

"That don't look like an inventory to me," said Ellis, handing the check to Hank.

Hank looked at the date and saw that the check had been drawn on the Cambridge Trust Company. "Mmm," he said, "interesting but hardly a collector's item. I seem to recall that my undergraduate days yielded several similarly marked. Eddie said he thought Chandler had found the inventory."

"When was this?"

Hank turned to Durrell for corroboration and told of Eddie's trip downstairs for pencil and paper.

"How long was he down there?"

"Four or five minutes. It's hard to say. I was kidding him about being a notary and Durrell was asking him about the insurance."

Durrell nodded agreement. "He seemed to think that Lloyd was going to take out the insurance with his company, just as Amos had intended."

"Where were the rest of them?"

Hank remained silent.

"Oh, all right"—Ellis seemed scornful of Hank's scruples—"I'll get to them in a minute."

And how! Hank thought to himself.

The doctor, who had been writing at the corner of the desk, handed a paper to Ellis and picked up his bag.

"I believe," he said, "that I'll just step in here for a moment and see Miss Currier, she's pretty old for all these goings on."

He went to the right of the bed and opened a door in the corner of the room. As he stepped through the doorway they could see that it led to a bathroom that connected Amos' room with Miss Currier's. Hank hadn't paid much attention to the door; he'd gone to bed in the dark and in the morning had thought, if he thought at all, that it was the door to a closet. That was probably what it had been originally, though there was another closet in the same wall, nearer the hall.

Ellis was looking at the door.

"Miss Amy wouldn't have heard a thing," said Durrell, "she's deaf as a post."

Mr. Chandler's call of "Amy, Eunice, Mrs. Leavitt," flashed through Hank's mind, together with the remark, "Why doesn't Amy come downstairs?" It occurred to him to wonder if Miss Currier was as deaf an invalid as she seemed. He heard her voice and the doctor's, then a third voice, presumably Mrs. Leavitt's.

Ellis edged himself in between the desk and the buckle bed.

"If he was standing here," he conjectured, "and somebody was standing beside him, why, he was trapped; he couldn't get away."

"And if," Hank suggested, "he had taken something from the desk, as apparently he had, and sat down on the bed to look at it, it would have been no trick at all to shove him over."

Hank picked up one of the pillows but put it down as Ellis roared at him, "I told you not to touch things."

Ellis looked on the floor, under the bed and at the papers strewn on the lid of the desk.

"What did this inventory look like?" he asked.

"Several sheets of paper," Durrell said, "sewn together at the top. I saw it once. Miss Amy showed it to me a long time ago."

"You look for it then." Ellis abandoned the search willingly as though already convinced that it was futile. "I suppose we better lock this room up till Morgan gets back. You go phone Morgan," he commanded Zubinsky, "and then take another look outside to see if everything's the same. I'll talk to the rest of them."

Durrell, unable to get his bulk between the desk and the bed, approached his task from the side. He ran his finger along the shelf that separated the row of drawers from the pigeonholes and shook his head at the dust he collected.

"Have to speak to Sally about that," he said. "Though I guess Amos didn't use this desk much. His pa did but Amos did his figuring in the library."

"So what?" asked Ellis, again impatient of Durrell's ramblings.

"So 'tain't surprising that there warn't a pencil here and that

Rawlins had to come downstairs for one."

Durrell went methodically to work on the papers from the first pigeonhole as though unaware that he had scored off Ellis very neatly.

Squaring his shoulders, Ellis marched to the door; Hank followed him.

The group in the hall confronted them mutely, apprehensively. Eunice was sitting on the top step; Emma, beside her, held her hand. Eddie, white but no longer shaking, stood with Shay by the window. Jeff stopped his pacing and jingled the keys in his pocket.

"Rawlins," said Ellis accusingly.

Eddie's hand went to his throat in a womanish gesture—Hank wondered if he were going to faint.

Ellis looked at his watch and back to Eddie, prolonging the agony of the uncertainty. "Rawlins," he repeated, "I want you to go downstairs with Fairbanks here and stay about the length of time you think you stayed."

Eddie's breath escaped through his teeth with a whistling sound. It took him a moment to get started, as though he had to overcome the force with which he had braced himself.

"Just a minute!"

Eddie stopped in his tracks.

"Did any of you hear any sound or cry that might have come from Chandler?"

They all shook their heads.

"Now go ahead!"

Eddie went hurriedly, followed more leisurely by Hank.

"The rest of you," Ellis ordered, "go where you were when you heard Rawlins shout and stay until I call you."

Emma went into her room, Eunice walked down the hall but paused at the door, Jeff sauntered to the head of the corridor that led to the ell—only Shay remained, abstractedly running his fingers through his hair.

"You," said Ellis, "get going."

"Me?" asked Shay. "Now let me see. Where was I at?"

"You don't need to bother," Eunice called, "I don't mind telling. He was in my room."

"Is that right?" Ellis asked.

"Oh yes. Stupid of me to forget. You see, there's a very handsome mantel in there that I wanted to photograph."

Ellis looked his disbelief. Behind her door Emma indulged in a snicker.

"Miss Marsh," Ellis called, "come across the hall."

Emma stepped out of the room. Ellis swung the door of Amos' room open and motioned for her to go in. All trace of amusement faded from Emma's mind. She walked in, focusing her eyes on Durrell and trying not to see the little black figure on the bed.

"Now go back to your room," said Ellis, his eyes on his watch. He was scribbling some figures on his pad when Hank and Eddie came back upstairs; he looked at his watch again and announced, "Four and three quarters minutes for you."

Then he called Shay, gave him the same instructions he had given Emma and marked again on his pad.

They heard Shay tell Eunice to keep a stiff upper lip and to shut her eyes. But when her name was called Eunice walked into the room where her father lay without a tremor. Only her hands, clenched at her sides, betrayed the control she put upon herself. Hank looked at Ellis' notebook and saw that it had taken Emma only forty seconds to open her door, cross the hall and return; Shay had made the trip in one minute, Eunice in two seconds more; and Eddie had been gone almost five minutes.

"All right, Graham," said Ellis.

Jeff moved a step closer to Amos' door. "This about right?" he asked.

"How should I know?" Ellis snapped.

"I wasn't asking you," Jeff snapped back. "I was asking Eddie. He saw me."

Eddie turned scarlet. "I wouldn't want to say," he stammered. "I guess I was too upset to notice. I suppose you were outside by the time I called?"

Emma, who had dutifully stayed in her room up to now, burst forth, her eyes dark with anger.

"Jeff wasn't in there," she declared, "and it's wicked of you to say things like that."

"Take it easy, baby," said Hank.

"Shut up," said Jeff. "I was too."

The doctor and Mrs. Leavitt, Shay and Eunice came out into the hall.

"Quiet!" Ellis roared. "Why didn't you say he was in there?" he shouted at Eddie.

"I—I didn't want to," Eddie demurred. "I thought it would look bad."

"You thought!" Ellis' voice was biting. Thumbs hooked in belt, he was his domineering self again. "I'm the one who does the thinking. This is murder. What was he doing in there?"

"Just standing," said Eddie meekly. "When I came back upstairs he was just standing there looking at Mr. Chandler."

"Eddie Rawlins," said Emma, "that's a lie."

"Cluck, cluck," said Shay.

Ellis ignored Emma and turned to Jeff. "So," he said, "you found him first. Why didn't you call somebody?"

"Cripes," said Jeff, "I didn't have a chance. Eddie was doing yelling enough for two."

"How long were you in there?"

"Just a minute."

"Long enough to kill him?"

"I suppose so."

"He did no such thing," said Emma.

Jeff glared at her.

"Only it happens that I didn't."

"I knew it," Emma cried triumphantly.

"If you don't keep still," said Ellis, "I'll lock you up."

Privately Hank thought that would save a lot of trouble but he spoke to Jeff. "What, exactly, did you do from the time you left us downstairs?"

"I got a sandwich," said Jeff calmly, "and then I came up the back stairs and went in my room. I thought maybe I'd shave and then I thought I'd look in and see how Eddie and Chandler were coming. I came up here and went in and saw Chandler, and then Eddie came up and began to yell. That's all."

"Was the door to Amos' room open or closed?"

"Neither. It was swung to but not shut."

"But I left it open," said Eddie. "I know I did."

Emma looked at Eddie as though she would like to tear him to pieces but she remained silent.

"You took the ice pick"—Ellis was reverting to his original tactics—"and came upstairs and killed him. Was it because of the muffineer?"

"I didn't see the ice pick," said Jeff, "until I saw it sticking out of Chandler and I've told you once, I didn't kill him."

"Mrs. Leavitt," Hank asked quickly, "was Mr. Graham carrying the ice pick when he went through the kitchen?"

Jeff started to speak but Mrs. Leavitt said it first. "I wasn't in the kitchen: I must have been up here."

"Birds," said Shay suddenly, "crumbs for the birds. It's a pretty thought, isn't it?"

All of them except Hank and Mrs. Leavitt looked at Shay as though he had lost his mind.

"If that young man," said Mrs. Leavitt with some asperity, "is talking about what I had in the pan, it was the sandwich trimmings for my chickens."

Durrell came out of Amos' room. "'Tain't in that desk," he said.

Ellis turned from one to the other like a man beset by midges.

"Crumbs! Chickens!" he shouted. "Don't talk nonsense. Why was he killed? That's what I want to know!"

"Sho," said Durrell placidly, "Lloyd warn't never what you'd call popular."

Hank avoided looking in Shay's direction. Durrell's understatement was the weakest excuse for murder he had ever heard.

"Go see if Graham had a razor," said Ellis. "Lock that room up first, though."

"Mrs. Leavitt," Hank began. As long as Ellis permitted he was going to get in as many questions as he could. "Why did you come upstairs?"

"To bring Miss Amy some sandwiches."

"Did you see anyone?"

"I suppose you mean Mr. Graham. No, I didn't see him. He must have been in his room."

"Never mind that. Did you see Mr. Chandler and Mr. Rawlins in there?" Hank hoped that she might determine, one way or the other, whether the door had been open or closed, and that in turn might explain why none of them had heard Mr. Chandler cry out.

Mrs. Leavitt shook her head. "I didn't look," she said. "I wanted to get home to my dinner and I didn't want Lloyd to ask me to stay and hunt for the inventory. I waited outside Miss Amy's door," she went on, "until he was through talking to her. Thanks be they went in there through the bathroom and didn't see me."

"Eddie," said Hank, "was the door from the bathroom to Amos' room locked?"

"What? Oh yes. Mr. Chandler unlocked it."

Mrs. Leavitt sniffed. "And I locked it after him."

"You what?"

"I said I locked it after him. He'd got no call to be traipsing through there, though I was glad he did, and there warn's no sense to leaving it unlocked with all the goings on that's going on," she added darkly.

Hank felt the first warm glow of accomplishment that he had experienced yet. It might just be that the secret of their troubles lay with the invalid who supposedly never left her room. Chandler had been a small man, and, as Ellis had pointed out, he had been practically trapped between the desk and the bed, but how Miss Currier could have killed the very husky Amos or how she had obtained the ice pick with which to kill Chandler, Hank hadn't yet decided. Mrs. Leavitt could have brought up the ice pick, but if she had known that the door was unlocked after the discovery of Chandler's body, it seemed unlikely that she would have been so insistent about having locked it. He would let the matter of the door rest for the time being.

But the doctor spoke up. "Who unlocked the door then?" he wanted to know. "I went into her room that way."

Mrs. Leavitt studied Hank's face for a moment before she spoke. "It'll do you no good," she said, "to try to make out she did it. Them as know her know better than that, and there's others got better reason."

"She hated him," Eunice cried out. "She hated my father and you know it, because Father always said she could walk as well as anyone."

"I wasn't going to say it"—Mrs. Leavitt did not look at Eunice—"but something made me look around just as I got to the back stairs, and Eunice Chandler was coming out of Amos' door."

"You, you old woman," Eunice screamed, "you were in love with Amos—"

Shay put his hand over Eunice's mouth and stopped her tirade.

Hank wished Shay would mind his own business.

From the back hall came the whir of Jeff's electric razor. Durrell was audibly proving the existence of that.

Ellis, his hope for accusations justified at last, sprang into action. He realized, as well as Hank, that all the others had been to the kitchen and could have obtained the ice pick, but Eunice had admitted ownership of the skull with ruby eyes. One and one, for Ellis, made two.

"Eunice Chandler," he bellowed, "I arrest you for the murders of Amos Currier and Lloyd Chandler."

Eunice's mouth made a round, silent o, and then she fell forward, striking her head on the banister before Shay could catch her.

Dr. Pratt, Hank and Eddie sprang forward, but Shay had her in his arms first.

"You dumb cluck," he roared at Ellis, "she would have told you about it. She went in there to get her boots and saw him."

"Take her in there," said the doctor, pointing to Emma's room.

"Oh, dear," said Durrell, whom the shouting had finally brought to the scene. "I'm afraid that was a mistake." He nudged Jeff with his elbow. "How do you manage that thing," he asked, "around the end of your chin?"

Chapter 7

AN HOUR LATER Eunice had regained consciousness and had been given a hypodermic to quiet her incoherent babblings. Mrs. Leavitt was with her and the doctor had gone home, having determined that the bruise on Eunice's head was not serious and having officially confirmed the already pretty generally held notion that Amos and Mr. Chandler were dead.

Morgan had returned and reported that there was only one set of fingerprints on the ice pick. Everyone had been fingerprinted and Morgan had departed again.

A rather subdued Ellis was in the dining room taking statements, a process that, Hank thought, might well have been resorted to sooner. The manner of Ellis' denunciation of Eunice Chandler, if not the actual charges, had set everyone against him again. The information he would get now would corroborate the facts already established; no one would volunteer anything new.

There was a different feeling in the house. It was as though Chandler's death had, in a curious way, lightened their spirits. Amos' death had been a shock. As far as they knew, Amos had been, in Mrs. Leavitt's words, a good man. They had, with the possible exception of the murderer, no reason for disliking Amos. On the other hand, Chandler's death, surprising though it had been, had been an anticlimax. Chandler could not have been said to have made a favorable impression on those who had not known him before; Durrell had magnificently understated the opinion of those who had. The human system can sustain an emotion only so long, and the killing of Chandler had, instead of adding to the horror of Amos' death, released them from it.

To complete the cure Jeff and Shay had gone to the buttery and mixed themselves a drink.

Miss Currier had readily admitted to Ellis that she had gone to the bathroom sometime after Mrs. Leavitt's departure and unlocked the door to see what Chandler and Eddie were up to. She had thought the room empty, she said, and had gone back to her chair. Both Ellis and Hank had stood in the bathroom door and found that the frame of the four-poster was so high that they could not see Chandler's body. If Miss Currier's story were true, he had been dead when she looked in, but Miss Currier could not say how long after Mrs. Leavitt had gone that that had been. She had eaten two sandwiches first and drunk her tea; and Ellis had shown that a minute would have taken the murderer into Amos' room and out again.

There was, however, one flaw in her story. Ellis had not picked it up, so Hank stayed behind when the others went downstairs.

Miss Currier had received them from the depths of the big wing chair in which Hank had first seen her, but now there was a blue-and-white coverlet across her knees falling in voluminous folds to the floor. The gold-headed cane leaned against the coverlet, and Miss Currier's hands were quiet in her lap.

"Why didn't you lock the bathroom after you looked in?" Hank asked.

"What for?" Miss Currier seemed surprised. "It isn't usually locked; that was just one of Sally's notions."

"Aren't you afraid to stay here alone?" It wasn't what Hank had been going to say at all, but Miss Currier seemed older than when he had first seen her. He couldn't imagine how he had suspected her of killing Amos and Lloyd Chandler. She looked old and feeble and helpless. Someone ought to be taking care of her.

"No," said Miss Currier. "Right now I'm a little tired. Death wouldn't be so bad if it weren't painful."

"Do you think someone will try to kill you?"

"No," Miss Currier said again, "but that's what you were thinking, wasn't it?"

"Perhaps. The mortality in your family has been rather high in the last twenty-four hours."

Miss Currier sat forward a little and life came back into her eyes. "You're a detective," she said. "Have you got any clues? Who did it? Nobody tells me anything."

She was so childishly eager that Hank laughed. "The usual procedure," he said, "is for the detective to ask the questions."

"Pshaw," said Miss Currier, "can't you violate the rules for once? I never had a chance to find out how the police actually work before." She broke off, flushing, and pointed with her cane.

"There's some brandy in that closet. Sally put it away for fear someone might see it. I always keep a little, for my heart, you know."

Amused, and willing to humor her for whatever information he might gain, Hank went to the closet as he was bidden. A few dresses hung there, a shawl and some night clothes. On the floor were slippers and on the shelves were many boxes neatly tied with string.

"What's in the boxes?" Hank asked.

"My dolls." There was a pause. "I look at them sometimes. I was saving them for Amos' daughter."

Quickly, from a decanter frosted with cutting as intricate as a snowflake, Hank poured two glasses of brandy. Miss Currier sniffed hers delicately.

"That's better," she said. "Now begin."

Hank edged his chair to one side so that the light was not directly behind Miss Currier. It wasn't a bad idea to go over the facts. She had a right to know them, even if she couldn't understand them, and he could watch her as he talked.

"What do you think Amos was killed with?" he asked.

If the question was a trap, Miss Currier avoided it. "Why, I thought Ellis said the ice pick?"

"Can you keep a secret?" Hank leaned forward, watching her closely.

Miss Currier nodded over her glass, her face alight with eagerness.

"I think he was killed with the ice crusher."

"What's that like?"

Hank explained the nature of the implement that he had found in the bucket. "I took the crusher," he went on, "and a sample of the water from the pail. I'm going to have a friend of mine in Boston analyze them for me and I have obstructed justice to the extent of not telling Ellis what I'm going to do. He must have seen them but he apparently paid no attention to them."

"Conflict," said Miss Currier, "between the police and the detective; that's good."

"Good for the criminal, you mean?" Hank asked. "I'll turn the findings over to Ellis, of course. Nobody's paying me to investigate these murders, but Ellis was so cocky I couldn't resist putting one over on him."

"Miss Marsh," said Miss Currier irrelevantly, "is a pretty woman; but go on. According to Sally anyone upstairs had plenty of time to kill Lloyd, including me. Did everyone go back downstairs last night after they were supposed to be in bed?"

"They all admitted it except Eunice. Ellis assumed she had because he found the skull from her bracelet."

"What about this Mr. Rawlins?"

Hank explained that the noise of the lock on Eddie's door would certainly have aroused Amos.

"That's right," Miss Currier conceded, "you told me about that before. You see"—she smiled at him—"I've heard about most of you from Amos. One hates to suspect one's friends of murder so I was trying to pin it on Mr. Rawlins."

"Assuming," said Hank, "that he could have left his room without warning Amos, who may have lain down but who was still partly dressed, how could Rawlins have killed Chandler, and what earthly motive would he have for killing them both?"

"You know him better than I do," said Miss Currier, "and I'll admit he didn't strike me as the killer type."

"Hardly," Hank laughed. He was amused to find himself talking man to man with Miss Currier. She might be old but Shay would have admitted that her command of the vernacular was excellent.

"Is Mr. Rawlins well to do?"

The quaint phrase was startling in her otherwise modern speech.

"He lives in a boardinghouse and drives a Ford but he has better clothes than I do. I think he makes a good living selling insurance. The company thinks well of him. About this insurance, now. That would have been a big policy."

Miss Currier giggled. "You sound just like Ches."

"First thing you know I'll be raising hogs too."

"There's no money in hogs right now, or fruit trees either." Miss Currier sighed and took a pull at the brandy. "Forgive my saying so but you seem to me to lack the energy required of a successful farmer."

"The sedentary type."

"Quite."

They both laughed; but Hank realized that they had wandered away from the subject of insurance and went determinedly back to it. "Eddie and Durrell agreed that the commission would be over six hundred dollars. That wouldn't be lettuce to anyone, and Eddie was right after Chandler to take out insurance as soon as he lost Amos. He might inadvertently kill one customer but it hardly seems likely that he'd kill two. You didn't have any objection to the insurance, did you?" he finished bluntly.

Miss Currier pursed her lips reflectively. "The best angle I can think of," she said, "would be for me to want Ches to write the insurance. Then Ches could kill them because he knew I'd give it to him rather than Rawlins. How does that strike you?"

"Weak," Hank admitted, "very weak." But he put away in his mind the fact that Miss Currier had not suggested that she had killed in order that Durrell might write the insurance.

"As a matter of fact," the old lady went on, "I urged Amos to take out insurance and I think he might have done so sooner—though as a rule Amos did not take kindly to suggestion—if Lloyd hadn't so continually badgered him about it. Amos was very casual about the family heirlooms, but I don't think he was as indifferent to the traditions of this house as he pretended. He was always very careful about locking up."

"Does it strike you as odd," Hank broke in, "that Amos was going around to lock up in the dark?"

"Not at all. Amos knew this house like the back of his hand. It was a fetish of his father's that nothing ever be moved. Amos was wholly indifferent to interior decoration and had no wife to want to rearrange the parlor. Sally puts things back where they were from habit. And, besides, a house seems cooler in the dark."

"Mrs. Leavitt," Hank offered, "seems a little vague about the muffineer."

"Sally has enough to do without keeping a mess of silver clean. Amos had sense enough to keep it locked up."

"You can force that lock with a piece of wire," said Hank. "I did."

"That's fortunate for Mr. Graham, isn't it? So long as Sally couldn't say when she had seen the muffineer."

Hank nodded gloomily. "Deprived of Eunice, I'm afraid Ellis could build up quite a case against Jeff."

"He had the key"—Miss Currier checked Jeff's misdemeanors off on her fingers—"he knows the value of antiques; he came downstairs with that flimsy pretext of returning the ice pick; he could have picked it up when he came upstairs this morning, and Mr. Rawlins found him in the room with Lloyd."

"That's about the ticket." Hank could have added that Jeff had quarreled with Amos and had struck him but, like Emma, he hated to be the one to spread that story; he rather imagined that Eunice would recall the incident when she was in a condition to be questioned. "I don't suppose," he went on, "that either you or Mrs. Leavitt could say absolutely what was in that silver cupboard or when, if you follow me."

"Not without the inventory."

"And the inventory seems to have been conveniently mislaid."

"Young man," said Miss Currier, "I don't like that 'conveniently'; just stick to the facts. The inventory is missing."

Hank looked around the room, at the many photographs on the walls, the crowded mantel, the drop-leaf table—pad-foot, he thought Emma would call it—piled with books and magazines and the sewing cabinet—the multitudinous though orderly objects of a life lived in a confined area.

"Ellis," he said, "will be hunting for the inventory."

"I tore it up," said Miss Currier, "and flushed it down the drain." She laughed at Hank's astonishment. "Of course I did no such thing, but you sounded exactly as though you were warning me that I'd better come across with it."

"Fortunately I've got a sense of humor, but don't try any jokes like that on Ellis or he'll have you in the jug. When did you see the inventory last?"

Miss Currier hesitated. "Not for a long time. Really, I don't remember."

"Did you describe the inventory to Chandler and Eddie?"

"Why no, Lloyd knows what it looks like."

"When Eddie came downstairs he said that he thought Mr. Chandler had found the inventory; would Chandler have any reason for destroying it?"

"None that I know of; I thought he wanted to find it to prove that Mr. Graham had taken the muffineer?"

"Suppose he took the muffineer himself, suppose that tantrum downstairs was all bluff, wouldn't he want to destroy the inventory to protect himself?"

Miss Currier rotated her cane slowly between her palms, considering Hank's suggestion. "You're implying that he killed Amos because Amos had found out that he took the muffineer. Lloyd's ways were past understanding so we'll concede that. Then he'd try to find the inventory and destroy it, but who would kill him?"

"Suppose he didn't find it and committed suicide because he thought someone else had?"

Miss Currier shook her head. "Even if the fingerprints on that ice pick are Lloyd's, I won't believe that. Even if he killed Amos he'd never kill himself, he'd bully it through on a claim of self-defense. Pour me some more brandy and think up something else."

"He's part of your family. You think you know him and you don't really think he killed Amos, for the same reason that I don't think Jeff did it: loyalty."

Miss Currier set her glass down with a thump. "Get this straight," she said, "I detested Lloyd Chandler. He may have been a Captain of Industry but his employees hated him, he bullied his wife and he tried to keep Eunice penned up with no allowance in this day and age. I wouldn't be surprised if she sneaks out and goes to joints where they smoke marijuana."

"It's nonhabit-forming," said Hank, who thought that Miss Currier had Eunice about right.

"I know that," Miss Currier snapped. "Tell me about Miss Marsh."

"She's a nice kid"—Hank spoke lightly—"a little forgetful and apt to jump at conclusions and firmly convinced that Jeff Graham can do no wrong, but a nice kid."

"Go on," said Miss Currier, "you can do better than that. Amos told me you were in love with her."

Deep down inside Hank knew that Amos was right but he resented Amos' knowledge. Hank was not one to wear his heart on his sleeve; he was so sure of his feeling for Emma that he did not have to think about it and he was equally sure that Emma knew the feeling existed and returned it. He did not like to protest his love; it embarrassed him, because traditions of reticence and reserve were the foundations of his character. If two people loved each other, that was a fact. But the fact was an emotion, and no emotion could stand constant prodding and turning and examination. It was safer to joke about one's affections and pretend they didn't exist. He couldn't tell Miss Currier how he felt about Emma.

He was conscious that he had been silent a long time. He looked up and would have sworn that Miss Currier opened her eyes as he did so.

"That's very nice," she said drowsily.

It was small wonder, Hank thought, that she was tired. If she had been fond of Amos, his death must have been a shock to her, and the added excitement of Chandler's death had told on those who were much younger. There was one more question he wanted to ask, and then he would leave her to her nap.

"About that check. You told Ellis that Gillespie was a friend of Amos'. Could the check have had any significance to Chandler?"

"What?" Miss Currier stared at Hank uncomprehendingly, then her eyelids drooped again.

The goings on, as Durrell called them, and the brandy had been too much for Miss Currier. Her head fell sideways against a wing of the chair and her breath ruffled her lips with a sound that was much too delicate to be called a snore. Hank got to his feet and tiptoed quietly from the room.

Miss Currier waited a long time. She recited the Declaration of Independence, the "Gettysburg Address" and as much of *The Aeneid* as she could remember. Then she said the multiplication table up to the sevens just to make sure.

When she opened her eyes there was a triumphant gleam in them. After a cautious survey of the room she peeked under the blue-and-white coverlet. It would be a long time before Sally got back. Gently, the more so because she herself could not hear a telltale crackle, Miss Currier lifted several sheets of paper from beneath the coverlet.

Chapter 8

DOWN IN THE DINING ROOM Ellis was getting nowhere with Emma, and Emma was wishing that Durrell would look at her and not over her shoulder at the mantel behind her. The windows were open and the door to the buttery was propped back to catch any movement of the hot, dry air, but the motes in the shaft of late afternoon sun that lay along the buttery floor were motionless. Durrell mopped continually at his face and neck, mopped and stared over Emma's shoulder as though thinking of something else.

In the kitchen Shay and Jeff were playing casino, with Eddie an admiring kibitzer.

As Hank had predicted, Ellis had obtained no new information from any of them, though Shay had admitted that he worked for the *American* and had seen his cherished camera turned over to Morgan.

Emma had repeated her statement that she had come downstairs on Saturday night to talk to Amos about the insurance. Concerning Chandler's death, she claimed that she had heard no outcry from Amos' room. She thought she had heard someone moving around but she had been changing her clothes and hadn't paid much attention. It might have been Chandler and Eddie that she had heard or Shay and Eunice in the next room. She had never seen the Coney muffineer and she knew nothing about any trouble between Mr. Graham and Mr. Chandler over a house. Mr. Graham had heard the Kimball-Haskett house was for sale and had told a customer about it. If Mr. Chandler had also wanted the house, that was too bad. Maybe he hadn't offered enough money for it.

"Cards *and* spades." Jeff's voice came exultantly in from the kitchen.

Ellis threw a quick annoyed glance in the direction of the buttery door, but Durrell did not take his eyes off the mantel. Every time he looked toward the buttery he remembered Amos' body.

Ches Durrell had gone to the Westham Academy with Amos Cur-

rier and had been familiar with the Currier house and the Currier
buttery, and he hadn't liked the sight of Amos' body caught there in
the door. He was remembering winter nights after school, the cookies that had been in the stone jar, the careful tiptoeing upstairs in
order not to disturb Amos' father and the fantastic tales of adventure
that Miss Amy had told to two small boys and a freckle-faced girl. And
now Amos was dead and he ought to do something about it, if only
for the sake of Miss Amy and Sally Leavitt.

"Paul and Virginia," said Ches Durrell triumphantly, "and an In-
dian."

Emma looked at Durrell, amazed. It was pure coincidence, she
thought, that she knew what he was talking about. If she hadn't seen
the figure in Miss Carey's shop, if she hadn't gone in to ask about it
because she had never seen one before she would have thought, in
Shay's words, that the chief of police had blowed his top.

"Been worrying me ever since this morning," Durrell explained
apologetically. "It used to stand over there on the mantel. Miss Amy
told us the story about them, said some Frenchman wrote it. Funny
how a thing like that'll worry you if you can't remember it."

"Has the guy gone nuts?" Ellis demanded.

But Emma said kindly, though with the superiority of great wis-
dom, "It was a Staffordshire figure."

"That's it," said Durrell. "There was a palm tree on it. I wonder
what ever happened to it?"

Ellis pushed back his chair with a violence that boded no good
for its delicate legs. "God-a-mighty," he said, unconsciously reverting
to Durrell's idiom, "you might as well go home. You might as well all
go home. And I'll go somewhere where they take murders seriously."

He stalked into the kitchen to dismiss the others. Zubinsky, coming in from outside, followed him. Zubinsky was hot, his shirt was
darkened with perspiration and he carried disdainfully a small black
cylindrical object.

"Where did you get that?" Emma, getting no answer to her question, followed Zubinsky.

At that moment Hank appeared in the dining-room door. There
was something in the twitch of Emma's skirt as she sailed into the
buttery that warned Hank of something brewing. He said, "Just a
minute," when Durrell hailed him, and followed Emma.

Zubinsky had handed a cigarette holder of standard manufac-
ture and prophylactic popularity to Ellis, and Emma was asking again
where he had found it.

"What's so important about that?" Ellis wanted to know. "Is it yours?"

"Certainly it's mine." Emma was very positive.

"On the contrary," said Hank, "I think it's mine."

Jeff put down his cards. "I've got one like that."

"Me too." Quickly, before Ellis realized what he was doing, Shay took the cigarette holder and handed it to Jeff. "You can tell by the teeth marks," he said, "if there's a big one, it's my left upper canine."

Ellis reached for the holder but Jeff warded him off.

"Canine nothing," he said, "that's where my bridgework gouges it."

"My bite isn't even"—Hank peered over Jeff's shoulder—"so the teethmarks ought to be farther ahead on one side."

"You should have worn braces," Emma admonished him. She did not reach for the cigarette holder; by now it had two sets of fingerprints on it and, wherever Zubinsky had found it, it wouldn't incriminate Jeff.

The same thought had been only too uppermost in Ellis' mind; he refused the holder when Jeff finally handed it to him.

"I ought to jail every one of you," he declared, "for obstructing justice." He turned to Zubinsky. "Where was it?"

"Out in that summerhouse sort of thing."

"Gazebo is the word," Shay corrected him, "from the Greek."

"Is it really Greek?" Emma asked. "I always wondered."

"And I suppose"—Ellis was reduced to the futile weapon of sarcasm—"that all of you were out in that what-do-you-call-it?"

"I wasn't"—Eddie spoke up—"and I don't have one of those holders, but if you're all using them, I think I will."

"That's why we love him," Shay explained, "he says such funny things."

"Miaow!"

It was only the stable cat at the kitchen door but the appropriateness was too much for them. They rocked with laughter, all but Ellis and Emma.

"Shame on you," said Emma, "the poor thing is probably hungry."

"Get out of here," said Ellis. "Get out of here and don't come back. When I want you I'll come and get you. And that goes for you, Fairbanks."

"I'm sorry," Hank said rather stiffly, "I only tried to help."

"Oh yeah?" Ellis was unconvinced. He spoke to Zubinsky. "Go with them when they get their bags and see that they don't take nothin'. Did you search the cars?"

Zubinsky nodded and followed a rather abashed contingent upstairs. Hank and Shay, having not so much as a toothbrush, remained in the kitchen. Ellis, to avoid the sight of them, went outside. Then Durrell ambled out of the buttery.

"You folks going home?"

"Pardon us," said Shay, "for eating and running."

Durrell looked at Shay for a minute, then, "I don't know's you got so much to eat that it need worry you none."

He walked to the woodshed door, motioning for Hank to follow him.

"About them pillows," he said softly, "that you was so anxious to look at. Well, I was in there alone looking for the inventory and it didn't seem like 'twould do no harm. I thought maybe the inventory had got hidden in the bedclothes."

Hank was listening attentively.

"Well, 'twarn't. But there was kind of a wet spot, like, on one of them pillows."

"Saliva?"

"Could be."

Eddie and Emma came into the kitchen and Durrell put out his hand. "Sorry to see you folks go," he said, "but I guess you ain't none too anxious to stay. Don't you worry about the cat, miss, Sally'll tend to her."

Durrell might be dumb, Hank thought, but he didn't miss much.

"Can I give anybody a lift? No?" Eddie shook hands all around, got in his car and waited for Hank and Durrell to open the garage doors.

"I meant to give him that holder," said Shay as Eddie drove off. "I don't think Ellis wants it."

"I'll thank you," said Hank, "not to make so free with my property."

Emma went to the table and picked up the holder.

"You better leave it," said Durrell. "It won't do nobody no harm now."

Then Jeff stormed into the kitchen, followed at a safe distance by Zubinsky. Jeff shook his razor under Durrell's nose.

"Hairs," he said darkly, "all clogged up with hairs. There was a pipe cleaner on the dresser. Why didn't you use it?"

Before Durrell could defend himself Jeff stamped out to his car.

There was an ominous crash as he failed to miss the fender of Hank's roadster and his engine roared as he hit the road.

"I'll sue him," said Hank.

"You say something to rile him?" Durrell asked Zubinsky.

"Pay no attention," Emma answered him. "He's terribly fond of that razor and it's the first time he's been normal all day."

Hank drove slowly and carefully. There was small chance of his overtaking Jeff but he did not want to pick up the more cautious Eddie. When they were well past the filling station, out of the village, he pulled over to the side of the road and got out of the car.

"What's the matter?" asked Shay. "Can't you wait?"

Hank opened the back of the car and removed from among the tools a half-filled whiskey bottle and an object carelessly wrapped in a piece of waste. The back of the car had been a risky place to put them, but the handle of the crusher might have been mistaken for the handle of a jack, and anybody might carry a whiskey bottle. Search had been certain and he had taken the chance that his booty would be overlooked if it were perfectly obvious. As he got back into the car Shay caught sight of the bottle.

"A noble idea, as I hope to crochet."

"Keep your paws off that." Hank carefully stowed his treasures away in the gadget trap. "That's not booze, that's water out of the ice bucket that will, I hope, have traces of blood in it. And that other thing is what the papers will call the murder weapon."

"Mercy me," said Emma, "what was I going to ask you and what will Ellis say?"

"Thank you, I trust, when I give them back to him, plus the laboratory report."

"Fingerprints," said Shay, "the hairs out of your head "

"No fingerprints, I'm afraid." Hank sent the car forward toward the turnpike. "It was covered with rust and any kid that reads the funny papers knows enough not to leave fingerprints. But there may be some of Amos' hair and a little skin left on it."

"Ugh!" said Emma. And then she hated to ask but she had to know—"Did you take it out of Mr. Chandler when you stayed upstairs?"

"Good heavens, no. I wouldn't touch the ice pick, goose. What pretty things you think of. That's the crusher."

"Oh." Emma was relieved. "That's why you were being so nice to Mrs. Leavitt, and if it wasn't the ice pick, why, then, Ellis can't pretend that Jeff did it."

"Don't she non-sequitur to beat all get-out?"

"You get so you can translate," Hank explained, "when you know her better. Jeff could have killed Amos with the crusher," he went on, "but this ought to nullify the effect of that story about trying to take the ice pick to bed with him."

"Come on, Jack, open up. Who did it?"

"Honestly, I haven't the foggiest."

"Well, if it's all the same to you, I'd rather Mrs. Leavitt was the one."

"Goody," said Emma, "that means you got her in the pool. I knew I'd find out sometime. Thank heaven, nobody drew Jeff. He's the one I tore up."

"So of course he didn't do it."

"You know he didn't."

"Ellis is going to think so when he gets all his facts. I wish we had told about that fight."

"Why? I was glad nobody did."

"Because when he does find out it's going to look worse because we didn't."

"Who's going to tell him?"

"Eunice."

There was a pause while they all thought about Eunice.

Finally Emma said, "It's funny, isn't it? We're all sure that it was Eunice or Mrs. Leavitt or Miss Currier and I bet they're just as sure it was one of us, because we know us and they know them."

"You've said it," said Hank, "in quite a mouthful. Ellis is the only neutral there."

"And he's biased or I never saw one." Shay was emphatic. "What about Durrell, the master mind?"

"He doesn't like Ellis and his natural sympathies are with the Curriers, but don't let the old boy fool you, he's cuter than he looks."

" 'All I know,' " Emma quoted, "'is hogs and insurance.' I'm so hungry I could gnaw a bone."

"Just any old bone?"

"Preferably a large steak bone."

"You got any money, Jack?"

"Not me, Jack. How about you?"

"Positiville nawthing."

"Too bad."

"All right." Emma had had that worked on her before. "You can just let me out at the Boylston Street Childs. I can walk home from there."

"At this hour of the night? Why, it'll be dark pretty soon. You might be kidnaped."

The Missing Witness or *Who Sat Down in the Gum?* Don't worry, honey chile, we all's gwine to sit droolin' while you eats them poke chops and then we is goin' take you home."

Hank wanted to know if Shay got his dialect out of *Gone with the Wind.* Shay claimed it was straight from the Old Howard.

"Be serious," said Emma. "We've got to hurry up and decide who did the murders before Ellis does. I think Mr. Chandler killed Amos and committed suicide and I don't want to be argued out of it."

"That would explain why nobody heard him yell."

"Exactly," said Emma. "If he'd been in the pool and I'd been sure of getting him, I'd have drawn."

"If you had fifty dollars."

It was just as well, Hank thought, not to upset her by telling her that the reason Chandler hadn't cried out was because he had probably been suffocated with a pillow. With suicide ruled out Ellis was going to recall Jeff's insistence that he was the last to see Amos alive and remember his unsubstantiated story that he had merely been standing over Chandler's body. Emma had been right, Jeff hadn't acted like himself all day. Or, no, he had been irritable enough in the morning, it was only after Chandler had discovered the loss of the muffineer that Jeff had quieted down. Hank was certain of Jeff's innocence but he didn't like Jeff's having had the key to the silver cupboard. He himself believed Jeff's statement that Amos had given it to him but, taking everything else into consideration, he was doubtful if Ellis would. Hank told himself that it would be time enough to worry about Jeff when he was accused; in the meantime: no pay, no work.

Emma remembered what she had wanted to ask Hank. She had wanted to ask about the letter and whether or not Shay had known Eunice before Saturday night but she hesitated to ask in front of Shay. Shay was odd about women. They were a part of his life that did not include her. Hank had once said that women were Shay's work and photography was merely his avocation.

Shay was wondering when Eunice would be well enough to call him. He was anxious to see her again. The fact that Eunice had become very wealthy in her own right did not disturb Shay a bit. Neither was he greatly concerned by his failure to call his paper. He would say that the police had prevented him and confiscated the pictures he had taken. He hoped he got the packs back. He thought he had a good one of Eunice.

Chapter 9

THE NEXT MORNING Emma left the roadster cautiously around the corner on Chestnut Street instead of blatantly, as was her wont, in the No Parking space reserved for customers in front of the shop. She sauntered past the corner door casually, as though the shop of J. Graham, Antiques, was no concern of hers. Maybe, she thought, she ought to have bought a paper, then she would have the official story and would know what to say to them. The lad from the *Transcript* was sort of cute and was a friend of Hank's. Emma squared her shoulders; she could handle them.

Jeff's car was not there yet, which was no surprise. Emma was the one who was supposed to open the shop; the surprise to Emma was that the sidewalk in front of the main entrance was encumbered only by the usual scurrying pedestrians who, like Emma, were late to work. The shop door looked peaceful, a little dusty and undisturbed; it was not surrounded by the eager crowd of reporters that Emma had expected. Emma was surprised, relieved and then a little annoyed. Didn't the dopes know that there had been a couple of murders and that she and Jeff were good for the front page on account of their apparent predilection for corpses? Emma unlocked the door and reproved herself sharply for ever thinking of such a thing. Things had come to a pretty pass if she wanted to get into print to the extent of hanging around murders.

The air in the shop, tight closed for a day, was hot and heavy and stale. Emma opened both doors wide, so long as Jeff wasn't there, and let down the awnings; then she decided that she really ought to have a paper after all, if Hank wasn't going to be decent enough to come around and tell her what was going on.

The account, when she got it, seemed hardly worth the trouble. The headline, SLEUTHS SLIP UP, capped a story that made more of the fact that murder had been done with a detective in the house and that the additional presence of the police had not prevented a suicide than of the identity of the others who had been present.

"Body of Host Discovered by Weekend Guests," the subheading went on, and the guests were listed by initials. As E. L. Marsh, Emma hardly recognized herself, and Jeff, thanks to a mistake on someone's part, was J. G. Grahme. The fact that Lloyd Chandler had committed suicide, the paper assured its readers, was well authenticated. His fingerprints, and his alone, had been found on the handle of the ice pick. That Mr. Chandler had been responsible for the death of Amos Currier was only delicately hinted, out of consideration, no doubt, for the stockholders in the Chandler Woolen Mills. In fact Emma decided that the reporter must be a stockholder, for Chandler's position in industry filled the article, almost to the exclusion of Amos, and ill health was given as a reason for any and all of his acts.

Still reading, Emma skirted the back of a limousine, stubbed her toe on the curbing and finally heard the telephone ringing furiously in the office. The caller was Jeff and he opened the conversation with the remark that Emma seemed a little bit late getting to work. Emma said that she had been there a long time; she had just gone across the street to get a paper. Jeff didn't seem to believe her but forbore to press the point as the purpose of his call was to announce that he was going to Narragansett and wouldn't be in that day.

"Why, Jeff, you can't. Ellis might want to know where you were. Have you seen the papers?"

"Yes. That's why I'm telling you. Now pay attention. If Tiny Bloom comes in with a message, write it down and leave it on my desk."

"What kind of a message? What are you up to?"

Jeff snorted with exasperation. "It'll be a name, the name of a horse, a hot tip for tomorrow."

"I'll take no such message and you oughtn't to go to Narragansett."

"You'll do as I say." Jeff ended any further criticizing of his actions by hanging up.

Emma was still holding the telephone when a young man came in.

"Well," said Emma, "what can I do for you?"

"Is your name Emma Marsh?" the young man began abruptly.

"I was never baptized," said Emma, "but they let me use it."

"Are you by any chance E. L. Marsh?"

"No, I'm Andy Devine in disguise."

"Come on," said the young man. "E. L. Marsh is supposed to live at 87 Melrose Street and the old gent over there said she worked here."

Emma thought that she would speak to M. Lebotien, her land-lord, about giving her address to strange young men.

"So," she said frigidly, "you're a reporter."

"You make it so hard for me. This is practically the first break I've had, their sending me out to check up on E. L. Marsh."

He didn't look very well fed, Emma thought, but aside from that he was rather nice looking. She wondered if someone was out ringing the bell at Jeff's apartment; maybe it was a good thing Jeff had gone to Narragansett.

"How'd you happen to be out at this Currier's?"

"Because he asked me," said Emma without thinking.

"Oh, so you are E. L. Marsh?"

"No," said Emma, regretting her momentary sympathy, "I'm Flora Temple. She was a trotter or a pacer or something and we have a fine print of her, and if you'd like to buy it well and good, if not please get out, because I'm very busy."

"Weren't you mixed up on another murder a couple of years back?"

"As it happens," said Emma, "I had no connection with it what-ever, though I suppose you're too young to know."

"Sort of the 'find-the-body' gal, aren't you?"

Emma went a little white around the mouth. "If I ever find an-other body and it isn't yours I'll be disappointed. Now I think you better get out." She was afraid someone would come in and ask for Jeff, someone who knew about their friendship with Amos and who would recognize the names. Mr. Chandler had killed Amos and com-mitted suicide and everything was all right, if only the fire of her dead past wasn't rekindled by more dead.

"No." The young man sat down on the sofa and put his hat be-side, him. "I think I'll just wait here."

Emma didn't know what she could do about him; in spite of his slenderness, he was too big for her to attack bodily. She decided to ignore him, picked up the morning mail and stalked, nose in air, back into the office. She sat down in Jeff's chair because, turned as it was to face the door, it commanded a better view of the shop than hers. She opened the mail: bills, bills, bills. People were always ask-ing J. Graham's to have a mattress made or to find a lampshade and then never remembering to pay for it. Didn't other people open their bills? Because if they didn't, Emma was going to quit opening hers. And Jeff off to the races! She couldn't imagine where he got the money.

Whoop-de-do! There was a check from the major's wife who had hounded Jeff into finding her a pair of card tables and then apparently forgotten the whole transaction. Emma hunted back through the files for the slip and vigorously marked it paid.

Emma found that she was humming the tune that her voluntary guard was whistling, broke off and turned abruptly to the stock book to cross off the tables. Two hundred and thirty-eight dollars wasn't much of a profit if you had to wait eight months for it. Jeff had bought the tables from a dealer in Millinocket—funny name—they had taken to putting down the names of people from whom they bought things to protect themselves against stolen goods. Emma remembered that she had not crossed off the purple overlay lamp and turned to the last entry in the stock book. But the lamp wasn't the last entry. Jeff hadn't entered it at all and would she give him what-for for his carelessness!

The young man was looking at the gilt lettering on the window; then he looked at his notebook. "By gum," he said, "the boss is dumb. That name should be J. O. Graham and he's the feller the police thought killed Richard Norwitch. Say, you're quite a pair, aren't you? I'd think twice before I was a customer of yours."

His thought coincided too closely with Emma's opinion for comfort. "Mr. Currier," she said with dignity, "wasn't a customer of ours: he was a friend."

"It makes no never mind. 'The Haunted Shop!' Say, how would that do for a heading?"

"Please," said Emma, "can't you see that this is awful for us? We just happened to walk in on this murder; it had no connection with the shop at all. And I think it's terribly unfair to persecute us just because we happened to know Mr. Currier."

The reporter, who didn't know Emma and failed to recognize the signs that her right hand was now energetically covering up what her left had been doing and who, being young, had just decided that he had fallen in love with Emma, looked acutely miserable.

Emma, feeling that she had scored a shot, though unaware how complete the devastation had been, was magnanimous.

"Look, if you leave your name and go away and forget about us, I'll promise to call you if anything new breaks." Emma opened her eyes wide and put on her best smile. "Is it a bargain?"

The young man got to his feet, a confused speech about the Fourth Estate being an honorable estate whirling in his mind. He couldn't get it to go just right, so he said "Thanks" gruffly, "name's Anderson" and went out.

The telephone began to ring; the competitors began to drop in with condolences that were more or less sincere, but the tenor of the remarks of friend or foe alike were about the same.

"It was too bad about Currier."

"Didn't they have any idea who did it?"

"Who was this Chandler anyway?"

"Isn't Eunice Chandler a mess?" (This over the phone from one of Emma's female friends.)

And then, invariably, "You're sort of unlucky, aren't you?" or "Just like old times, isn't it, with a body around?"

"Oh, you say Jeff's out of town?"

"Well, it's lucky young Fairbanks was there, eh?"

They said it over and over again until Emma was almost relieved when Mrs. Logan came in, though ordinarily she didn't think much of her. Mrs. Logan was pale and ethereal and usually wore a veil—she had welcomed snoods with open arms—and, Emma thought, played up to Jeff shamefully.

Mrs. Logan dismissed the deaths with a "Too, too sad" and wanted to know if Jeff had anything put away for her.

One of the things Jeff had discovered in his years of dealing with a capricious public was that people were more likely than not to buy something that had been put away and saved for them especially; they liked the flattery and, because Jeff had discerning taste, they usually liked what he picked out.

As a result the lower drawer of Jeff's desk had become the catch-all for the foibles of the specialist as well as the resting place for odds and ends for which only Jeff could think up uses. Emma never knew, when she opened the drawer, whether she would find a petit-point bag or a stuffed rattlesnake.

"Now let me see," Emma began, "didn't he tell me?"

She opened the drawer, prepared to sell Mrs. Logan whatever it might contain, but the drawer held only two objects: one was swathed in tissue paper and the other was a patch box. The patch box, Emma knew, had on the reverse of its lid the picture of a corpulent washerwoman bending too far over her tub. Mrs. Logan didn't collect dirty patch boxes and one of the local bank presidents did, so Emma felt of the tissue paper bundle, felt the hard turned shape within and wished that she had never done it. The tissue paper crackled like a splitting board, and Mrs. Logan was holding out an up-turned palm to Hank and caressing Shay with a languid "How do you do?"

Emma shut the drawer with a snap, wondering why Hank always had to act as though it was an unutterable joy to meet anything with a skirt on and what she would say if either of them chanced to look in that drawer.

"I thought Mr. Graham had something," she said, "but I can't seem to find it. He'll be back tomorrow."

"Back from where?" Hank wanted to know.

"Narragansett."

Mrs. Logan pressed Hank's hand and got up.

Hank held the door for her and then flopped down on the couch with a "How's my little crime wave?" as greeting to Emma.

Shay sat down in the wing chair, got up again, prowled around among the trivets, andirons and Bennington crocks piled in the aisle and asked what the pile of junk in the window was.

Emma said it was Surrealism and wanted to know if they weren't supposed to be working. She shut the door that Hank had left open and walked down the aisle to shut the corner door. She hadn't had time to think it out; maybe if she just didn't think about it at all she could face them with equanimity. Maybe they wouldn't talk about it; perhaps they'd come to tell her about Chandler or Eunice or something. Emma walked back to them and asked if Mr. Chandler really had committed suicide.

"Isn't she wonderful?" Hank asked. "Puts her finger right on the spot. No, my little duck, he didn't. How do we know? Because somebody stuffed a pillow in his mouth and held him down. Durrell, the old snoop, found a wet spot on one of the pillows."

"Mrs. Leavitt"—Shay paused in his pacing—"has a hefty biceps."

"So does your girlfriend Eunice. Sit down, boy, you exhaust me."

"But the papers said—" Emma began.

"Angel face, haven't you known Shay long enough to know even the pictures they print are fakes?"

"If I wasn't so hot," said Shay, "I'd clip you for that."

"It could be," Hank went on, "that Ellis is being cute, pretending to think it was suicide so the murderer will give himself away. I think it much more likely that old hogs and insurance is holding out on him. Understand me, I don't give a hoot. As long as I'm not paid or personally accused my interest in this affair is purely academic."

He looked so placid lying there with his head on the arm of the sofa that Emma had half a mind to tell him what she had found in Jeff's bottom drawer but she quickly thought better of it. Perhaps she was wrong. She wished they'd go away so that she could make sure.

"You suppose Donovan's got my camera back yet?"

Hank shut his eyes. "Pray," he said, "don't mention that name in my presence."

"Why?" Emma was surprised. "What's the matter with Donovan?"

"We went over to see him last night. Really to see if he could do something about Shay's camera, but we just happened to mention the murders, as long as they're in his line of business, and leave the crusher and what do you think that blue-faced Irishman did?"

"What?"

"He laughed. He thought it was a great big, supercolossal, howling joke that I was in on the ground floor of two murders and didn't know who did 'em and wasn't going to be let work on them."

"I think he's mean," said Emma loyally. "Did he have any bright ideas?"

"He said"—Hank recalled with relish—"that day after tomorrow you'd probably remember something that would clear the whole thing up. I told him that you had learned your lesson and came to Papa with everything."

"Why, of course," said Emma.

"Look," said Shay, "I think I'll go over to Stuart Street and see if he's had any luck. When this thing breaks it's going to be bad enough so that I'd better be working."

"Gimme a ring if the report on the crusher is ready. If I'm not right here I might be at the office."

Shay said good-by to Emma and went out into the sunlight.

"Sometimes," said Emma, "Shay doesn't even make sense." She had been so preoccupied that she was only dimly aware that Shay had not been his amiable, ungrammatical self.

"Never mind about Shay." Hank turned on his elbow so that he could look at Emma. "Now that he's gone suppose you tell me what you went downstairs to talk to Amos about."

"Insurance," said Emma. "I told you once."

"Phooey. Is that the best you can do?"

"You'll laugh at me," said Emma, "but after I went upstairs I got to thinking about Jeff's getting mad at Amos—though he was all over it in a minute, as you very well know—but I was afraid Amos wouldn't think so and would be annoyed at Jeff and might cancel the policy, and we need all the money we can get, what with Mrs. Graham's trip and all, and I thought maybe I could explain it to him."

"You could talk an arm off the Iron Virgin," Hank conceded graciously. "What did Amos say?"

"He said"—Emma blurted it out—"that nothing Jeff had done made any difference."

"For cat's sake, what are you blushing for?"

"I'm not."

"You are too. What's the matter? Did Amos make a pass at you?"

"Don't be absurd."

"Oh, all right. I suppose"—Hank's tone was tinged with sarcasm—"that you were too engrossed in your pleading to see whether anyone else came downstairs?"

"I couldn't, smarty, I told you it was dark."

"Oh yes"—the sarcasm deepened—"you were talking to Amos about insurance in the dark."

"See here." Emma was a little guiltily annoyed. "I came downstairs in the dark and I heard someone moving around and I said, 'Who is it?' softly, the way you do in the dark, and Amos said, 'It's Amos,' and I said, 'Can I talk to you a minute?' and he said, 'Come on in.' Only I was halfway in by that time anyway."

"You're so plausible," said Hank, "that I almost believe you myself."

"If that's the way you're going to act," said Emma shortly, "you might as well go home. You're not the one who's investigating this case."

"Alas, no."

"Isn't there something that you're being paid for that you ought to be doing?"

"If, by any chance"—Hank rolled over on his back—"you are trying to get rid of me, give it up. I am going to stay right here and think."

"You'll go to sleep," said Emma, "and that'll look pretty if anyone comes in."

"You said yourself business was terrible."

"I really ought to change the windows but it's too hot. Tell me"—baffled in her attempt to get rid of Hank, Emma thought of something else—"did Shay tell you what he went downstairs for?"

"A drink. Does that surprise you?"

"You don't think it could have been anything else?"

"What's on your mind?" Hank was used to Emma's devious method of approach. It might just be, as Donovan had suggested, that she knew something.

"When you and Shay went out to Amos', right when you first got there, I mean, did Shay act as though he knew Eunice?"

"He nearly ran over her, if you think that's a sign of friendship.

What are you getting at?"

Emma began again, from a third angle. "How did you know the way out to Amos'?"

"We didn't. We stopped in the village and asked a man at the filling station. I drew a map on the back of an envelope that Shay gave me. The directions weren't very hard but we weren't remembering so good. Nice feller at the filling station, though, we had quite a chat about something."

"Hank, when I went out to put your car away I saw that map."

"Did you now? Pretty, wasn't it?"

"Pay attention to me. That letter was from Eunice Chandler."

"Eh?"

"I say that that letter you drew the map on was from Eunice Chandler."

Hank's interest brought him almost to a sitting position. "How do you know?"

"Because her name was printed on the outside."

"You don't say. What was on the inside?"

"Now, really, you don't think I read it?"

"I gave up trying to figure out what you'd do years ago. It'd be a lot more use if you had read it."

"Well, of course, after Amos was killed I was sorry I hadn't."

The couch shook with Hank's laughter. "Your ethics are wonderful, but never mind. Thanks for the hot tip." Hank relaxed again.

"Well, go on. What does it mean? Did she know him? Does it do anything to that picture of yours? Do you think she's good looking? Because I don't."

Hank squinted up at the ceiling where a pair of fire buckets, once the property of T. Simms or E. Pluribus Unum, vibrated gently to the outside traffic.

"Every time I tell you something," he said, "it backfires on me. You're always so sure I'm wrong that you get yourself into some scrape trying to prove it. But I'll try it once more. Eunice Chandler knew you were downstairs and, believe me, I was in a cold sweat for fear you'd think up some reason for denying it. But the point is, she agreed to say nothing about you if Shay would keep still about something concerning her. The letter may be part of the deal."

"If she knew I was downstairs," Emma began excitedly, "she must have been down there too. And she lost the skull and she was very odd about Amos. Oh, Hank, do you think she did it then? Would she kill her own father? Oh dear, I wonder—" Emma broke off because it had just occurred to her to wonder if Eunice had overheard her conversation with Amos.

"There you go," Hank said resignedly, "drawing conclusions all over the walls. Ponder these thoughts, my little artist: Amos had planned to go to New York; Papa was supposed to be in Worcester. Saturday afternoon Shay put in a telephone call between every other drink, and when I said you and Jeff were at Amos' he insisted we go out there."

"Oh." Emma was aghast. "You mean that Mr. Chandler didn't go to Worcester at all and that he and Eunice planned to steal the muffineer"—Emma choked on the word and wished she hadn't said it but went on anyhow—"and put the blame on Shay?"

"That wasn't," said Hank, "what I meant at all."

"Oh." This time Emma was shocked. "Henry Fairbanks, you have a dirty mind. Eunice is a nice girl."

"Aren't women wonderful?" Hank addressed the fire buckets. "Eunice is too nice to have a date with Shay but perfectly capable of murdering her uncle and her father."

"That's entirely different. Of course"—Emma began to consider the practical aspects—"Miss Currier is deaf as a post and Eunice brought those fancy pajamas over to impress somebody. Mrs. Leavitt goes home early. I've got it! Amos found out about the affair and Shay killed him, and Mr. Chandler wouldn't think Shay was a very good match so Eunice killed him. How perfectly dreadful!"

"And now Eunice has the money and they'll live happily ever after if you keep still, because even Ellis wouldn't think of anything so completely fantastic."

"All right, know-it-all, who did do it?"

"Durrell. He wanted to write the insurance."

"How'd he get in? Both Jeff and Eddie say everything was locked up."

"He stole the key from Mrs. Leavitt."

"He's too nice. Try again."

"Miss Currier. I don't think she's bedridden at all. She killed Amos because he had the house full of drunks and lewd women—that includes you—and she killed Chandler because he was on to her. Mrs. Leavitt brought her the ice pick to stir her tea with."

"You're not being the least bit serious."

"Why should I? Try waving a retainer fee under my nose and see the difference."

"I haven't got any money and I don't need your assistance." Emma hoped devoutly that she was right.

"You're lucky. Just keep your nose out of things and you'll stay that way. Seriously, my dear, let Ellis handle this. If he makes a mistake he'll get set right without any of your help. I'd just as soon not have to get you out of jail again."

"You had nothing to do with that." Emma went indignantly to answer the phone, made a face as she heard the frosty "Mr. Fairbanks is there, I presume?" and beckoned to Hank.

"Good morning, sweetheart," Hank said airily. "All right. Miss Sweetheart to you. I'm just going out to lunch." Then, "What? She does? Well, bless her little heart. Oh, in a while."

He waltzed away from the telephone and then sank again on the couch, fanning himself with the paper. He paused and looked at the weather report.

"Continued warm," he read, "that's conservative journalism for you."

"Very interesting," said Emma. "And how are carloadings?"

"Mmm, let me see." Hank turned the pages briskly. "High tide at ten forty-seven," he offered.

"You goon. What did old pickle-puss have to say that set you off like this?"

Hank folded the paper firmly and began to read. "Famous sleuth hired by ex-ex-debutante. Mr. Henry Fairbanks, whose mental wizardry solved the baffling mysteries of the Case of the Coughing Gorilla, Old Uncle Asey on the Mud Flats and the Versailles Treaty, has been chosen by Miss Eunice Chandler, Hasty Pudding '99 and Pins and Needles '39, to reveal the dastardly slayer of her father, Mr. Lloyd Chandler, the old dastard."

"Hank," said Emma sternly, "you're making that up."

"Honest injun. And it's likely to cost me three hundred and fifty dollars."

"Cost you." Emma was indignant. "Make her pay you; she can afford it."

"Don't worry, my little flower; but, you see, I drew her in the pool, along with Shay, which was a waste of money."

"Why is she hiring you?"

"Because I'm good, stupe. Or maybe it's a guilty conscience."

"Hank, whose cigarette holder was that?"

"It was mine."

"Just so it wasn't Jeff's."

"Thanks."

Hank's tone was rather grim and Emma forgot to ask what Hank had been doing in the gazebo in her haste to correct the impression of partiality.

"Darling," she said, "you know I love you but I have to look after Jeff."

"Mrs. Hen." Hank smiled at her. "I wonder that Jeff grew to maturity without you."

Hank's words were light but he understood why Emma felt that Jeff might need looking after. Jeff had struck Amos because of the insinuation that he could control the dice; he would just as promptly strike if Amos had hinted that he was responsible for the absence of the muffineer. It was common talk on Charles Street that Jeff's hair-trigger disposition would get him into trouble sometime. Maybe this was the time. And if Jeff had gone into the room while Eddie was downstairs and Chandler had accused him of taking the muffineer—

Hank brought himself up short. Jeff's fireworks were not premeditated. Whoever had taken the ice pick had planned to use it at the first opportunity; that wasn't like Jeff. And Chandler had already accused Jeff and Jeff had sat still and taken it. That wasn't like Jeff either.

"I was," said Hank, "going to take you to lunch but I feel that I should have a conference with my client. Only it won't do to let her think I'm overanxious so I shall go see if the report on the crusher is ready and take the opportunity to thumb my nose at my late friend Donovan."

"You wouldn't be above asking for a little advice either."

"The picture," said Hank loftily, "will become perfectly plain as soon as I have ascertained the facts. Good-by and try not to tell all you know."

Under the circumstances, Emma thought, that was a pretty funny remark.

As soon as Hank was out of sight she took the bundle from Jeff's drawer—carefully, as though the crackle of the tissue paper still might give her away—and went down into the basement. There, amid the litter of crates and broken furniture, Emma sat down in the rickety wing chair where Jeff sometimes napped and with trembling fingers unwrapped the bundle.

The object she drew forth was about five inches high and was shaped somewhat like an aluminum kitchen saltcellar only it didn't look at all like one. Its baluster turning was graceful and sure, from the delicate tiny pineapple finial to the quadrooning of the flaring base. Its metal gleamed and was soft to the touch. Emma let her hands go over it gently; it was one of the loveliest things she had ever seen, except that it was the Coney muffineer. There on the side was the Coney hallmark: J. C. with a little star below it.

And what was the Coney muffineer that belonged in Amos Currier's cupboard doing in Jeff Graham's drawer? Emma told herself that it was perfectly all right; the bundle that Jeff had brought in on Saturday had contained the muffineer. Jeff had just come from Amos. Amos must have given him the bundle.

Perhaps the muffineer was broken and Amos had sent it in to be repaired. Emma turned the muffineer over in her hands and discovered a slight dent on one side.

But why hadn't Jeff spoken up when Mr. Chandler discovered that the muffineer was missing? Why hadn't he said that Amos had given it to him, instead of sitting there saying nothing? What would Eunice Chandler think if she knew he had it? What would Ellis and the chief of police? Even Hank would expect some explanation. And Jeff had gone off to Narragansett as though he hadn't a care in the world. That was it, of course; he had a reasonable excuse for his possession of the muffineer, but he might have told her what it was and not left her to worry her head off. Wishing that she had never opened the bottom drawer, Emma wrapped the muffineer up again and went upstairs.

Eddie Rawlins telephoned and asked cautiously if Jeff was there. Emma said that Jeff had gone out of town on business and that she was about to go out to lunch. Lunch with Eddie, Emma thought, would be just the peaceful soothing that she needed. But Eddie said that he was very busy and hung up quickly. She might have known, Emma thought ruefully, that Eddie would avoid them like the plague. In the best circles, as Eddie conceived them, murder was not done.

On the way to lunch Emma passed Miss Carey's shop and noticed that the Staffordshire figure of Paul and Virginia was still in the window. It was odd how two rare things always popped up at once. Once they had found two Bible boxes in a month and had had to hide the second for a year to keep from glutting the market. She had seen the Paul and Virginia in Miss Carey's window and then Durrell had talked of one. Probably there were two Coney muffineers and the one in Jeff's drawer had nothing to do with Amos'. Somewhat cheered by the thought, Emma told Charlie the Greek that everything was fine and that his ham hocks were delicious.

It was nearly four o'clock when Tiny Bloom came in. Tiny was a meek, shuffling little runner who was easily talked out of a reasonable price for the odds and ends that he picked up. Jeff, though he always shouted that he was being robbed, paid Tiny's asking price and was rewarded with an occasional treasure as well as a worshipful affection.

Tiny asked hesitatingly for Jeff.

Emma said sternly that Jeff was away and that she would take the message, though she didn't approve of betting and Tiny knew it.

Tiny backed away from her, blinking.

Emma smiled reassuringly, not wanting to frighten the message entirely out of Tiny's mind.

"Jeff said to tell me," she urged.

But Tiny shook his head, fumbled in his pocket and produced a folded slip of paper and handed it slowly over.

"Give him this," he said. "He's not in trouble, is he, over this murder?"

"Oh my, no," said Emma, not feeling it necessary to tell Tiny that the murder was plural, "we just happened to be out there."

Tiny blinked at her. "Tell him to be careful," he said. "It's a risky business."

Emma wasn't sure whether Tiny meant betting or murder but she wished he would go because she was itching with curiosity. It wasn't that she cared what horse Jeff was going to lose his money on, it was just that she couldn't see what was written on the slip and she didn't want to spoil Tiny's secret by unfolding it in front of him.

"Tell him"—Tiny shuffled toward the door— "if he wants me he knows where to get me."

Emma thanked him, wondering if touting was to become a regular business with Tiny, waited until he was well down the street and then went into the office to open the paper.

"Rockingham," it read, "1st."

Rockingham, in the first race. What she ought to do was tear it up. But she refolded the slip and put it under the snowstorm paperweight on Jeff's desk.

Chapter 10

ON TUESDAY MORNING Emma was not feeling any too chipper. She had spent a hot, restless night thinking about Jeff and the muffineer and berating herself for not caring more that Amos was dead. She had not heard from Hank or Jeff; she felt neglected and disturbed, and the sight of the dusty shop-windows sent her spirits even lower. There was a lot to be done and nobody seemed to be doing any of it, or, if they were, they weren't telling her about it. She was in the mood to do something herself but it seemed futile to rearrange a window when there were two murders waiting to be solved.

Hank hadn't been serious enough about the murders; she hadn't been very serious either. Emma sat down in Jeff's chair and gave herself a lecture on her lack of the finer feelings. Of course Hank didn't know that the muffineer was in Jeff's drawer—waiting to be repaired, of course—but right there to make things extremely uncomfortable for Jeff if anyone found it, because Jeff had certainly had the key to the silver cupboard, and Mr. Chandler had been very disagreeable about it.

Why did it have to be only the muffineer that was missing? A couple of chairs and a table gone, too, would reduce the importance of the little object in Jeff's lower drawer.

Emma sat up straight. How could they tell whether anything else was gone or not with Amos and Mr. Chandler dead and no inventory? Miss Currier couldn't remember things that she had not seen for nearly a lifetime; Mrs. Leavitt had no certain knowledge of the things in the house. Mr. Chandler might have but he was dead.

The telephone rang, and when Emma picked up the receiver it seemed to her that someone was already talking.

"—Miss Emma Marsh," a voice was saying, "if this is Miss Emma Marsh, will you please hang up? I will call back in a moment."

Emma hung up, completely mystified as to the identity of the voice and the meaning of the curious request. In a few moments the

116

call came again and Emma took it quickly. "Who is this?" she asked.

The voice paid no attention. "There is a warrant out for Mr. Graham's arrest. I thought you should know."

"What? Who is this?" Emma was screaming into the phone but all she got was a repetition of the previous statement. Then the line went dead.

Emma got up and locked the shop doors. The act was instinctive and, she realized, useless. Jeff wasn't there and if he were, locking the doors wouldn't prevent his arrest. Who was going to arrest him? Ellis, of course.

Hank had told Ellis that Mr. Chandler hadn't committed suicide. That, added to Jeff's story about the ice pick and his possession of the key to the silver cupboard, had been enough for Ellis. It was all a horrible mistake. Jeff didn't murder and Jeff didn't steal. There was some very good reason for his possession of the muffineer.

The muffineer! Without that what proof would Ellis have? She would see to it that he didn't find the muffineer. She'd get rid of it if she had to melt it up. What was a thousand dollars compared to Jeff's safety? Emma pulled open the bottom drawer of Jeff's desk and stared into it stupidly. There was a lot of dust in the back corners, there were two rubber bands and a paper clip and the patch box, but the tissue-paper-wrapped bundle was gone.

Ellis had broken into the shop, searched it and found the muffineer. That was why he was going to arrest Jeff.

Emma got up and examined the locks on the doors; they showed no signs of violence. Whoever had got in had done so with a key, and only she and Jeff had keys to the shop. Jeff had removed the muffineer because he realized that its presence was incriminating; perhaps Ellis had found it at Jeff's apartment or in his possession, perhaps Jeff was already in jail.

She considered calling Hank but Hank would tell her that if Jeff were innocent he would be set free.

But she wasn't sure that Jeff was arrested. Ellis couldn't arrest him if he wasn't there. That was it. She had to think up some way to keep Jeff from being there; but that was difficult and complicated by the fact that she hadn't the faintest notion where he was now.

Emma got up, unlocked the doors and went to the washroom. The cracked Stiegel flip mug that served as a drinking glass stood in the sink. Emma sniffed at it and wrinkled her nose; it had contained something besides water. Jeff had come back to the shop on his return from Narragansett, had mixed himself a drink and taken the muffineer. He had been alone because there was only one glass. What had he done then? It was just possible that he had gone home. Emma went back into the office, picked up the phone and put it down again. If she called Jeff up and told him there was a warrant out for his arrest, he would say "So what?" and come swaggering into the shop. She had to do better than that. Then she noticed that Tiny Bloom's folded slip of paper was gone and condoned, for once, Jeff's favorite failing. If Jeff were at the races, Ellis couldn't arrest him.

A woman came in "just to look around"; Emma told her to go ahead and tried to think. The woman wanted to visit; she asked how much everything was and then assured Emma that she had one at home just like it, only better. Emma had played that game before and found it dull.

"You must have quite a houseful of things," she said politely.

The woman assured her that she had. Dealers were always trying to buy something from her but they never did, no siree.

Emma smiled, not to be polite but because an idea had come to her. She edged the woman toward the door and, finally rid of her, rushed back to the telephone.

Jeff's voice when he answered was grumpy, and he was grumpier when he recognized Emma. He had been, he asserted, halfway down the hall and had to go back to answer the phone. He'd never get to the office that way.

Emma was so relieved to find Jeff safe and sound that she almost forgot what she was going to say. She shut her eyes to concentrate on making her voice natural. She wanted to know, she said, if Jeff was coming to the office after lunch because she sort of thought she'd go buy a dress. Jeff said she didn't need a dress and that he was going to be busy. Emma said, well, another time would do.

It was a shame they were both tied up, she went on, because she thought she had something terribly good spotted. Jeff said yeh? Emma said a woman had just been in. Jeff wanted to know what was so terribly good about that.

"She's got a Hepplewhite sideboard and six Hepplewhite chairs and a pair of girandole mirrors. She has a gate-leg table that she says is either mahogany or walnut, a banjo clock, a barrel-backed wing chair and what she calls a lot of maple things—"

"Judas priest," Jeff managed to get in, "where does she live?"

Emma laughed merrily. "Oh, I got her address all right, but it won't do us any good, for a while."

"I asked you where she lived?"

"North New Portland." Emma positively purred it into the telephone.

"Where, for cripes' sake, is that?"

"In Maine." Emma had been through North New Portland once on a vacation and remembered it as a long way off. "It's a crime you can't go right up. It's her sister's house; her sister just died here in the hospital and she's gone back on the train. I guess the sister sat on the steps with a shotgun to keep the dealers off, to hear her tell it."

Emma was having a hard time with her story because Jeff kept interrupting her.

"What's her name and how do you get there?"

"But, Jeff"—Emma was aghast—"you couldn't possibly go up. What would Ellis think?" What Jeff would think and say when, if ever, he got to North New Portland was not bothering Emma.

Jeff did not seem to be particularly concerned with what Ellis would think.

"Well"—Emma let the information be dragged from her—"her name is Hattie B. Woods and first you go to Lewiston. North New Portland's five miles, she says, from West New Portland. No, I'm not being funny; there's even a place she referred to as the South. No, it's north of Portland. Lewiston's somewhere near Augusta, isn't it?"

Jeff said that if the place was on a map he could find it.

From Emma's recollection of the combined general store-gas-station-and-blacksmith shop that was North New Portland, she thought it would have to be a pretty large map but she only asked what Jeff was going to use for money.

Jeff, it seemed, had a lot of money; what he wanted to know was what she had done with the purple overlay lamp.

Emma said proudly that she had sold it to Mr. Finegold and why hadn't Jeff entered it in the stock book?

Jeff said "Cripes" and hung up.

Emma realized that she had not asked him about the muffineer. Perhaps it was just as well, she thought; any distracting ideas and Jeff might not have gone so meekly off to Maine. Well, she had taken care of him; all that remained was to find out who had really done the murders before he got back.

Emma sat down at her desk, got out a sheet of paper and took pen in hand. The fact that three other people had been working on her problem for several days did not discourage her. She might have gone to Hank with her worry if there had not been in the back of her mind a faint idea that he might not approve of what she had done with Jeff. Of course, she reasoned, when Hank had told her to keep her nose out of things he could not have imagined that Ellis would do anything so silly as to try to arrest Jeff. That put an entirely different face on the matter. Still, it might be just as well to say nothing until she had her own case worked out.

Emma wrote down a list of all the people who had been at Amos' on the night of June thirtieth. Next she made a list of all the people she was sure hadn't killed Amos: Jeff, Hank and herself. Then she added the names of those that she didn't think had killed Amos: those of Shay and Eddie. That left her with Mrs. Leavitt, Miss Currier and Eunice. She asked herself which one she would pick if she had to choose one of them and without hesitation jabbed her pen point into Eunice's name.

Emma was no prude. She would have denied indignantly that Hank's interpretation of Eunice's letter to Shay made suspicion of Eunice easier. She told herself that she was considering only the truth and not being influenced one jot or little by the fact that Eunice had called her a shopgirl. Emma leaned over backward in her endeavor to be fair. She even omitted the warning that she would never marry Amos. She had enough against Eunice without that and she preferred not to remember the conversation by the back steps.

She would concede, however, that Eunice had been disturbed at the thought that Amos might marry. Furthermore, Eunice had disliked Amos; that was apparent from her manner toward him. She had gone downstairs on Saturday night and the charm from her bracelet had been found in Amos' hand. On Sunday Eunice had gone to the kitchen to get her father a glass of water and could have taken the ice pick. She had left Shay and gone to Amos' room. Shay had said that she went to get her boots and the boots had been found in the closet, but Amos' closet was a queer place to leave her boots.

Aside from the actual facts against her, Emma felt that Eunice had done a lot of queer things. She had pretended not to know Shay. The manner in which she received the news of Amos' death had been distinctly artificial. She had agreed to say nothing about having seen Emma downstairs in return for something from Shay. She had shown no especial grief at her father's death but had fainted when Ellis accused her of it. In addition to all that, she had put her boots in Amos' closet. Even if she had gone to Amos' room for a bootjack, Emma couldn't understand why she had left the boots there, unless she had wanted an excuse to go back.

But how could Eunice have been sure, on Saturday, that Mr.

Chandler would be in Amos' room on Sunday? Only if she knew the inventory was there and that her father would be looking for it.

Emma, who herself did things spasmodically and on impulse, assumed that everyone else proceeded rationally from cause to effect. Reasoning thusly, it seemed to her that Eunice had left her boots in Amos' room because she wanted to go back there on Sunday. She knew that her father would start looking for the inventory when he found that the muffineer was gone. How did she know the muffineer was gone? Because she had taken it herself and sold it to Jeff. That explained everything: Eunice's nervousness, the presence of the muffineer in Jeff's drawer and Jeff's meek acceptance of Chandler's denunciation. Jeff wouldn't have known, until Sunday morning, that Eunice had stolen the muffineer from Amos and he would be too chivalrous to give her away.

Emma scowled at the clock. Her reconstruction was all very fine. That was the way Jeff would act under those circumstances, but why would Eunice Chandler, who was rich, steal the muffineer and sell it? She might take it because she liked it or because she was a kleptomaniac but she wouldn't sell it, because she wouldn't need the money.

Thoroughly disgusted with the collapse of her edifice of ideas, Emma looked at the clock again and saw that it was past lunch time. She braved the Greeks across the street and had a large plate of boiled shrimp because she was very fond of them and because she could think better if her hands were busy.

She wondered what Hank was doing. She was a little surprised that he had not appeared with his customary demand that she repeat over and over the incidents leading up to the crime. He claimed that she never told a story twice alike but that by superimposing all her versions he got a fairly complete picture. He was, of course, wrong; she was always very accurate but there was no reason why she shouldn't employ that method for her own information.

She went back to the moment when Jeff had walked into the shop with the paper-wrapped bundle

By the time she had finished the shrimp she was down to the discovery of Chandler's body, and the only new ideas that her mind had dredged up were Mrs. Leavitt's implication that Miss Currier was busy because it was the thirtieth of June; Durrell's concern about the Staffordshire figure of Paul and Virginia, and the fact that on Sunday morning she herself had seen Eunice twice outside Amos' door.

Because Miss Carey's shop was on the shady side of the street Emma walked past it. Miss Carey was addicted to batik scarves and amber beads—Jeff called her The Rattler because of the noise she made as she moved—but she was an outspoken soul and honest. Emma noticed that the Staffordshire figure was no longer in the window and had a sudden curiosity to know what had become of it.

"I saw that you'd sold something," Emma said as Miss Carey rattled to greet her, "and I came in to congratulate you."

Miss Carey denied that she had sold anything in six months.

Emma asked what about the Paul and Virginia. Miss Carey sniffed. Selling something back for what you paid for it wasn't her idea of a sale. Emma looked interested.

Miss Carey went on to explain that she had bought the figure in the winter and had sold it that very morning back to the person from whom she had purchased it. Had Emma, she wanted to know, ever bought anything from a tall redheaded girl? Emma hadn't but she felt as though her nose was twitching with excitement.

"Well, don't," Miss Carey advised. "She acted as though she was doing me a favor when she sold it and she was just as uppity when she came in this morning. She didn't look like the sort of a person who would be selling antiques anyway. I couldn't make her out at all."

"Red hair," asked Emma, "and tall and a very white skin and a bad disposition?"

Miss Carey nodded.

"Thanks," said Emma. "I'll watch out for her."

She left hastily before Miss Carey had time to realize that Emma had given a very accurate description of a person she had supposedly never seen.

Emma sailed across the street as happy as though she had been reassured of the existence of Santa Claus. It didn't make any difference whether Eunice Chandler were wealthy or not; she had stolen Paul and Virginia and sold them to Miss Carey and then bought them back. It wasn't sensible, but there it was; so there was now no reason why Eunice hadn't stolen the muffineer and sold it to Jeff. Eunice had been hanging around Amos' room trying to get at the inventory herself but Emma's presence had prevented that.

Emma magnanimously decided to call Hank so that he could give Eunice back her fee and would not suffer the ignominy of having Ellis arrest his client. She would give him the pleasure of telling Ellis to tear up the warrant. She would wire Jeff to come home.

She was advised that Mr. Fairbanks was out. Unwilling to demean herself to Hank's secretary by further inquiry, she called Shay and was told that Mr. Horrigan was no longer in the employ of the *American*.

From the tone used by her informant, Emma gathered that Shay had committed a heinous offense. Probably the paper thought he was guilty of the murders; she could fix that up for him.

She called Old Cape and asked for Mr. Rawlins. Eddie was in a hurry. He was going to Mr. Chandler's funeral and expressed surprise that Emma was not going also. Emma said she didn't like funerals, that she had to go to Amos', and that she felt one was enough.

Actually she had forgotten all about the funeral, but it explained what Hank was doing. He would certainly feel that he had to go to his client's father's funeral. It really was going to be an awful joke on Hank to win the pool with his own client. Emma told Eddie to tell Hank to come right to the shop after the funeral. Eddie could come too, she added graciously; she had something important to tell them.

It was just as well, she thought, that she had not reached Hank before the funeral. It would be terribly embarrassing for Eunice to be arrested at her own father's funeral. Probably Ellis would go to the funeral and come around afterward for Jeff. He was due for a jolt and she would enjoy giving it to him. She smiled with self-satisfied anticipation.

She wondered, though, who had warned her about Jeff. The repetitious way of talking had obviously been to disguise the voice, which had been deep enough to have been a man's but could have been a woman's. It hadn't been Hank, Emma was sure of that; it might have been Durrell. Hank had suggested that Durrell might withhold information from Ellis, and Durrell, sure that Ellis was on the wrong track, might have wished to keep him from making the arrest. Durrell was a nice old bozo.

Emma wrote her initials in the dust on Jeff's desk, put on her smock and began to rearrange a window.

Chapter 11

SHAY came in so quietly that Emma did not hear him. Not until the customer who was picking out transparent slides for a lamp shade gave a half-smothered exclamation did Emma turn and see Shay standing behind her. Shay was hatless and more disheveled than ever. The front of his coat was wet, and his necktie was jerked away from his collar in a hard knot, and there was an unmistakable reek about him. Emma had supposed that Shay would be at the funeral, what with his feeling for Eunice and all, but she realized that if Shay had done any crossing of the bar it had not been in church. She was annoyed with him for coming to the shop in the condition which he was obviously in. Then she remembered that Shay had lost his job and felt sorry for him.

"Just a minute," she said as though he were a repair man, "and I'll see if we have something for you." She turned to the customer and said apologetically, "One of our best workmen, but, you see—"

The woman tsk-tsked appropriately.

Shay swayed his way down the aisle, turned and announced dramatically, "'But she is in her grave, and, oh, the difference to me!'"

"Educated too," said the woman. "What a pity."

"Oh, very," said Emma, wondering how Shay had guessed about Eunice and feeling sorry for him on that count too. She had quite a serious chat with the customer on the Evils of Drink, sold enough slides for two lamp shades and was very grateful to Shay for turning up as a Bad Example.

"'Then my heart,'" Shay was announcing as Emma bowed the customer out with the enthusiasm attendant on a good sale, "'it grew ashen and sober—'"

"Shay," said Emma, "I'm awfully sorry. Did you guess?"

"'Revile me not—'" Shay hung his head. "'The Tempter hath a snare for all.' '—it was charged against me that I sought to destroy institutions.' Say, my little beetle, can I borrow your car?"

"Oh, Shay." Emma cherished her roadster like a spinster's canary. "Do you think you should? I mean, do you think you're in any condition to drive?"

" 'Over the hills and far away, to Grandfather's house we go.' I will be the epitome of caution. That means I will be cautious."

"No, Shay," said Emma. "Let me go across the street and get you some coffee. I know it's a shock but it had to be someone."

"That's gratitude for you." Shay's voice grew sullen. " 'The dear love of comrades.' Bah!"

Shay was presuming, Emma thought, or else he was just saying words. She would try to stall him off until Hank got there.

"Sit down," she said, "and try not to think about it."

But Shay came closer to Emma.

" 'The hound was cuffed, the hound was kicked.' "

" ' "U-lu-lo," howled the hound.' "

Shay's howl was so realistic that it sent a sharp chill up Emma's spine. Shay came closer.

" 'He lept, he seized the throat, he tore—' "

Shay's hands were coming up from his sides; his eyes blazed.

Emma fell back. Her throat was constricted, as though Shay's fingers were already upon it. "You can have the car," she managed to say. "You can have the keys."

She fled to the office, snatched her purse and handed over the keys with trembling fingers.

" 'Good hound.' " Shay's eyes were glazed but he laughed. "Scared you, didn't I?"

"Don't be ridiculous. I was going to let you take it anyhow."

"You're a spunky little beetle. Thank you very much. Say"— Shay paused with his hand on the door—"how about coming with me and getting all unglued?"

"Thank you. Some other time."

The arrival of a customer saved Emma further argument. She watched Shay drive away with a silent prayer for the roadster and the hope that Shay might break his neck. He certainly, she thought, was in a dreadful state. It was small wonder that Hank referred to him as "my drinking friend." Shay did peculiar things when he was drunk. Shay had been very drunk at Amos'. If it hadn't been for Paul and Virginia, Emma might have transferred her suspicions to Shay.

Emma was concocting a wedding present for a customer when Eddie got to the shop. He sat down quietly in Jeff's chair and listened appreciatively to Emma's sales technique.

With a large English pewter platter, an unmarked porringer and two mended beakers Emma had assembled the perfect smoking set for an Early American house.

"Most people," she told the customer firmly, "like two beakers: one for matches and one for cigarettes; fortunately I have two beakers that are almost exactly alike."

The coincidence was too much for the customer. She took the lot at Emma's figure, which was not quite double what the pieces would have brought separately, gave the address for delivery and sighed the sigh of one rid of a harassing problem.

"Where'll we go?" Emma waved the bills under Eddie's nose. "My, this has been a day."

"You seem very cheerful." Eddie had the slightly reproving tone of one who had been preoccupied with things of another world.

"Cash money," said Emma, "practically makes me break out laughing, and I've made two good sales even if Shay did scare the life out of me and I've found out something. Where's Hank?" Emma would save her big news for him.

Eddie said that Hank had been intercepted by a dowager who had been a friend of his mother's and inquired for Jeff.

Emma said that Jeff was on the trail of some furniture and felt that she was telling the truth. Eddie didn't need to know that the trail would lead nowhere.

Eddie frowned. "Wouldn't it be advisable for him to be here? There might be questions."

"Not questions," said Emma, "exclamations of surprise and delight when I unfold what I shall unfold."

"What have you found?" Eddie sounded interested.

"Oh, something. I'll tell you when Hank gets here. Who do you think did it—them—I mean the murders—Mrs. Leavitt, Miss Currier or Eunice?"

"Miss Currier," said Eddie promptly. "Patricide is unnatural; Mrs. Leavitt had a key and that makes her too obvious. Miss Currier is supposed to be an invalid but it is going to be shown more and more that she isn't."

"You sound as though you were analyzing a detective story."

"I read quite a lot of them," Eddie admitted.

"I used to," Emma said darkly, "before I got to going round with one. You don't think Eunice had anything to do with it?"

Eddie shook his head. "During the brief time that Mr. Chandler talked to her Miss Currier impressed me as being rather strange. She asked Mr. Chandler if he expected her to go to an old ladies' home; Mr. Chandler, of course, ignored the remark, but I imagine that Amos must have discussed such an idea with him and that Miss Currier killed them both because she did not wish to go. I shall warn Eunice that her aunt is probably senile and possibly insane. That reminds me, there's something I wanted to ask you. What is the formal period of mourning?"

"Eh?" said Emma.

"How soon would it be all right for me to call and offer my condolences?"

"Oh, for heaven's sake," said Emma, "skip the condolences. If she likes you she'd probably be darn glad if you called her up and took her to a movie. Here's Hank."

Hank came in, took off his coat, his necktie and unbuttoned his shirt before he spoke. Then, "Lovely funeral," he said. "Dignified."

"What did the ushers wear?" Emma wanted to know.

"Point d'esprit. Bouffant. With just a soupcon of garlic."

Hank was hot and tired. Eunice Chandler had been irritating in her insistence that she had hired him to discover the murderer of her father and not to concern himself about the death of Amos Currier. The natives of Westham had all swallowed their tongues when he tried to talk to them; Ellis had been angry because he had taken the crusher, and if it had not been for Durrell, he would not have succeeded in dissuading Ellis from his avowed intention of arresting Jeff.

Funerals were depressing, at best. Hank wished he hadn't gone. The notion that he might spot the murderer at the funeral was absurd. The directors, trustees and bondholders who had attended Chandler's funeral were much too respectable to have committed a murder. That was silly, Hank told himself, a murderer might look just as respectable as the next one. He was so tired that he felt silly.

"Pay attention," said Emma, "because I have something important to tell you."

"I'd rather go swimming," said Hank.

"That's a good idea— Please don't distract me. Eunice did the murders."

"You wouldn't tell me."

"Oh, I say." Eddie was shocked.

"Will you listen to me ?" Emma launched into the tale of Durrell's preoccupation with the missing Staffordshire figure, her location of a similar figure at Miss Carey's and her discovery that Miss Carey had not only bought the figure from Eunice but had sold it back to her.

Hank conceded that Emma might have something.

"So, Mr. Smarty-Pants," Emma wound up, "if she stole the figure she probably stole the muffineer and sold it to—somebody."

Emma had caught herself just in time. She had said nothing about her discovery of the muffineer in Jeff's drawer because, of course, it wasn't there now, and there was no sense in dragging it into the story when the Staffordshire figure was proof of Eunice's guilt.

"I bet," Emma went on quickly, "that Eunice puts Paul and Virginia back in a cupboard or up in the attic and pretends it was always there."

"If I were she," said Hank, "I'd put it at the bottom of the Basin in small pieces and deny that I was ever in Miss Carey's shop."

"Couldn't this Miss Carey identify her?" Eddie wanted to know.

"She described her perfectly." Emma felt that Hank was not giving her discovery its deserved importance. "There couldn't be two people like Eunice Chandler and her little skull was in Amos' hand and she left her boots in Amos' room, and I thought I had it all fixed so they wouldn't arrest Jeff."

Hank had to laugh. Emma's motive for accusing Eunice of the murder was as transparent as her disappointment at his failure to agree that Eunice was guilty. That Eunice had taken the figure he did not doubt; but he did not want to discourage Emma by pointing out that should Eunice choose to deny the whole matter it would be difficult to prove that she had taken something that might have existed only in Durrell's imagination. Miss Carey could claim that she had purchased a Staffordshire figure, but there was no proof that it was the same one that Durrell thought he remembered. Hank supposed that the incident of the figure meant something, but what, exactly, he was too tired to figure out.

"What made you think Jeff was going to be arrested?" he asked.

Emma told them of her peculiar phone call.

"How very extraordinary," said Eddie.

"Did you trace the call?" Hank wanted to know.

"Why, no. I never thought of that until it was too late. I just assumed, somehow, that it came from Westham. I thought it was Durrell."

"It probably was. He's the only one I know of, besides me, who knew what Ellis was up to."

"Oh, then it's true." Emma wrung her hands. "When is he coming? What will we do? Will you tell him about Eunice? We have to do something. Don't just sit there."

Hank did not move. "Take it easy. I talked him out of it, temporarily."

"You did? Darling, I could kiss you. How did you do it?"

"Mostly on Durrell's evidence that Mr. Chandler didn't go to
Worcester but was seen heading for Amos' about eight-thirty Saturday night."

"You don't mean it?" Emma's jaw dropped. "Oh, that means that
they were in it together, Eunice and Mr. Chandler, and they were
going to kill Amos, and Eunice was going to get the house and give it
to her father for the Preservation Society, only I bet he would have
taken all the credit."

"Then who, might I ask, killed Mr. Chandler?"

"Miss Currier," said Emma promptly. "She found out what they
were planning to do. That makes it better than having Eunice kill her
father."

"Could be. Your guess is as good as mine, right now." Hank had
another interpretation of Chandler's presence in Westham.

"Seen anything of Shay today?" he inquired.

"I should say I have. He came in here in a perfectly dreadful state."

"Rhode Island, Vermont or collapse?"

"Drunk, if you must know."

"Blind staggering or running stumbling?"

"He was quoting poetry and he scared me half to death and took
my car and he thinks Eunice did it, and I know he's fond of her but
that's no excuse for acting the way he did."

"Shay thinks Eunice did it?" Hank was puzzled. "Last I knew he
was going to marry her on the three hundred and fifty he was going
to get because Mrs. Leavitt did it and he was off to prove it. Did you
tell him about Eunice?"

"Why—no. But he was going on about somebody's being in their
grave and his heart was broken and not to blame him because he had
been tempted, and then he howled like a dog."

"Ah, yes. *The Song for the Jacquerie*. He does that very well. He must
have been in wonderful shape." Hank sounded rather envious. "But I
don't think he was mourning Eunice; he has other things to howl
about."

"Oh, you mean about his job?"

If only, Hank thought, Emma wouldn't tell everything she knew.
It concerned her and it was bad publicity. He caught Emma's eye and
said firmly that it was only a little trouble concerning some pictures.

"About Mrs. Leavitt," Eddie began, "she said she hoped we

wouldn't see her when she went down the hall, but I did and she was carrying something."

"Crumbs," said Hank, "for the birds."

"No, this was a tray covered up with a cloth."

"The remains of Miss Currier's lunch. Mrs. L. is a great one for carrying things." Hank wished they wouldn't talk about the murders. There wasn't any use in trying to think when your brain felt like a dry sponge. He wished Eddie would go away so that he and Emma could go swimming and get cool and eat a nice comfortable dinner. Emma wasn't half bad in a bathing suit. She swam without a cap, throwing her short hair out of her eyes like a boy, and Hank liked to watch her.

"Eddie," said Emma, "what made you think Mr. Chandler had found the inventory? I mean, did you know what it looked like?"

Almost in spite of himself, Hank listened for Eddie's answer. Miss Currier had said that she had not described the inventory to Mr. Chandler, and, if Hank remembered correctly, Eddie had not been in the dining room when Chandler spoke of the pages sewn together at the top.

"No," said Eddie. "I suppose I thought I knew what an inventory would look like, and he was so upset that I didn't want to bother him with questions. He wouldn't let me touch a thing in the desk and as he was going through a bundle of papers he said 'Aha,' as though he'd found it, and told me to go get a pencil and paper."

"He must have eaten it." Eddie had made the right answer and Hank lost interest. "Durrell swears it's not in that room."

"Of course not, dummy." Emma was determined that Hank should solve the case, if she had to do it for him herself. "Miss Currier was watching and came in and took the inventory."

"No," said Hank, "Eddie took it so that you and Jeff would have to make another one." Perhaps, he thought, if he insulted Eddie, Eddie would go away. "Eddie killed him," he went on, "because Chandler wanted to save money by using the old inventory."

"Hush," said Emma, "you mustn't say things like that in front of people."

"No," said Eddie gamely, "I killed him because he was going to let Durrell write the insurance."

"Now that that's settled," said Hank, "let's go swimming." He hoped that Eddie couldn't swim. He was partially right.

"It gives me the hives," said Eddie.

"You don't say? What do you do about washing?"

"I can swim in a pool. It's only salt water that bothers. It's kelp or polyps, or maybe the fish bite me."

Emma laughed. "We'll find a pool then. Some one of Hank's rich friends must have a pool."

"Uh-uh. They all have themselves dry-cleaned. How about some of your wealthy customers?"

"All of our customers," said Emma, "have pools but they don't recognize me socially."

"Because you're in trade or because of your gaudy past?"

"Because I go around with you."

"What's wrong with me? I'm a good guy. I don't ask much; all I want is a drink and a little natation."

"From the Latin, as Shay would say."

"Yeh. I'm a Rhodes scholar, once removed."

"The term is 'sent down.' "

Eddie wished that he could talk that way. He envied their pat-ter—although he sometimes wondered if they knew what they were talking about—because it seemed to him a chummy, friendly sort of thing. Without it one was left out; and it wasn't a matter of birth or background that gave one the ability. Shay Horrigan talked that way. Shay Horrigan had a brother who had been a bootlegger and Shay was their friend. Maybe it was just another mannerism that one ac-quired by practice.

"There is always," he said, "the pond in the Garden."

"That's out," said Hank. "My grandmother—sweet old lady she was, too, when we could keep her off the gin—told me you weren't a true Bostonian until you'd been in the pond and I refuse to be insu-lar."

"Was that your grandmother Fairbanks?" Emma wanted to know.

"No, no," Hank corrected her. "*She* took dope. I mean Grand-mother Shaunnessey of the Maverick Square Shaunnesseys."

"I thought that was Shay's grandmother."

"We're related. All the fine old families are inbred."

"Are you really? " Eddie asked. "Anyhow, Boston isn't an island, it's a peninsula."

Hank and Emma looked at each other and laughed. Laughed because they were pleased with themselves, because the pun was bad and because Eddie's factual naivete was sometimes amusing.

"Let's not drown him," said Hank. "Let's keep him. I like the black spot on his tail."

"I shall call him Spot," said Emma, "and teach him to jump over a stick."

"Come on, Spot." Hank stood up and buttoned his shirt. "Let's get out of this sweatbox and go where we can be intellectual."

They took Hank's sapphire-blue Rolls because Eddie's coupe was safe in a downtown garage. Emma drove at Hank's direction and soon they were walking down a flight of steps to a large low room, lit from converted gas chandeliers, where red plush benches and small tables still lined the walls.

Eddie eyed the place suspiciously.

"Hank," Emma explained, "is a fugitive from chromium furniture."

"I let 'em put in air conditioning," said Hank, "but that's as far as I go."

"Yes-sir." A waiter took them to a table. "What'll-it-be-sir?"

"Two planter's punches and an orangeade for the little girl."

"Isn't that pretty strong?" Eddie asked, not meaning the orangeade.

Hank chose to be obtuse. "They'll kill her," he said, "but she will drink them." Perhaps he could pass Eddie out and get rid of him that way. Still and all, Eddie wasn't such a bad sort; just a little overanxious to do the right thing. He wished Shay were there; Shay, who had none of the milk of human kindness, would have been rid of Eddie in ten minutes. Without Shay he would have to think of something tactful.

"Well," he said as the drinks came, "here's to crime."

The word was unfortunate; it set Emma off again on her theoretical sleuthing.

"The more I think about it," she began, "the surer I am that Eunice killed Amos and Miss Currier killed Mr. Chandler."

"Why did Eunice kill him? I forget."

"Because she stole the Paul and Virginia, the way I told you."

"Pardon me. I thought it was because she wanted the house to give to the Salvation Army."

"Well, a little of both. I had it straight once but you get me all mixed up."

"Look here, my little Dick Tracy, how much was that ceramic novel worth?"

"Thirty-five or forty dollars. They must be fairly rare, I never saw one before."

"Well, rare or not, even if Eunice's father kept her short of petty cash and she did sell the thing, she wouldn't kill Amos over forty dollars. She's not a bad kid. Dumb and opinionated, but I never saw a woman who wasn't."

"Oh, is that so? I might have known she'd get you on her side. You're positively imbecilic where women are concerned. Who did do it then?"

"I told you, Eddie, I mean Spot, with the crusher. I gave Ellis the report and he's going to arrest him instead of Jeff."

"What did the report say?" Emma asked. "I mean, was Amos really killed with the crusher?"

Hank nodded. "The hair from his head, as Shay would say, and blood in the water. Only Eddie wiped off his fingerprints."

"Oh, I say"—Eddie flushed—"a joke's a joke. Let's have another drink. This one'll be on me. The same," he said to the waiter.

"No," said Emma, "I'm grown up now; I think I'll have something else. What'll it be?" She appealed to Eddie because it was beginning to dawn on her that Hank was half irritated by his presence.

"Champagne?" Eddie suggested.

"Why, bless its little heart," said Emma, "I think that would be elegant, with lots of gold foil and a large bucket."

Hank snorted. "You're just wasting money. She couldn't tell champagne from Rhine wine and seltzer."

"Some champagne," said Eddie firmly.

"Yes-sir," said the waiter, "any-particular-kind-sir?"

"Larson," said Eddie, "'34."

"That's a good wine," Hank conceded. He had wondered if Eddie knew one brand from another.

"Tell me"—Emma ignored Hank—"were all the windows and doors really locked?"

Eddie nodded. "I went around with Jeff myself and looked at all of them. That is," he corrected himself, "all except the windows in that place you call the buttery. I hated to stay in there. I wished," he went on, "that we could have found something open because that would have meant that it wasn't someone in the house."

Emma nodded too. "I know. Of course, Mrs. Leavitt had a key."

"Oh, for heaven's sake," Hank cut in. "I'm trying to have a good time. If you have to do something, find the muffineer, find the inventory, find me any honest-to-God motive for killing both Amos and Chandler. Here's your fizz water. I'm going to get a paper so I won't have to listen to you."

"He doesn't sound as though things were going very well." Eddie had waited until Hank was out of earshot. "Or does he know something that he's keeping to himself?"

"Don't you worry," said Emma loyally, "he'll find out who did it—

them. He just mopes around and you think he's not doing anything, and then, bang, he has the picture all in one piece."

"Of course"—Eddie watched admiringly as the waiter poured the champagne—"as he says, the apparent absence of motive makes it difficult."

"There's the house," said Emma, "and about a quarter of a million dollars' worth of furniture. That isn't lettuce."

"No. But Eunice will be wealthy in her own right."

"Them as has wants."

"By the way. Whose cigarette holder was that?"

"Hank's, I guess; he keeps saying so."

"Really? He must have been out there before I came. I don't remember his leaving the house."

Hank was coming toward them reading the paper, guided by remote control, it seemed, between the tables.

"Hank," asked Emma, "what were you doing out in the gazebo?"

"Gazing tenderly at your window, my sweet. I wished I'd stayed longer."

"How very touching." Emma didn't believe him for a minute but she wouldn't press the point in front of Eddie.

"Who wants the funnies?" Hank divided the paper. "The funeral made the front page, but if you want to read about that you'll have to buy a paper of your own. Hey, who drank my drink? Waiter, two planter's punches."

Eddie, who had thought to taper off on champagne, assumed a do-or-die expression as the drinks were set before them. Emma stirred the bubbles out of her champagne with her finger. "Somebody told me it took out the headache," she said.

"And you believed it."

"It sounds reasonable," said Eddie. "The bubbles are carbon dioxide—"

"I wanna go swimming!" The loudness of Hank's tone caused the people at the adjoining table to exchange significant glances. Emma, also, was surprised. Hank was not given to creating disturbances in public places, except, Emma claimed, when Shay led him on. She had also seen him down more than three planter's punches and maintain his decorum. It was the heat, she decided, and the fact that he was very tired.

"We're gonna take Eddie swimming." Hank pinched Emma under the table and Emma glared; such an action was very unlike him.

"Think of somebody with a pool," Hank went on, "a large pool, preferably tiled, because I scraped my shins once on one of those stone ones. I like urns on the corners too; give a flossy effect. Spot likes urns. Don't you, Spot?"

"Why do you have to make it so difficult?" Emma asked. "I suppose you want a diving tower too?"

"Sure; so Spot can do a swan dive."

"You don't need a very high board for that."

"Yeah, Spot can do a swan dive from the edge of the bathtub. Good old Spot."

Good old Spot was looking rather flushed from the drinks and rather pleased with all the attention he was getting. Emma picked up the paper, feeling at a loss for convivial conversation.

"Put that paper down," Hank commanded, "and put your mind on this thing. Who's got a swimming pool?"

"The Drapers," said Emma. "You know them and it would be all right to go out there."

"A fishpond," said Hank. "A measly fishpond. She wants us to swim in a little old fishpond."

Emma folded the paper for surreptitious reading and found herself in the society section. She also finished her glass of champagne because she didn't want to be left too far behind. The Leeds, she read, had gone to Lennox. That explained why Mrs. Leeds hadn't come in to see about the lamps they were wiring. Emma wondered if it was cool in Lennox.

"We want a big pool," Eddie was saying, "a great big pool."

"And we don't care who owns it, we'll swim in it anyhow."

"Oh, really"—Eddie had a grain of caution left—"we couldn't do that."

"All right, quitter." Hank started to get up from the table.

But Eddie didn't want to be a quitter, he appealed to Emma.

"Sure," said Emma. "I know just the thing." The Leeds were in Lennox, she reasoned, but it would serve Hank right if a caretaker caught them. "Big as the Atlantic," she continued, "but it's got statues instead of urns."

"Spot doesn't like statues. Do you, Spot?"

"Sure I do."

"It's got green tile and is landscaped to beat all get out."

"I want urns."

"Sheep," Emma offered. "These people keep sheep on the front lawn and once, for a wedding, they tied blue bows on them."

"Suppose it had turned out to be a girl?"

"Don't be vulgar," said Emma primly.

"Bathing suits," said Eddie. "We can't swim without bathing suits."

"Sissy. Go on home and go to bed then. I'll buy Emma a suit in a drugstore."

"Drugstores," said Emma tartly, "were invented for people like you. You never buy anything until you want it and then you throw it away. That's planned economy."

"Darling," said Hank, "it isn't as though I were offering you a mink coat. Please, please let me buy you a bathing suit."

"Idiot," said Emma but she laughed. Maybe it would be fun.

"Yoicks and forward the Buffs." Hank got to his feet and started toward the door.

The waiter came running.

"All this good champagne," Emma mourned. "It seems a pity to leave it."

"Take it along."

"It'll get hot."

"Take the bucket."

"Yes-sir: there-will-be-a-slight-deposit-sir."

Eddie, who had been ready with the exact price of the wine, slowly handed over two more bills and received the chilly bucket in reluctant arms.

"I wonder if I ought to be doing this?" He spoke aloud, but Hank and Emma were already going up the steps, and Eddie followed them because he knew that more than anything else he wanted to be with them, wanted to do the sort of things they did. He lurched into a table and found himself apologizing a little thickly. He didn't care; just for once he was going to have a good time and not worry about what the company would think.

He protested only mildly when Hank put him in the rumble seat with the bucket and no more than it seemed reasonable when Hank insisted that he go into the drugstore to pick out the bathing suit.

Hank bought a large green rubber frog, a pair of water wings for Eddie and a crepe-paper bathing suit for Emma. The Japanese, he told the clerk, were a wonderful little people.

The bathing suit, the clerk assured him, was made in Framingham, and Hank tried to get Eddie to stay with the clerk on the grounds that they had a lot in common.

The frog and the water wings necessitated a stop at a filling station. Emma put the inflated objects in the seat with Eddie and said that all he needed was a derby hat.

Eddie said that he had a derby but that it was home.

Hank and Emma leaned against the car and laughed until they cried.

Eddie wanted to know what was so funny about his having a derby hat and that kept them laughing until they got to Coolidge Corner, where Hank spied a bar.

He offered Eddie the choice of taking another drink or going home on the subway, and Eddie manfully added a scotch and soda to the rum and champagne.

"Just so she knows where she's going." Eddie blinked at Emma in an attempt to make the two faces that he saw come into focus.

"Do you know where you're going, my dear?" Hank half suspected that Emma would stop at a restaurant and demand to be fed. Hank was becoming a little hungry himself and beginning to despair of ridding the party of Eddie, whose capacity, apparently, was only surpassed by his tenacity.

"Certainly I know where I'm going"—Emma was thoroughly enjoying herself by now—"but I'm not going to tell. Sh-sh—the Fifth Column."

"All right, men, what are we waiting for? We may be outnumbered but old soldiers never die. Remember the Maine, remember the Marne, remember Munich."

They left the bar, retrieved their souvenirs, which Hank had carefully checked, and climbed back into the roadster. Eddie clasped the frog lovingly in his arms and for a while Hank sang a long rambling song with great stretches of tum-tums in it. From the context Emma decided that the tum-tums represented expurgation rather than forgetfulness but that it was just as well not to shock Eddie too much.

It was quite dark now; the way wound in generous curves between hedges, brick walls and the darkness of tree-shaded lawns. Emma chose the blackest spot between two streetlights and suggested that they leave the car and walk around the block. Hank dissuaded her on the grounds that a mechanized retreat was faster than his best gallop, so they drove along to the high hedge that screened Emma's objective.

"This," said Hank as they stopped, "is beyond my wildest dreams."

"You asked for it," Emma reminded him. "You're not going to back out now."

"Not in a thousand years."

They helped Eddie from the back of the car. He had long since ceased to protest and followed blindly, happily.

"Shall we deploy or invade in a swarm? And don't the military have lovely terms?" Hank wanted to know.

"We better stick together." Emma touched the hedge gingerly and was relieved to find that it was not barberry. They explored the hedge, looking for a vulnerable point, and were rewarded with the steps of a stile.

"Very pastoral," said Hank, poised on top with the champagne bucket. "But that reminds me of the sheep. Suppose they start baaing or booing or whatever it is they do, or suppose they are herded by a faithful canine with a fine set of teeth in his head?"

"The hazards of war, my friend," said Emma, "but get going because we'd look funnier to a cop than we would to a herd of sheep."

"Sheep come in flocks. Please be accurate."

The darkness was even more complete inside the hedge; it seemed cooler, the turf was thick and moist from frequent watering, and Emma took off her shoes for the pleasure of the resilient softness. She led the way and the others followed her. Away to their right a street lamp picked up a reflection of light from a gingerbread-trimmed cupola, but of the house itself showed only the silhouette of a square, boxy roof line. Emma said "Watch it" and stepped onto a flagstone terrace covered by a long trellis. Two ghostly white figures marked the corners of the pool.

"There are fancy dressing rooms down below," Emma informed them, "but if you'll just go to the edge of the flagstones you'll find some nice bushes. I'm going over here."

She got into the bathing suit gingerly and by the time she was back, her eyes by now more accustomed to the gloom, she could see Hank's trunk-clad figure poised on the end of the diving board. Emma giggled.

Hank's arms fell to his sides. "Don't do that," he said. "I'll have you know that I'm considered a perfect Adonis."

"Oh, are you?" Emma was unimpressed. "Well, it's really too dark to tell. I was thinking wouldn't it be funny if they had drained the pool."

Hank came back down the board. "I know who killed Amos," he said. "You killed him, just for a laugh."

"No," said Emma, "not Amos. Mr. Chandler, maybe, but not Amos."

"You kind of liked him, didn't you?" Hank was referring to Amos.

"Kind of," said Emma. "Listen, there's something I want to tell you and a lot I want to talk to you about."

"You and me both, sister, when we get a moment's privacy."

"Oh, dear," said Emma, "have I done something?"

The water rippled smoothly below them and a hand was thrust over the splash rim.

"What are you waiting for?" Eddie, revived by the water, was having a very good time.

"The evening mail," said Hank. "A streetcar—"

"Rain," said Emma.

"No, stupid, you pray for rain."

"Ouch!" Emma stubbed her toe on the champagne bucket, sat down to investigate the damage and began to laugh.

"Sh-sh. You'll wake the sheep."

"I just thought"—Emma suppressed her giggles—"we made Eddie cart this stuff all the way out here and didn't bring a glass. I should feel so elegant," she went on regretfully, "sitting here sipping champagne, pretending it was the cocktail hour and that we had been invited."

"Empty it into the pool and swim in it. That ought to please your elegant soul."

"You do think of the nicest things."

Emma, watching the champagne fizzle from the bottle, did not see the beam of light that, traveling slowly behind her, was aimed at the windows of the house.

"There," she said. "Shay would love to take a picture of this."

She sent the bottle hurtling into the shrubbery and was surprised at the sudden crash of glass against concealed masonry. The beam of light shifted and darted quickly over the pool, too high up to reveal them.

"That cuts it," said Hank. "Get your clothes and beat it."

"What?" asked Emma.

"A patrol car." Hank was already away in the darkness. "Run for it."

Emma did not need to be told three times. She grabbed bag, dress and hat and sprinted for what she fervently hoped was the stile in the hedge. The beam of light was still now; she heard the quiet opening of a car door and, away to her left, an audible exclamation as Hank went headlong over the wire boundary of a flower bed. The paper bathing suit tore on a bush, something stabbed her foot, but Emma kept on running; she ran the wrong way along the hedge and had to retrace her steps, panic-stricken at the thud of feet behind her. She was over the steps and in the car fumbling for the keys before she saw Hank appear at the top of the stile and realized that he had been her pursuer. Hank flung himself into the car; he was smeared

with rich black dirt and sprinkled with the petals of many pink gera-
niums but Emma did not look at him. Automatically she switched on
the lights and Hank quickly switched them off.

With the starting of their car they heard a shout and saw the
forward movement of lights on the other side of the block. How she
was to proceed in the dark, Emma didn't know, but around the first
bend Hank turned on the lights and Emma began a series of swoops
and turns that finally brought them to an unknown intersection. Either they had lost the patrol car or been mistaken in the idea that
they were being chased, for nothing appeared to molest them as they
waited for the light.

"At last," said Hank, surveying his spattered front, "we are alone."

"Oh-my-goodness-gracious-heavens-above! We've forgotten
Eddie."

"Go on!" Hank yelled as Emma failed to take advantage of the
light.

"We've got to go back." Emma went slowly forward.

"We'll do no such thing. All night I've been trying to get rid of
that lad and, while I'll admit the final measures were a little drastic,
I'm not going back now, at least not in this Battle-of-the-Flowers cos-
tume."

"Aren't you tight?" Emma asked suspiciously.

"I am not."

"Didn't you want to go swimming?"

"Not with him along."

"And you really meant it when you kept trying to get him to go
home and I just thought you were being silly?"

"You're very dumb sometimes."

They looked at each other and began to laugh, because of Emma's
misunderstanding of Hank's foolishness, because the evening, however ridiculous, had been a relief from their worries and because they
looked as ridiculous as they felt.

"What did Eddie have on?" Emma wanted to know.

"Shorts," said Hank, "with a stripe; green, I think."

Then they laughed again until Emma pulled over to the side of
the road and leaned weakly on the wheel. "Stop it," she begged, "I'll
cry in a minute and dissolve what there is left of this bathing suit."

"What there is left of it," Hank repeated. "All you'd have to do to
get me in jail is to start screaming."

"You go to jail for trespassing."

"As a matter of fact," said Hank reproachfully, "if you'd just stood your ground and said the whosits had given us permission to swim in their old pool, we'd been all right."

"Me stand my ground!" Emma was indignant. "Alone? Correct me if I'm wrong, but it seems to me that you were the one who sounded retreat."

"Maybe so. Whose pool was that anyway?"

"Leeds'."

"What Leeds?"

"J. Sherman Leeds."

Wherever they were Hank's shout of laughter could have been heard in Boston.

"J. Sherman Leeds," he said, "is president of Old Cape. Eddie's Old Cape and Eddie will swoon."

Concern for Eddie's plight stilled Emma's mirth.

"We've got to go back," she insisted. "We've got to find out what happened to him and do something about it, poor lamb."

"We will not."

"We will so."

"All right," Hank grumbled. "Keep your shirt on, or rather put your shirt on. When we find out where we are I'll call the police station."

Behind a billboard, in an empty lot, Emma got back into her clothes. Hank dressed in the car. He had lost his necktie so he left his shirt unbuttoned, but when he had washed at a filling station he looked reasonably presentable. At the filling station they found out that they were still in Chestnut Hill, but a call to the police revealed that no one by the name of Eddie Rawlins had been picked up for any offense. No one had been picked up for prowling or trespass, which seemed to indicate that Eddie was still at large.

"We've got to go back just the same," Emma said when Hank came to the car to report, "maybe the cops got his clothes and he can't come out of the pool."

"I hope that's it. I get rid of him"—Hank settled himself resignedly in the car—"and you hunt him up again."

Very casually, as though they were a couple out for an evening ride, they found their way back to the Leeds'. They drove around the block twice and Emma risked a whistle that went completely unnoticed by anyone. Eddie was safe, Hank argued, and there was no necessity for searching the pool.

Later, after they had eaten, Emma sighed contentedly.

"It is nicer—with just us, I mean. Isn't it?"

"I think so." Hank let the smoke from his cigarette veil the intensity of his expression.

"There were a lot of things I wanted to talk to you about, but I'd rather just sit."

They sat for a while and then Hank drove Emma home.

"Good night," he said as he left her. "Don't worry."

Right then Emma felt that she had nothing to worry about. Shay had returned the roadster to the alley beside her apartment and the keys to her mailbox. The telegram tucked under her door read: "I drew Eddie protect my interest." That was Jeff's idea of a joke and nothing to worry about either.

And tomorrow was the Fourth and she didn't have to worry about getting to the shop on time.

Chapter 12

AT TEN O'CLOCK the next morning the sapphire Rolls was in front of Emma's apartment with Hank's hand on the horn button. Shay was with Hank and the two of them perspired gently in the sun as Emma put on her hat and powered her nose. The hat was a diminutive sailor perched over one eye and with it Emma wore a dark sheer dress that looked crisp and cool. Hank would have said that Emma looked very nice, but Shay, who could generally be counted on to be more articulately appreciative of feminine pulchritude, merely eyed her with cold disfavor.

He heaved himself out of the car to let Emma slide in next to Hank, put himself back in and slammed the door in disapproving silence.

"Is he sick?" Emma wanted to know.

"Daddy's disappointed." Shay assumed a fine "this-hurts-me-more-than-it-does-you" manner. "He can't trust his little girl."

Hank winked at Emma.

"I only took two drinks." Emma was meekly penitent. "Did I do wrong?"

"Probably; The minute I let you out of my sight you do something crazy."

"*I* do something crazy. You're a swell one to talk after the way you acted yesterday."

"Pay no attention," said Hank. "He's just jealous because he wasn't along with us."

"I was led astray," said Emma, "by a couple of low companions."

"You mean Eddie was led astray. Have you bothered to find out what happened to the poor devil?"

"He stayed in the pool—the cops didn't see him—then he got out and dressed and took a streetcar home. He called up this morning to see what had happened to me. You'd think he would have called up last night. We spent a lot of time looking for him."

143

"His boss's pool. And to think I missed it."

"Did you have a nice time on your ride?" Emma wasn't quite sure whether or not she should bring up the subject of Shay's job.

"I had a flat tire right in front of the Leavitts' farm. A strange coincidence. I put on your spare. I hope you don't mind?"

"That spare's no good. It's a wonder it got you home." Hank had been right, Emma realized; Shay had gone sleuthing on his own.

"Find out anything?" she asked.

"That the key to Currier's hangs by the back door and that Mrs. Leavitt went to bed early Saturday night. At least that's where the boys think she was at. I, personal, think different."

"Jeff drew Eddie in the pool. I got a wire last night saying so."

"He better give up gambling, his luck is slipping." Shay began to laugh again, thinking of Eddie. "Boy, I wish I could have got a picture of his face when you poured that French champagny wine into the water."

"Where was the wire from?" Hank asked casually.

"Really, I didn't notice."

"All race tracks have wire service," said Shay, "or so they tell me."

"Not any more. They're using carrier pigeons."

"No kid'?"

Emma was glad that the talk had steered away from Jeff. She had the guilty feeling that she ought to tell Hank about the muffineer but she didn't want to—not yet, not until it was well established that some-one else had killed Amos.

"I wish I didn't have to go to this funeral," she said, "but as long as you're going to be there it won't be so bad."

"Thanks," said Hank, bumping over a stretch of ancient cobble-stones.

Still under the spell of the previous night, Emma wiggled down a little in the seat because that brought her closer to Hank. She looked at the straight line of his nose, the angle of his jaw and decided that she liked him, even if he did drive a car from a semi-recumbent posi-tion that must certainly limit his field of vision. Hank looked down and returned her gaze.

Shay sighed deeply. "Don't mind me," he said. "But why not let me drive? It might be safer."

"Safer than what?"

Shay seemed willing to waive the point. "I wish I could have some beer. They sell beer there"—he pointed to one of the stands beside the turnpike—"and Roman candles."

"You'd smell," said Emma. "How about some fried clams?"

"Uh," said Shay. "My spies tell me that Ellis was nosing around down at the office yesterday trying to find out my life history."

"Is he still there?" Hank wanted to know.

"He got hold of Harris, who thinks a photographer ought to punch a time clock, and Harris told him I was a Communist, among other things."

"Are you?" Emma was curious.

"Don't be a dope—but Ellis looks like a witch-hunter and he'll have me a one-man crusade to kill all the capitalists."

"He does act a little storm trooperish," Hank admitted, "but he's a good Yankee from Billerica. Don't let him bother you."

"Authority," said Emma, "is a dangerous weapon for the uneducated."

The two men looked at Emma. "Don't use words you don't understand," Hank advised.

"But I do understand," Emma insisted. "The Paul and Virginia made me think of it. I mean people laugh at Rousseau now, but his innate goodness of the natural man isn't any more preposterous than thinking that people who don't know anything can run things by instinct any better than they're run now. On a dark night I'd prefer a few sublimations to a bunch of instincts."

"A pretty thought," said Hank, "and not necessarily invalidated by the fact that Rousseau didn't write *Paul and Virginia.*"

"Who did then?"

"Bernardin de Saint-Pierre, in 1788."

"Say, what is this? Information Please?"

"Why don't people learn what they're taught now?" Emma interrupted him. "I mean the Sermon on the Mount and the Golden Rule and the Bill of Rights? There've been a lot of good ideas around loose for a long time and do the majority of people cooperate or arbitrate? Well, take a look."

"Now I know it's the Fourth," said Shay, "I've heard a speech."

They rounded the last bend and Emma thought again how proudly Amos' house sat its knoll. It was still Amos' house to her, though she supposed that it was Eunice's now. There were many cars parked beside the road, and they ranged from white-tired limousines to dusty model Ts. Emma was a little surprised at the number; she had supposed that Amos' funeral would be a family affair and therefore small. Hank parked the car and they walked through the woodshed to the lawn; their entrance, this time, would be made decorously at the front of the house. Knots of men and boys dressed in Sunday suits that were dark and heavy or of too bright a blue fell silent as they approached, drew closer together and watched their progress around the house. Emma felt that these, Amos' neighbors, were curious and a little hostile. They didn't know her. They might even think that she had killed Amos. A pebble hit the ground at Emma's feet and, turning quickly, she saw a tall man catching at the arm of a small boy. Hank took her elbow and marched her steadily on.

"The bastards," said Shay, "shall I go back and take a poke at them?"

"That wouldn't help. It was just a kid trick."

There was another group of men at the corner of the house; several of these nodded or said a stiff good day. At the steps were several that Hank knew but he took Emma inside, surveyed the rows of chairs and benches that filled the hall and the parlor, put Emma in a seat near the door and admonished Shay to stay with her. Emma wished Hank would stay, too, partly because, while Shay was nice, she felt safer with Hank. But Hank, with a whispered request to save him a seat if she could, went away. If he could find Durrell perhaps he could find out if there was some definite reason for the local hostility.

Durrell was helping Mrs. Leavitt and her husband carrying chairs. In the kitchen Hank found Ellis dodging the spoon in his coffee cup but meeting a fat sandwich more than halfway.

"Good morning," said Hank.

Ellis bit off another mouthful before he answered. "Got the warrant?" he asked. "Everything all ready for the big moment?"

"Why, no," said Hank. "I don't know anything more right now than you do."

"Oh, is that so? Then it didn't do you any good to take the crusher and to send that Communist snooping out here yesterday asking questions the minute my back was turned?"

"I gave you the report," said Hank peaceably, "and he couldn't ask you questions when you weren't here." That was it then. Harris had probably only included the word "Communist" as a string of derogatory epithets but Ellis had taken it seriously.

"No"—Ellis gave his lips an anticipatory lick—"I was asking a few questions myself. But you better get this straight right now. I'm in authority here and you work under me or I'll see to it that you don't work at all. There are certain kinds of people that a God-fearing community don't want hanging around."

"I don't believe I exactly understand you."

"Oh, you don't?" Ellis thrust out a thick puttee-clad leg, leaned back and hooked his thumbs in his belt. He apparently relished what he was about to say.

"You're a fine bunch, all of you. You call yourself a detective but you never solved a case in your life. You couldn't even find out who killed your uncle; the police had to do that for you. You high-pressured Miss Chandler into hiring you and what have you done? Nothing. All you do is to hang around with the Marsh girl and Graham and that drunken Communist. Graham is a gambler and was in jail for the killing of your own uncle. I let you talk me out of arresting him yesterday but today I got different ideas. He'll go with me when the funeral is over. Shut up," he said as Hank started to interrupt him. "I'm not through yet.

"You know why Horrigan was fired from his paper: for taking pictures of Graham and the Marsh girl out of the morgue and destroying them. He's a drunk and a bum. He came snooping out here yesterday trying to pump the Leavitt kids; you're so lazy you probably sent him to do your dirty work for you. He was jailed for leading a demonstration when Sacco and Vanzetti was being tried. He's a dirty Red and you're a half-baked Pink that thinks it's cute to go around with guys like him and Graham and this Marsh gal, who goes around with all of you when she ain't running after fellows like Currier. You're a rich man's son and you think you can do anything and get away with it, but this is one time you don't."

Hank counted ten. If he were Shay, he thought, he'd punch Ellis in his ugly mug and go to jail and be glad of it. It was so easy, sometimes, to be a hero; but it would be very difficult to solve the murders from a cell.

"I'm afraid," he said, "that it isn't going to do any good to argue with you because you obviously want to believe what you've said. But just for the record, as you would have found out if you'd gone to the police station instead of to Harris, it is absolutely untrue that Jeff Graham was in jail for the murder of my uncle—there was never any charge against him—he was held in protective custody, fortunately, as it turned out, and he gave us the clue to the real killer.

"Furthermore, my drunken friend Horrigan, as you choose to call him"—Hank smiled wryly at the use of his own phrase—"was not jailed for thinking Sacco and Vanzetti innocent, he was hauled away for hitting a cop: a practice that appeals strongly to me this minute. Just wait a bit." Hank held up his hand as Ellis started to get to his feet.

"I'm not through either. Horrigan removed that picture from the files a long time ago because Miss Marsh objected to the hat she was wearing in it. It's the sort of a trick friends do for each other but you wouldn't understand that. My father didn't have any money, but that is beside the point. My money and my friends are my own business. I came out here in the kitchen to ask you why no one would talk to me yesterday and why a stone was thrown at us as we came in. I don't need to ask. You're so scared for fear someone else will break this case that you're spreading a lot of lies to turn public opinion against us. Go right ahead. You can't arrest Graham because he took advantage of the holiday to go look at some furniture. Arrest him tomorrow and you'll be the laughing stock of the force. Go right ahead, but leave Miss Marsh out of your stories, or, when this case is over—"

Durrell came to the door. "You folks coming in?" he wanted to know.

Hank was conscious that he and Ellis were the sole disturbers of the hush that had fallen on the rest of the house. He went back, through the pantry, the dining room, to the hall and took a seat in a small uncomfortable chair because it was too late for him to get to Emma and Shay.

The rustle of best dresses died away. The parson began to speak. Hank, from where he sat, could not see the parson, but from his voice and his manner of speaking judged him to be an elderly serious man. A native too; from the scholarly resume of the Currier family history with which he began his oration. Hank slumped down a little in his seat and thought that if one changed Currier to Norwitch or to Fairbanks the history would read very much the same. There was a certain uniformity in the background of all New Englanders that at times distressed him. They had all come over with the first wave of immigration, farmed a little, fought a little and raised the same broods of lawyers, preachers and teachers. Once in a while there had been a black sheep. If the black sheep were a smarty, the family became wealthy; if he were just black, his name was erased from the family Bible and no one but the neighbors talked about him.

The parson temporarily abandoned the Curriers in order to justify Amos' death—if not the manner of his passing—with the idea that God moved in a mysterious way. God wasn't the only one, Hank thought, who had them all mystified. At least this old codger—Hank had by now added a round white beard to the minister's appearance—didn't pretend to be privy to God's secret mysteries. " '—blessed is he that endureth temptation.' "

Hank wondered what temptation had troubled Amos. It seemed hardly fair to bring it up now; well, whatever it was, the minister wasn't going to tell. Two women several rows in front of Hank turned to each other and nodded solemnly. Hank bet they thought they knew what Amos' temptation had been. He bet everyone in Westham knew it but they wouldn't tell him about it. Oh no, they'd fold their lips together the way Mrs. Leavitt did and let him find out for himself.

"—apple trees—" Surely Amos was not being compared to an apple tree. No, but the Currier Bell, a veritable gem among apple trees, heir to none of the ills that beset apple trees, and the result of Amos' own crossing, had been given to the State Experimental Station; Amos had also contributed generously to the Westham Academy. As Hank's late uncle would have reckoned philanthropy, these were pretty small potatoes, but surely it was every man's privilege to give as he saw fit. In Westham too lavish giving would have been thought ostentatious and Amos had been well liked in the village. Yet someone had killed him. Hank moved restlessly, recoiling his long legs under his chair. It had to have been someone in the house, unless Shay had his money on the right horse or they were all wrong about the windows.

To Hank both murders had an impromptu air about them, as though someone had seized on the confusion of Saturday night to kill Amos, knowing that suspicion would fall on the strangers present, and had taken the same opportunity on Sunday. No, the killing of Chandler had been done at the risk of immediate discovery by someone who was watching for an opportunity; someone, Hank was certain, who did not want the old inventory to be discovered. Why? Well, it looked as though it was because of the muffineer, and it looked to Hank as though Miss Currier, who was nobody's fool and who could get as far as the bathroom door, was the one who had had the best opportunity to kill Chandler.

If he had made up his mind, Hank asked himself, why didn't he do something about it? The trouble was that in front of the picture of Miss Currier slipping through the bathroom door to kill Chandler there passed the pictures of Jeff, who had had possession of the key to the silver closet, of Eunice with the Staffordshire figure and of Mrs. Leavitt, who must have supplied Miss Currier with the ice pick. Working backward from Miss Currier and the ice pick, that would mean that Miss Currier had killed Amos for some reason connected with the muffineer, had confided the muffineer and the story to Mrs. Leavitt and had been forced to kill Mr. Chandler when she found that he was looking for the inventory. Mrs. Leavitt had helped her and had disposed of the muffineer.

It was a pretty picture, but Hank decided it didn't make a lick of sense. The muffineer was gone, everyone admitted that, so the fact that it was listed on the inventory didn't mean a thing. The only importance the inventory could have would be if, as Mr. Chandler had pointed out, something else that was listed there was unaccountably gone. Hank almost sat up straight. That was it. Something more important than the Staffordshire figure was gone and that was why somebody didn't want the inventory found.

Hank squirmed again as he thought of Eunice and the figure. He would find himself trying to convict his client yet. The little fool. He supposed she had taken the figure to sell because her father kept her short of cash. He hated to have to accuse her of it but it was beginning to look as though it would be necessary. There were too many loose ends that he was overlooking. Ellis would be finding them out and raising a stink. And one of the loose ends was why Jeff had taken it into his head to go off without leaving definite word of his whereabouts. Only Hank didn't really think he had. Emma would loosen up if the occasion demanded, he was sure, unless Ellis got after her and then she'd get stubborn and wouldn't tell anyone. Her loyalty was on occasion a nuisance.

There was a stir about him. People were getting up and moving toward the front of the house. Some of them would go to the cemetery; Emma wouldn't have to do that. He wondered how she had felt during the eulogy of Amos; she had liked Amos all right but not the way she liked him; he had been an ass to let her know that her coming out to Amos' had riled him.

Hank moved forward as fast as the crowd would allow him. He saw Miss Currier, supported by Eunice and a blue-jowled man, leave the house. A tall hearty man was talking to Emma. Hank was too far away to hear what was said but he could see the expression of surprise on Emma's face.

Hank waited impatiently at the foot of the stairs. He wished they would hurry; he had things to do.

"I have to stay until they come back," Emma said as she reached him. "Amos' lawyer just asked me to stay until the will was read. I suppose"—she seemed confused and apologetic—"Amos left me something."

Hank said, "That's O.K. Why shouldn't he?"

Emma smiled at him gratefully.

"I hope it wasn't the muffineer," Shay whispered, "on account of where is it at?"

"I think," said Emma, "from something he said once, that it'll be

Slocomb and what on earth will I do with a horse?"

"Can he run?" Shay wanted to know.

"Really," said Emma, "wouldn't you think he'd have more sense?"

"What makes you so sure it's the horse?"

"Because"—at the memory of the incident Emma blushed a deep red—"because that Saturday, before he was killed, I mean, we were out in the barn and he told me to be good to Slocomb."

"Probably he just meant for you to quit hitting him." Shay pointed in the direction of the kitchen. "Can't we go out there? I've got something to tell you that is more important than horses."

"Ellis went out there; do you want him to know?"

"That louse. Where then?"

Nearly everyone had gone now and the undertaker's boy was stacking chairs with only a nominal attempt at quiet.

"Come upstairs," said Hank. "I'll need some help."

"You won't believe this," Shay began, "but I saw it with my own eyes. It was during the prayer and I was looking around. There was a little silver box on the edge of that desk thing and she just reached out and put it in that big bag she was carrying."

"Who?" said Emma.

"Who do you think? Mrs. Leavitt, of course. She's my baby and I'm going to win that three hundred and fifty yet."

"What a way to talk," said Emma. "I didn't see her."

"No, you had your eyes shut, like a Christian."

Hank paused at the head of the stairs. "My researches have pried out the fact that the Leavitts could use a little extra money. I don't mean that they're in danger of being evicted by the villain with the black mustaches and the mortgage, but Durrell says that Ruel is just naturally unlucky. Even his hogs die."

"Maybe," said Emma, "Durrell sells 'em to him. Where are you taking us?"

"To the attic. On the very remote chance of finding the inventory. Ellis swears it isn't anywhere in the house, but Zubinsky told me it was so hot in the attic that they didn't half search it."

As he opened the door that led to the third floor they fell back from the wave of hot, musty air that broke over them.

"It smells just like the shop," said Emma.

"The state police," said Shay, taking off his coat and throwing it over the banister, "being a puny crew, can't take it." He removed his necktie. "But what are a couple of fried friends to Kid Fairbanks?" He added his shirt to the coat and tie.

"My" said Emma, "what a nice tan you have."

"I," said Shay, "do my swimming in broad daylight."

"Come on," said Hank. "Play Tarzan in the attic, if you must, or they'll all be back from the cemetery before we get started."

The Currier attic was stifling but it was tidy and not too dusty. The great chimneys, softly red, rose from the loose plank flooring to the timbers of the roof but around them was no litter of trash. No splayed out piles of yellowed newspapers, no cardboard boxes spilling their contents marred the monumental effect of the chimneys. No bunches of withered herbs, no dusty clothes hung from the rafters.

Emma was faintly disappointed. An attic ought to be more exciting; an attic was where one found discarded treasures: a chair with a broken rung, a drop-leaf that would have inlay under its paint, or at least a box of old bottles. A spinning wheel and a smaller walnut flax wheel stood in one corner but Emma sniffed at those. Even Jeff had never thought up any use for a spinning wheel.

She took off her white gloves and laid them atop her bag, on the floor. Her head swam a little as she stood up and she could feel the perspiration trickling down her back. She would look a sight when she got through, she thought, envying Shay.

"Get going," said Hank. "Begin over there."

He pointed to one end of the row of trunks and chests under the eaves.

Shay, his hair already limp in his eyes, held up a sextant.

"What do you do with this?" he wanted to know.

"Find out where you are."

"I don't need any gadget to tell me where I'm at; not even the presence of a couple of gray shades that used to be my friends."

"It's all in your mind." Hank lifted the tray out of a trunk and paused to wipe at his forehead. His sleeve came away wet and he ruefully took off his coat.

"The Seven Hinges of Hell," said Emma, "may have been hotter—why are there seven hinges?"

"The ancients"—Hank prodded a blue broadcloth greatcoat to see if it would give off a revealing crackle—"considered the numbers three, seven and nine to have mystic properties."

"My birthday's on the ninth," said Emma. "February, in case anyone is interested, and I want a pair of silver foxes or a grand piano."

"How about a pair of rabbits?"

"I'm a seventh son of a seventh son"—Shay nibbled at a twig of cedar that had fallen from the folds of a cashmere shawl— "and my mystic powers tell me we are not getting anywhere in this Augean stable. The Curriers were a tidy lot and they wouldn't have hidden that inventory in with Great-grandfather's red flannels."

"That's what gets me." Hank slammed down the lid of his trunk and tackled a round-topped chest. "You'd think the inventory ought to be in Amos' desk and that they all would know it. Instead they all go into a daze at the word 'inventory' and say, 'Oh yes, it's here somewhere.' "

"Mrs. Leavitt," said Shay, "burned it. She saved the old home place by selling off the Currier knickknacks and doesn't want to be caught."

Emma sniffed. "She didn't, but I know who did. But even if we found it — Ouch!" Emma rescued a finger that she had inadvertently shut in the trunk, sucked it for a moment and went on. "It would take a long time to prove that anything else was missing."

Emma was wondering how many days it would take Jeff to get to North New Portland and discover that he had been had. His trip home, she was quite sure, would be speedy and Emma wanted everything cleared up before Jeff came back.

"Because," she continued, in spite of the fact that no one seemed to be listening, "the old inventory wasn't made out by rooms and we'd have to hunt all over the house for the things and then check them off."

"How do you know so much about the old inventory?" Hank inquired casually.

"The night we were all out here, before you came, I mean, I said something about using the old inventory to help make the new one, and Jeff said—or Amos, I forget which, they were both talking about it—that we wouldn't use it because it would be more nuisance than it was good."

"Who'd you say said it?"

"Now don't try to catch me up like that. I said I didn't remember."

"If Jeff said it," Hank mused, "it would mean that he had seen the inventory."

"I think it was Amos," said Emma promptly, "because it was right after that that he told me how he didn't like antiques because he'd been spanked for whittling them and that his family had run out and people ought to use what they had instead of saving it. I remember that because it was then that he gave Jeff the key to the silver cupboard and Jeff made a dumb remark about locking the stable door after the horse was stolen."

"You do it every time, don't you?" Hank's voice was tinged with exasperation.

"Do what?"

"Finally come out with something that you should have told in the first place."

"I haven't told you a thing," said Emma sharply. "Everybody knew that Jeff had the key to the silver cupboard."

"Yes," said Hank, "but it sounds to me as though Amos and Jeff knew that something was missing from the silver cupboard. Whatever has been going on, they suspected it, and Amos got killed, and Jeff beat it. Where did you say he went?"

"I didn't say and don't you go hinting that Jeff ran off."

"Don't be a dope," said Hank, "I don't think Jeff ran off any more than I think he killed Amos, but I think he knew something that he's holding out on me. You don't suppose"—Hank scowled at Emma—"that the dirty pup has gone off to solve this by himself."

"Certainly not," said Emma, "he went to look for some furniture. I mean that's what he said, only he didn't tell me where."

"Mmm"—Hank regarded her suspiciously—"so you won't talk. Well, let it go; it'll leak out sometime. For the love of Mike, will you look at that."

Shay had abandoned the hunt; seated cross-legged on the floor, he was deep in the contents of a gaudily covered magazine.

"*Ace Detective,*" read Hank. "Where did you get that?"

Shay looked up. "Who, me? Trunk's full of them. All kinds of them. Very interesting." He turned a page.

Hank and Emma peered into the trunk. "*Dime Detective, True Detective, Sleuth Samples, Amazing Mysteries;* it's all wrong," said Hank. "It spoils the picture. *Atlantic, Harper's, Century*—even old copies of *Life,* yes—but detective stories are simply not appropriate to this house. Did Amos read them?"

"I wouldn't know." Emma shook her head.

"Not lately, he didn't," said Shay. "They're all ten-fifteen years old. Maybe they had a cook that read them."

"More likely the hired man. Anything else in the trunk?"

"It's the last one," said Emma. "There better be."

She looked in the tray that Shay had set aside. In a basket, still faintly redolent of sweet grass, were sea shells. There was a pewter doll's tea set and a leather bag of marbles. Emma eyed the tea set covetously but picked up instead a dog-eared leather-bound book. On the brown-edged flyleaf was written: Amy Prescott Currier.

"Listen to this," said Emma and began to read:

"Jan. 1, 1875. I have decided to keep a journal. Mr. Wilson says it is the way to develop an unconscious style. Many famous people have kept journals. It was cold at school this morning. Ruel was late and hadn't started the fire. Mr. Wilson has very elegant hands. I do not think he likes to start the fire—"

"Put it back," said Hank. "I hear a car and Shay's got to get his clothes on."

Shay started downstairs and Hank, picking up his coat, followed him. Emma was fumbling with her bag.

"Hey, put that tray back," Hank called over his shoulder.

Emma did so with only a conventional protest. Her bag was now in her hand, but she did not need to put the book into it surreptitiously because Hank was halfway downstairs exhorting Shay to hurry.

Anyone could see, Emma thought, that the diary would probably tell what kind of person Miss Currier really was and why she had chosen to spend her life in her room. Anyone should see that, but as no one did Emma was perfectly willing to take the glory of discovery for herself.

Stowing the diary away beneath the compacts, cigarettes, old letters and bills in her bag, Emma went downstairs.

Chapter 13

THEY were all coming into the hall: Miss Currier, flanked by Eunice and the dark man, Mrs. Leavitt, Durrell, Ellis and a solid woman in sensible shoes and a voile dress who turned out to be one of the cousins from Grafton. The lawyer appeared and ushered Miss Currier into the sitting room. Eunice whispered to him and he went over to Hank.

"Hinckley is my name, H-i-n-c-k-l-e-y. I have been out of town or we would have met before. Are all these people"—he was presumably referring to Shay—"concerned in the reading of the will?"

"More or less," said Hank. "This is Mr. Horrigan; he was here at the time of the murders."

Mr. Hinckley winced at the word "murder" and said, "How-do-you-do? A most distressing circumstance."

Shay put on a long face and said, "Yes indeed."

Emma wished they hadn't chosen the sitting room for the reading of the will. In spite of the shining knobs on the Franklin stove, the enormous hooked rug—the bright, patient product of long winter evenings—the curly maple highboy, the Chippendale sofa with its faded covering and the chairs that seemed more comfortable than those anywhere else in the house, she had conceived a certain dislike for the room. She picked a banister-back armchair in a corner and sat down, making herself as small as possible.

Miss Currier and the two with her sat on the sofa. Shay took a stool, much too small for him, beside Emma, leaving Hank to dispose himself with the others where he could. It so happened that he faced Emma, across the room.

Eunice ignored Emma. Miss Currier looked tired, though she sat bolt upright, immobile, except for her eyes which darted from face to face, watching, it seemed, and noting any change of expression.

Mr. Hinckley drew the mate to Emma's chair up beside a butterfly table, took a blue-backed paper from his briefcase, glanced around the room, felt his necktie and cleared his throat. The room became silent.

156

Mr. Hinckley cleared his throat again. "This will is dated June twenty-second," he began. "Well, perhaps I better just read it." He paused again and then plunged in, stilling the murmur that arose as the recent date of the will dawned on those present.

"I, Amos Currier, being of sound mind and body and firmly convinced of the folly of too great preoccupation with things of the past, do give, devise and bequeath my estate to my niece, Eunice Chandler—"

Mr. Hinckley paused and took a drink of water.

Emma was sure that she heard a sigh of satisfaction in the room but she did not look at Eunice. She was glad if Eunice had what she wanted. She couldn't see the point of putting in the dig about Chandler if Amos were going to give the farm to Eunice. He couldn't have known that Chandler would be dead and not able to turn the place into a museum. Or had he anticipated not only Chandler's death but his own? The will was so new. Well, it wasn't her business. She'd probably come at the end, along with the minor bequests. If she wasn't down for Slocomb she might get the second-best bed.

Mr. Hinckley put down his glass, drew a deep breath and continued:

"—with the exception of the farm known as the Currier Place"—the room seemed to hold its breath— *"two hundred acres, situated in Middlesex County—"* There followed a metes and bounds description, *"—the buildings thereon and the furniture and appurtenances pertaining thereto."*

A rustle of anticipation ran over the room.

"Upon these conditions: that my aunt, Miss Amy Currier, shall have a life estate therein and that the horse Slocomb be maintained, I do hereby give, devise and bequeath the aforementioned property, so excepted, to Emma Larabee Marsh."

Emma felt as though she were alone at the bottom of a well, dropped into a steep-sided abyss from which no one would help her. She looked across the room to Hank. His face was stony, aloof. She did not hear Shay's whistle of astonishment.

"He can't do it." She was conscious that her voice was much too loud, as if she were calling for help. "I can't take it," she went on and then, more normally, "Whatever possessed him?"

Eunice Chandler stood up; her face was flushed and her eyes blazed at Emma. "You tricked him," she accused, "into changing his will. You hung around him and flattered him—you'd have married him if you'd had to, just as you told me, because you and that man you work for wanted this furniture. But you'll never get it; I'll break that will. I'll show them the kind of person you are; you got that man to kill Amos so you wouldn't be bothered having to marry him—"

"My dear young lady—" Mr. Hinckley tried to stem the shocking flow.

"You just try to break that will." Emma wasn't at the bottom of her well any more; she was unconscious of everything around her except that she was facing Eunice Chandler and that she wanted very much to scratch her. "If Amos wanted me to have this place, I'm proud to take it—"

"Yea, bo," said Shay but nobody heard him.

"—and I won't put Miss Currier in an old ladies' home or Slocomb in a glue factory the way you would—"

"Why, you, you—sneaking down here at night and kissing him. You didn't think anybody heard you, but I did. Trying to make up for telling him he was a meddling old fool—"

"Ladies, ladies! Unfounded accusations—"

Eunice turned on Hinckley. "She told me she was going to marry him. Mrs. Leavitt heard her. Then they all got drunk and that Graham hit Amos and she was afraid their plans would go wrong so she came down to this very room, and I heard Amos tell her that what Jeff Graham did didn't make any difference, and then he kissed her."

Emma was no longer alone with Eunice. She saw Mrs. Leavitt nodding affirmation; she saw Hank coming toward her and heard him ask, "Is this true? Did you tell Miss Chandler that you were going to marry Amos Currier?"

And then it seemed to Emma that she and Hank were alone, only they were miles apart and every second she kept silent increased the distance.

"Answer me."

Emma's head went up and her jaw went out a little.

"Yes," she said.

"And how about coming down here? The part you didn't tell me before?"

"Yes," she said, "Amos kissed me."

"Thank you," said Hank. He went back to his chair and sat down. Hinckley and the man who had been with Miss Currier were talking to Eunice. Eunice was sullen now but still determined.

"Leave me alone," she was saying. "I don't care what you say; I'm going to break that will."

They led her out into the hall.

"So"—Ellis was leering at Emma—"you were going to marry the old man but you and your boyfriends thought up a way so you wouldn't have to? As soon as he makes a fresh will he gets killed. Come out in the dining room."

A few moments ago, Hank remembered, he had wanted to punch Ellis; now he no longer cared how Ellis talked to Emma.

His brain was very clear and cold and keen. He spoke to Durrell, "Who's that man with Miss Currier?"

"Name of Gillespie," said Durrell.

They exchanged looks. Durrell heaved himself to his feet and guided Hank out the door.

Still seated on the sofa, Miss Currier caressed the knob of her cane with sinewy fingers. She was sure everything would work out beautifully. The expression on her face as Mrs. Leavitt came across to her was one of intense satisfaction.

"Have they found it?" she asked.

"I don't think so. They'd been up in the attic. There was a piece of cedar stuck to Mr. Fairbanks' coat but they didn't look excited about anything."

She opened her bag and held it close to Miss Currier so that no one else could see in. "From the parlor," she said.

"Better put it back." Miss Currier's brows wrinkled faintly. "They're all mixed up now but somebody might notice."

Mrs. Leavitt sniffed. "A stupider bunch of dopes I never saw," she said.

"Sally!" said Miss Currier. "Such language! Help me upstairs!"

"That Ellis"—Mrs. Leavitt spoke softly—"says he's going to remove the guard tonight."

Eunice was sitting on the stairs, pale but quite in control of herself. Mr. Gillespie would take her to the Chandler place, and Hank would go there after he had talked with Durrell. Eunice looked up at Hank.

"You're not going back on me? Because of what I said? Are you?"

"Why should I? It was true."

Hank felt very old and disillusioned. Emma and Jeff didn't matter to him any more. He was concerned only with the case. It was as though a barrier had been removed, a barrier of personalities that

kept him from seeing the case in its true light. He could understand
Ellis' feeling about Jeff. Maybe Jeff had done it. The recent will would
give Ellis a case against Emma. Maybe she had done it. He didn't
care. If Eunice had done it, he'd help her out of it somehow. He
thought cynically that no jury would convict her—she was too good
looking. He didn't care who had killed Amos Currier but he was glad
someone had. He thought of himself out in the summerhouse and
was filled with great disgust.

He went to the car with Eunice and then back to the library where
Durrell was waiting for him.

He sat down on the worn black leather couch that was broad and
flat and comfortable and not at all antique. Except for the fireplace,
the window casings and a glass-doored secretary, Amos had, in this
room, vanquished the past. Durrell sat in an oak swivel chair in front
of a roll-top desk that bulged with papers, pamphlets and letters. There
was a spray gun on top of the desk and a roll of tar paper beside it.
The walls, where they were not filled with books, were hung with photographs: family pictures, school pictures, a group of young men in
sweaters and shorts, most of them shoeless. So Amos had rowed on
the crew, had he? Hank got up to look. Yes, there was Amos on the
end; he'd been a good-looking kid. Hank's eyes ran over the rest of
the faces and came to rest on a square full face that showed dark jaws
even then. That explained Gillespie; he had been in school with Amos,
possibly in his class. That explained the check, too, but not why it had
been kept all the years or why Mr. Chandler had expressed pleasure
at the sight of it. Hank's eyes dropped to a picture of a horse that was
probably Slocomb, parked exaggeratedly, head up, ears pointed. A
faded blue rosette was affixed to the picture. Well, Emma had been
right about one thing. She had got the horse. She must have known,
surely she had known that Amos had willed her the property; and yet,
at first, back there in the sitting room, Hank would have sworn that
her surprise was real. Would have sworn it if he hadn't seen her hoodwink Jeff or bamboozle a customer, seen her do it a thousand times,
all, of course, for her own good.

If Hank hadn't been hurt and angry, it might have occurred to
him to wonder how the man in whose room he stood had come to be
friends with Jeff Graham. The room emphasized Amos' disregard for
the one bond they might have had in common: the furniture. And
surely they had never met at any meeting of the Horticultural Society
whose framed award also hung on the wall. All Hank could think of at
the moment was that Amos Currier, dead, had taken from him the

one thing that he prized most.

"Well," he said, sitting down again, "what's on your mind?"

Ches Durrell tipped back in the chair and folded his hands across his stomach.

"It don't make no difference to me," he began, "what a man's politics may be; they come and they go—all these highfalutin' notions about how to run the government. Give us a good year, with enough rain but not too much, and I notice folks get along all right. It's this drouth and not being able to get cool nights that's got folks so riled up."

Hank was by now accustomed to Durrell's rambling introductions and waited for him to make his point.

"Now you take Ellis; he's not such a bad feller, only he's been out in the heat too much chasing after people that's trying to get somewhere out of the heat in too much of a hurry. He's got it in for this Horrigan boy because he don't like his politics. God-amighty, I can remember when old man Ellis, Moe's grandfather as was, gave away all his property and stood on a hill in a bed sheet waiting for the end of the world. Of course the trump didn't sound like he'd figured it would, and the Ellises had to move over to Billerica. Disappointment like to have killed the old man; he never spoke to a living soul after that, though he lived to be ninety-seven. You see how it is; folks had crazy ideas even in them days, but I guess maybe Moe's kinda sensitive."

Durrell reached out and fiddled with a bunch of wooden tags.

"I wouldn't know nothing about that. Live and let live, as the feller says, but there's two things I do know about and that's hogs and insurance."

Now they were getting to the point, Hank realized; he hadn't been brought in here just to have Moe Ellis' motives explained to him.

"Amos Currier knew that, and Amos and I was pretty good friends. I ain't said nothing about it because I guess I was kinda sensitive, too, but it don't seem logical that after all the years I talked insurance to Amos he'd go and take it out with somebody else."

Durrell sighed. "There must have been a reason. I kinda figured I'd talk to Graham and Rawlins about it today but they ain't here. You'll be going in to Boston, won't you?"

Hank nodded.

"Well." Durrell relaxed. "That's one angle. And you can find out from this Gillespie about the check?"

Again Hank nodded. He had already planned to see Gillespie, but the point about the insurance was a good one, and it amused him that Durrell's lethargy prevented him from following up his own idea.

"You don't suppose"—Durrell was pondering again—"that Amos suspected Graham had taken the muffineer and was trying to cozy him along by giving him the key to the silver cupboard and letting him make the inventory?"

Hank shook his head. "I can understand how you and Ellis might suspect him but I think you're wrong. I don't think Jeff took the muffineer or had anything to do with the murders, because I know Jeff Graham and he's a good man."

It was true, Hank told himself, and the fact that Emma had proved herself deceitful didn't alter it.

"Now I've got a couple for you."

He told Durrell of Eunice and the Staffordshire figure but Durrell was unimpressed.

"Sho," he said. "Eunice's always been kinda scatterbrained and Lloyd was awful close but I had it figured out that she was pretty fond of Amos."

"All right, listen to this."

He retold Shay's story of having seen Mrs. Leavitt put the silver box in her bag.

Durrell looked at him, aghast. "Young feller," he said, "you get the notion that Sally Leavitt had anything to do with the murders right out of your head. Why, I've known her all my life."

Hank had to laugh. "There we are," he said. "You know Mrs. Leavitt and I know Jeff Graham."

"Of course"—Durrell tactfully avoided mention of Emma and the date of the will— "it was Amos' business where he left his furniture but how well do you know this Rawlins?"

"Enough," said Hank. "I've thought about him, too, because you had to think about everybody in this case, and Eddie hasn't a sign of a motive, even supposing that he could have left the parlor without Amos' hearing the key screech or that he could have killed Chandler from downstairs."

"He'd written a lot of insurance," Durrell insisted, "thanks to Mr. Graham. If Amos had got the wind up about Graham, it would lose Rawlins a mighty big policy."

"It would take more than Amos' policy," said Hank dryly, "to make Eddie do anything that would injure his career."

"Well," said Durrell, "you go to Boston and I'll talk to Sally. Ellis says he's taking the guard off the place tonight."

As they left the library they could hear Ellis' voice raised in the dining room and a low murmur that might be Emma answering him. She'd take care of Ellis all right, Hank thought. The twenty-second of June; only a week before Amos' death: it had to be a new will. She'd taken care of herself pretty well, it seemed, with no help from him. He inquired the way to the Chandlers' and, on being told that it was only a short walk across the fields, asked Durrell to have Shay take his car back to town. He could get a ride with Eunice or Gillespie or someone; he did not want to ride back with Emma. As he crossed the lawn to the lane by the fence he reminded himself that the last time he had quarreled with Emma he had come near to throwing up the detective business and sailing for the South Seas. Well, he hadn't done that this time; he must be growing up.

In spite of the sun, Hank had the momentary feel of rain in his face and remembered Emma's voice asking him to love her enough to let her solve her problems her own way. That had been different; that time she had only withheld facts about Jeff that he had felt he had had a right to know, that time she hadn't pretended to love him and engaged herself to marry a man old enough to be her father. Why had she done it? It couldn't have been money; heaven knew he had enough money for any mortal need, even if he did try to live on what he made himself. Maybe she had loved Amos. Well, all right, why hadn't she come out and said so? It looked very much as though, after Amos' death, she had seen the chance **to** have her cake and eat it too, especially if she knew she was going to inherit. Maybe, if she had known about the will, she and Jeff had killed Amos for the property? It was a nasty idea and Hank wished he hadn't thought of it. He kicked at a little brown snake that suddenly parted the grass in front of him. But the idea wiggled into his mind just as the snake wiggled away through the grass. Emma had admitted that Amos had told her that she would get Slocomb. She had only told him part, just as she had only told him part of the story of her trip downstairs in the night. She had told Jeff that Amos was leaving her the furniture and together they had planned Amos' killing. Or maybe, half sense made Hank take that back in favor of the idea that Jeff, knowing of Emma's prospects, had plotted the murder of Amos alone.

What ailed him? Hank wondered. He had defended Jeff to Durrell and here he was making Jeff a murderer for gain. It was, he supposed, that Emma's action had undermined his confidence in everyone. He had thought he could type mentalities and prophesize actions, had he? It looked as though he might as well have failed the courses in psychology and turned his attention from people to something predictable, like apple trees, say. Or did apple trees sometimes confound the prophets?

He was passing a planting of young trees. Somewhere there was a street called Young Orchard Street. He liked streets with names like that. If he was naming a street right now he'd name it the Street of the Disillusionment of Henry Fairbanks. That would be one for the sign painters. And people would wonder what it meant, but Emma would have to walk down that street every day and she would know. And he hoped she choked. The wench. She'd had him coming and going for four years now; he'd taken it for granted that she loved him, and all the time she had just been looking around for someone else. Women were a mess, but he had always thought that Emma was different. There was certainly no fool like an old fool, except a young one.

Back in the Currier dining room Ellis was bending over Emma shaking his finger and Emma was saying no. It seemed to her that she had said it a hundred times already. No to the idea that she had known she was Amos' beneficiary; no to the statement that she had killed him for his money, no to all the implications that she knew who had killed him. She denied that she had made a secret of the fact that she was going to marry Amos; after he was dead there was certainly no point in mentioning it. She denied that her relations with Shay were anything but friendly or that she had ever been engaged to Henry Fairbanks. She denied that she knew the whereabouts of Jefferson Graham.

It didn't make any difference what happened to her, she thought, now that Hank was really angry; it just seemed easier to deny everything except that she had said she was going to marry Amos. If she was going to marry him, she pointed out, she wouldn't have had to kill him to get his property.

Ellis, who obviously thought Emma no better than she should have been and who could not forget that he had seen Emma weeping on Shay's shoulder the Sunday of the murders, assumed that Emma's affections went where they would do the most good. She had promised the old man she'd marry him, she'd buttered him with soft words until he'd drawn up a new will in her favor. Then she'd popped the old boy off and sneaked across the hall to kill Chandler because she knew he'd make a stink about the will. Ellis knew that he didn't have a stick of proof to bolster his opinions but he thought he could save time by bullying a damaging admission out of Emma.

A little more investigation on Ellis' part might have revealed the fact that Emma did not bully easily; working for Jeff, added to a certain native stubbornness, had seen to that.

"No," said Emma.

Shay had followed Mr. Hinckley outdoors to ask about the will. Mr. Hinckley had assured him that it was a perfectly sound will; it had been drawn in his office. Mr. Hinckley had no idea of the amount of the estate that would go to Eunice. He implied that even if he had known he wouldn't have told Shay. As far as he could see the only way for Miss Chandler to break the will was to charge duress, fraud and undue influence. That was her business. He wished Mr. Horrigan a rather hasty good day.

Shay thought that Eunice showed every indication of making it her business; though maybe, if the estate was big enough, she'd be satisfied with her share. She had enough anyway; what did she have to be so ornery for? It just looked bad. Emma had done pretty well for herself. Emma was a cute beetle too.

Shay went back to the house with the intention of hunting up Mrs. Leavitt. The incident of the silver box had increased the value of his draw in the pool but he didn't know exactly what he was going to do. You couldn't walk up to a person and say, "Come on, let's see what's in that handbag." He had no official excuse for asking questions—he didn't even work for a paper any more—but maybe he'd think of something.

As Shay crossed the hall to the stairs he looked into the parlor, emptied now of the little folding chairs, still and grim as when Eunice had first showed it to him. He remembered that he had called it a swell place for a funeral. He must have been fey; it must have been the Scotch in him. Shay grimaced at his own bad joke, scowled and looked again. Then he went into the parlor to make sure. The little square box that he had seen disappear into the maw of Mrs. Leavitt's bag was sitting just where it had been on the lid of the secretary.

"Well I'll be damned," said Shay.

He put out his hand to see if it was real but drew back, remembering that it would be just as well if he were careful of his fingerprints. He couldn't prove it—Emma hadn't seen it. Probably Ellis wouldn't believe him but Shay knew that Mrs. Leavitt had taken the little box. And now Mrs. Leavitt, or somebody, had put it back.

Shay felt as ineffectual as though he were trying to swim in molasses. He could hear Ellis giving Emma what-for in the dining room;

he couldn't butt in there. Hank had vanished. The significance of the silver box had vanished.

Shay ran his fingers through his hair. Nothing he could do seemed to help or hinder. Events would run their course, and then it would all come out. But just in case, just on the off chance, he'd go upstairs and see if Mrs. Leavitt was still there.

He knocked on Miss Currier's door. Mrs. Leavitt opened it for him; she had been pouring Miss Currier a cup of tea and asked Shay if he would like some. Shay could see no harm in that; so he said yes. Mrs. Leavitt went down the back stairs to get another cup.

A thin cashmere shawl had replaced the blue-and-white spread across Miss Currier's knees. She arranged the fringe, where it lay on the floor, with the ferrule of her cane.

"If I cared at all," she said suddenly, "I suppose I should apologize for my niece's behavior, but all the Chandlers were grabby."

Shay murmured something about the nature of the will being rather a shock.

"Speak up, young man, and look at me when you talk."

"Oh yes," said Shay, "I'd forgotten that you were deaf."

"Thank you, young man. You don't think that my niece killed Amos and her father?"

"No," said Shay, "I don't. In fact if I had half a chance I'd be in love with your niece."

Miss Currier brought her cane down smartly. "If she marries you," she snapped, "she'll show more sense than I give her credit for."

"Thank you." Shay bowed politely.

Mrs. Leavitt entered the room and handed Shay a large deep saucer of pale, greenish glaze; there were tiny red flowers painted on it and in it was a little handleless bowl of steaming tea.

"Like a Scotchman's whiskey," said Miss Currier, "it warms in winter and cools in summer."

The little bowl slid slowly across the wide saucer; Shay took both hands to steady it. "It smells good," he said. "Am I just supposed to inhale it?"

"Sally," said Miss Currier, "you didn't bring Mr. Horrigan a cup plate."

"The system"—Shay still held the saucer in his two hands—"is complicated enough already. Chinese restaurants simplify matters considerably by omitting the saucer."

"Let me show you." Miss Currier took the saucer airily in one hand, tilted a little tea from the bowl and sloshed it around to cool it.

"Now," said she, "if I had a cup plate I would put the cup in it, so." She set the cup on the stand beside her and drank from the saucer.

"I'd like to see you eat peas with a knife sometime," said Shay admiringly; "I bet you could make that look ladylike too."

"Mannerisms change," remarked Miss Currier, "but not manners. Of course you know what a cup plate looks like?"

Shay shook his head. "You shame me but I'm afraid the Horrigans drank out of the saucer without further refinements." The conversational control seemed to have been taken out of his hands. He wondered why Mrs. Leavitt hadn't brought him one of the blue-and-white cups to which Miss Currier had returned. His little bowl had cooled now; he picked it up and finished the tea.

"It's pretty, isn't it?" he asked, turning the pale thinness in his hand.

"Oh, you know what that is?"

Did he imagine it, Shay wondered, or did both women wait breathlessly for his answer?

"Lennox?" Shay was willing to be helpful.

"Lennox!" Mrs. Leavitt entered the conversation with a sniff. "No, and it's not Haviland either. That's Lowestoft."

"Fancy my not knowing that." Shay wondered why the dickens he should and felt that it was his turn to embarrass Mrs. Leavitt.

"Do you know," he asked, "what a little silver box in the shape of a book is for?"

"Silver?" asked Mrs. Leavitt.

"Shaped like a book?"

Their guileless faces looked as though they had never heard of such a thing.

"Snuff?" Mrs. Leavitt suggested.

"Come to think of it," said Miss Currier, "I believe there was a box like that in the silver cupboard."

"Well, it isn't there now. It's in on that bookcase in the parlor."

"For mercy sakes," said Mrs. Leavitt brazenly; "anyone could have picked it up."

"I wonder," said Miss Currier, "how it could have got in there? Now that these things belong to Miss Marsh, we shall have to be more careful. I don't think that nice young Mr. Fairbanks liked the will very well, do you?"

"No," said Shay.

"I couldn't see all that was said but Sally told me about it. It's rather absurd to be jealous of a man that's dead, isn't it?"

"I'd think so." Shay was wondering if Miss Currier had known about the will. She seemed not at all concerned about it.

"Miss Marsh is very fond of her employer, isn't she?"

"Only to the extent of her right eye."

"He wasn't at the services?"

"No."

"Amos was very fond of him."

"He's out of town." Shay found himself apologizing for Jeff's behavior. "Business."

"Selling something?"

"No, buying. I don't know. I'd be the last person Jeff would confide in." Shay was aware that he was the well instead of the pump and he was fearful that his last drop of information would be sucked from him.

"Has anything been heard of the muffineer?"

Before Shay could answer, Emma came to the door and said that she was ready to go home. She resisted Miss Currier's urging to come in, saying that she was tired and hungry.

Miss Currier nodded. "Please," she said, "come again. Come and talk to me."

Mrs. Leavitt turned her face away from Miss Currier. "The place is yours," she said, "but she doesn't need any help except what I'm glad to give her."

Emma nodded.

Miss Currier's hand was on the gold head of her cane and her palm caressed it with a circular motion. "It would be nice if you would come out for the weekend; Sally is a very good cook and we would be very comfortable, just the two of us, for Ellis says he is taking the guard away tonight."

"Thank you," said Emma, "perhaps I will. I'll let you know. Ready, Shay?"

After they had gone downstairs Mrs. Leavitt sniffed again.

"He didn't notice a thing," she said scornfully.

"He doesn't know a snuffbox from a muffineer. Lennox, my eye!"

"Do you think she'll come?" Mrs. Leavitt asked.

Miss Currier's hand tightened on the cane. "She's unhappy," she said. "Yes, I think she'll come."

Chapter 14

HANK went across the Chandler veranda and rang the bell. After a too-long interval a sour-faced servant came to the screen door. Hank waited to be let in. The sour-faced man waited too. Hank gave in first and briefly stated his name and business. The man said that Miss Chandler was not at home.

She had to be, Hank insisted; he had an appointment with her.

Miss Chandler was not in. She had, sour-face conceded the information grudgingly, gone into town with a gentleman.

Hank thought damn and asked for a message.

There was no message.

Hank said damn, turned on his heel and walked away.

The servant shut the door inside the screen and locked it.

Hank stood in the sun and cursed all women for a bunch of deceitful, inconsiderate wretches. Then he went back to the shade of the veranda and wondered what he should do. His watch confirmed his impression that he was hungry. It was half after three and by the time he walked back to the Currier place it would be almost four o'clock. By that time, if not already, Shay would be gone with his car and he would have either to beg a ride from Ellis, if he was still there, or phone for a taxi. He wondered what had possessed him to walk over there in the first place.

Well, there was nothing else to do, Hank decided; he had walked over; he would have to walk back. He started across the lawn with a purposeful stride; he took life much too easily anyhow. He ought to get up earlier, take more exercise and, in particular, concentrate on the elusive facts of the case at hand. Work was said to be a fine substitute for emotion; perhaps he ought to try it.

He thought about Shay's story of the silver box. If Mrs. Leavitt was robbing Amos' house of unconsidered, she hoped, trifles did she do her robbing in cahoots with Miss Currier or by herself? The middle of a funeral was a curious time to pick for a snatch at the parlor orna-

169

ments. But wasn't that it? Didn't something always occur just when
Amos' usually calm household was disturbed? And who was more privy
to forecasts of probable disturbance than Miss Currier and Mrs. Leavitt? Weekend guests, of which they both had had warning, came and
there occurred two murders. In the concentration of the prayer Mrs.
Leavitt had taken a silver box. Hank had to admit that the taking of
the box was a little anticlimactic. But the interregnum between the
change in ownership from Eunice to Emma would be a fine time for
more serious robbery because, of course, there was no inventory to
prove what had been there; there was only Miss Currier's memory
and Mrs. Leavitt's word. And right now, right after the funeral and
the shock of the will, would be an excellent time for something to
happen; and Ellis had said that he was going to remove the guard.
Hank thought of his previous vigil in the summerhouse. He would
watch again, for a different purpose. He was supposed to be with
Eunice, but not even Eunice would know where he was. The only
drawbacks to staying at Amos' on the chance that something might
happen were the facts that it would not be dark for several hours and
that he was very hungry. He could not go to the kitchen, on the chance
that Ellis had not eaten everything, without running the risk of revealing his presence.

Where the lane branched Hank avoided the path that led to the
house and went on toward the stable, his movements well enough
screened by a row of hazel and alder bushes. The lane led up to the
side of the stable farthest away from the house to a small paddock
and door. As Hank crawled through the bars a brown head was thrust
out of the open upper half of the door.

"Hello," said Hank. "You must be Slocomb. Do you mind if I come
in?"

Slocomb put one ear forward but flattened the other close to his
head and blew a long breath through his nose.

"Come, come," Hank went on softly, "I know we've never met and
the chances are that our paths will rarely cross in the future, but right
now I crave sanctuary. That's a mighty fine picture of you up at the
house."

Slocomb put his other ear forward, reached for Hank's battered
Panama, removed it and dropped it inside his stall.

"Well, well," said Hank, "the reverse of 'Here's your hat'!" He
opened the door, retrieved his hat and let himself out onto the main
floor of the stable. There he paused and, turning, eyed Slocomb reflectively. It would be a lot of bother but he supposed he could do it;

after all, four feet were better than two. He moved toward the tack room, pondering the situation that had brought him to this pass and the lengths to which hunger could force one, but his course was halted by the approach of someone whistling "Barney Buntline," and the clang of a bicycle being dropped on the ground sent him swarming up the ladder to the hayloft like a whole crew of sailors. The twelve-year-old Leavitt boy, one stocking sagging below his knickers, sauntered up the ramp to the stable door, stumbled over the sill and moved in the general direction of the pitchfork. Hank remembered that "Barney Buntline" had been in his grade school singing book and decided that the Leavitt boy was probably doing his chores early so that he could go to a movie. Someone taking advantage, again, of the unsettled routine.

The boy raked down hay with the fork from the mow, bundled it expertly together and trailed it into the stall. Then he returned to the grain chest, scooped up a measure of oats, let them dribble back slowly, scooped again and bore the measure finally to its destination.

Hank watched, pleased with the boy's coltish naturalness, liking the smell of the clover hay and the purr of a lanky cat that rubbed against him. In a moment the boy would be off. Hank could see him coasting down the long hill to the village, feet on the handlebars, and felt a deep regret at the complexities of adulthood.

The boy came out of the stall, fastened the hook and hung the grain measure on a familiar nail. But instead of closing the chest, he plunged his arm deep down in it and pulled out a package wrapped in brown paper and tied securely with many turns of string. The package was about nine by twelve, Hank thought, and thick—three or four inches thick. With a maddening finger the boy traced out the address but Hank was too far away to see what the letters spelled. Possibly the boy's own name. He might have sent for a joke book, a water pistol, imitation ink spots or bugs, useful for scaring girls, and hidden it here against a safe unwrapping. But as the boy flicked away the oats that were caught in the string Hank could see that there were no stamps on the package. It was, then, something to be mailed; but what?

Hank had a swift decision to make. Should he go down as quickly as he could and demand to see the package or should he keep his presence a secret and try to follow the Leavitt boy? The boy was already walking to the front of the stable. Startled by a sudden hail, he might easily reach his bicycle and be away before Hank could stop him. Hank would then be none the wiser concerning the package and would have revealed his own secret. Without moving, he watched the boy put the package in a wire carrier, cover it with an old sack and pedal away, no longer whistling.

Hank came down the ladder, saw from a window that the boy was indeed going in the direction of Westham and went into Slocomb's stall. Slocomb ignored him; he had finished the oats and was busily munching hay. He suffered himself to be led away reluctantly, but when Hank reached to fasten a rope to his halter reared and dodged back to his stall. Exasperated, Hank led him out again and this time succeeded in hitching him. Hank's childhood had been punctuated with stubborn Shetland ponies, but either he had forgotten his skill or the ponies had not been as stubborn as he remembered, for he had considerable difficulty with the saddling. Slocomb held his head as high as the rope would permit and clamped his teeth together. Only after Hank had shut off his wind would he take in the bit and he swelled his sides obstinately against the tightening of the girth. Hank could feel the sweat trickling down his back; a drop ran down the side of his nose, tickling him. He jerked off his coat and threw it out of sight in the loft where he had left his hat. Then Slocomb swung himself sidewise and stepped on Hank's foot—only for an instant, for Hank slapped at his flank and he moved away again—but the pain, though slight, roused Hank's irritation to frenzy. He raised his hand to strike at the horse. Then his anger melted away as the pain in his foot died out, and weak, and a little sick, he leaned against the horse instead. Slocomb stood quite still and Hank felt a shameful need for apology.

It was not the horse he wanted to hurt, it was Emma; Emma, who was the indirect cause of his hunger, his ludicrous efforts to go sleuthing on horseback and the direct cause of the pain that, put it in his heart or his mind, was very real. He wondered if Emma had any idea of how he had felt when she had answered yes to his questions there in that awful sitting room? Probably not. If she had any feeling about the matter at all, it was probably merely chagrin at having lost both her beaux so suddenly. She'd never really cared about him; she couldn't have and have said that she'd marry Amos. Amos was well out of it. Emma hadn't cared about him either. All she wanted out of life was a lot of stuffy old furniture and Jeff Graham to boss and wheedle. Well, she had both now, and if it looked as though he were doing her a kindness in investigating the murder of Amos Currier, he could assure one and all that that was only incidental to the discovery of the killer of Lloyd Chandler.

He led Slocomb through the stall and out to the paddock bars. Slocomb eyed the bars as suspiciously as though he had not seen them every day of his life and shied at each one Hank let down. Hank wished that he had done a little more riding in the last ten years and hoped that Slocomb would not take advantage of him. Slocomb let Hank mount and then backed a few steps, ducking his head.

"You," said Hank, "come up."

Slocomb surged forward.

"Easy does it."

Slocomb sidled away from a small and quite motionless stone and proceeded down the lane with the careful step of one treading on eggs.

Hank decided that he could avoid the highway and possibly reach Westham ahead of the Leavitt boy if he retraced his steps, for the road from the village to the Chandler house was so uninhabited as to be almost a private drive. He hoped for a shed of some kind on the edge of the village where he could leave Slocomb, for the horse would certainly be known to some of the townspeople, and a man on horseback, minus a parade, would certainly cause comment, even on the Fourth of July.

As they left the lane Slocomb broke into a canter and Hank let him go. It was rather fun, though he knew he would regret it next day. It was only as they neared the little wooden bridge that Hank realized his mistake. On the grass of the meadow they made almost no sound but they would clatter over the bridge like a troop of cavalry and doubtless bring old sour-puss to the window. Hank tried to pull Slocomb down but the horse wanted exercise. His only response to Hank's tuggings was to abandon the bridge and head straight for the brook. He had jumped the brook many times with Amos but Hank did not know that. Hank had visions of himself again on the Chandler lawn, deprived of his only means of locomotion, probably with two broken legs and hungry. He closed his eyes. Slocomb took the brook in his stride—it wasn't a very big brook—and Hank was so pleased to find himself still atop the horse that he laughed. He was sitting down in the saddle now where he felt right and comfortable. They skirted the lower slope of the lawn, almost out of sight of the house. Hank waved to a dormer window.

"I can't come in," he said, "I'm Paul Revere. Giddap! The British are coming."

They swept through the gate which was fortunately open—though Hank felt that it would have made no difference to Slocomb if it hadn't been—and only checked their course on the upward slope of a hill. At a walk Hank could feel the sweat bursting from his body and the greater heat from the horse between his legs. Slocomb's hide was wet and there was a white froth where the reins rubbed his neck. The saddle creaked rhythmically. Hank let his feet dangle out of the stirrups; the moist leather of the reins felt good in his hands.

They walked up the hill and down the other side, then Hank picked up on the reins and Slocomb broke into a smooth trot. It was not until they had gone almost the last of the four miles to the village that Hank bethought himself of what he had to do. For the last three miles, ever since they had crossed the brook, actually, he had not thought at all. The comfort of bodily motion had lulled his mind until it was something of a shock to remember that he was not happy, that he was not completely carefree. With a sigh he pulled Slocomb to the side of the road to recapitulate. He was not a summer resident out for a ride, he was trying to solve a murder. He must eat, he hoped to find some trace of the Leavitt boy and he wished to assure himself that he could lay his hands on Slocomb for the return trip.

Through the trees ahead of him Hank could see a farmhouse that he did not wish to pass on horseback; beyond that was the village. Warned by a cloud of dust of an approaching car, Hank turned Slocomb onto the stubble of a hayfield and almost into the half-overgrown depression of an abandoned cellar. Skirting the cellar, he came to the spot where the outside entrance had been and rode the horse down the now irregular ramp. There was a wild cherry tree there, stout enough for tying, and Slocomb would be completely concealed from passersby.

"Be a good horse," Hank admonished, "and don't whinny and don't bust your bridle. I'll be back."

Once in the village, Hank slouched his way down a back street toward a lunch place that he had spotted the day before—a cafe, so called, in the corner of the two-story wooden block that was the town's business district.

As he neared it, however, he dodged into a doorway, snorting with disgust. There was a car in front of the lunch place, his own car, and sitting in it were Shay and Emma. Hank resented the proprietary way in which Shay lolled back, one hand on the steering wheel; he disliked the sight of Emma sitting there in her accustomed place, but he would have given a good deal to know what the two of them were saying to the Leavitt boy, who rested beside them, still on his bicycle, balanced by one foot on the running board of the car. Of the package there was no sign; the sack, flipped lackadaisically now and then, dangled from the boy's hand.

Then there was a spurt from the exhaust, the boy flung the sack over his shoulder, and the car pulled away in the direction of the highway, the boy pedaling furiously after it.

Hank went into the lunchroom, began with bean soup and worked his way through to pie a la mode, thinking furiously the while. He tried to track down his concern about the package, for it seemed to him that he might have worked himself up over a matter of no importance. One explanation of the conference between the bicycle and the roadster might be that the Leavitt boy, having chosen the Fourth on which to try to mail a package, had seen a chance to start it on its way by giving it to Shay and Emma. If that were so he could easily find out about it from Shay, though of course he would not dream of asking Emma. That would mean that the package was some boyish triviality, not worth the attention he was giving it. It was not until he was on his second glass of iced coffee that the pictures of Mrs. Leavitt came to him: Mrs. Leavitt as Eddie had seen her, carrying the tray covered with the napkin; Mrs. Leavitt standing in front of the stable door as he himself had hailed her from the upstairs window after the discovery of Chandler's body. Mrs. Leavitt had not turned around; she had halted, and then gone into the stable. It had been the action of a person carrying something in front of him that he did not wish seen, and Mrs. Leavitt had been carrying something. To be sure it had turned out to be a pan of bread crusts. Shay had seen it. But if the pan had been big enough, there might have been a package in it along with the bread crusts, and the package might have contained the muffineer. What more likely than that Mrs. Leavitt, called back to the house, had set down her pan of crusts and hidden the package in the oatbin? Ellis had had a man at the house, but today, under cover of the confusion occasioned by the reading of the will, she had risked sending the boy after it. But why in a package tied with a string? That was easy; she was sending the muffineer to someone to be sold. He had to know the address on the package. The Leavitt boy knew the address; he had spelled it out there in the stable.

Again Hank had the feeling of being obsessed with trifles. He wanted to know about the package; he wanted to watch Amos' house; and here he was, prevented from inquiring about the one for fear it put someone on guard about the latter.

The counterman approached him, wiping up crumbs with a damp rag.

"Fellow and a girl just in here?" asked Hank. "Kind of a big fellow?"

"Maybe," said the man.

"I saw them outside. Fancy-looking car they had."

"Yeh?" said the man. "I seen better."

Ordinarily Hank would have been glad to argue the point but he could not see that it would get him anywhere. "Get a lot of business here?" he ventured.

"A lotta bums," said the counterman.

Before Hank could think of a suitable retort the screen door slammed behind him and a man in overalls approached the counter.

"Hot damn," he said, throwing a leg over a stool.

"Hi, Lafe," said the counterman. "What'll it be?"

Lafe expressed a preference for custard pie and ran his eye over Hank, who was grateful for his wrinkled trousers, his sweat-soaked shirt and his grimy hands.

"Boy, oh boy," Lafe went on, "you ain't heard nothin'."

The man refused to be excited but he leaned his arms on the counter in front of Lafe.

"They buried Amos Currier today."

Apparently that was old stuff to the counterman, for he grunted and turned to Hank. "You want something else?" he said.

"Yeh," said Hank. "Gimme some more coffee."

Again Lafe eyed Hank and, satisfied of his appearance, included him in the conversation. "Feller got buried here today," he repeated. "Local boy; family used to have a lot of money."

"Yeh?" said Hank, stirring his coffee.

"Some of 'em still do," said the counterman darkly.

"Hot damn," said Lafe, "wait till you hear. Well, this Currier got himself killed last week—"

"It was in the papers," said the counterman.

"I thought there was two of 'em killed," Hank put in.

"That was the next day. Currier's brother-in-law—meaner than dirt he was too. I bet he's doing flip-flops in his grave right this minute." Lafe paused to savor the situation along with a bite of pie. "Well, this Currier had a nice place out here and a lot of old furniture that they say is worth a quarter of a million just because it's always been in the house, though I wouldn't know about that."

"Antiques?" asked Hank.

"That's what they call them. Well, Chandler and his daughter have been waiting around for Currier to break a leg or something so they could get hold of the place, and Amos goes and gets himself killed, only Chandler don't live long enough to enjoy it. But what do you think that old son-of-a-gun Currier does?" Lafe was at the climax of his story and paused dramatically for another bite.

"Go on," said the counterman.

Hank, although he thought he knew the answer, tried to look interested.

"The cute old devil"—Lafe slapped his thigh—"leaves his estate to the Chandler girl all right enough but he left the farm and the stuff to another one."

"Go on," said the counterman, "where'd you hear that?"

"Up at the filling station. Feller got it from a feller that drove one of the relatives over to the train."

The counterman almost chuckled. "That's a good one," he conceded.

"Hot damn," said Lafe, "ain't it? She's a looker too."

"Who?"

"The dame he left it to. That Marsh girl they say was out here the night he was killed. Works for the one Ellis is trying to pin it on. She just stopped for some gas with the big feller in a Rolls about a block long. She don't do so bad for herself."

The counterman looked at Hank, hating to concede an answer, even to a long-past question, but anxious to keep up with Lafe.

"Was she with kind of a big feller? There was a couple in here but I didn't notice her much."

"A big feller; sort of all sprawled out."

There could be, Hank thought, no better description of Shay.

"We seen her." The counterman nodded to Hank as though confirming a question that they both had asked. "Kind of skinny with a big mouth."

Hank nodded back, relishing the description sourly.

"You fellers use a drink?" The counterman made the supreme gesture of apology for his previous coolness to Hank.

"I could use one."

"Same here."

Two glasses were filled below the counter.

"Stow it if Ellis comes in. I ain't got no license."

The noise Lafe made expressed his opinion of Ellis.

"Cop?" asked Hank.

"State police," Lafe answered but both men looked at Hank speculatively.

"I got a friend in Boston who's a cop," Hank put in to establish himself as a usually law-abiding citizen.

"You in Boston much?"

"When I can get a job." Hank grinned and the counterman poured another drink.

"Here's luck," he said.

"I ain't got nothing against Ellis," said Lafe in a tone that indicated that he had, "but I ain't telling him nothing either."

"You know something?"

"Let him find out for himself. He's going around telling that the big feller is a Communist and that maybe he killed Amos so that the girl could get his money, but it was the other guy in the car that was going to kill him."

"What other guy?" asked Hank.

"The detective, the one that owns the blue Rolls. They stopped at the station the night Amos was killed."

Hank looked at Lafe in amazement. He could have sworn that he had never seen Lafe in his life. Apparently he had been tighter than he had realized.

"Of course I didn't see them—"

Hank almost sighed aloud with relief.

"—but Joe was telling me. They stopped and inquired the way and the detective drew a map and all the time the big feller was pleading with the detective not to kill Amos just because he'd swiped his girl, because no girl was worth it. And the other guy kept saying that dawn would see one or the other of them stretched upon the sward—grass, he meant. But he ain't telling Ellis what he heard because he hopes Ellis goes ahead and makes a fool of himself."

Hank thought he would stop around sometime and thank Joe. It was all true. It had been Shay's idea in the first place that Hank challenge Amos to a duel. Shay had thought it would be nice if he could get some pictures of a duel. But once Hank had agreed that he would fight Amos with horse pistols, Civil War sabers or whatever the attic afforded Shay had turned about, with the inconsistency of a man in his condition, and had tried to argue him out of it. Hank had then, of course, been forced to defend his determination to be avenged. They had been very serious and, apparently, very convincing.

"The big feller was right," said the counterman. "No woman is worth it."

"She must have something. Look what she did to Amos."

"He'd-a burned the place down before he'd see the Chandlers get it."

"Hot damn." Lafe slapped Hank so enthusiastically on the back that Hank flinched. "I bet that Chandler girl is fit to be tied."

"She's not so bad off." Hank felt that Eunice must have made herself pretty generally unpopular that these two should so enjoy the fact that she had missed part of her inheritance. "She gets the rest of the estate. You just said so yourself," he added as the two stared at him.

Then Lafe roared with laughter, and even the counterman grinned as he said, "You forgot to tell him."

"That's it. Hot damn. I forgot the point. There isn't any other estate. Amos didn't have a nickel."

"Hot damn," said Hank. "That's a good one, but I thought you said this Currier was rich?"

"He was," said Lafe. "And I'll say this for Amos, he didn't spend it on women."

"Careful," said the counterman.

A stout blonde woman, who in the days of trotting horses would certainly have been the town milliner, came in, followed by a man who might be anything. The woman spoke to the two men at the counter and sat down at one of the little tables.

Lafe slapped his money down on the counter and stood up to go.

"Hey, wait a minute," said the counterman. He pulled out a brown paper parcel tied with many turns of string and shoved it across to Lafe. "You'll see Leander before I do in the morning. The Leavitt kid left this in here, said he'd be in to pay the express."

For the moment before Lafe picked it up the package lay there on the counter, the address plain for Hank to see. Burns and Whitman, it read, with a New York address that Hank noted carefully.

"Okey-doke," said Lafe. He nodded to Hank and went out the door.

The man with the blonde came up to the counter to order; it was clear that confidences were over for the evening. Hank paid his check, counting out the money carefully, a little fearful lest he had eaten rather opulently for a man who was out of work, said, "Thanks, pal" and went away, hoping that his rather stiff-legged walk would be taken for the result of manual labor.

It was just after six and would not be dark for several hours, but Hank felt that he would do better if he got Slocomb home before night concealed any object at, or over, which Slocomb might want to jump. He had plenty to think about.

Slocomb greeted Hank with a whinny of relief when Hank came

down into the cellar. He had eaten all the grass within reach and had nibbled at the bark of the cherry tree. Hank hoped he would not show up the next day with the horse equivalent of a stomachache. He also hoped that Slocomb's lunch would make Slocomb less anxious to get back to his unfinished meal.

If Slocomb was not hungry he was certainly anxious for bed. He pressed against the bits, broke into a canter when Hank let him trot and, instead of walking, jogged with a stiff-legged bounce that shook Hank's spine and exhausted the grip of his tired legs. By the time they had reached the Chandler place the inside of Hank's knees was raw and his arms ached from pulling. He wanted very much to get off and walk, but a certain stubbornness stopped him, along with the fear that his legs would buckle under his weight. Horseback riding, he thought, was not conducive to mental activity; either it felt so good that one didn't want to think or so bad that one couldn't.

When Slocomb stopped bouncing to step trimly over his paddock bars and came to a halt outside his stall door Hank could only drop the reins and sit. He had eaten and he had discovered the destination of the package; he knew how the people in the village felt about the murders and he had found out that, except for the farm, Amos had been supposed to be penniless, but it wasn't worth it; he doubted if he would live to make use of his knowledge.

Hank dismounted stiffly and led Slocomb into his stall. His legs felt like two stumps. Slocomb was sweat-stained and the mark of the saddle showed plainly on his sides. Hank didn't care; if he got the leather to the tack room he would do well.

Slocomb shook himself and stretched his mouth comfortably.

"You, you red horse," Hank addressed him, "whoever sees you in the morning will think you've been hag-ridden. Someday, when I get my strength back, I'm going to run you over a plowed field."

Then he remembered that he wasn't going to see Emma or Slocomb any more and was doubly unhappy.

He hung the bridle on its peg and put the saddle on its rack, then he let himself down gingerly into a backless chair by the window to wait for darkness. He supposed he should climb up to the hayloft; from his seat he could see the back door of the house and the main door of the stable, but if anyone came in through Slocomb's stall or from the shed entrance, he would be caught with no place of concealment. The climb up the ladder, however, seemed an impossible effort; for the time being he would stay where he was. He rubbed his aching muscles slowly.

So Amos hadn't had any money. The willing of the estate to Eunice had been nothing but a practical joke over which Amos could laugh in anticipation, knowing that when it was discovered he would be free from the danger that the practical joker always ran: retaliation. Hank wished that he had known Amos better; the man had undoubtedly had his points. Hank had paid no attention to Amos until Amos had begun to show an interest in Emma, and then only to the point of teasing her about her middle-aged beau. Possibly his lack of concern had piqued Emma—Hank was nearer to the truth here than he realized—but it need not have driven her to duplicity and deceit.

Hank felt that the introduction of Emma was bound to cloud the picture of Amos that he was trying to get and erased her from the canvas of his mind. Not even the newness of the will could make Hank seriously suspicious of Emma, and if he could not think of her as a suspect he would not think of her at all.

But if Amos hadn't had, in the words of Lafe, a nickel, on what had he lived? Slocomb might get along on the fruits of the ancestral acres but Hank doubted that Amos could. True the man had not been extravagant, but in dress, manner and methods of entertainment he had succeeded in creating the impression of a man of plenty. No one ever fed Emma on a bushel of apples or the proceeds from it. Hank knew that the word "poor" had come to be only a comparative term. Too many of the class to which he belonged by birth and the inheritance of his uncle's wealth complained of poverty when they only meant that they had been deprived of extravagances that others might have the necessities. Poverty, for Amos Currier, might not be the poverty of a laid-off mill worker. Hank stirred uneasily as he always did when the inequalities of an economic system, of which he was, perforce, a part, came home to him. He looked out of the window, past the long shadow now cast by the gazebo, to the stone-bordered fields. The time had been when these acres had been an economic unit supporting the people who lived on them. They would probably never be so again. He tried to imagine Emma feeding chickens, running a separator, tending a garden, canning beans—the picture would not come.

Instead he saw Mrs. Leavitt in the flesh come around the corner of the house on her way to the back door. She carried a picnic basket, containing, Hank guessed, Miss Currier's supper. He wondered if the basket would contain something else when she came out. With the inventory gone, she could have been robbing the place for years. But the inventory hadn't been gone for years. According to Emma, Amos had spoken as though he could lay his hand on it to help in the making of the new one. Perhaps Amos had been wrong; maybe the inventory had been destroyed long before by someone who knew Amos' general disregard for the furnishings and memorabilia of his house, someone who knew that if Amos could not find the inventory he would merely shrug his shoulders and do without it. And who knew Amos better, or would have more opportunity, than Mrs. Leavitt? It almost looked as though Shay might win the money.

No. Hank recalled the picture of Amos watching the crap game, meticulously correcting the sloppy play of his guests. He saw Amos making the rounds of the downstairs windows. These were the actions of a man of precision and habit. Amos might not have been greatly impressed by the historical or financial importance of his possessions but he was not a man whom one could bamboozle or hoodwink. If he had thought he knew where the inventory was, Hank believed that it was because he had seen and handled it recently.

Amos hadn't missed the china figure, though. Or perhaps he had; perhaps that had been the basis of the coolness between him and his niece. Perhaps Eunice had feared that Amos would expose her theft as well as her dalliance to her father. It came to him suddenly that Eunice had gone to the stable on Sunday morning to look after her horse; perhaps the muffineer had gone with her. Perhaps he would win the pool with Eunice. Perhaps nothing. Hank told himself that he was wandering far afield; he was making things up instead of looking for facts to go on.

Mrs. Leavitt came out of the house, locked the door and went away with her basket on her arm. A light showed dimly in the upper hallway. In a little while it would be dark enough for him to go to the gazebo where his view of the house and its approaches would be more complete.

If he were going to be sensible, if he were going to look facts in the face, if the muffineer was the loose end in the snarl that confronted him, he might as well admit with Ellis and Durrell that Jeff Graham was the most likely murderer. Jeff was quick to anger and he would know the value of the piece. He might have offered to buy it—Jeff would have offered to buy the Park Street Church if he had had a customer—have been incensed at the manner of Amos' refusal and have struck him. He had probably not meant to kill—in his new unfriendliness toward all those connected with J. Graham, Antiques, Hank would not go quite that far—but he had struck harder than he intended—

Hank broke off in disgust, jerked himself upright in the chair and winced. Was he losing his mind? What was he going to have Jeff do next? Tie the muffineer up in a box, stuff it in the oatbin and then kill Lloyd Chandler for fear he'd find out that it was gone? All Jeff would have had to have done was to put the muffineer back in the cupboard and there would be no visible motive for his having killed Amos. Jeff might be short on temper but he was long on sense. Ellis was crazy. Durrell was crazy. They didn't know Jeff.

Hank got up slowly, straightening his back inch by inch. His wishes, more limber than his back, were for the coat in the loft to cover the whiteness of his shirt; his eyes, practical even in the almost darkness, sought for a coat or sweater in the tack room and were rewarded with an old leather jacket kept there by Amos against frosty mornings. The evening was anything but cool but Hank put on the jacket and the wrinkled cap that hung beneath it. If Emma could see the cap, he thought, she'd keep still about his hat. Then he reminded himself that his hats were no longer any concern of Emma's. He went down the lane behind the bushes and back on the path that lead to the house. Keeping in the shadow of the shrubbery on the edge of the lawn, he gained the gazebo and settled himself as comfortably as he could for his vigil of hopeful watching.

At first it seemed very quiet; then his straining ears began to pick up the myriad tiny sounds that went unnoticed in the day. Leaves rustled, although there was no breeze; chirps, shrills and chatterings came from the orchard behind him; there was a skittering and a scampering beneath the boards at his feet. Far away a dog barked and another answered him. There was no moon and, as the darkness increased, the white house that he watched seemed to shimmer and go farther away. Hank blinked his eyes and the house came closer. He straightened up and pressed his aching back against the latticed wall behind him. After the discomfort that he had gone through there was no point in going to sleep and missing whatever it was that he hoped was going to happen. If nothing at all happened— Well, no one knew what he had been planning to do; not a soul knew where he was. He would go to a Turkish bath and get rid of his aches and pains and not have to explain to anyone. He yawned sleepily. The keen-eyed detective. That was him all right!

He forced himself to trace the outline of the buildings from the front of the house, along the ell and woodshed, to the stable. All was perfectly serene. No shadow moved; no black skulking figure was revealed against the grayness.

His eyes came back along the shed. Convenient, that. On a frosty

morning one could go to the stable without sticking one's nose outdoors. The architects thought they had something new, did they, with
their office buildings and apartments where one could live and die
without ever going outdoors? That had been old stuff in 17— when-
ever it was the house had been built.

He wished the house had never been built. He wished that profi-
teering ancestor of Amos' had been sunk by the British or the pirates.
He wished he had never sat there on that other night, sat there like a
love-sick sophomore, watching Emma's window, waiting for a glimpse
of her. She had fooled him all right. He supposed that was what made
it hurt most: the confidence, the trust he had given her, only to find
out that she had been stringing him along and planning to marry
Amos all the while. He wondered how she would have felt when she
found out that Amos didn't have any money? It would have served
her right!

Hank looked up suddenly from his gloomy contemplation of the
gazebo floor, conscious that something had happened. The light had
been turned on in the library and a shawl-wrapped figure was moving
slowly across to the corner where stood Amos' desk. Miss Currier had,
of course, every right to go through Amos' papers but why did she
pick this night, right after the reading of the will? Was she looking for
the inventory or for something that concerned Amos' penniless condition? Hank crept across the lawn to a spot by the window where he
was out of range of the light but almost looking over Miss Currier's
shoulder. The window was closed but he could see her sigh as she
faced the clutter and the crowded pigeonholes. Surely Ellis and Durrell
had gone through the desk looking for the inventory? What, then,
did she expect to find?

Miss Currier leaned her cane against the desk and began with
the left-hand pigeonhole. Apparently she knew what she was looking
for; she shuffled through the papers rapidly, not pausing to peer into
envelopes. Once or twice she shook her head and made as though to
throw a bunch into the wastepaper basket but each time she put the
papers back. It was not until she had exhausted the pigeonholes and
turned to the little drawers below them that she found what she
wanted: a folded sheet of blue or gray paper. With it in her hand she
rose, took her cane and steadied herself across the floor, through the
hall and into the dining room.

With mounting excitement Hank slipped around the corner of
the house to the rear window, where he would have at least a partial
view of the dining room. Had she found the inventory? If so, she had

fooled them with her description of the three or four pages sewn together. But this single sheet could not possibly list everything in the house. He waited anxiously while Miss Currier fumbled with the light switch.

She must have had the key in her hand, for she unlocked the glass doors to the silver cupboard, let them swing wide and stood gazing at the contents. Was she choosing what to take next? Was she planning to make a last haul before the new owner checked over her possessions ? It almost seemed so. Miss Currier picked up a silver mug and ran her hands over the worn surface. But she put the mug back, unfolded the sheet of paper, ran her pencil down it and made a check near the bottom.

By gum, Hank thought, as he pounded silently on the window-ledge with his fist, if she hadn't found the inventory, at least she had found a list of the silver. Sweat broke out on his face again and ran trickling down his nose; he reached to his pocket for his handkerchief but his hand never got there. It fell nerveless to his side as he slumped over from a quick, sharp blow on the head.

Chapter 15

ORDINARILY Emma, who prided herself that she could read a customer's thoughts almost before he had them, would have noticed the looks of the men at the filling station. Tonight, however, she sat slumped down in the seat, wishing that she could get home—away from Shay, away from everyone—to hide the hurt that was getting bigger and bigger inside her. It hadn't been so bad at first. She had been angry, angry at Eunice for her nastiness and angry at Hank for not trusting her; but now her anger had worn away and she could see herself as Hank must have seen her—a grasping, deceitful little schemer. Emma knew she wasn't any of those things, but that wasn't the point. She could explain to Hank, she supposed, wheedle him around to understanding what she had done, but, again, that wasn't the point. Hank was supposed to know her well enough to trust her, to be confident that her feeling for him was there, deep underneath, no matter what her actions might be. If he couldn't do that, then their years of companionship counted for nothing, and it was just as well to know it now. Only it was going to take a little while to cut something out of her life on which she had come to count and depend. She wished Jeff was there. He would say, "What the hell, what the hell?" and offer her a stick of gum.

While Emma reasoned thus with herself Shay let the attendant fill the tank, fill it while the motor was running, for Shay, with the photographer's eye for a picturesque group, saw the expressions on the faces of the men squatted on the shady side of the filling station. Shay hadn't liked the stone that had been thrown at Emma. Whether it had been meant for Emma as an immoral wench or for himself as an immoral political thinker, Shay didn't know; but he knew the lengths to which bigotry could go and he knew that Ellis had done considerable talking in the village. So when the long overalled man with the stubble of beard nudged his neighbor and pointed as they drove up, Shay left the motor running. A short fat man, still in the

186

dark clothes that he might have worn to the funeral, leered at Emma and whispered something to the others. They all laughed but broke off and looked at Shay as a bald-headed man whispered something else. Then the tall whiskery man got up, hooked his thumbs around his suspenders and started toward them.

"Check the oil, mister?" asked the filling-station man.

Shay handed over a bill. "You owe me the change," he said and shot out of the station toward the highway. In the mirror he could see the tall man and the attendant gazing after them.

"Shucks," said the tall man, "I was going to congratulate her."

Shay looked at Emma, but Emma, who had been oblivious to the misunderstood good will of the villagers, was gazing straight ahead.

Presently she said, "Shay, I feel terrible."

"Daddy'll buy it some supper."

It was just like a man, Emma thought, to assume that food would cure a broken heart. "Would you mind stopping," she asked, "before we get to the highway? I think I'm going to cry."

Obediently Shay pulled over to the side of the road. Emma opened her bag and hunted for a handkerchief; a tear was already working its way down her cheek.

"Do—do you have a handkerchief? I can't seem to find one."

Shay felt unsuccessfully in his pockets. "I changed my pants," he apologized.

"Then I'm afraid I can't cry." Emma sniffed and wiped her cheek with the back of her hand. "You might as well go on; I can't cry without a handkerchief."

"What were you going to cry about," Shay asked, "if you could have found a handkerchief?"

"Because I acted so and made such a scene."

"*You* made a scene?" Shay was emphatic. "It was that screwy Eunice that caused the trouble. Somebody ought to fan her britches."

"Why, Shay, I thought you liked her. I mean Hank told me—I mean—" Emma paused, not liking to involve Hank in a betrayal of confidence. "Shay," she went on, "you had known her before, hadn't you?"

"Young Fairbanks," said Shay, "talks too much. Yes, since you want the not-too-sordid details. I met her in a bar, a very respectable bar; but you know how such things go. We got to talking, the way one does in a bar, and one thing led to something else. I got to know her rather well; so well, in fact, that Papa threw me out on my ear. Hence the assignation at Amos'."

"Yes, I see." Emma was willing to skip that part. "What is she like? I mean, did she really go after her boots and why did she leave them in Amos' room?"

"That's what she said. I think she got the wind up when she found you all over at Amos' and was so jittery for fear Amos would find out about us that she didn't know what she was doing. As it turned out it was a good thing you came out, because Eunice says one of the servants squealed to Papa and he wasn't in Worcester at all; he was hanging around waiting to put the peek on us."

"Oh, so that's why he didn't go to Worcester."

"If he hadn't found a howling mob at Amos' he'd probably have come busting in with a shotgun."

"But if she loves you"—Emma was puzzled—"why does she care who knows it?"

"She doesn't love me," said Shay. "I'm excitement; I'm adventure; I'm different."

Emma put her hand on Shay's arm. "I'm sorry. If you love her, I mean."

Shay looked down at her. "Not being a man," he said, "you may not understand this. I'm in love with her but I've been in love before. When Eunice gets bored and throws me over, as she undoubtedly will, I shall fall in love again. My sustaining philosophy of life is that there is always another pretty face just around the corner. I have known moments of anguish when the pretty faces turned out to have bow-legs or a bad disposition or another fellow; but I always get over it. Hi, ho for the open road, and all that sort of thing. Don't worry about me and don't worry about Eunice. With the addition of Amos' shekels I'll replace awful easy."

"Did Hank tell you"—Emma wasn't liking Eunice any better for Shay's description of their relationship—"about the Staffordshire figure? "

Shay, cutting out around a truck, only nodded.

"What did she take it for, another thrill?"

"Sure. I tell you she's nuts."

"She's greedy and hateful and deceitful and—and not very nice. I think she killed Amos and I'm not going to let her get that place away from me."

Shay took a quick look at Emma. In her righteous indignation she was almost as prim as Mrs. Leavitt. Women were peculiar creatures. Emma would suspect Eunice of murder because she didn't like her morals; but it seemed not to occur to Emma what some people would construe from the fact that Amos had recently made a new will.

"Have you any idea," Shay asked cautiously, "why Amos left you that place?"

"Oh yes," said Emma. "It's perfectly simple, now that I think about it. Amos didn't like the Chandlers and he had a horror of museums. Too many museums, I mean. He said that possessions were made for people, to be used and worn out and replaced. I guess that he'd been told once too many times as a child to keep his hands off Great-grandfather's shaving mug. He knew I liked old furniture, but I don't think he would have cared whether I lived with it or sold it. He just wanted the place to stay alive."

"Well, of course, if you put it that way."

"What other way is there to put it?"

"Don't be goofy." Shay was exasperated. "That will is only a week old; if Amos thought he was going to marry you, of course he'd will you the property."

"Amos didn't know he was going to marry me," said Emma. "Eunice Chandler was the only one who knew that and she didn't know it until the night Amos was killed. Put that in your pipe and smoke it."

Shay slowed down the speed of the car in order that the irony of his words might not be lost. "I'm just a stranger here," he remarked, "but, leaving Eunice out of this for a minute, isn't it customary for both parties to an engagement to know about it?"

"I suppose I might as well tell you"—Emma was thoughtful—"but you have to promise not to tell Hank. It was this way: Eunice made me so mad, that night out at the farm, twitting me about chasing Amos that I just up and told her I was going to marry him and she could like it or lump it. Did you ever do anything like that? Just say something you didn't mean at all, I mean, because you were mad?"

"Frequently," said Shay. "Is that honestly all there was to it?"

"Positively."

"Pardon me if I'm being too bold, but what about that kissing in the parlor?"

"That wasn't so good," Emma admitted. "I went down to talk to him, just as I told you, and I guess he'd had one too many drinks or maybe he did want to marry me, I don't know. Anyhow, he got all puffy and snorty and said it didn't make any difference about Jeff and grabbed me and kissed me. Now I ask you, what was a girl to do, scream?"

"You'd been kissed before," said Shay. "Didn't that give you any ideas?"

"Kissing's funny." Emma ignored him. "A lot of people kiss me and it doesn't make any difference—you, for instance—"

"Thanks," said Shay dryly. "I wasn't really trying."

"I suppose"—in the full flood of confession Emma became thoroughly honest—"I'd been sort of impressed by Amos all along, because he was older and handsomer and not silly like you and Hank. And then Jeff and Hank started kidding me about him and I got self-conscious and wondered if he really was in love with me and what it would be like to be married to him and so on. Amos never gave himself away, though, and I couldn't find out how he felt, and that got me a little steamed up too. But when he kissed me, and I knew he meant it, and that I could probably marry him if I wanted to I didn't like it at all; and I was ashamed of the way I'd been acting—sort of leading him on, you know, just to get a rise out of Hank—and oh, damn, look at the mess."

"You could write it up for the movies," said Shay. "What happened next? What did you do when he kissed you?"

"Does it matter?"

"I don't know. I just thirst for facts, like your friend Fairbanks."

"I said for him not to be silly and ran upstairs. And you're not to tell my friend Fairbanks anything about this."

"Why, in the name of heaven, didn't you tell him yourself?"

"How could I, there in front of everybody?"

"I see what you mean; but you could have explained it to him afterward."

"He could have trusted me then."

"You don't expect much, do you?"

They were well into the city by now and the heat was upon them again, radiating from the pavements and the buildings.

"Judas," said Shay, "I thought it was hot in the country."

"Want to go swimming?"

They both laughed. Then Shay put his arm around Emma and kissed her.

"Grade A, brotherly kiss," he said and then he kissed her again.

This time the kiss wasn't so brotherly and Emma, stiffening, drew back. Shay shouldn't kiss her like that, not when he knew how she felt about Hank, not when he had just finished telling her that he loved Eunice. Emma was silent the rest of the way home.

They turned into Emma's street, in a quarter where rows of two-story eighteenth-century houses had not quite been elbowed out of existence by hotels and office buildings. Emma had an apartment over a grocery store run by an elderly and very French Frenchman. Emma liked her house in winter because it had two fireplaces with delicate mantels and warm-looking yellow-painted pine floors; and because the grocery store was handy on cold nights when she did not want to eat out. In summer she was forced to admit that the pine floors were always dusty, the fireplaces were useless and the odors from the grocery store were distinctly noticeable. In spite of these drawbacks, she stayed on because M. Lebotien was a lenient and unobtrusive landlord and because there was a convenient alley beside the house where she could park her roadster. Usually she was content, but tonight Emma wished that she had a lofty air-conditioned penthouse whose broad rooms were only sparsely furnished with cool, smooth furniture that would not remind her of the trumpet-turned highboys and the Spanish-foot chairs of which she was now the possessor.

"Good night," she said rather coolly as Shay stopped in front of her house.

"Good night," said Shay. "Write when you get work."

Chapter 16

EMMA got out the key to the front door and let herself in. In the daytime Emma and M. Lebotien let in each other's visitors with phlegmatic impartiality.

Whew! Just as Emma had thought, the little hall was stifling and smelled more than mildly of garlic and sausage. As she started up the stairs M. Lebotien opened the door of his shop and spoke to her. He wore carpet slippers, an old velveteen jacket and a muffler. Emma wondered if he had been sitting in his own icebox.

"Good evening," said M. Lebotien.

"Good evening," said Emma.

"About an hour ago," M. Lebotien went on, "there was a young man here to see you."

For one happy moment Emma thought that it had been Hank, come to tell her that he didn't believe what she had said about Amos. But, "A strange young man," said M. Lebotien, "very correct."

That would be Eddie, Emma thought, glad that she had missed him. She didn't feel up to Eddie tonight.

"He said he would return"—M. Lebotien thus blasted her hopes —"and a special-delivery package also arrived."

"Thank you," said Emma. "Golly, isn't it hot?"

"Have you ever been in Indochina?"

Emma shook her head.

"It is hot there, but one manages; the real cause of the war is that both the Japanese and the Germans want Indochina."

"If it's any hotter than this," said Emma, "they can have it."

M. Lebotien looked pained; Emma usually listened attentively to his pronouncements on international affairs. Because he liked Emma and because he knew of the murders from the papers he ventured a personal remark: "Things do not go so well?"

"Things go swell," said Emma. "I've just been left a farm and about a quarter of a million dollars' worth of furniture."

"Alors," said M. Lebotien, his eyes sparkling, "a farm."

"Yes," said Emma, "a farm, and the Japs and the Germans can have that, too, because it cost more than it's worth."

With this generous offering Emma went upstairs, leaving M. Lebotien shaking his head.

The package leaned against the door, address to the wall; Emma picked it up, unlocked her door, put the package on the desk and opened doors and windows, not because the air outside was any cooler but because she hoped it was different. She stumbled over a candle-stand, delicate, with tiny spade feet, that she had persuaded Jeff to sell her at cost and then left in the middle of the room because she could not decide where to put it. What did she want with a maple candle-stand? she thought viciously; she didn't have to buy odds and ends now out of her salary, she had mahogany stands with eagle inlay. She switched on the light and looked around her. Who wanted an Empire sofa, even if it were a swan-necked one, well carved and graceful? Sheraton, Chippendale—she could take her choice from the best. The piecrust table that she had bought when she couldn't afford it had a mended foot; the wing chair had a new stretcher. All the savor had gone out of her own peculiar possessions; beside the furniture in Amos' house, her own looked mended and second-rate. Only her desk stood up under the comparison. Fondly her eye traveled over its gleaming blocked-out front, over the solid lid to the intricate, many-drawered interior. That was her very own and it was as good as anything Amos possessed; she had found it in a carriage shed, miraculously protected from a broken window by the discarded top of a surrey. It had all its brasses, even the heavy ones on the ends for lifting. Repair for one drawer and polishing had been all it needed. She touched it and was reassured by its perfection.

She turned the package over and saw that it was from Jeff, just as she heard M. Lebotien at the door say that she had only that moment come in. Why hadn't she told him that she was going to bed and didn't want any visitors? Through the still-open door she saw Eddie coming up the stairs, trim, shaven and spotless.

"Hello," she said, not very graciously. "Come in."

"Hello," said Eddie. "I just stopped by; I hope you don't mind. Funerals are rather depressing, and I thought perhaps—"

Emma smiled at him. He meant to be kind. "Take off your coat," she said, "you'll die in here."

"That's it," said Eddie. "I thought perhaps you'd like to go out somewhere where it's cool."

"Swimming?" asked Emma wickedly.

"My God, no," Eddie said quickly. "Excuse me. I say, that was pretty awful, wasn't it?"

"We were dogs to go off and leave you like that. Look, Jeff's sent me a present and it's not even my birthday. Well, will you look at that?"

Eddie looked over her shoulder. Across one corner of the package was carefully printed DO NOT OPEN UNTIL CHRISTMAS and underneath Jeff's name was the address Rockingham, heavily underscored.

"Jeff isn't supposed to be in Rockingham," said Emma, and then added quickly, "What do you suppose is in it?"

"I wouldn't know," said Eddie. "Does it rattle?"

Emma shook the package and prodded it. No rattle. She put it down and looked at it.

"Well, I'll be darned," she said finally.

"Are you going to do what it says, not open it until Christmas?"

"My goodness gracious, no, I'd go crazy before then, only I can't imagine why he sent it or what's in it." Emma turned the package over, peered at it, smelled it.

"Well, then," said Eddie, "why don't you open it?"

"You're making fun of me," said Emma, "and you're just as curious as I am. Got a knife?"

Eddie hadn't but the desk yielded a pair of scissors. When Emma had cut the string she paused. "Maybe I shouldn't," she said. "Maybe it's like Pandora's box and something dreadful will come out."

"You could put it away in a drawer," Eddie suggested, "and pretend it had never come."

"Not me, I couldn't. Here goes."

The box inside the paper was about nine by twelve and said "Munsing Wear" on its end. That was not illuminating.

"I bet it's a pair of wool socks," said Emma.

"But you don't wear wool socks."

Sometimes, Emma thought as she lifted out tissue paper, the gap where Eddie's sense of humor should have been was irritatingly noticeable.

"Oh," she said and tried to put the tissue paper back.

But Eddie had seen it. "What is it?" he asked. "It looks like a salt shaker."

"Yes," Emma repeated, "it looks like a salt shaker." For there in the tissue paper, the light twinkling from its little finial, the fluting and the quadrooned foot, lay the Coney muffineer.

"Take it out," Eddie urged, "and let's see what it looks like. It looks like a wedding present."

Without answering, Emma handed him the muffineer. She didn't know what to do or say, for the significance of the word "Rockingham" had suddenly come to her. Instead of going straight to Maine, Jeff had gone up to Rockingham for the Fourth of July races. If she had only thought of that in time she would have heeded the warning on the outside of the package. That was why Jeff had put it there and why Rockingham was underscored; that was why Jeff had sent the package to the house instead of the shop. He had done his best to have her receive the muffineer in private and unwrap it only under favorable circumstances and she hadn't caught on at all. She was a stupid dolt and what was she going to tell Eddie that would put him off the track?

"I've got it," Emma began; "it isn't a present at all, it's something he picked up and he sent it back so he wouldn't have to carry it around with him."

"Oh, it's old, is it?" Eddie asked. He turned the muffineer over. "J.C.," he read. "What does 'J.C.' stand for?"

"John Coney," said Emma without thinking.

Eddie put the muffineer down on the desk as though it were red hot.

"'It looks like a salt shaker,'" he quoted. "That's what they said about the muffineer that was missing from Currier's silver and they called it the Coney muffineer." He looked accusingly at Emma. "Is this what you call a muffineer?"

"Yes," said Emma because he could easily find out. "But it doesn't have to be a Coney muffineer. J.C. could stand for John Coburn or Jonathan Clark or—or Jesse Cox." (Emma wasn't sure about Jesse Cox, but the others were real enough.) "There are lots of J. C.s and they made lots of muffineers, lots and lots, and people liked them. They're really quite common and this must be one that Jeff found in Rockingham and sent down for me to sell. Now if it were only a Revere piece—" Eddie wouldn't know, she thought, that by craftsmen Coney was esteemed as highly as Revere.

"I don't understand it at all," Eddie said dubiously. "You say Jeff isn't supposed to be in Rockingham—"

Emma silently cursed herself for that slip.

"—but he is and he sends you a muffineer that could be a Coney muffineer. You say it isn't worth much but Mr. Chandler made an awful fuss about the one that was missing. I really don't know what to think."

Emma wanted to suggest that he mind his own business and not think about it at all but she was afraid that wouldn't work.

"If this could be identified as the missing muffineer"—Eddie was going on slowly—"perhaps it would help catch the thief—of course I don't mean Jeff," Eddie added hastily as he caught Emma's hostile look, "but perhaps he bought it from the thief. I think Miss Chandler ought to be told about it."

"Why Miss Chandler?" Emma wanted to know.

"Because, of course, it's hers now."

"Because nothing," said Emma, seeing a loophole out of the difficulty. "If this is Amos' muffineer it's mine now, and if it's mine I don't have to do anything about it."

"What do you mean it's yours?"

"Just," said Emma sweetly, "that Amos left the farm and the furnishings to me."

"What?" Eddie plainly couldn't believe his ears. "You mean he didn't leave everything to Eunice Chandler?"

"Nope." Emma felt that she was enjoying her bequest for the first time. "I get the farm and the knickknacks; Eunice gets the rest of the estate."

Eddie sat down in the mended wing chair.

"You get the house and everything in it?"

Emma nodded.

"But Eunice gets the rest of the estate?"

"That's it."

"Whew," said Eddie. "I shall have to think this over."

"It is rather a surprise, isn't it?" Emma couldn't help feeling a little complacent. "Rags to riches. Shopgirl to chatelaine. At least," she added, "that'll be in the way it'll be in the papers."

"Why, it's swell," said Eddie finally, "we certainly ought to celebrate."

They put the muffineer in a drawer and went to the Ritz. There were no fried nightingale's tongues but Eddie ordered champagne.

Chapter 17

IT MIGHT HAVE BEEN the excitement of the day followed by chicken Tetrazzini and champagne that would not let Emma sleep that night; it might have been her fear that Eddie had not been convinced by her explanation of the identity of the muffineer; it might have been the realization that Eddie was a nice boy but that she would not trade an evening of his company and all the champagne in the world for ten minutes with Hank; it might, of course, have been the heat.

Emma lay on her back and wondered what Jeff was doing with Amos' muffineer, why he had taken it from the desk drawer and why he had sent it to her. The immediate danger of arrest having abated, Emma felt that Jeff should come home and do a little explaining. But the jaunt to Rockingham—here Emma rolled over onto her left side— had delayed his start for Maine and therefore his return, for who knew what other detours he might think up?

Emma punched her pillow and wished that she had an atlas so that she could figure out where he would go next. If he left early the next morning it would take him half a day to get to North New Portland. It probably wouldn't take him very long to find out that he had been hoaxed, and then he would come flying back ready to break her into small bits. But even if he didn't get jailed for speeding, she couldn't expect him before sometime Friday afternoon and Emma did not think that she could carry the burden of the muffineer alone until Friday. But suppose he had left Rockingham right after the races? Suppose he hadn't? Well, then he was still there.

Emma rolled over on her right side, picked up the phone and dialed long distance.

"I want," she said when she got the operator, "to talk to Mr. Jefferson Graham, who is somewhere in Rockingham. If there are two hotels there, he's in the most expensive one."

Emma got up and got a drink of water and was raising the screen on the fire-escape window for M. Lebotien's dog-eared yellow tomcat

197

when the phone rang. She flew to answer it, thinking that the operator was going to get an earful when Jeff replied to her explanation of
why it was not necessary for him to go to North New Portland. But
Jeff was not in Rockingham; he had checked out of the hotel, she was
informed, at two forty-seven and had left no forwarding address. There
would be a ten-cent charge for the report.

Emma said thank you and composed herself for sleep. If Jeff had
left Rockingham at two forty-seven, where would he be now? She supposed he would sleep somewhere. Exactly where was Rockingham
anyhow? Maybe she ought to buy an atlas—Rocking-ham, Rock-ing-
ham; it was a silly name if you said it over times enough but it didn't
seem to put you to sleep. A silly name for a town and a silly name for
a horse.

Emma sat bolt upright in bed. If Jeff had checked out of the hotel at quarter of three he hadn't been at the races. And Tiny Bloom's
message hadn't been a tip on a horse, it had meant for Jeff to go to
Rockingham. What for? Had Jeff tried to sell the muffineer quickly
and, failing that, returned it to her? Emma didn't like that; it made it
look as though Jeff had wanted to get rid of the muffineer. But "1st,"
the other part of the message, could have meant First Street or the
first dealer in the phone book or to take the first offer. Emma didn't
like any of it and she would have to wait until Jeff got back from Maine
before she could find out.

Now she never would sleep a wink. Maybe aspirin would help.
Emma got up and went into the living room to look for her bag. The
aspirin was in the bag, right enough, but Emma didn't take it out.
Instead she took the leather-bound diary that had been Miss Currier's.
That would put her to sleep fast enough, if the opening entry was any
sample. Emma paused for a last admiring look at her desk and then
went back to bed.

She adjusted the light, wadded the pillows up behind her and
went back to a cold day in January 1875.

Jan. 6 (read the diary). *Still cold. Ma rubbed my chest with goose grease
last night because I coughed; but I got up after I had gone to bed and scrubbed
it off. Very cold in my room, but goose grease smells bad. Coasted after school.*

*Jan. 7. One of the sows littered yesterday and Pa fixed a place for them in
the woodshed next to the chimney. Ma was mad and said the neighbors would
say we kept the pig in the parlor, but Pa said the pigs would freeze in the sty.
The little pigs are very clean.*

Hurray for Pa, thought Emma, almost shivering out of sympathy
for the pigs.

Jan. 8.I do not seem to write the right things in my diary. Mr. Wilson says that one should write one's highest thoughts and not the trivialities of every day. I do not seem to have very high thoughts. Nellie went out to the end of the shed and stayed until the dishes were wiped, so I would not help her with her algebra and she told Ma that I scrubbed off the goose grease. She put some more on.

Jan. 9. Mr. Wilson called me up after school to talk about my essay but he kept his head turned away all the time. I think he smelled the goose grease. I still cough. Amos (that would be Amos' father) *has the mumps.*

Time fell away from Emma. She forgot her worries, forgot the heat, so absorbed did she become in the trivialities of life in a bygone era, trivialities that crept in in spite of the writer's noble efforts at higher thoughts. After the first flush of enthusiasm the entries in the diary were irregular, but they recorded the important events of a life that was full, vigorous and normal.

The little pigs, when Ma permitted, were dressed in doll clothes by the younger Nellie and played with in the kitchen; there were taffy pulls and sleigh rides; Mr. B. the minister—a mothy man, Amy described him—came to supper and so did the schoolteacher, Mr. Wilson. A little brother Frank arrived with modest suddenness, and Amy, celebrating her sixteenth birthday, was allowed by Ma to put her hair up.

As she read Emma began to develop an active dislike for Mr. Wilson because he turned out to be a sissy and because of his interference with young Amy's literary style; but by the end of the school year it became apparent that to Amy he had become not only her urge to higher thoughts but the object of a very sincere, if youthful, affection that was in part reciprocated.

May 16 (read the entry for the last day of school). *Mr. Wilson is going to tutor in Cambridgeport. He pressed my hand when I said good-by and said that the summer would be very long. For me it will be interminable.*

The interminable summer was not recorded in the diary, but with the opening of the Academy in the fall it became apparent that something was wrong. The entries took a decidedly religious turn with speculation as to early death and the life hereafter. It was not until the Thanksgiving entry that the little tragedy came out.

"No school yesterday," said the diary, "Mr. W. left early for Cambridgeport to visit his intended. Oh, death, where is thy sting?"

The louse! Emma thought, so he got himself another girl, did he? She did not laugh; she was too absorbed in the story and she was in the mood to be sympathetic with unrequited love.

With the winter Amy's cough came back and this time it did not yield to goose grease. Finally: "I write this in bed. The doctor says that I have consumption. I hope it is the galloping kind." But Amy was disappointed, for in January 1876 she wrote: "It seems that one does not die of a broken heart. It is rather nice to lie here. I read a great deal. Ma says that I will hurt my eyes, but eyes were made for looking and surely it hurts no more to look at words than out of the window at the belfry of the Academy."

At this point a large tear splashed from Emma's eye onto the yellow page. She sniffled and read on.

The mothy minister turned out to be rather nice. His visits were anticipated because he brought books and discussed them with the invalid; books that were not mothy—books that substituted new visions for the sight of the Academy belfry and new ideas for the inward turned thoughts. By spring Amy was able to write: "Mr. W. here today. I had never thought to bear the notion of his marriage so equably. "

The cough was better but Amy stayed in bed. Her legs, she wrote, would not support her and she felt safer in bed. After six months in bed it seemed reasonable that she would be weak, but her strength would have come back to her if she had not feared, probably unconsciously, a repetition of the hurt that the outside world had given her. She excused herself with the doctor's diagnosis of "weak lungs" and became in the mind of her family and herself a confirmed invalid— an invalid who withdrew more and more into herself, relying more on books than on her family for enjoyment, becoming increasingly critical of both. Whitman she admired for his rhythms but she caviled at his concept of democracy. Poe and De Quincy seemed to have been her especial favorites.

Of her family, she thought Amos opinionated and Nelly silly. Frank, her favorite, died of "inflammation of the bowels."

Prosaically, the invalid shelled peas, wrote labels for the preserves and helped with the sewing; but she did it with a book propped at her elbow or with her eyes out the window noting the progress of the seasons in the fields below her.

With Christmas of the year 1878 the diary broke off and the next entry, undated and cryptic, was in a more mature hand. It was simply: "Sent it off." Then, "Mr. B says not to despair so I have sent it off again."

What, Emma wondered, was going on?

"A very nice note from Mr. Howells. He does not feel that the

Atlantic can use the poem but asks to see more of my writing."

Amy had written a poem.

"Acting on Mr. B's advice, I sent the essay, 'Juncoes in Snow.' Back without comment."

Then there was a list of titles, whether of poems or essays, Emma could not tell: *Meditations from a Window, The Smell of Clover, Some German Poets, On Lying in Bed, First Love* and *The Cider Press.* Beside each title were check marks: four, five or, in the case of *Cider Press,* eight representing the departure and return of manuscript.

Then there was the date March 10, 1896, in large letters, surrounded by flourishes and stars, and, following it, *"Argosy* accepted my story of the experience of Captain Amos with the Hottentot chieftain which I had thought so fanciful and outlandish as to be almost unworthy. They ask for more stories of similar adventures. I had not thought to write in that vein but I find the cheque very beautiful."

There followed a problem in multiplication, from which the writer deduced that if she sold ten stories at fifteen dollars a story she would be the proud possessor of one hundred and fifty dollars. Emma rejoiced with her, conscious of the triumph and justification that the sale of the first story must have been. She yawned sleepily and ran her eye down another list of titles of which few were followed by the fatal check mark.

The Scottish Skipper.

Typhoon—Maybe the estate could sue the Conrad estate.

An Adventure with the Malay Pirates.

The Eating of the Sacred Cow—Emma bet that was a corker.

A Chinese Gentleman—Around the world with Captain Amos, Emma thought.

Mystery on the Barque Mary Harris.

Emma turned out the light and went to sleep to dream that a cannibal chief would have stuffed her in a boiling pot except for the intervention of Miss Amy. This was, of course, directly traceable to the champagne or, perhaps, the heat.

Chapter 18

WHEN HANK OPENED HIS EYES the first thing he saw was the picture of Slocomb. This seemed appropriate since Slocomb was responsible for all his aches and pains. He moved his head and was lost again in a black cloud of dizziness.

"Thank God, he's coming to."

This time Hank opened only one eye, carefully, and saw Ellis bending over him. Ellis looked worried, Hank thought, but nowhere near worried enough. Hank wanted to say, "Did you get him?" but the words wouldn't come out. He shut his eyes and lay very still because his head hurt so much that the rest of him felt pretty good.

"He's gone again," he heard another voice say. "I told you we ought to call a doctor."

Hank groaned as an arm was thrust underneath his head. "Drink this," he heard Miss Currier's voice say, felt a glass pressed to his mouth and drank.

He hadn't expected whiskey. He spluttered, coughed and sat up. "What the Sam Hill?" he muttered thickly.

"Mr. Fairbanks, I hadn't any idea it was you. It scared the living daylights out of me when I see who I'd hit."

Hank braced his head with his hands and looked up. He saw Ellis, with his thumb hooked in his belt, Miss Currier, still in her shawl and holding a glass, and finally Durrell, ashen and contrite, literally wringing his hands, his fat jowls quivering as he tried to explain.

"Ellis thought maybe, if he said there wasn't going to be anyone here tonight, something might happen. So we come over soon as it got dark and he was going to watch by the road and I was going to watch from the gazebos—"

It was a fine idea, Hank thought ruefully, only it wasn't very original.

"—only Sally was late coming with the supper and we got talking and then we saw Miss Amy come down, and then I just thought maybe

202

I better come around here and, by gum, just as I come around the corner I thinks I see this feller pull a gun so I let him have it, and then it turns out to be you and, by cracky, I'm sorry."

"It's a good thing I gave him the club instead of the gun," said Ellis.

Hank nodded agreement and then wished he hadn't for he lurched sideways and everything swam before him.

"Steady on," said Ellis, bending to catch him.

"I'm all right," Hank said after a minute, "if I just sit still."

"I'm awful sorry," Ellis went on. "I should have told you what I was going to do. I was going to this morning but you got me all riled up "

"Forget it," said Hank; "I was mad too."

"It's my fault," said Durrell; "I'm just a numskull that's got no business trying to be a detective. All I know about is hogs and insurance."

"I—I think I'll sit down," said Miss Currier. She sank into the chair by the desk and took a sip from the glass still in her hand. "For my heart," she explained. Then, "If Mr. Fairbanks is feeling better, I suppose I better tell you what I was doing when this regrettable incident happened."

Hank motioned for her to go ahead.

"On the third of January my late nephew allowed the Currier silver to go on display in a loan exhibit at the Boston Museum. Mr. Graham persuaded him to do it, though Amos cared little for such things and had refused Mr. Lloyd Chandler permission to display the silver in Worcester. I had, of course, the highest regard for the museum's integrity but I had not at that time met Mr. Graham and I persuaded my nephew to make a list of the silver. He promised me that he would do so, and when the silver came back said that he had checked the list and that the museum hadn't stolen a thing, that was his idea of a joke. There has been so much said about the inventory that I wonder I didn't think of this before; I suppose I thought Amos had destroyed the list—" She paused and peered at her three listeners to see, Hank thought, if they believed her.

"Tonight it occurred to me that the list might be in his desk. If I had seen his desk before I would have known it. I don't think he ever threw anything away. But no matter. Eventually I found what I was looking for—" She paused again and looked from face to face, as though expecting some comment.

"Did you think something else was missing besides the muffineer?" Ellis asked cautiously.

"There was a little silver box in the parlor," said Miss Currier. "It should have been in the silver cupboard. That just made me wonder if anything else might be gone."

"Well?"

"If Amos didn't lie to me, and I don't think he ever did, though mercy knows he had plenty of opportunity, a Revere marrow spoon and a Hurd cream pitcher are missing from the silver that came back from the exhibition."

"You say Mr. Graham persuaded Amos to take those things to Boston?" Durrell asked slowly.

Miss Currier nodded.

"Then he knew all about it?"

"See here." Hank forced himself to speak. "If that silver was on exhibition a lot of people saw it."

"Yes," said Ellis. "But don't forget that Graham knew where it came from and would know how to get rid of it. I'll go to every dealer in Boston and make them talk."

"The pieces wouldn't have been sold in Boston," Hank explained; "and I know from watching the antics of my late lamented uncle that once a piece goes down the maw of some collectors it never sees the light of day again. You'll have a sweet job trying to trace them."

"Maybe they're still in his shop," said Ellis, "or his house—Rawlins would know where that is. I'll go see him first thing in the morning, and if we can trace one piece to Mr. Jefferson Graham—" He stopped suggestively.

"My goodness me," said Miss Currier.

"Where's that list?" Ellis asked quickly.

"Why, I don't know." Miss Currier looked around vaguely. "It must be in the dining room; I must have dropped it when you came in."

Ellis went into the dining room; then they heard the creak of the swinging door and his heavy steps in the buttery; then he was back. "I can't find it," he said shortly. "Are you sure you didn't go anywhere else or bring it in here?"

"Now, let me see—did I go into the kitchen? I guess I did because I thought of tea before I thought of the whiskey. Did you look in the kitchen?"

Ellis went to the kitchen, muttering, and Durrell said, "Think, Miss Amy, try to think what you did with it."

Miss Currier shook her head. "The excitement, you know, has driven it clear out of my mind."

Ellis came back empty-handed; had it not been for the chastening events of the early evening, he might have been sterner, but even he could not fail to see that Miss Currier was nearly exhausted. Her head drooped and her hands shook against the shawl.

"Look," Ellis said, "will you hunt for it in the morning and call me if you find it; but just in case you don't, tell me again what is missing."

Miss Currier gathered herself together with an effort. "The Revere pitcher and the Hurd spoon—"

"Miss Amy." Durrell spoke quickly. "That's not what you said before. You said the Revere spoon and the Hurd pitcher."

"Oh, did I?" Miss Currier's voice was so weak as to be hardly audible. "I don't really remember. It's the silver box in the parlor that's important."

Durrell and Ellis exchanged glances. She was old, they said to each other, and though normally pretty bright for her age, she tired easily.

"I've got to go home," said Hank.

Miss Currier seemed to come to life. "You'll do nothing of the kind," she said. "You'll stay right here, and then when it's light I'll call the doctor. We had a hired man once that got kicked by a horse, but doctors get called enough at night as it is."

Durrell came close to Hank. "You better do as she says," he said, his face turned from Miss Currier. "You want I should stay with you?"

Hank shook his head. All he wanted was not to have to move or think.

"I shall stay right here in this chair," said Miss Currier. "He'll be all right."

Ellis and Durrell went out. Hank lay back and did not know presently whether the pain in his head was dream or delirium. Miss Currier waited until there was enough light outdoors to see that there was no one around the house. Then she went to the kitchen and pulled a wadded-up ball of blue paper from the pocket of her dress. She spread out the ball and burned it in the kitchen sink, carefully washing the charred scraps down the drain. Then she called the doctor.

The doctor said concussion. Mrs. Leavitt came, and between them they got Hank up to the front bedroom and into the Chippendale bed. Hank did not seem to care much what happened to him. He slept most of Thursday, rousing only occasionally. But Friday morning he startled Mrs. Leavitt by asking her what had happened to the china figure that used to be on the mantel in the dining room.

Mrs. Leavitt wasn't sure whether or not he was yet rational but she thought it best to humor him.

"Why," she said, "I knocked that off when I was house-cleaning but, praises be, it lit in the scrub bucket instead of on the hearth. It scared me so, though, that I put it up in the buttery cupboard so's I wouldn't do it again."

Had she seen it lately?

Mrs. Leavitt wasn't sure.

Would she please go and look?

Mrs. Leavitt came back with the report that the figure was there right enough.

Had Eunice Chandler visited her great-aunt at any time since the murders when Mrs. Leavitt had not been present?

Yes, Mrs. Leavitt remembered mention of at least one visit.

"Fine," said Hank, "things are shaping up; all I needed was a fresh viewpoint. Or perhaps, as one of my former friends has often said, I think best in a horizontal position.

"Now"—Hank folded his hands demurely on his chest—"go away. I have some more thinking to do."

At noon Hank awoke with the feeling that someone was watching him. The room was dark because the shutters were closed, the thick wooden shutters that shut out light and sound. Hank raised his head and saw Miss Currier sitting by the door, her hands folded on the top of the ebony cane. Her hair was silver in the shaft of light. Silver, always silver; muffineers and boxes. It was wonderful what rest in bed did for one.

"You think you're cute, don't you?" he asked.

"If you're quite rational and not trying to be complimentary"— Miss Currier rose and went over to the bed—"I want to talk to you. I knew that Amos was going to change his will; it hadn't anything to do with this."

"Do you," asked Hank, "object to a large telephone bill?"

Chapter 19

EMMA AWOKE the next morning with the feeling that she had made a great discovery. She lay looking at the ceiling, trying to recall what it was.

"Mystery on the Mary Harris," she said finally. "Imagine."

She reached for the phone to call Hank and remembered that he wouldn't be speaking to her. She got up, took a cold tub and dressed, examining her new idea carefully before she jumped to any conclusions. It was too hot to make coffee; she drank some tomato juice and gnawed at a hard roll. She would be late to work but it didn't matter; Jeff wasn't there and he was in no position to criticize her. She reminded herself that she must get some butter, went to collect her bag from the top of the desk and stopped in her tracks, overpowered with the good fortune of not one but two discoveries. She knew where the inventory was. It was as plain as the nose on your face, only you had to know about desks to think of it. She wrapped a pair of shoes that needed reheeling in the paper from Jeff's package and went downstairs feeling very pleased with herself.

By the time she got to the shop she was so puffed up at her own cleverness that she half expected to rise buoyantly into the air. She had to tell someone so she forgave Shay his osculatory enthusiasm and called his room.

"Olson's grocery," came a sleepy voice.

"Listen, Shay, I know where the inventory is and Miss Currier writes detective stories—"

"But I read about it in her diary. She took to her bed and never got up, like Hank's great-aunt who went to Baden for a broken heart and died there when she was ninety-seven—"

"No, you dolt, Hank's aunt didn't write detective stories, but Miss Currier does. She tried for the *Atlantic* and wound up in the pulps. And you know she doesn't talk like an old lady and she said it was in the desk—"

"Sure, it does tricks like mine—"

"Well, I haven't given up Eunice entirely, but right now I think it was Miss Currier and I'm going out there Saturday—"

"I'm not scared. You heard her invite me."

"No, I can't tonight. I'm going out with Eddie. I'm on a champagne diet—"

"Good-by. I've got company."

Mr. Finegold and Mrs. Garfinkle were coming into the shop. Coming was really too mild a word for it. Mrs. Garfinkle squeezed the bulging confines of her expensive hand-knit through the door and expanded into the shop, brandishing in one hand a purple overlay lamp. Mr. Finegold teetered and hopped excitedly behind her.

"We'll see what she has to say about this." Mrs. Garfinkle advanced on Emma threateningly.

"Good morning," began Emma soothingly.

"This is my lamp." The words were vehement.

Emma wondered if Mrs. Garfinkle had caught Mr. Finegold trying to sell the lamp to someone else. "Why, of course," she said, "Mr. Finegold bought it from me expressly for you."

"There, you see"—Mrs. Garfinkle turned around and nearly crashed the lamp into Mr. Finegold's nose—"you see, she admits it."

"But I'm already telling you"—Mr. Finegold's extended forefinger stabbed the air—"I bought it from her."

"And it's my lamp and you're just as responsible as she is."

"I am telling you"—Mr. Finegold's hands shoved responsibility away from him—"I didn't see your mark, my mark was not on it—"

"Just a minute," said Emma, "if you'd just explain to me what this is all about before you get too excited—"

"Who's excited? Who's excited?" Mr. Finegold hopped up and down. "She is saying it's stolen and I'm responsible."

"Why, that's ridiculous, Jeff bought it himself —"

"Nobody bought it, I tell you it was stolen. See there." Mrs. Garfinkle's fat finger pointed to a bottom corner of the marble base of the lamp where the date 5/18/40 was faintly marked in indelible pencil. "Everything I buy I mark it, and last week, when I come back from Herbie's wedding in Watch Hill, the house in Magnolia has been broken into. This lamp is gone, and a salt glaze plate, and a silver luster sugar bowl that I kept cigarettes in; and now he tries to sell me my own lamp back."

Emma didn't know why on earth she said it. It just popped into her mind and out of her mouth: "Did you have insurance?"

Mr. Finegold stopped jittering and looked at her.

"Not the kind where you get what you paid for it back; Herbie said that was too expensive. Where did you get this lamp?"

"We bought it last Saturday"—Emma bravely included herself in any possible misdemeanor of Jeff's—"but Mr. Graham won't be in today and I can't tell you from whom we purchased it." Emma could almost see the words "stock book" forming in Mr. Finegold's mind, but the lamp wasn't in the stock book. "I'm terribly sorry," she hurried on, "that this has happened, but you mustn't blame Mr. Finegold"—Mr. Finegold looked a little startled to find himself included in the blame—"all of us get hold of stolen things once in a while—some of the runners, you know. You have your lamp back now," Emma went on persuasively, "and of course we wouldn't think of charging Mr. Finegold for it; we'll just take the loss and we'll certainly keep an eye out for those other things, won't we, Mr. Finegold?"

"Oh yes. Yes, yes, yes." Mr. Finegold seemed to have been thinking of something else.

Mrs. Garfinkle appeared to deflate a little. It was true she had her lamp back, which was more than she had expected. She would have to withdraw her claim but she wouldn't have got the price of the lamp anyway. It was better to have the lamp. "You don't suppose it could have been the servants, do you?" she asked.

"I expect your servants have been with you for years," said Emma. "I'm sure it couldn't have been any of them."

Mrs. Garfinkle, who always had trouble with her cooks on account of her nervous stomach, looked pleased. "There are so many people about in the summertime," she said vaguely.

"Exactly," said Emma, edging them toward the door because she had caught sight of Ellis and a man in a blue suit outside the shop window. It wouldn't help Mrs. Garfinkle's opinion of her, she decided, to find out that she was mixed up in a couple of murders. And it wouldn't improve the situation to have Ellis know— She stopped short. Even if Mrs. Garfinkle's lamp had been stolen, Jeff hadn't taken it, any more than he had stolen the muffineer. There was some reasonable explanation for his not entering the lamp in the stock book, if only she could get time to think of it.

"Good-by," she said. "I think Mr. Finegold has a vase about the color of that lamp."

"A vase? Why didn't you tell me?" Mrs. Garfinkle led the way out. "I can use a vase."

"Good morning, Lieutenant." Emma spoke affably, but mentally she had her fingers crossed. Ellis looked too pleased with himself to be up to any good.

"Morning," said Ellis, "this is Mr. Saunders."

"How do you do?" said Emma. "Do you think it's ever going to cool off, and what can I do for you?"

Mr. Saunders extracted a card from his billfold. Ellis sat down on the Chippendale sofa, still with the pleased smirk on his face. She would have to watch out, Emma thought; something was doing.

"I represent"—Mr. Saunders handed over his card—"several insurance companies, among them, Old Cape."

Emma started to say, sweetly but firmly, that they did all their business with Mr. Rawlins, but her eye caught the word "investigator" on the card and she thought of Mrs. Garfinkle's lamp.

"Yes?" she said.

Mr. Saunders seated himself on the sofa and smiled reassuringly.

"I will be brief," he said, "and put the case as simply as possible. The people I represent"—Mr. Saunders looked down modestly—"have had too many losses; losses of a particular kind." Mr. Saunders paused and looked around the shop. "The average policy covering burglary," he went on, "makes no specific mention of antiques. Furnishings are usually listed at a blanket value. Perhaps I am telling you something that you already know? But," Mr. Saunders went on as though unmindful of Emma's murmur of assent, "in the last two years Old Cape has written several policies in which antiques, on the appraisal of an expert, were given full coverage."

Mr. Saunders drew a blue-bordered handkerchief from his pocket and patted his forehead. Emma didn't know what he was getting at but she had the feeling that she wasn't going to like it.

"Some of the people I represent," Mr. Saunders repeated with maddening slowness, "other than Old Cape, have paid a great many claims for burglary, and adjustment has been difficult because the majority of these claims have been for objects said to be antiques and to which it has been felt, in the absence of expert opinion, that the owner attached a sentimental rather than a real value."

Emma felt that she could nod understandingly at this point. Mr. Saunders hadn't accused Jeff of fee splitting, or whatever insurance people called it. Not yet.

Mr. Saunders smiled at Emma. He was smiling as he said, "It has been brought to my attention that those patrons who have taken on full coverage with Old Cape have never been robbed since the taking out of that policy."

Emma jumped to her feet. "How dare you"—her voice quavered with rage—"how dare you come in here and make such an accusation?"

Mr. Saunders shrank back, as people usually did when Emma attacked them, but his expression was one of surprise.

"My dear young lady," he broke in, "I assure you that you have completely misunderstood me. The idea that Mr. Graham had any connection with the robberies had never occurred to me—" He paused and Emma could have kicked herself at the realization that he was mentally adding "—until this minute."

"The embarrassment," Mr. Saunders went on carefully, "is entirely Old Cape's. They felt that the smaller policyholders might consider that they were inadequately protected. No results from previous investigations." Mr. Saunders paused and looked at Ellis.

Emma realized that she had made a blunder. Saunders' words, coming right on top of Mrs. Garfinkle's visit, had tricked her into thinking that Saunders was accusing Jeff of stealing from people whom he could not persuade to buy insurance, that Saunders knew about Mrs. Garfinkle's lamp and that he had heard the rumors of fee splitting at which Mr. Finegold had hinted.

But Saunders couldn't know where Mrs. Garfinkle had found her lamp, even if she had turned in a claim, because she had only just then found out herself, and what the other dealers gossiped about didn't prove anything. Jeff had made enough inventories for Old Cape so that he would be the one to whom they would naturally turn for information; but now, if they did hear about the lamp, they would really be suspicious because she had flown off the handle at a fancied accusation. She was an idiot, and it was certainly up to her to fix things somehow.

"I'm sorry," she said with her most disarming smile. "Of course you know Mr. Graham's reputation as well as I do. You came to us for help and we'll be very glad to do anything we can for you ''

Emma remembered that she had used almost the same words to Mrs. Garfinkle and sounded insincere, even to herself,

"Are you looking for anything in particular?" She hoped he wouldn't mention a purple overlay lamp. "I mean if we're to be on the watch for stolen things we ought to know what we're looking for."

"A Hurd cream pitcher"—Saunders glanced at Ellis—"and a marrow spoon—"

"Revere," said Ellis, "didn't you say?"

"That's it," said Saunders. "Revere."

"Heavens, no," said Emma. "I haven't seen a piece of Revere silver in years. Who lost it? I mean we know most of the silver collectors. Is it Mr. Dwight? Because if it is I can imagine that he's in a hissie."

She stopped because she realized that Saunders was not paying any attention to her; he was looking at Ellis as though waiting for something.

"Yeh?" said Ellis. "Cut out the applesauce. I figured it was Graham but I guess I was barking up the wrong tree. You know as much about antiques as he does; you were the one who was after the old man's stuff; anybody could open that silver cupboard. You did it and you took the muffineer."

"I did not," said Emma.

"No? Then maybe you can explain what it was doing in your apartment?"

From the side pocket of his tunic Ellis produced the Coney muffineer. There was no mistaking it. Emma felt that she would recognize the muffineer if she saw it in China. She was beginning to believe that there was only one muffineer in the world, but she felt that for an inanimate object it got around an awful lot.

"Where did you get that?" she asked weakly.

"Don't kid me." Ellis was very happy. "You know where I got it: out of the top drawer in your desk."

"You can't do that," said Emma. "You have no right—"

"It was quite regular," Saunders explained, "we got a search warrant."

"Come on," said Ellis. "You stole the muffineer, along with the rest of that stuff. What have you done with it? Did you kill Currier? Did you kill Chandler?"

"I did no such thing." Emma was outwardly defiant but she was shaking inwardly. She had been keyed up to defend Jeff; for herself she could think of nothing to say. She couldn't tell them that Jeff had sent her the muffineer; implicate Jeff. And, anyhow, she didn't have the wrapper. She had left it at the cobbler's.

"You can't prove that that is Amos' Coney muffineer," she said finally.

"Oh, yeh? Well, the guy out at the Museum identified it fast enough. Come on, come clean."

"If," said Emma with dignity, "that is the muffineer that you took out of my desk, you can just put it right back. Amos gave it to me." Surely that wasn't lying, Emma thought. Amos had supposed he was giving her that, along with the rest of the things.

Ellis stood up. "Cut it out," he said. "I've got the goods on you; maybe you'll talk better in jail."

Ellis felt that he was proceeding slowly and cautiously, accusing only when he had proof. He didn't have any proof, yet, that she had done the murders, but there was the will.

Emma was thinking fast. She would make one last desperate attempt. If they didn't believe her, she supposed she would have to go to jail and wait till Jeff got back to straighten things out.

"Sit down," she said. "I suppose I might as well tell you, though Jeff wouldn't like me to." That was probably the truth, she thought. She shut her eyes for a moment to beg forgiveness and launched into the realm of pure fiction. "Amos didn't exactly give me that muffineer," she went on, "he gave it to Jeff and me to sell. He wanted some money quick"—nobody was going to believe that, she thought—"and he didn't want anyone to know that he was selling the family silver." Why, she wondered, hadn't she thought to say that Amos had borrowed money and the muffineer was security? Well, it was too late now. "This was way before Amos was killed, but Jeff couldn't find a customer and of course after Amos *was* killed he knew it would look funny for him to have the muffineer, it does to you; and he gave me the muffineer to take care of."

"Why didn't he tell all this when Chandler first discovered the muffineer was missing?"

"And let Chandler and Durrell and Miss Currier know that Amos had been selling the family heirlooms? Jeff wouldn't do a trick like that, particularly when Amos wasn't there to defend himself."

"That's a likely excuse. And, anyhow, Currier didn't need money, he had plenty. That story doesn't hold water. You better put on your hat and—"

"Just a minute," said Saunders, "you don't want to do anything too hastily. It may just be that what Miss Marsh says is true."

Emma gaped at him.

"Huh?" said Ellis.

"Haven't you seen the morning papers?"

"When would I have time?" Ellis was indignant. "I'd seen half-a-dozen people before I met you—"

"Currier didn't have any money. The estate that he left his niece is entirely mythical. Miss Chandler spent yesterday afternoon with the lawyer and is—er—quite disturbed about it."

Ellis looked at Saunders as though betrayed by an ally.

"You're kidding me," Emma said incredulously.

"You might have suspected it," Saunders went on, "if he was selling off his things. Perhaps that's the way he lived and kept up appearances."

Ellis looked crestfallen.

He turned to Emma. "Then that's true, what you just told us about Currier's giving Graham the muffineer to sell?"

Emma took a deep breath. "Absolutely," she said.

"Damn," said Ellis. "I thought I had something."

"Don't be discouraged," said Saunders. "There are lots of other angles." He turned to Emma. "Will you have Mr. Graham get in touch with me when he gets back?"

"I'll be glad to," said Emma fervently. It seemed the least she could do for one who had practically saved her life.

"Yeh, "said Ellis, "and if he's keeping quiet about who killed Currier for fear of hurting the family's feeling, have him get in touch with me."

Outside the door Emma could see Mr. Finegold wavering between his desire to come in and his fear of a uniform. She hoped he didn't have a fresh tale of woe from Mrs. Garfinkle.

"Good day, gentlemen," she said, "any time I can help you—"

"By the way." Emma spoke to Saunders. It had just dawned on her that the two of them had been working together. "That spoon and pitcher you were talking about. Has somebody really lost them or was that part of the game you were playing with me?"

"Why, no." Saunders almost blushed. "He—we thought it would be better if I asked you about them before the muffineer was mentioned."

"They're gone from the cupboard too," said Ellis shortly.

"How do you know? Have you found the inventory? Where was it?"

"No. Not exactly." Ellis was loath to tell what had happened the night before. Hank's accident was partly his fault and he did not wish to admit any errors in front of Saunders. "Miss Currier," he went on, "found a list of silver that had been sent to some exhibition—"

"Why, of course," said Emma. "I remember about that. Amos didn't want to but Jeff made him. I didn't know what was sent and I didn't know there was a list of it, but that'll be a big help, won't it?"

Ellis grunted something, not feeling it necessary to explain that since Miss Currier had promptly lost the list he had no proof of the existence of the pitcher or spoon.

"And now," said Emma, "may I trouble you for the muffineer? I'm not quite sure whether the money from it is going to belong to Eunice or me, and we want to keep everything straight."

Ellis handed over the muffineer without a word and followed Saunders out into the street.

Mr. Finegold tiptoed in, eyebrows raised in question.

"Whoopee," said Emma. "Tell me, did you ever make something up and have it come true?"

"You mean being rich? I am thinking about that all the time but for me it does not come true. Tell me, this furniture that you are getting, is it very good?"

"You've been reading the papers," said Emma accusingly, "when you should have been tending to business. Yes, the furniture is super-colossal, but I can't sell it, even if I wanted to, because there's an old lady who lives there who will probably hang on for years and years, if I don't get her electrocuted in place of me."

"Oh, dear me," said Mr. Finegold, "I don't understand—"

"That makes it unanimous."

"I was afraid," Mr. Finegold began, "when I saw that man from the insurance company, that I had got you in trouble "

"You couldn't," said Emma, "there isn't room for any more."

Mr. Finegold was used to Emma and ignored the interruptions.

"He is coming in the other day," he continued, "asking about a purple lamp, and before I know what I am doing I am telling him about the one I got from you "

"You're a rat," said Emma cheerfully, "but that is such a little fire compared to the large red-hot skillet that I just got out of that I forgive you. Have you seen a customer lately or have they all melted in the heat?"

So Saunders had known about the lamp too. She wondered why he hadn't mentioned it.

Business, Mr. Finegold said, was terrible, but a couple of young men had inquired for her earlier in the morning.

"Reporters, I bet," said Emma. "I hope you told them I had died."

No—Mr. Finegold seemed a little unhappy—he had told them that the shop was closed for the day.

"Honey, you're wonderful," Emma complimented him.

"I didn't know," said Mr. Finegold. "I thought they was customers."

Emma laughed. "You're a crook," she said, "but what do you think of this?" She handed him the muffineer.

Mr. Finegold took it in his hands, touching it softly.

"It's beautiful," he said, his face alight with something that was almost reverence.

"Look"—Emma pointed to the pineapple finial—"and look at the way the bottom swirls around."

"And here"—Mr. Finegold pointed a stubby finger—"the leaves, so delicate."

They beamed at each other.

"How much you are asking for it? Nine hundred? A thousand, maybe?"

"Maybe," said Emma.

"I give you eight hundred cash."

"I'm sorry. I can't sell it. Because why? I don't even know who it belongs to. It might even belong to me."

"Stolen, eh?" Mr. Finegold handed the muffineer back to Emma quickly.

"It was stolen from me this morning, by a policeman."

The phone began to ring and Emma went into the office to answer it. Mr. Finegold started out but paused to call back over his shoulder, "When you find out, remember, eight hundred, cash."

Emma waved him away.

The call was from an acquaintance who had also read the papers and wanted to congratulate Emma. She was discreetly curious for details, and Emma, feeling that it was a reflection on Amos to say that he had no one else to leave his property to, said that he was an old friend.

A reporter called. Emma said that she had no statement to make and that she was leaving the shop immediately. Several customers called, and a competitor. They were all pleased, they said, but Emma couldn't help gathering that they thought the whole affair was a little odd. When Police Lieutenant Donovan called he was inclined to be facetious. "You might as well confess," he said, "you killed Amos for his money."

"I'm a trained nurse," said Emma. "I held Amos' hand and took his temperature through a long and lingering illness."

"That's worse," said Donovan; "either you poisoned his gruel or you made him sign a new will when he was unconscious. Where's your boyfriend?"

"I don't know. If you were on this case you wouldn't be so funny."

"I got a cousin on the force in Cambridge. If the case comes up there, I'll tell him to look out for you. You say you don't know where

Hank is?"

"Probably urging Eunice Chandler to sue me."

"You two had a tiff?"

"Something like that."

"You're old enough to know better."

"Tell that to your chum."

"Sure I will."

"Don't bother. It's all over and I'd almost forgotten about him until you brought it up."

"Tell him to call me when he comes in."

"O.K. but you better not wait. Good-by."

Emma wished that he hadn't brought it up. She had been so elated over getting rid of Ellis that she hadn't, for a time, thought about Hank. She didn't ordinarily see him in the daytime, but it was chilling to know that around five o'clock he would not call up or drop in. If she stopped to think how much she was going to miss him she would burst into tears right then. She wanted to tell him that what she had said about Amos was only literally true and didn't alter their relationship one bit. She wanted to ask him what she should do about the muffineer, for, of course, Ellis would find out that there wasn't a word of truth in what she had told him and she would be in the soup again. She wanted to tell him where the inventory was; maybe that would give him an idea. Ellis seemed to have been having most of the ideas up to now, and she didn't want Hank to come in second, that was, second to Ellis. It would be an awful joke on him, though, if she solved the murders herself. That would, too, justify her taking the furniture as well as keep her out of jail. Then Hank would be sorry he'd ever imagined he could get along without her. Serve him right. Who did he think he was, telling her what to do? She thought they'd had that out once, long before. That had been a little different, though. Emma was forced to concede that concealing evidence was not exactly like saying you'd marry someone, though she would have expected Hank to think it worse.

Well, if she was going to solve the case and make everyone look silly and save her neck, where was she going to begin? Owing to Hank's inertia and Ellis' secretiveness, practically all she knew, except what she had found out for herself, was what she read in the papers.

She shut the doors, on the chance that Jeff might come home suddenly and find them open. Then she sat down in the office to turn over the little knowledge she had. Knowing where the inventory was didn't do her any good unless she had the inventory. But actually what was that going to tell her? Except, perhaps, that something was missing. There were enough things missing now. She'd told Hank about Eunice and the Staffordshire figure but he'd done nothing with that. She'd work on what she had left herself. And what was that? The knowledge that Miss Currier had written one mystery story (probably more, else why the piles of magazines in the trunk?) and the decidedly startling information received from Saunders that Amos didn't have any money. But he had to have had money; he had acted that way and places like his didn't run themselves for nothing. But suppose, just for once, that the paper was right and Amos was broke; who did have the money that had bought her lunches, Amos' expensive-looking clothes, Miss Currier's China tea and Slocomb's oats?

Emma rather imagined that she was the only one who knew the answer. Miss Currier wrote. She had written and she was keeping on writing. She paid the bills, supporting her nephew in the manner to which he was accustomed just so long as she approved his expenditures. And then, Emma whirled along on the wings of her suppositions, Amos got to spending the money in ways that his aunt did not like so she up and bopped him—Emma came to earth with a crash. Why would Miss Currier do that when she held the purse strings? And surely she wouldn't kill Lloyd Chandler because Amos had been squandering her money. But if she found out—say through Mrs. Leavitt— that Amos had been augmenting her stipend by selling off the silver and that Mr. Chandler knew about it, might not family pride compel her to get rid of the culprit and the one who would take malicious pleasure in revealing the disgrace? Emma thought it might. But the Curriers had had money once. What on earth had Amos done with it? Somebody must know. Simultaneously there came to Emma the memory of the blue-jowled man who had been at the funeral and the check that had been found in Mr. Chandler's hand.

Emma grabbed the telephone book, found two Anthony Gillespies and called the one with the State Street address. When she got Mr. Gillespie on the wire she explained who she was. Mr. Gillespie was very polite. He congratulated her on her good fortune and didn't seem at all surprised at it.

"Maybe you know about it," Emma began, "and maybe you think it's none of my business, but that check that they found in Mr. Chandler's hand. It was an old check of Amos' but it was made out to you and it was marked 'no funds.' Do you suppose that has any importance? I mean anything that Mr. Chandler's knowing about would make somebody want to kill him? You don't have to tell me if you don't want to, but I'd like to know."

Mr. Gillespie was very gracious. He was sorry, he said, that the matter had ever come up; he had no idea that the check was still in existence; but as long as he had already explained the matter to a Lieutenant Ellis and to Mr. Fairbanks he did not see that it did any harm to tell her.

Emma found herself feeling like the man who had invented the automobile, only to discover that someone had already done it.

Amos, Mr. Gillespie went on, had overdrawn his account to pay a college debt and his father had refused to make the check good, with the idea of teaching Amos a much-needed lesson. Mr. Currier had written the bank that it would have to get the money from his son; the college authorities had got wind of it, and there had been the makings of a rather unpleasant mess until Amos borrowed the money to cover the overdraft. Mr. Gillespie paused. "I didn't tell the police this," he continued, "but it may amuse you. I loaned Amos the money to make the check good."

"Well, you were a sap," said Emma bluntly.

"Not at all," said Mr. Gillespie. "I knew the Curriers had plenty of money; Amos was a nice kid and his father was an old hellion."

"What was the debt for in the first place?" Emma wanted to know.

"Bad luck in a poker game. I suppose I felt a little guilty because I won a lot of Amos' money by filling an inside straight. It was a very fine game. I remember it to this day. It started one noon and went on all night. It would have probably been going yet except that a fire started in a lumber yard in East Cambridge. But I mustn't bore you with undergraduate reminiscences."

"Not at all," said Emma. "It sounds like fun. But there's one more thing I want to know. You see, if there isn't any other estate, I feel sort of like a worm taking what there is. Are the papers right? Didn't Amos have any money?"

There was a long silence, one so long that Emma finally said "Hello," thinking that she had been cut off.

"I'm right here," said Mr. Gillespie, "but my best advice to you, young lady, considering the fact that I have been retained as legal counsel by Miss Chandler, is not to talk like that."

"Oh," said Emma. "I see what you mean. Thanks."

She hung up, decided that if Eunice Chandler was going to be mean, it was no more than one could expect and went back to her previous train of thought.

She was beginning to get a clear picture—idea. She would have to give up using the picture comparison; that was Hank's. The story, then, was that Amos had gambled away the family fortune, and Miss Currier, who had at first written for personal justification, had continued writing to support Amos. That was fine, but when Miss Currier discovered that what she could supply was not enough and that Amos was buying meals for questionable women (that was Emma) on the money obtained from the sale of the silver Miss Currier hadn't liked it, had brooded—hurt pride would come in there, too, Emma thought—and had killed Amos. Then, when she discovered that Mr. Chandler was hell bent to reveal all this by means of the inventory, she had killed him too.

It was a fine little theory. Emma patted it on the head and hoped it would grow. *Murder for Pride.* It was too bad Miss Currier couldn't write her own story. Now all she, Emma, had to do was to go out to Westham and prove her theory. Finding the inventory would help. There would be more things missing on the inventory; with Jeff's help they would trace the sale of these—Emma broke off again. At this point it occurred to her that Jeff undoubtedly had been making sales for Amos and could locate the spoon and the pitcher as well as the muffineer. That would prove that Amos had been selling things but it wouldn't prove that Miss Currier had killed him. Well, say that Miss Currier had gone downstairs the back way, had heard Jeff and Amos discussing the sale of the muffineer, had waited until Jeff went to bed and had then killed Amos. And Jeff had kept quiet about the muffineer, just as she had told Ellis, out of loyalty to Amos. What was wrong with that picture—idea? Nothing, except that Miss Currier was stone-deaf.

But if she told Miss Currier that she knew where the inventory was, maybe Miss Currier would try to kill her. That would be proof—if she lived through it. A prickle of excitement ran up Emma's spine. If that were going to happen, it would be rather nice to have someone along for protection. No—Emma squared her shoulders—if she were going to solve this thing herself she would ask help from no one, and the presence of a third person might put Miss Currier on guard. She would have to fight the war alone. She turned resolutely to answer the phone.

"Hello," she said guardedly.

"Hello." Eddie's voice sounded surprised. "Are you there?"

"Where'd you expect I'd be—in jail?" Then Emma went on to explain her witticism by telling of Ellis' visit.

"I hadn't thought of that," Eddie said. "I was afraid you'd be out to lunch."

"I will be in a minute. About tonight—"

"Oh yes," said Eddie.

"You better meet me over at the apartment so that I can do you justice by putting on the equivalent of a clean shirt."

"That'll be fine—"

"And I've got a surprise for you. I've got the Currier-Chandler case all solved. Or at least"—as Eddie made an incredulous sound into the phone—"I know where the inventory is. I thought of it this morning.

"No, I'll not tell you now. I want to show you."

Emma went to lunch at the Greek's, suffering the congratulations of Charlie the proprietor, the countermen and the bus boy as graciously as she could.

"You're rich now, eh?" asked Charlie. "You eat up the street now, at the hotel?"

"Don't be sil'," said Emma, picking out salami and potato salad; "it isn't money, it's furniture; and besides I haven't got it yet; and, furthermore and besides, the hotel doesn't make its potato salad with bacon."

"And the pastry cook has leprosy," said the fat counterman, winking; "the doorman told me so."

"He told me you had smallpox," said Emma and they all laughed.

The afternoon was surprisingly busy. Several people came in, drawn, Emma supposed, by curiosity but a few of them bought things. Emma's sad young reporter came and reproached her for not telling him of her good fortune. Emma said that she would make up for the omission by tipping him off to the fact that the case was nearly solved. He could say, she told him, that new developments promised a break by—well, Emma thought she ought to give herself a little time—by Sunday.

Then another thought struck her; she could provide for a slight measure of safeguard, not that she would need it. She looked at the wall beside the telephone and read off a number.

"You call that number Saturday afternoon about five," she said, "and if I'm not there you find out why not."

"Hot-ziggety," said the reporter. "If you're not there where'll you be?"

"At the bottom of the well," said Emma, "with my head bashed in."

After the reporter had gone Emma felt very pleased with herself.

When that came out in the paper it would set them all on their ears. By them she meant Hank and she was equally pleased when Hank's secretary called and she could say loftily that she hadn't the faintest idea where Mr. Fairbanks was. She sold a broken toasting fork by sheer charm and hardly noticed the heat until five-thirty came and she realized that she was dirty and exhausted.

On the way home she stopped only long enough to buy a bottle of sherry, hoping to wean Eddie from his taste for champagne, then hurried on and into a cold tub as fast as she could.

When Eddie arrived, wearing what Shay would have described as a pearl-gray ensemble, Emma was dressed and almost still cool. Eddie went right to the point.

"I say," he began, "what do you know? I mean, what do you really know?"

Emma smiled sweetly. "Sit down," she said, "and have some sherry. You look as though your blood pressure was up to boiling now. So I guess I won't tell you."

"Oh, but, Emma." Eddie looked so sad that Emma knew he had taken her seriously.

"Oh, but, Eddie." She mimicked him. "How's the sherry? Are you quite comfortable? Did you have a good day at the office? I saw simply millions of people, among them our friend Ellis, as I told you."

Eddie looked so acutely disappointed that Emma didn't have the heart to go on tormenting him. "Do you see that desk?" she asked.

"Yes," said Eddie. "It's pretty. I suppose it's old, too, but I wish you'd tell me—"

"Keep still," said Emma; "I'm trying to." She went across to the desk and put her hand on one of the two half columns that flanked the center compartment. "See this knob?" She tugged at a small brass pull. "Well, it's a fake. On most desks like this these columns pull out and are little thin up-and-down drawers, but on this baby it works like this."

Emma opened the sunburst-ornamented door between the columns, pulled at the underlip of a flat facing and produced a small drawer. "Secret number one," said Emma, "but you ain't seen nothin'." She put her hand into the thin opening left by the drawer, pressed on a wooden spring and pulled out the whole center section of the desk.

"Oh, I say," said Eddie, "I never saw anything like that."

Emma pointed to two worn leather tabs, one at each side of the back. "The little thin drawers are here, at the back of the columns instead of at the front. The column secret drawer got to be old stuff, and some smart guy thought of this. You don't see many like it, though; he must have patented the idea. That's a joke," she explained, not wanting Eddie to get his periods mixed.

"But," said Emma, not without pride, "it's my business to notice if the feet are cut off of chairs and if all the brasses are on a chest, and I noticed that the desk upstairs, the one they call Amos' father's, the one where the inventory was supposed to be, was like this. I didn't think of it until this morning, but all of a sudden I thought that I bet all the people who had searched the desk hadn't known about those drawers. I bet that's where it is."

"Oh," said Eddie, "then you don't really know?"

Emma collapsed on a chair. "Shucks," she said, "haven't you any enthusiasm? Haven't you any imagination? Where else could the silly thing be? Miss Currier said it was in the desk, and Ellis claims that he has gone over the rest of the house with a fine-tooth comb." Emma thought it was just as well not to mention the activities in the attic. "It has to be there and I'm going out Saturday afternoon to find it, just to prove I'm right."

She went on to tell of her conviction that Miss Currier had killed Amos to protect the story of his betrayal of the family traditions. Eddie listened attentively.

"So she writes detective stories?" he commented. "I say, that's funny, isn't it? Because if she did it, it would be like writing a plot for her; but if she didn't do it, why, she's no quicker than the rest of us at solving the plot before the last page."

"You mean she's laughing up her sleeve or that she's just as burned up as we are only more so?"

"Well, something like that. Where do you want to eat?"

They had a very nice meal and went to a movie. Emma thought she saw Mr. Saunders leaving the theater behind them but she did not mention him to Eddie.

Chapter 20

FRIDAY MORNING, after another hot, sticky night, Emma decided that if a completely strange man came along and asked her to go to Alaska, she would probably go. It was cleaning day at the shop and the long, wet swings of Mary's mop helped some. But Mary's gloomy nature was depressing.

"I wish we had a sprinkler system," said Emma. "I'd turn it on."

It did no good, Mary replied darkly, to try to change the ways of nature. Her rheumatism was worse, she said, as the result of working in one of those air-conditioned places where it was that cold the water nearly froze in the pail. Mary also felt that Emma should not accept the legacy about which she had read in the papers. It was tainted money and would do her no good.

"'Tain't money," said Emma; "'tis furniture."

Mary did not laugh; she advanced grimly with mop and Emma had to put her feet up in a chair to avoid being swept away by the flood. When the waters had ebbed Emma decided that she might as well start making out some bills for the middle-of-the-month attack. It wasn't the middle of the month yet but it would be by the time she finished them. Emma regarded Jeff's idea that bills should be sent twice a month as a device calculated to keep her chained to the typewriter. And it didn't seem to do any good; Emma couldn't recall that there had been any response to the batch she had sent out the day before they went to Amos'.

She paused to consider how she was going to act when she went out this time. She would be very casual and very friendly. She wouldn't mention the inventory until she was upstairs; then she would sneak up on the desk and say: "My, that's a pretty desk; I wonder if it's like mine?" Then she would open up the front of it, whisk out the inventory—and see what Miss Currier did. Maybe she ought to wait until the phone call came at five o'clock, tell the reporter to hold the line and dash upstairs and look. Then she'd have the inventory but Miss

Currier wouldn't have time to do anything. No good.

If she went up in the attic and started rummaging around—she guessed she could, in her own attic—and found the magazines and opened one and said, "Oh, do you write detective stories? Is it hard?" What would Miss Currier say? "Yes," probably, which didn't seem very incriminating. Emma decided that she would get a bright idea when she got out there and that in the meantime there were the bills. Emma addressed an envelope without very much enthusiasm, heard the corner door of the shop open and got up. Walking around the pile of furniture to the front aisle, she found herself approaching Eunice Chandler. They continued to walk toward each other, stiffly, for all the world, Emma thought afterward, like two strange dogs. Emma waited for Eunice to speak, to set the tone of the interview. She expected to be insulted, but all Eunice said, rather meekly, was "How do you do?"

"How do you do?" said Emma neutrally.

Eunice looked around as though seeking inspiration on how to begin from the sideboards, four-posters, figureheads and bread troughs about her. Emma offered no help.

"I just wanted to tell you," Eunice began finally, "that I'm not going to do anything about the will. Amos wanted you to have the things and it's quite all right with me."

Since when? Emma thought; but aloud she said, "It was nice of you to come and tell me."

"And I'm sorry about the things I said," Eunice went on as though speaking a piece, "out at the farm, after the funeral. I knew they weren't true; I don't know what got into me. I imagine" —there was a burst of emotion in her voice—"that I was jealous that Amos liked you better than he did me. I don't expect you to like me but at least I want you to know that I'm sorry." Eunice stopped suddenly and her face flushed darkly with embarrassment.

Emma put out her hand impulsively. "Thank you," she said. "I know that it must have been hard to come here and say that. I'm sure I shall like you, because Shay likes you. Come on back and let's talk about it."

Eunice followed her to the Chippendale sofa and sat down stiffly, not exactly sure, yet, of Emma's attitude.

"It's funny, isn't it," said Emma, "how you get off on the wrong foot with people sometimes. We couldn't possibly dislike each other as much as we thought we did because we don't know each other well enough."

"I do that a lot," said Eunice; "get off on the wrong foot, I mean. I quarreled with Mr. Hinckley yesterday because he told me to do just what I'm doing now."

The thought came to Emma that in the meantime Eunice had engaged the services of Mr. Gillespie, but she put it aside. "I'm sorry," she said, "about there not being any other estate "

"It doesn't matter. I suppose Amos just spent it. Wouldn't that be fun? To spend a lot of money? I imagine I'll spend quite a lot now," she add naively. "What really hurt was to have Amos want someone else to have it. I've always been terribly fond of Amos."

Emma pricked up her ears. She had been under the impression that Eunice rather cordially disliked her uncle.

"Amos never liked me, though." Eunice was going on as though anxious to pour out all the thoughts that had been troubling her. "I imagine it was because of Mother—he was very fond of her and he didn't like Father. And then she died and Father—" She broke off and added, "But you know all about that."

Emma nodded and Eunice went on. "I don't suppose I was a very appealing child. I was scared of everything. I was scared of horses but I made myself get over that because Amos liked them. I was scared to death of Miss Amy, although that was Father's fault."

"How do you mean?" Emma asked quickly.

"Father said she wasn't an invalid at all and she told me such bloodcurdling stories, all about pirates and things. Amos said he used to like her stories so I listened to them, but I used to go home and dream that at night she turned into a witch and went out doing all the things she didn't do in the daytime."

"Did you know she supported Amos with her stories?" Emma asked and went on to tell of the diary and the piles of magazines in the attic.

"So that was it," Eunice said; "I wonder if Father knew that? Father used to say that Amos didn't have any money sense and it galled him terribly that Amos seemed to get along. I wish I'd known—not that I'd have ever told Father."

"See here"—Emma leaned forward confidentially—"Miss Currier didn't like your father, did she?"

"I should say not." Eunice's words came quickly. "It wasn't that she regarded him as an upstart, the way some people did, because he had worked in the mill and made his money the hard way, she was too much of a lady to care about that; she disliked him because he was mean and niggardly and overbearing and prying—"

There was such bitterness in the last words that Emma must have looked startled, for Eunice said quickly, "I know I shouldn't speak that way of him, but it was true. At first I used to wish that Amos had been my father."

"But let me ask you"—Emma was anxious to get corroboration for her theory—"do you think that Miss Currier hated your father enough to kill him if she thought he was going to find out something that would reflect on the integrity of the Curriers, something that would give him the last laugh after all his years of feeling inferior to them?"

"Absolutely," said Eunice.

Emma's eyes gleamed and she leaned forward on the edge of her seat.

"Now I want to ask you something else. I just want you to say what you think, for of course we have no way of knowing yet. Suppose Amos was the one who was doing the thing that would, in Miss Currier's eyes, disgrace them, would she kill Amos?"

"Why, yes," said Eunice, "I think she might."

Emma leaned back with a sigh of gratification. "I should have met up with you sooner," she remarked. "You're no end of comfort to me." She went on to explain why she thought Miss Currier might have killed Amos and then Mr. Chandler; she told again of her conviction that the inventory was in the desk and signified her intention of going out Saturday afternoon to prove it. "It will please me tremendously," she wound up, "to pull a fast one on Mr. H. Fairbanks."

"It all sounds dreadful," said Eunice, "but perfectly possible. By the way, do you know where Hank is?"

Emma did not.

Eunice knitted thin eyebrows. "I suppose he's working," she said, "but I haven't seen him since the funeral."

"He's asleep somewhere," said Emma.

"Why don't you go out to the farm now?" Eunice wanted to know.

Emma waved her arm to include the bread troughs, the fourposters and the sideboards. "I can't," she said. "I'm supposed to be working, and Jeff isn't here or I would—go out, I mean. I figure"— Emma was very nonchalant—"that Saturday afternoon and maybe Sunday ought to just about clean it up."

"It must be marvelous," Eunice sighed, "to be like that—independent and able to do things."

Emma gaped at her. "I just told you," she said firmly, "that I'm a wage slave, not able to call my soul my own."

A suspicious noise came from the direction of Mary and the scrub bucket but Emma did not even hear it.

"As far as I'm concerned," said Eunice, "I'd change places with you in a minute because you look as though you always had a good time."

Which just showed, Emma thought, how well she concealed a broken heart. "That's life for you, isn't it?" she said profoundly.

Eunice stood up. "Is there anything I can do? To help out Saturday?"

"No," said Emma, who was not above wanting the glory, if any, for herself. "I think the surprise attack will work better if I'm alone." She also hated to admit that all there was so far of planned attack was the surprise. "You might go out to your place Saturday," she added, "I may scream for help."

"You're awfully nice," said Eunice. "Good-by."

"Now what," said Emma to Mary after the door had closed, "do you think of that?"

"Is that," Mary wanted to know, "the one as calls herself the Chandler girl?"

"Sure an' it is," said Emma. "She don't favor her paw none, though, except, I used to think, in disposition."

"There's a lot of them," said Mary, burrowing under a radiator, "as has bad dispositions, but I ain't saying nothing."

"If you mean me," said Emma, "who wouldn't? If you mean our absent employer, I thoroughly agree."

"I don't tell all I sees." Mary padded to the washroom for clean water.

"Mary," said Emma sternly, "are you threatening to blackmail us?"

The sound of running water drowned out Mary's answer. She climbed into Emma's surrealist display, surveyed the objects therein distastefully and swept them all together, preparatory to cleaning the window.

"Ingrate, that's what she is." Mary brandished the rag doll. "Talking that way about those as done everything for her."

"Oh," said Emma, "I see what's eating you. You mean 'honor thy father,' even if he is a blackguard. I think it would have been very difficult to honor Lloyd Chandler, even if he had been my father."

Mary muttered something.

"What did you say?"

"I got no cause to tell it."

"You said, 'He's as much your father as hers.'"

"What are you asking me for then?"

"Mary"—Emma went over to the window—"you're just itching to tell me something. Put down that rag and don't stand there hinting that Eunice Chandler is an illegitimate child."

"I never said no such thing. I guess her parents was married just the same as anybody's, only they wasn't the Chandlers. There, you've drug it out of me with your questions and your nagging, though I promised myself I'd never tell a soul." Mary abandoned her bucket and leaned closer to Emma. "I was in the outer office—night before last it was—and I didn't know that she was in there with him, or that he was in there either, for that matter, until I heard her say she'd do no such thing and him telling her that if she made a fuss, the fact that she was adopted was bound to come out. Then I banged the bucket against the filing cabinet and Mr. Hinckley got up and shut the door. 'Tis no disgrace to be adopted, but she shouldn't talk that way about them as done everything for her, so help me."

"Mary, Mary, are you telling me the truth?"

"I cleans that office every night of the world, excepting Sundays and holidays."

Emma groped for a chair and sat down. "Then the baby died, too, when Eunice's mother, I mean Mrs. Chandler, died, and Mr. Chandler adopted another baby. I wonder who else knows about this? Do you suppose Amos knew it?"

Mary picked up her rag. "As to that, I couldn't say. 'Twarn't none of my business to find out and it don't make no difference, only she hadn't ought to talk that way—"

"Mary"—Emma was thinking out loud, her eyes fixed on the bootjack—"it makes everything different. He wasn't her father, and if she knew it, it would only make his meanness harder to bear. She said she wished Amos had been her father and that she was jealous of him— why, she was in love with Amos. It's just as plain as day from what she said. And when she told me, out by the kitchen door, that I'd never marry him she meant that she'd kill him first; but she'd taken the figure, so when Mr. Chandler began to scream for the inventory she got panicky and killed him, not liking him very well anyhow. Oh, Mary, this is dreadful."

Mary waved her rag threateningly at Emma. "I never told you no such things," she said vehemently, "and don't you go saying I did."

"No, no, I know you didn't, but she said she wasn't in the pantry when she came back downstairs and yet there was the little skull from her charm bracelet. I thought Miss Currier did it, but now, as Shay would say, I don't know where I'm at."

"It's time you went to lunch," said Mary, "and if you go around telling I told you that—may the saints forgive me—'tis like I'll lose my job."

"Don't worry"—Emma went dutifully to the washroom for her hat—"if she's adopted, there are a lot of ways of finding that out. Probably all of Westham knows it. I bet Ellis knows it; that's why he didn't stick at accusing her of killing Mr. Chandler."

Damn, she thought to herself, if Eunice did the murders, then she wouldn't win the pool for Jeff, but it would be just as much fun to have Hank win the pool on the client by whom he had been hired. She'd tell that story to the young reporter. No, Emma knew she wouldn't. Suddenly she didn't want to be the one who proved Eunice Chandler guilty. It was different about Miss Currier—she was old and queer and scary—but Eunice was young and pretty, and the underlying bravery of her story, the very bravery of coming to tell it, had appealed to Emma. But Eunice had only decided not to sue on Hinckley's advice—no, she had said herself that she had quarreled with Hinckley—then she had gone to Gillespie and probably he had told her the same thing. She had decided not to sue because the fact of her adoption would make it seem to others, as it had to Emma, possible for her to kill Mr. Chandler.

With her head in a whirl Emma stepped out into the street and directly into the path of an oncoming truck. The truck stopped with the scream of brakes and curses and Emma stepped back sheepishly. Once safely within the restaurant she burned her mouth on the coffee that she hoped might clear her thoughts.

Nick brought her the noon edition of the young reporter's paper. Uncorroborated, her story was featured as an article rather than as news: UNDISCLOSED SOURCE PROMISES BREAK IN CHANDLER KILLINGS—"Amateur sleuth gazes in crystal ball and sees location of missing paper—Psychic to triumph where cops failed." There was a lot of hugger-mugger along the same lines and the article wound up with the idea that the whole story was only a trap to frighten the criminal into a false move. It wasn't a bad story; Emma was pleased to see that it had earned the boy a byline. She told Charlie that it sounded like a lot of bunk to her and had a dish of ice cream to cool her mouth.

Emma might have fooled Charlie, but when she got back to the shop there were three reporters waiting to see if she knew anything about the undisclosed source and anxious for the interview that Mr. Finegold had deprived them of the day before.

What was she going to do with her money?

Who was the undisclosed source?

Where was her boss?

Where was Mr. Fairbanks?

What did an inventory look like?

Did she think she knew where it was?

Had she been engaged to Amos Currier?

Had she done the murders?

Who had?

Why was there an insurance detective on the case?

What was a muffineer?

Emma tried to be polite; she tried to appear dumb; she attempted to appeal to the combined better natures of her questioners by being appealingly feminine; and she ended by getting belligerent and ordering them all out of the shop.

And then Jeff walked in, walked in as casually as though he had himself just been out to lunch.

"You boys scram," he said.

And the boys all scrammed for the nearest telephone.

Jeff turned a cold eye on Emma. "That goes for you too," he said.

"Jeff Graham, where have you been?" It was a rhetorical question, Emma knew, but she felt that she had to preserve some semblance of authority.

"What's it to you? You heard what I said, get out of here."

"Jeff," said Emma, "there's no need to get that sore; I only did it because—""

Jeff picked up Emma's bag from her desk and threw it at her.

"You've got your hat on and you understand English. Get out, vamoose. You're fired!"

"Now be reasonable—"

"I'll not have you around. I read the papers. Making up to Amos behind Hank's back and getting his money— All women are alike, just a bunch of dirty—"

And then Emma got mad too. "I hate you, I hate you, I hate you," she repeated. "I've stood up for you and protected you for years, and this is the thanks I get. You don't understand—"

"I don't want to understand—"

"I'll not listen to such talk." Mary slammed down her pail and added her voice to the confusion.

"Will you get out of here?"

"I'm going too."

"I hope Ellis proves you did it."

"Come along, dearie." Mary hooked her arm in Emma's and led her outside.

Emma climbed into the roadster, buried her face in the steering wheel and burst into tears.

Finally, when she could control herself, she drove Mary home. She tried to pay Mary for the time she had worked but Mary would take no money. It was just as well, for Emma found that she had sixty-three cents in her purse. Sixty-three cents and no job. But that wasn't what hurt. The tears came again and she drove blindly ahead, unconscious of where she was going. In all the years since Jeff had advanced the money for the appendix that had become acute the day after she went to work for him Emma had never questioned Jeff's friendship. They had quarreled and argued; they had carried on long feuds over important trifles such as whether the shop doors should be open or closed in summer; they had pointed out each other's shortcomings openly to others; but if Emma's forgetfulness or Jeff's quick temper precipitated a business crisis, they had presented a united front of mutual defense. Emma had tried to be a tactful buffer against the depredations of Jeff's spendthrift wife; and she had tried equally to curb Jeff's passion for gambling, and Jeff had shown his appreciation, though he never would have admitted it, by paying her more than she was worth and claiming that she was worth it. Jeff howled with protest when she took the afternoon off to buy a hat or was an hour late to work but he had patiently taught her the difference between Sheraton and Hepplewhite and the all-important doctrine that if you could think up a use for something you could sell it. Jeff told her in picturesque language that she couldn't add two figures correctly, but if she made a mistake in a bill, he took the blame. Jeff kidded her about Hank and Shay and Charlie and Amos and Mr. Finegold and other occasional beaux, and now he had fired her because of Amos. Emma could not understand it. Her world was quite upside down as well as knocked into a cocked hat. She felt as though she had been abandoned on a doorstep and snarled at by a Saint Bernard.

Saint Bernards, she had heard, sometimes turned mean, and Jeff had acted very strangely ever since Amos' death: not telling about the muffineer, going off to places, trying to pretend that Rockingham was a horse, getting angry about Amos— A brilliant thought came to Emma. She was trying to do it; Shay was trying to do it. In some round-about fashion Jeff was trying to solve the murders.

He wasn't angry about Amos at all; he'd fired her so that she wouldn't know what he was up to or tell Hank what he had discovered.

Well, she had discovered a thing or two herself and she'd solve the murders first. She became so incensed at this betrayal of their years of partnership that she forgot to be reasonable. She thought of the pool and decided that Jeff wanted to win that too. For a paltry three hundred and fifty he would fire her.

Oh, he would, would he? The old meany. Fire sparked in Emma's eyes.

She found herself approaching Franklin Park, went through it and turned the roadster northward. No duties now prevented her from going to Westham at once. In Somerville she decided that she would be more welcome and least suspected if she gave warning of her visit. Miss Currier probably would not answer the phone so Emma spared some of her precious change to call Mrs. Leavitt.

Mrs. Leavitt assured her that she would be most welcome. And then Emma had a hunch. "I'm coming out to solve the murders," she said; "I think the inventory is hidden in the stable."

That, she thought, would show whether there was a connivance between Mrs. Leavitt and Miss Currier, because if Miss Currier tried to do anything to her before she found the inventory, it would show that Mrs. Leavitt had warned her. Emma thought she was very smart.

It had been a day of catastrophes, and more were to come, for about a mile out of Westham came the ominous sound as of a pop bottle being broken. The car lurched to the side and bumped along.

"This," said Emma to a large maple tree, "is the worst."

There was no use looking in the back of the car; Emma knew she didn't have a jack; Jeff had borrowed hers and strenuously resisted returning it. Then Emma remembered that even if she had a jack it would do her no good; it was the feeble spare that had blown out. The tire which Shay had punctured had not yet been repaired.

The maple tree offered the one bit of shade along the sizzling road. Emma set her teeth and thumped, thumped to the filling station at the corner of the square.

Lafe surveyed the damage sadly. "You'll need a new tube and a blowout patch and you ain't helped that casing none, and I ain't got a tube the right size. You going over to the Currier place?" he asked tentatively, not sure that Emma wanted to be recognized.

Emma nodded.

"Somebody'll be along by'm'by'll give you a lift. Want to wait inside?"

Emma agreed and spent an extravagant nickel for a bottle of tonic.

Lafe filled up a car that was headed for the turnpike and then joined Emma. "You know a short stocky feller in a '38 Packard?" he asked.

"With a dented front fender?"

"That's the one."

That was the last dent Emma supposed she'd put in a car of Jeff's. "Yes," she said, "I know him."

After a pause Lafe said, "Well, anyhow, this feller was in here this morning asking a lot a questions— Hi, Georgie!" he yelled as a battered Ford chugged by. "You going past Currier's? Got a lady in here wants a lift."

Aha, Emma thought to herself. "What kind of questions?" she asked.

"Georgie'll take you up. 'Tain't a bit out of his way. Huh? Oh, about who stopped by here the night old Amos was killed. Say, what you aiming to do with the place, turn it into one of them tearooms?"

"I don't know," said Emma, getting into the Ford; "maybe I'll just live there." Jeff knew who had been out at Amos'. What, she wondered, had he been asking that for? He was way off the track.

Georgie was as battered as his car, grizzled and taciturn. He did not seem to know or care who Emma was and his impersonal stolidity was a relief. As they rounded the last turn, and the house between the elms came into view, Emma was struck again with the peace and graciousness of the scene. Maybe she would live there. She wondered if she could make a living on a farm. M. Lebotien was always talking about the waste of land in America; maybe he would like to come out and run the farm for her. They could take the yellow tomcat and get a dog and she wouldn't be lonely but would turn into a nice eccentric spinster in tweeds and flat heels—overalls and rubber boots was probably more like it.

Georgie stopped by the woodshed and Emma let herself out of the car. She wandered what she ought to pay for her ride, but Georgie drove off before she could ask him. A fine man, Emma thought.

Emma walked around to the front of the house. The west lawn was cool and shady in the lengthening shadows of the trees, but Emma noticed that the grass needed cutting and that the dry, brown patches were larger. Clearly a man was needed around the place, but a man was just what she didn't have at present. She wondered where the hose was; it wouldn't do to let the place run down. The front door was open, and as Emma opened the screen she saw Miss Currier coming carefully down the stairs, cane in hand. Miss Currier wore a blue muslin dress, her cheeks were pink under her white hair, and Emma thought that she did not look at all like a murderess. But—

"I was watching for you," she said and she looked behind her quickly as though someone was following her.

"I had a flat tire," said Emma, "and had to catch a ride."

Miss Currier clucked in sympathy. "Then you don't have your car? That's too bad; maybe you will have to stay longer than you intended. Come into the dining room. Sally has fixed some raspberry shrub."

As Emma followed the tap-tap of the cane she felt that the hall was suddenly chill. What did Miss Currier mean: she didn't have her car? Did she mean that Emma couldn't get away? That she would have to stay longer than she intended because Suppose it really was Miss Currier instead of Eunice? Emma told herself not to be silly; she could break Miss Currier with one finger—if she saw her coming.

The raspberry shrub was pink, in tall glasses; there was a cold chicken and cucumber sandwiches, thin as paper. The polished mahogany table had lights as deep as a pool; the blue-green woodwork of the room was soothing and the silver gleamed like water behind the glass doors—

What if, Emma thought, the food was poisoned?

Miss Currier sipped her drink; Emma did likewise. Miss Currier passed the sandwiches; Emma took one, so did Miss Currier. The swinging door to the buttery opened slowly. Emma jumped, but only a gray cat squeezed through the aperture. Miss Currier paused in her carving to offer a crumb of chicken.

"Amos didn't like cats in the house," she said, "but I do."

Amos was dead and Miss Currier was doing the things she wanted to—

"I've lost my job," said Emma suddenly.

"Oh, my dear," said Miss Currier, "how despondent making."

Ooo-o, Emma thought. And despondency leads to suicide, and suicide might cover up a murder—

"Men are an odd lot," said Miss Currier, "although you may think I'm in no position to judge; but I wonder why he did that?"

"He said"—Emma kept her own opinion to herself—"that I'd been making up to Amos behind his back."

"Tush," said Miss Currier, "you didn't have to do that. Amos cared for you very deeply. Will you have some more chicken?"

"No," said Emma. "I mean, thank you. I really didn't know that. I thought he left me the house and the things partly to spite the

Chandlers and partly because he really wanted them used and you're—I mean, of course you'll live a long time but it isn't as though you were young."

"You're right. I'm old and Lloyd Chandler said I was senile. Amos did not expect me to outlive him. If he willed the property to me with the understanding that, should he die first, I would leave the place to you he was afraid that the Chandlers would break the will. Do you think I'm senile, my dear?"

No, whatever she thought, Emma didn't think that. Insane, perhaps—Amos hadn't expected her to outlive him, but she had; and, with Emma out of the way, Miss Currier had a better claim to the property than Eunice.

"No indeed," said Emma.

The cat jumped up on the table with a soft thud.

"Scat," said Miss Currier. "That's another nice thing about a cat"— she changed the subject abruptly—"you can attribute all the strange night noises to them. You will find that an old house like this has many noises at night. Or perhaps you have noticed it?"

Cats didn't use canes, Emma thought, and Miss Currier couldn't hear noises. Eunice's story of her childhood dreams came back to Emma; she envisioned Miss Currier flying about at night on her ebony stick doing all the things she wrote about in her stories

The rocking-ship clock in the hall struck six. Emma wondered if she would hear it strike seven.

"I like this house," she said defensively.

"So do I," said Miss Currier.

She wants it for herself, Emma thought; she doesn't really want me to have it.

"I have lived a very strange life in this house," said Miss Currier, "and now I suddenly find that I am just beginning to live."

And Emma wasn't to interfere

"I like the house," Emma repeated; "I wouldn't change a thing in it, except, perhaps, the position of the furniture in the parlor."

Miss Currier's hand moved agitatedly to the top of her cane. "Not just yet," she said; "don't change—anything—just yet. I'm an old woman"—she smiled disarmingly—"and I need a little time to get used to change."

In a little while, Emma thought, she'll have the place to herself. She'd thought she was smart to come out here but who was she to go up against this old woman who had accomplished two successful murders? Emma almost bade life a sad adieu then and there but she remembered what Jeff had said once, that she was a fool for luck—

The telephone rang. Miss Currier made no move.

"The phone," said Emma. "Shall I answer it?"

"What?" Miss Currier seemed disturbed. "Yes, please. If it's Sally tell her everything is all right."

All right for what? Emma wondered.

It was the young reporter, a day ahead of himself.

He was just curious, he said. Did she need any help?

Emma said no and added firmly that he must have the wrong number. There was nothing else to do. She couldn't tell him that he had called too soon, to call again; that might make Miss Currier suspicious. Not until she had hung up did she remember that Miss Currier could not have heard her conversation. Too late Emma realized that she had unnecessarily cut herself off from all help.

It had grown very dark in the dining room and a cool draft of air suddenly bellied out the curtains at the windows. Far away there was a distant grumble of thunder; something soft rubbed against Emma's ankles. It was, of course, the cat.

"Oh, dear me." Miss Currier got up, closed the windows and locked them. "Of course we need the rain, but mud tracks so. If you will excuse me, my dear, I believe I will go up and lie down. I always try to sleep through a thunderstorm; then I'm not afraid of it."

Miss Currier couldn't hear thunder, Emma thought; if she was afraid of lightning, it was only because it forewarned her of hellfire— she was not going to be caught.

"I think I'll lie down too," she said. "This has been a bad day." She realized that she was very drowsy. Suppose there had been something in that pink lemonade? If she could only get upstairs and into a room with the door locked, then, for a moment, she might be safe. She could make a rope out of the sheets—unless Miss Currier had taken them away— She groped her way out of the room behind Miss Currier and down the hall.

Miss Currier paused to lock the front door. "Now we are safe," she said.

Safe—

"I have put you in the room you had before," she went on.

If I can only get there, Emma thought.

"—it is the most comfortable. I hope you don't mind the distance to the bathroom—"

Miss Currier opened the door for her, and, in the half-light, Emma could see the furtive little look over the shoulder. Emma shut the door and didn't care if Miss Currier heard her lock it. She fought down a wave of black dizziness long enough to get to the bed and fling herself upon it. The dizziness passed and came again and with it a sudden nausea. Emma could feel the sweat break out all over her body. She had been poisoned; she was going to die there, writhing horribly, the thunder drowning her screams as well as Miss Currier's ghoulish laughter. And Miss Currier would say it was suicide or bury her body and say that she had never been there—but Georgie knew, Georgie and the man at the filling station. Miss Currier better stick to the story of suicide or this murder would be her undoing.

There came another spasm of nausea, and Emma knew that she was going to vomit. She lurched up from the bed before she realized that she must not go to the bathroom. She got to the window, managed to raise the screen and was violently sick into a bed of Rosy Morn petunias with the thunder crashing in her ears.

As the thunder rolled away Emma felt better. Weak as a kitten, she rested her head on the sill and let the first slow drops of rain cool her face. She crouched there a long time, waiting for another fatal onset. The rain came faster, the ringing left her ears, and Emma began to feel surprisingly well. Gingerly she lifted her head and experienced no dizziness. If she had been given poison she was rid of it. Or perhaps it had been the cucumbers. Cucumbers sometimes did that to her but she loved them dearly. Excitement and cucumbers and raspberry shrub. Heavens knew what was in that, maybe raspberries. Emma began to feel a little silly at finding herself alive, because she had been so sure she was going to die. She went cautiously to the bed, lay down and took an almost guilty pleasure in wiggling her toes.

If Miss Currier *had* tried to poison her, she would be dead by now, and they would find her body in the morning. Of course Miss Currier wouldn't do that—Mrs. Leavitt, perhaps, with screams and shouts, and Miss Currier would say, "Poor dear, she lost her job." And Jeff would be sorry because he had driven her to it, and Hank would realize that he had loved her after all— Say, maybe Hank would get suspicious and find out that she, like the others, had been most foully murdered. No, Emma was darned if she was going to die so that Hank could solve the murders. Ellis, perhaps—but she didn't like Ellis very well either.

Emma sat up. If she were dead and Miss Currier couldn't hear her anyway, now was the time to look for the inventory. It was funny how she always forgot about Miss Currier's being deaf. And you couldn't hear a ghost.

Emma took her disembodied body off the bed and quietly unlocked her door. Quietly, in spite of the thunder and Miss Currier's deafness. A flash of lightning showed that the hall was empty, and Emma was grateful for it, not thinking that the lightning would reveal to Miss Currier what the thunder would not hide. Emma slipped across the hall and into Amos' room, feeling as light as ectoplasm. She wafted herself around the bed to the corner where the desk stood. The lid was down. With soft fingers Emma opened the center door. She was quivering with excitement; she felt giddy and light-headed.

The little drawer was thinner than the one in her desk but it worked the same way. In the darker darkness after the lightning Emma could not see, but her fingers found the spring and she felt the center section come loose in her hand. In only a minute, now, she would know. A crash of thunder covered the sound as she set the section down on the lid. She felt for the tab on the drawer at the back, pulled it out—even in the darkness she shut her eyes, afraid, like a child, to look lest she had found the wrong thing. The top edges of the drawer were cut down in a scallop; Emma could feel thick folds of paper held together by stitching. She had found the inventory!

In the instant after the sound of the thunder had died away it was very quiet. Emma did not know whether a sound or a breath of air made her look up. Then in the close-following flash of lightning she saw Miss Currier standing in the doorway, her eyes dark and staring, her cane upraised—

Emma forgot that she was a formless spirit and let out a piercing, full-bodied scream.

There was the sound of swift steps in the hall, someone turned on the light, and Emma saw Hank enveloped in a nightshirt of Amos', a cold compress wrapped to his head with a towel. For an instant all Emma could think of was that he looked like an illustration in a long-forgotten volume of Dickens. Then she flew to him.

"Save me, save me," she wailed, burrowing into his nightshirt.

Hank extricated her face from the folds and kissed her, kissed her thoroughly, as though he had not done so for a long time.

"You're safe, you silly little goat," he said.

"I'm not little," said Emma. "What are you doing with that thing around your head? Did she try to kill you too?"

"Will you please explain to her"—Miss Currier's voice was somewhat acid—"that I haven't tried to kill anyone?"

Hank grinned at her. "Don't you think," he asked, "that we ought to keep up the suspense as long as possible?"

"She poisoned me," Emma insisted, "or else it was the cucumbers."

"Hush your mouth"—Hank chided Emma—"she's my first assistant or, rather, I should say that I'm a poor second to her because it was she—"

"Sh-sh," said Miss Currier. "The suspense."

"And now"—Hank took Emma by the shoulders and shook her gently—"suppose you tell us what you were up to prowling around in the dark."

"You think you're so smart," said Emma. "I found the inventory. I told them I could."

"You told who?" Hank asked quickly.

"Oh," said Emma vaguely, "everybody, I guess. Shay and Eddie and Mary and Eunice and Mrs. Leavitt—I forget if I told Jeff or not, I was so mad at him. He fired me," she explained, "because he was trying to solve the murders, though he said it was because Amos left me the furniture. Oh, I forgot"—Emma drew away from Hank—"you're mad at me, too, about that."

Hank pulled her back against his shoulder. "I find," he said, "that I really do not give a damn about Amos."

"You mean you don't want to know why I said those things?"

"Did you say something? I'd forgotten."

"Oh," said Emma blissfully, "this makes everything perfectly lovely. But if," she conceded, "you ever want to know you can ask Shay; I explained it all to him. But aren't you proud of me about the inventory? I thought it all up myself, just to make a monkey out of you."

"Oh yes," said Hank, "the inventory. And you told every mother's son where it was." He turned accusingly to Miss Currier. "You let her come out here in hopes that we'd do just this very thing: make up. I can see the self-satisfied expression on your face. You sprung this on me. But I could have told you that she'd gum things up somehow if you let her in the house."

"I found the old inventory," said Emma defensively, "and I nearly died I threw up so hard, and this is the thanks I get."

"Pet," said Hank abstractedly, "you always do that when you get excited. I wonder—"

"I don't think she's gummed things up," said Miss Currier. "I think she's set the trap we've been trying to set. I hoped it would be tonight but I was afraid the rain—"

"When did you say you were coming out here?" Hank asked quickly.

"Tomorrow. I told the reporter "

"Oh, my sacred aunt," said Hank, "a reporter."

"I wanted somebody to know if I got killed, but he called too soon. Do you want me to tell the rest of it or not?"

"Sure," said Hank resignedly, "we've got all night; go ahead."

"I said," Emma resumed with dignity, "that I was coming out here Saturday, only after I got fired there wasn't any reason for my not coming out here then. Do you think I ought to forgive Jeff and let him take me back?"

"Shut up," said Hank. "I'm trying to think." He pointed to the desk. "Put that thing back the way you found it, only give me the inventory."

Emma did as she was told. Hank took the inventory, felt for a pocket and, finding none, handed the inventory to Miss Currier.

Emma thought he might have given it to her. She had found it and she wasn't sure, yet, just what part Miss Currier had in the goings on. Hank turned out the light.

"I hope we haven't left it on too long," he said, "but it's only about eight. We will now go into Miss Currier's room and hole in."

"You ought to be in bed," said Miss Currier.

"Are you sick? Are you hurt?" Emma asked quickly. "I thought maybe that was a disguise."

Miss Currier giggled. "I can't hear what you're saying but I don't know when," she said, "I've had so much fun."

"Compassionate woman." Hank's voice came out of the darkness. "Who ever thought that up? I am dying, Egypt, dying, but pay no attention to me." He picked Miss Currier up bodily, put her on her bed and pulled the spread over her.

"I don't want to go to bed," said Miss Currier. "It's bad enough not to be able to see what you're saying."

Hank pulled the wing chair away from the bed at an angle, poked Emma in behind it and crawled in himself, extending his long legs under the bed.

"I wish," said Emma, "that I had some idea of what was going on."

"You couldn't get deaf, could you?" Hank's voice was low. "I find that deaf women are much easier to handle."

"I think you're whispering," said Miss Currier. "I wish I had a flashlight or that it would lightning more frequently."

"I thought she killed Amos," Emma whispered.

"You're goofy. Here—" A clap of thunder that jarred the house beneath them made Emma jump. Hank pulled her over against his shoulder; in the following flash of lightning Miss Currier saw, and beamed at them.

"Did you know she wrote detective stories?" Emma asked, still whispering.

"Sure, her agents are Burns and Whitman. She sent a manuscript off on Wednesday."

"You're so smart. How did you find that out?"

"By hard work."

"Any time. And Amos lost his money playing poker—"

"—the stock market. He and Jeff met on the mourners' bench."

"Does it matter? And got to selling off the family heirlooms and I thought she'd got wind of it—"

"Did ums think that up all by um's little self?"

"Oh, be still. It's perfectly logical."

"You're talking about me," said Miss Currier plaintively; "my ears burn."

"Just as logical as one, two, three," said Hank. "Maybe you're right."

"Then what are we playing hide-and-seek for? Did you know Eunice was adopted?"

"Sure. After Durrell told me. So did Ellis and everybody in town. It explains a lot of things."

"Well, if it wasn't Miss Currier, it was Eunice. She was in love with Amos," Emma hurried on, anxious to get her own interpretation of the facts in, "and when I said—what I said—why she believed me, too, and killed Amos and then Mr. Chandler was going to find out about the figure so she killed him because he wasn't her father— Are you laughing at me?"

"Heaven forbid. I think you're wonderful."

"Only I wanted Miss Currier to have done it so Jeff would win the pot."

"I'll win it on Eunice. Isn't that all right?"

"The lightning doesn't seem so close now," came the voice from the bed. "Doesn't somebody hear something?"

"No," Emma went on in a small voice, "somehow I don't want Eunice to have done it—them. I think I could like her."

Hank squeezed Emma's hand. "It's a dirty business, puss. People try to keep you out of it but you have the happy faculty of landing in the middle of things with both feet."

"Didn't you know I was coming out here?"

"I should say not. I'd have had you forcibly detained."

Emma sighed comfortably. "You're so sweet to me," she said;

"but then what did you mean about trying to keep me out—"

"Sh-sh," said Hank as a soft thud came to them. "What was that?"

"That?" Emma giggled. "It was the cat."

Miss Currier prodded Hank with her cane.

"I suppose," said Emma, "I ought to be scared but I'm too happy."

"You better be scared," said Hank rather grimly; "you can be happy any time. Damn that thunder. I thought I heard a noise."

Emma giggled again. "It is like the *Pirates of Penzance*. I have the feeling that if you turned on the light the room would be full of policemen."

Hank made no answer. Emma could feel the tenseness of his body. He coiled up his legs, gave Emma a reassuring squeeze and remained half crouched beside the bed.

It was raining steadily now, but above the drumming of the rain Emma could hear the scratch of cloth as Hank moved slightly. The thunder grumbled in the distance and there was no lightning. Something creaked, somewhere. Hank inched forward.

"Softly now, on tiptoe creeping " Emma hummed to herself and broke off as another creak set her scalp to prickling. This time the creak was definitely in the hall. "In an old house," she remembered, "there are many noises." Or were they really waiting for someone?

She could hear a faint rustle from the bed, then nothing, until there came the faint scratch of wood on wood.

Hank dashed through the bathroom; Emma collided with Miss Currier in the doorway then stopped, aghast, as the light revealed Eddie standing in front of the desk, the empty drawer in his hand.

Eddie blinked. "Damnation," he said, "I thought I was going to solve the murders and win the pool. What is this? Another party?"

Emma leaned against the doorjamb and laughed. It was such an anticlimax.

"Every man a sleuth," she said. "I wonder if everyone I told about the inventory is going to try to beat me to it."

Eddie sat down on the bed. "Gosh," he said shakily, "you scared me."

"I should say so," said Miss Currier, "jumping out at you like that. Miss Marsh was scared, too, weren't you, my dear?"

"I should say I was," Emma said. "I thought you were going to kill me."

"The girlfriend," said Hank, "has, as usual, thrown the monkey wrench in the machinery. We thought we had a trap set for the criminal, but she goes and tells everyone where the inventory is and then walks into the trap herself."

"I wish," said Emma, "that I could remember whether I'd told Jeff or not; it would be such fun to jump out at him."

"You mean you told a lot of people and not just me?" Eddie spoke as though Emma had been disloyal.

"Cute, isn't she?" asked Hank. "So, of course, everyone will come, wanting to be the bright boy to solve the murders, instead of just the guilty one as we had hoped."

The One Who Stayed Away," said Miss Currier. "I wish I had my notebook."

"Maybe you've got something there." Excitement crept back into Hank's voice. "The guilty one is the one who doesn't come because he, she or it doesn't want the murders solved. But in the meantime, while we wait for the procession, come into my room. There's something I want to show you."

Hank waited at the head of the stairs for Emma and Eddie to pass him then hurried after them to turn on the light in the front room.

"I'll turn out this light," said Miss Currier. "Nobody's going to come in with the light on."

"She thinks of everything," said Hank admiringly; "you see, the light in here won't show." He pointed to paneled wooden shutters that were slid across the windows, closed the door carefully behind Miss Currier and escorted her across the room to a comfortable chair. Then he picked up a set of glossy prints from the corner of the washstand and sat down on the edge of the bed. Emma went over and sat beside him. Hank tantalizingly turned over the top picture.

"You see," he began, "the person who won't come tonight is the person, probably far away by now"—Hank looked at Emma—"who knows that listed on that inventory is a little silver object, call it a muffineer—"

Emma said "Oh" softly and sat still as death.

Eddie looked at Emma.

"What we have now is a very complicated picture." Hank was picking his words slowly. "Everybody had a hand in putting it together—Ellis and Saunders and your humble servant; but we owe most to Miss Currier; though"—he spoke to Eddie—"you come in for a bit of praise too. You see, my angel"—this time he spoke to Emma—"Eddie was the one who suggested that Saunders and Ellis search your apartment—"

"Oh, but I say—" Eddie began.

"Why, you, you underhanded—" Emma's eyes were blazing but

she turned to Hank. "That muffineer has nothing to do with the murders. Jeff didn't do them, I swear it."

"I thought you were mad at Jeff?" Hanks voice was casual. "Will you be quiet and let me finish my story?"

"You're wrong; you're dead wrong."

"Shut up, will you? As I was saying, Saunders was looking for someone who was stealing antiques from uninsured houses. Come clean, Eddie, hadn't you been suspicious of Jeff for some time?"

Eddie looked uncomfortable. "I'd hardly like to say that."

"It doesn't matter," said Hank, "now."

"Why, Henry Fairbanks!" Emma beat at Hank with her fist.

Hank grabbed her hand and held it, pressing it. Pressing it once, four times, three times, and then beginning over again. Emma's fingers pressed back involuntarily. It was the old handholding trick: I— L-O-V-E —Y-O-U. What a silly time, she thought, to be doing it.

"Much as I hate to disappoint you, my dove," Hank was going on, "the inventory is not important. Miss Currier found a list of the silver that was in the cupboard six months ago. It remained only for us to find an object on that list that was misplaced—stolen—and then to find that object in the possession of one of the people who were here on the night of June thirtieth. The muffineer was on that list and we have found the muffineer— Here," Hank broke off again and handed the pictures he held to Emma. "If you don't want to listen to what I'm going to say, look at these. Shay finally got them back from Ellis; they were taken on the fatal night."

Emma took the pictures. She wasn't listening to Hank anyhow. He had made a mistake and he would find it out sometime. Jeff hadn't killed Amos. Miss Currier had made the list up herself and found it just to throw suspicion on somebody else. She turned to the pictures. The first one was of Eunice laughing, Hank's hand holding her face. There was one of all of them dancing in the kitchen; there was a close-up of Emma spitting out a piece of ice. It was sad to have the pleasure of that evening recorded. Shay should have caught the bad moments. If only he had caught a picture of the murderer—

The next one was of Jeff cracking ice—Emma turned it over quickly and came upon the view of the parlor that Shay had taken from the doorway. It was a good picture. The woodwork showed up nicely—she could even see the inlay on the table flanking the secretary. The secretary's closed lid gleamed, smooth, glossy and bare. Bare. Emma glued her eyes to the picture. Hank was always talking about pictures. The lid was bare but it shouldn't have been. There should have been a little silver box like a book on one corner.

From the road Emma heard the honk of a car horn. It was a familiar honk, but she paid no attention to it. She had something that the others had missed—something that would save Jeff. Because Mrs. Leavitt had taken the silver box from the secretary and then had put it back.

"Here," said Hank, "let Eddie look at the pictures. The one of Jeff is very clear."

He handed Eddie the pictures and pushed back one of the shutters. "It's stuffy," he said, "and so late that I don't believe we will have any more murderers. What I said"—he whirled about suddenly—"was absolutely true, except in place of muffineer, read snuffbox—watch out!"

Miss Currier was on her feet brandishing her cane. Eddie dropped the pictures, gained the door and dashed down the hall. Shay was coming out of Amos' room. But Jeff was already dashing up the stairs, and Ellis, flanked by a wheezing Durrell, barred the way to the back hall. Mrs. Leavitt came from Emma's room.

Why, Emma thought, they were all there except Eunice. Was that what Hank had meant by the one who wouldn't come? But what on earth was Eddie doing? He had pulled something from his pocket, something long and gleaming.

"Good-by, folks," he said, "it's been nice know—" The word stopped in a gurgle. Before their very eyes, before anyone had the wit to stop him, Eddie cut his throat.

Emma and Miss Currier went down in a heap together and in the hall below the telephone began to ring madly.

Chapter 21

WHEN EMMA CAME TO she found that she had been dumped on Amos' bed and that no one was paying any attention to her. She could hear voices from the direction of Miss Currier's room so she got up and went rather gingerly in that direction. Miss Currier was lying on the bed, propped up with pillows. She was saying that she would be perfectly all right, if she didn't die of mortification at having fainted at the crucial moment. Hank said that she wasn't the only one.

Jeff looked up from a longing contemplation of Miss Currier's brandy decanter and saw Emma. "In walked a dead duck," he said sociably. "My, you're a sight."

"Surprised you, didn't we?" said Shay.

"Can't you be serious," Emma asked reprovingly, "after what has happened?"

"Eddie isn't dead," said Shay, "if you're worried about him. You have to be an expert to cut your throat. Ellis and Durrell are taking him to the doctor's now. He'll live to die again if vertigris doesn't set in, that means gangrene "

Emma went over to the bed. "First," she said, "I guess I owe you an apology."

"Granted, my dear," said Miss Currier; "it's always the people one doesn't know that one suspects. At first, before they told me how Lloyd was killed, I thought perhaps you had killed Amos yourself. And I'm awfully sorry about the cucumbers. Amos didn't like them but I am very fond of them."

Emma leaned over and kissed Miss Currier's cheek. "I hope," she said, "that you live to be a hundred, but do you mean to say that you suspected Eddie as soon as Chandler was killed?"

Miss Currier nodded.

"Go on and tell them," Hank urged.

Miss Currier blushed and fingered the spread. "I don't suppose it was original with me," she began modestly, "but, you see, I used that idea in a story once: having a man kill someone and leave, and then go back and discover the body."

"Cripes," said Jeff, "that took nerve."

"You bet you," said Miss Currier; "the man in my story was a nervy guy too. Dear me," she interpolated, "I shouldn't talk that way. Sally and I do it sometimes, just to get the phrases right, but you're correct. He ran the risk of having you or Miss Marsh or my niece or Mr. Horrigan find the body too soon after he had left. I almost found it myself when I looked in, but that, of course, was when Mr. Rawlins dashed out to call you, so that wouldn't have been so bad."

"Why didn't you tell somebody?" Emma wanted to know. "Everybody else was talking fast enough."

"Why, you see, at first I didn't have any proof. You must remember that Mr. Rawlins, along with the rest of you, was a perfect stranger to me. I couldn't imagine why he had killed Lloyd and I wasn't sure that he was the one who killed Amos. It really wasn't until Sally noticed the silver box in the parlor, where it shouldn't have been and where he had slept, that we began to get somewhere with our investigation. We ruled out Mr. Horrigan as soon as we found that he knew nothing about antiques—"

"I wish we'd known about you," said Shay; "we'd have let you in on the pool."

"What?" asked Miss Currier and Mrs. Leavitt together.

Hank explained.

"Yes," said Jeff. "I win, don't I?"

"Jeff," Emma exclaimed, "you aren't going to take the money?"

"Don't be a dope," said Jeff, "I most certainly am."

"But you didn't do anything to earn it and, besides, it doesn't seem nice somehow."

"Who didn't do anything to earn it?" Jeff belligerently ignored the ethics involved. "Who got the bright idea that Eddie knew his way out here? The filling station is the only place that's open at night and he didn't ask there. Who told 'em where the inventory was? Who found the marrow spoon in Eddie's apartment? Who went to Rockingham on Tiny's tip that he bought the lamp there?"

"Oh," said Emma, "that was it. How'd you know where the inventory was?"

"I put it there. Right after you found Amos' body. But I forgot I had the damn key until Chandler asked for it."

"Oh," said Emma sadly, "then I really wasn't any help at all."

"Yes"—Hank helped her out—"you precipitated the crisis and

got Eddie out here, and your having told everyone where the inventory was gave us an excuse to stall Eddie until Jeff got back with the spoon. If he hadn't found anything and hadn't come back, I'd have had to call in Ellis and Shay and arrest him on suspicion, though of course the way he got in the house really gave him away."

"I never thought to wonder about that," said Emma. "How did he?"

"It really wasn't a tight plot at all," said Miss Currier.

"Ellis thought of it first," Hank conceded, rubbing his head reflectively; "he had the house locked up, just the way it was the night Amos was killed, and then he waited to see if the criminal would come back. I think Eddie was too smart for that. I don't think he would have come except that he saw the chance to get rid of the inventory."

"But he was in the house," said Emma, puzzled; "why did he have to get in again?"

"Because, rabbit, he was in a room with a squeaky lock, but he knew that he could get in the way he had before, through the pantry window. So he went out his window and in through the other."

"But I thought it was locked?"

Jeff groaned. "It was my fault."

"You remember," Hank went on, "that Jeff and Eddie checked the windows—incidentally, that was a laugh, wasn't it?—the pantry window is up over the counter; Jeff is short so he didn't climb up to find out that the screws that hold the back half of the catch are rotted out of the wood. The window goes up slick as a whistle but it looks locked, and neither Jeff, Ellis nor I thought to try to open it. Savvy?"

"You mean Eddie had come in that way before and stolen things?" They all nodded.

"Why"—Emma turned to Jeff—"didn't you tell where the inventory was in the first place so we'd know things were missing?"

Jeff spread out his hands in a gesture copied from Mr. Finegold. "He didn't take it all," he said; "I was trying to cover up for Amos."

"You were half right," Hank consoled Emma. "Amos had been selling things for several years. Or rather Jeff had been selling them for him."

"That was his own business"—Jeff's tone was hostile—"and, besides, I had that damn muffineer in the shop that he'd given me just the day before. That was to pay for the insurance.

"I didn't tell you this"—Jeff glared at Emma—"because you always say no to everything I do, but the reason Amos finally decided to take out insurance was that he had checked over the inventory and found some things missing that he hadn't sold. He gave Rawlins the insurance instead of Durrell because he'd heard me tell that I was helping Saunders try to trace some other things. You didn't know that either, did you?"

Emma did not answer. The reason for the nonappearance of the overlay lamp in the stock book was dawning on her.

"Amos," Jeff went on, "didn't have any idea who'd taken his stuff, but that night, Saturday night, he asked me to come back down after you'd gone to bed. He'd got the idea it was Eddie. He'd seen him looking at the silver, sort of drooling at the mouth. I told him he was crazy but after he was killed I began to wonder. I'd bought that overlay lamp from Tiny because a purple overlay lamp was one of the things Saunders was yelling about—the one you sold to Finegold." Jeff threw another glare at Emma. "I had Tiny track it down. Feller he got it from got it from Murphy, on First Street, in Rockingham. You thought Rockingham was a horse, and I thought that was a good idea because it would keep you out of things, but I might have known— Anyhow, Murphy describes Eddie down to the last button and says he's bought a Hurd creamer and a lot of stuff from him. That's when I sent you the wire, as sort of a warning, but you were too dumb to catch on."

"Why did he do it?" Emma ignored the slur. "Steal things, I mean?"

"Champagne taste and a beer pocketbook," said Shay.

"Practically my entire contribution to this case—" said Hank.

"Here, here," said Shay.

"—is that I remembered that Eddie laughed when I called a Stiegal dish Sandwich and that I once called him a social climber. His trouble was that he wanted to climb too fast. He'll probably confess, if his windpipe is not irreparably damaged, that he is the one who has been responsible for most of the thefts that Saunders is worrying about. It looked too easy. Jeff was sending him to all these people who ought to insure their antiques and telling him how valuable the stuff was. This place was a perfect setup when Amos was away because of Miss Currier's deafness and the casual attitude they both had about their valuables."

"But the other places," Miss Currier put in, "everybody isn't deaf."

"He just had to take a chance, though that doesn't quite fit in with his innate caution."

"No, he didn't," said Emma suddenly. "Have to take a chance, I mean. Remember the night we went swimming? Well, all he had to do was look in the papers and see who was out of town or who had closed their house."

"Only a woman would think of that." Jeff's tone was belittling.

"If he hadn't thought of that before"—Hank defended Emma—"he liked the idea. He, or somebody with wet feet, tried to get into the Leeds' house the night we were there."

"I thought it was funny," Emma claimed, "that he wasn't more upset about our leaving him. Where's Eunice? I ought to apologize to her too."

"She's in the ditch," Shay volunteered. "She phoned awhile ago. Hank told her to get a horse."

Everybody but Emma looked at Hank and laughed.

"I think you're all hateful." Emma was indignant. "You try to keep me out of this and you don't tell me the jokes."

"You better go look at Slocomb," Jeff advised. "I've seen Hank but I imagine the horse looks worse."

"Hank Fairbanks, if you hurt that horse—"

"Stop teasing her," said Miss Currier. "Mr. Fairbanks merely rode the horse."

"You didn't. Whatever for?"

"I wonder myself, now. At the time it was to get some food and to find out that Miss Currier had sent a manuscript to her agents."

"It was late," said Miss Currier, vexed; "it was due on the thirtieth. I hope they'll understand."

"And Mr. Fairbanks," said Mrs. Leavitt, "was so curious to know what I had in that pan of scraps."

"I suppose it was silly," Miss Currier explained, "but I didn't think it was very dignified for an old lady to be writing detective stories."

"That's not it at all," Mrs. Leavitt burst out; "she didn't want people to know that she was supporting Amos."

"Tush, tush," said Miss Currier. "All that bothered me was that I had to sit and roast all Sunday morning with that quilt over my knees covering up the typewriter."

"Where it is now?"

"One of the boys hid it in the haymow."

"I wish I'd known," said Hank. "I'd have written you a letter."

"I wonder," said Emma plaintively, "if I shall ever find out everything?"

"You know all you can understand," said Jeff.

Emma made a face at him.

They heard the sound of Eunice's voice and heavy steps on the stairs.

"I hope Ches Durrell remembered to wipe his feet," said Mrs. Leavitt in a tone that indicated the wish was futile. "This house will be a sight, what with the mud and all."

"Don't pick on Durrell," said Hank; "he's the one who thought it was odd that an insurance salesman wouldn't have a pencil in his pocket."

Eunice came in first. Her dress was torn, her hair was wet and there was a smudge of dirt on her face.

"Isn't she gorgeous?" asked Shay.

"Auntie," asked Eunice, "are you all right?"

"I'm perfectly all right," said Miss Currier; "I'm just not used to so much exercise. How is Mr. Rawlins?"

"He isn't bad," said Ellis. "He missed the vessels here"—Emma turned her eyes away as Ellis demonstrated on his own neck—"on account of the muscle," Ellis went on, "and the Doc says the wind box here is pretty tough." Ellis fingered his Adam's apple speculatively. "Anyway, he was alive enough to sign a confession. Amos caught him in the buttery with the silver box, and he says he hit him with the first thing that was handy."

"I guess he didn't mean to kill Amos," said Durrell, "he just got scared. But he meant to kill Lloyd right enough."

"Don't kid yourself." Jeff wasted no pity. "He killed Amos rather than be exposed as a thief."

"He was a cold-blooded devil," said Shay. "He knew well enough that Jeff sent the muffineer to Emma but he didn't tell Ellis and Saunders that. He hoped that having the whatsis would put Emma on the spot because he'd drawn her in the pool."

"Oh," said Emma faintly.

"And when I think"—Jeff's tone was venomous—"of the business I got him—"

"Just the same," said Emma, "it'll be easier if he dies."

"Nuts." Jeff was unconvinced.

"They've been telling me"—Eunice, turning again to her aunt, changed the subject—"how smart you were to figure out that Rawlins must have taken the silver box out of his bag while Mr. Fairbanks was waiting for him to get dressed."

"If he hadn't been so greedy," said Jeff, "he'd have put it back in the cupboard after he killed Amos."

"Sally really thought of that," said Miss Currier.

"I did no such thing. But we had a time trying to make somebody else see that the box pointed to him."

"I had that list all the time," Miss Currier confessed to Ellis, "but I burned it because you were so set on making it point to Mr. Graham. I didn't want to tell you right out because I thought the police really ought to have the credit, but you were all so dreadfully slow."

"It was coming to me." Hank defended himself. "Another day in bed and I'd have had it, but Shay came out all steamed up about the picture without the box in it, and then Jeff came with the news that Eddie was selling antiques to a dealer in Rockingham and that the filling-station man claimed Shay and I were the only ones who had inquired the way out that night, and the pieces began to go together."

Durrell had edged his way over to Jeff and the decanter.

"Why don't you drink that," Miss Currier inquired, "instead of looking at it?"

"No glass," said Jeff, "and you can't drink out of a neck like this without spilling."

"I'll get you a glass," said Emma.

"Quite the little hostess," said Hank, but Emma laughed at him.

She came back in time to hear Durrell saying heavily, "If I could-a got to Boston to talk to him I reckon I'd-a caught on. You see, all I know about is hogs and insurance."

Emma said, "I've got a good mind to take these glasses right back downstairs. It makes me simply furious to think of you all getting together out here and figuring this out without me. How did you happen to come out here?" She withheld Jeff's glass. "I thought I sent you off to Maine?"

"I was just protecting my investment. Gimme that glass. Oh, all right," as Emma put the glass behind her. "I went to Rockingham because I didn't like having all the stuff stolen from houses that I couldn't insure any better than Saunders did. There'd been a lot of talk about my splitting commissions with Rawlins—"

"I never thought that," Emma put in quickly; "not for a minute."

"If I thought you had—" Jeff looked at her darkly. "So I find out that Eddie's been selling stuff—I suppose he'd picked up enough knowledge from me to know what to take—he was the only one who didn't have a motive for killing Amos but he's got a motive if Amos caught him stealing his stuff. So I come back here to tell Miss Currier that I've got to admit Amos was selling so that we can check with the inventory, and on the way I get to thinking about Eddie's knowing the way out here, and when I get here everybody's gathered round thinking the same thing. We tried to keep you out of it because—" Jeff paused, hating to admit even the impulse of consideration for

Emma's feelings. "But you had to stick your nose in. I'm going to Maine tomorrow so try to behave yourself."

"I wouldn't bother"—Emma hastily handed over the glass—"I got word from Mrs. Stone that the house burned down."

"Stone?" said Jeff suspiciously. "You said Wood before. Say, what is this? Did you send me off on a phony?"

"It's no worse," said Emma, "than your firing me to get me out of the way. I thought Ellis was going to arrest you." She turned accusingly to Miss Currier, who gravely winked at her.

"Oh, my goodness," said Emma, "didn't everybody make a mess of things?"

THE END

A catalog Rue Morgue Press titles
as of December 1999

Murder is a Collector's Item by Elizabeth Dean. "(It) froths over with the same effervescent humor as the best Hepburn-Grant films."—Sujata Massey. "Completely enjoyable."—*New York Times.* "Fast and funny."—*The New Yorker.* Twenty-six-year-old Emma Marsh isn't much at spelling or geography and perhaps she butchers the odd literary quotation or two, but she's a keen judge of character and more than able to hold her own when it comes to selling antiques or solving murders. First published in 1939. **0-915230-19-4 $14.00**

Murder, Chop Chop by James Norman. "The book has the butter-wouldn't-melt-in-his-mouth cool of Rick in *Casablanca.*"—*The Rocky Mountain News.* "Amuses the reader no end."—*Mystery News.* "This long out-of-print masterpiece is intricately plotted, full of eccentric characters and very humorous indeed. Highly recommended."—*Mysteries by Mail.* Meet Gimiendo Hernandez Quinto, a gigantic Mexican who once rode with Pancho Villa and who now trains *guerrilleros* for the Nationalist Chinese government when he isn't solving murders with the help of a beautiful Eurasian known as Mountain of Virtue. **0-915230-16-X $13.00**

Death at The Dog by Joanna Cannan. "Worthy of being discussed in the same breath with an Agatha Christie or Josephine Tey...anyone who enjoys Golden Age mysteries will surely enjoy this one."—Sally Fellows, *Mystery News.* "Skilled writing and brilliant characterization."—*Times of London.* "An excellent English rural tale."—Jacques Barzun & Wendell Hertig Taylor in *A Catalogue of Crime.* Set in late 1939 during the first anxious months of World War II, *Death at The Dog,* which was first published in 1941, features Inspector Guy Northeast, a lonely young Scotland Yard inspector who makes his second and final appearance here and finds himself hopelessly smitten with the chief suspect in the murder of a village tyrant. **0-915230-23-2 $14.00**

They Rang Up the Police by Joanna Cannan. When Delia Cathcart and Major Willoughby disappear from their quiet English village one Saturday morning in July 1937, it looks like a simple case of a frustrated spinster running off for a bit of fun with a straying husband. But as the hours turn into days, Inspector Guy Northeast begins to suspect foul play. Never published in the U.S., *They Rang Up the Police* appeared in England in 1939. **0-915230-27-5 $14.00**

Cook Up a Crime by Charlotte Murray Russell. "Perhaps the mother of today's "cozy" mystery...amateur sleuth Jane has a personality guaranteed to entertain the most demanding reader."—Andy Plonka, *The Mystery Reader.* "Some wonderful old time recipes...highly recommended."—*Mysteries by Mail.* Meet Jane Amanda Edwards, a self-styled "full-fashioned" spinster who complains she hasn't looked at herself in a full-length mirror since Helen Hokinson started drawing for *The New Yorker.* In this 1951 comic gem Jane goes looking for recipes (included between chapters) for a cookbook project and finds a body instead—and it's her brother Arthur who's holding the murder weapon. **0-915230-18-6 $13.00**

The Man from Tibet by Clyde B. Clason. Locked inside the Tibetan Room of his Chicago luxury apartment, the rich antiquarian was overheard repeating a forbidden occult chant under the watchful eyes of Buddhist gods. When the doors were opened it appeared that he had succumbed to a heart attack. But the elderly Roman historian and sometime amateur sleuth Theocritus Lucius Westborough is convinced that Adam Merriweather's death was anything but natural and that the weapon was an eighth century Tibetan manuscript. It it's murder, who could have done it, and how? **0-915230-17-8 $14.00**

The Black Gloves by Constance & Gwenyth Little. "I'm relishing every madcap moment."—*Murder Most Cozy*. Welcome to the Vickers estate near East Orange, New Jersey, where the middle class is destroying the neighborhood, erecting their horrid little cottages, playing on the Vickers tennis court, and generally disrupting the comfortable life of Hammond Vickers no end. It's bad enough that he had to shell out good money to his daughter Lissa a Reno divorce only to have her brute of an es-husband show up on his doorstep. But why does there also have to be a corpse in the cellar? And lights going on and off in the attic? First published in 1939. **0-915230-20-8 $14.00**

The Black Honeymoon by Constance & Gwenyth Little. Can you murder someone with feathers? If you don't believe feathers are lethal, then you probably haven't read a Little mystery. First published in 1944. **0-915230-21-6 $14.00**

Great Black Kanba by Constance & Gwenyth Little. "If you love train mysteries as much as I do, hop on the Trans-Australia Railway in *Great Black Kanba*, a fast and funny 1944 novel by the talented (Littles)."—Jon L. Breen, *Ellery Queen's Mystery Magazine.* "I have decided to add *Kanba* to my favorite mysteries of all time list!...a zany ride I'll definitely take again and again."—Diane Plumley in the Murder Ink newsletter. When a young American woman wakes up on an Australia train with a bump on her head and no memory, she finds out that she's engaged to two different men and the chief suspect in a murder case. **0-915230-22-4 $14.00**

The Grey Mist Murders by Constance & Gwenyth Little. Who—or what—is the mysterious figure that emerges from the grey mist to strike down several passengers on the final leg of a round-the-world sea voyage? **0-915230-26-7 $14.00**

The Black-Headed Pins by Constance & Gwenyth Little. It wasn't Santa's reindeer that caused the clatter on the roof in this wacky 1938 Christmas houseparty murder case. **0-915230-25-9 $14.00**

The Mirror by Marlys Millhiser. "Completely enjoyable."—*Library Journal* . "A great deal of fun."—*Publishers Weekly*. How could you not be intrigued, as one reviewer pointed out, by a novel in which "you find the main character marrying her own grandfather and giving birth to her own mother?" **0-915230-15-1 $14.95**

The Rue Morgue Press specializes in reprinting mysteries from 1900 to the 1960s. If you'd like to suggest titles or get our catalog, write to us at P.O. Box 4119, Boulder, Colorado 80306.